The Vault of Vishnu

About the Author

Ashwin Sanghi is among India's highest-selling English fiction authors. He has written several bestsellers in the Bharat Series (*The Rozabal Line, Chanakya's Chant, The Krishna Key, The Sialkot Saga, Keepers of the Kalachakra, The Vault of Vishnu*) and two *New York Times* bestselling crime thrillers with James Patterson, *Private India* (sold in the US as *City on Fire*) and *Private Delhi* (sold in the US as *Count to Ten*). He has also co-authored several non-fiction titles in the 13 Steps Series on Luck, Wealth, Marks, Health and Parenting.

Ashwin has been included by *Forbes India* in their Celebrity 100 and by *The New Indian Express* in their Culture Power List. He is a winner of the Crossword Popular Choice Award 2012, Atta Galatta Popular Choice Award 2018, WBR Iconic Achievers Award 2018, the Lit-O-Fest Literature Legend Award 2018 and the Kalinga Popular Choice Award 2021.

He was educated at Cathedral and John Connon School, Mumbai, and St Xavier's College, Mumbai. He holds an MBA from Yale University. Ashwin lives in Mumbai with his wife, Anushika, and son, Raghuvir.

You can connect with Ashwin via the following channels:Website www.sanghi.in

Twitter @ashwinsanghi
Instagram @ashwin.sanghi
Koo @ashwinsanghi
Clubhouse @ashwinsanghi
Facebook fb.com/ashwinsanghi
YouTube youtube.com/ashwinsanghi
LinkedIn linkedin.com/in/ashwinsanghi

Acknowledgements

It would be impossible to write the books that I do without the assistance, input, guidance, love and support of so many. Here are some of those without whom these books in the *Bharat Series* may not have happened.

My publishers, HarperCollins *Publishers* India—in particular, Ananth Padmanabhan and Udayan Mitra—who always ensure that my books reach my readers quickly and efficiently.

Prita Maitra, my primary editor, who continues to be indispensable in editing the series in addition to several other individuals including Karthika VK, Deepthi Talwar, Ashok Rajani, Aparna Gupta, Karthik Venkatesh and Swati Daftuar whose edits, inputs and guidance have been invaluable in various books of the series from time to time.

Rupesh Talaskar, my talented illustrator, who has meticulously executed maps and internal illustrations in various books of the series, and Semy Haitenlo, who has designed stunning book covers for each of them.

Ameya Naik, the versatile composer who has composed the haunting tracks used in the trailers of these books, and the teams at TwistStudio and Oktobuzz for their video trailers and social media support from time to time.

Deepshikha Kumar and Nijansh Verma of SpeakIn for their advice and input on my speaking tours and events. Also, Ashoo Naik and Chirag Nihalani of Collective for their efforts towards bringing my stories to a wider audience through cinema, television and OTT.

My parents, Mahendra and Manju Sanghi, and my siblings, Vidhi and Vaibhav, who have always encouraged me to follow my dreams. My wife, Anushika, and son, Raghuvir, who have been my constant support in my writing endeavours. Had it not been for their unconditional love, none of my books would have been possible. My little rakhi-sister Farah, who has taught me that not everything in life can be explained and that some things are better left unexplained.

Gautam Padmanabhan, my friend, philosopher and guide who gave me my first publishing break and has encouraged me through several stories of the series.

The late Ramprasad and Ramgopal Gupta, my maternal grandfather and maternal granduncle, who inspired me with their stories and books. Their blessings prevent the ink in my pen from running dry.

Finally, Ma Shakti, the One who puts power in my pen. I thank you, Ma, for your abundant blessings—forever.

Praise for the Bharat Series

The Rozabal Line (2008)

'In *The Rozabal Line*, Ashwin Sanghi does a Dan Brown by mixing all the ingredients of a thriller—crusades, action, adventure, suspense—and pulling off, with dexterity and ease, a narrative that careens through cultures and continents, religions and cults.' ~*The Asian Age*

'*The Rozabal Line* by Ashwin Sanghi is a kickass thriller that forces you to re-examine our histories, our faiths.' ~Pritish Nandy

'Sanghi's flair for religion, history and politics is clearly visible as he takes the reader across the world spanning different decades. A mixture of comparative religion, dangerous secrets, and a thrilling plot makes for an esoteric read.' ~*The Statesman*

'Sanghi has got the sure-fire formula right.' ~ *The Times of India*

'A provocative, clever and radiant line of theology, Sanghi suggests that the cult of Mary Magdalene has its true inspiration in the trinity of the Indian sacred feminine, thereby out-thinking and out-conspiring Dan Brown.' ~*The Hindu*

Chanakya's Chant (2010)

'With internal monologues and descriptions as taut as a-held-by-the-thumb sacred thread, we have Ashwin Sanghi's cracker of a page-turner, *Chanakya's Chant*. Two narratives flow like the Ganga and Yamuna … a brisk technicoloured thriller.' ~*Hindustan Times*

'I'm utterly enthralled. A delightfully interesting and gripping read. The historical research is deeply impressive …' ~Shashi Tharoor

'A gripping, fast-paced read, the novel is a true thriller in the tradition set by Dan Brown.' ~*People Magazine*

'Political grooming and conspiracy remain at the core of Ashwin Sanghi's historical thriller. Bloodshed, legal trials, betrayals, murders, assassination attempts and all that which make this into a page-turner.' ~*Sakaal Times*

'Released in India to wide acclaim, *Chanakya's Chant* is a political page-turner.' ~*Business India*

The Krishna Key (2012)

'Why should racy historical thrillers or meaty fantasy sagas come only from the minds of Western writers? Ashwin Sanghi spins his yarns well and leaves you breathless at every cliff-hanger. No wonder his books are bestsellers!' ~*Hindustan Times*

'While the plot is set in today's world, one can expect to travel back and forth in time with generous chunks of history and nail-biting fiction.' ~*The Telegraph*

'An alternative interpretation of the Vedic Age that will be relished by conspiracy buffs and addicts of thrillers alike.' ~*The Hindu*

'Just finished *The Krishna Key* by Ashwin Sanghi. Rocking story and incredible research. Loved it!' ~Amish Tripathi

'Sanghi manages to blur the line between fact and fiction and give a whole new perspective to history and the Vedic Age.' ~*DNA*

The Sialkot Saga (2016)

'*The Sialkot Saga* moves at a breakneck pace hurtling through time and space uncovering ancient secrets and burying modern ones.' ~*The Hindu*

'The book spreads across decades and centuries, till it reaches present day India and will sure have both historic and thriller readers in for a treat.' ~*The Times of India*

'There are books that take time to develop an interest and then there are books that grip you from the very first page. *The Sialkot Saga* is one such book that hooks you from the start.' ~*Hindustan Times*

'There's never a dull moment in the book. In fact, the story takes on such a pace that the overwhelmed reader is compelled to put the book down and take a deep breath on many an occasion.' ~*The Financial Express*

'Sanghi weaves a masterpiece building up the readers' involvement in the novel with every turn of the page.' ~*The Pioneer*

Keepers of the Kalachakra (2018)

'The book can't be put down till all pieces of the jigsaw puzzle are put together.' ~*The Financial Express*

'The author packs a powerful punch ... spicy and saucy, a survey of the past and the present ... without a dull moment, without a dull page.' ~*The Sunday Standard*

'Science and spirituality collide in Ashwin Sanghi's latest thriller.' ~*India Today*

'Spread over a vast canvas, the novel has an engaging plot laced with mythology, history and legends.' ~*The Hindu*

'Ashwin Sanghi's *Keepers of the Kalachakra* is as explosive as a time bomb ticking in your hand. Every chapter springs an unpredictable surprise.' ~*Deccan Chronicle*

'*Keepers of the Kalachakra* has it all: political characters that remind you of real-life politicians, a racy, complex plot and enough improbable twists to keep you hooked.' ~*Hindustan Times Brunch*

The Vault of Vishnu (2020)

'In an enthralling alchemy of myth and science, Ashwin Sanghi gives us the sixth book in his Bharat Series. As with all Ashwin's books, the research is meticulous and the technical(ese) leaves one gasping as *The Vault of Vishnu* takes the reader through the highs and lows of history, myth, physics, warfare technology, AI and biochemistry.' ~*The Times of India*

'*The Vault of Vishnu*, like all of Ashwin's books, is a heady mix of history, myth, science and thrills.' ~*The Hindu*

'A very interesting and intriguing thriller, thanks to the author's storytelling gift and painstaking research on Hindu metaphysics.' ~*The New Indian Express*

'Sanghi's latest work uses his favourite tool—mythology—and blends it with history to deliver some edge-of-the-seat action.' ~*Hindustan Times*

The Vault of Vishnu

Ashwin Sanghi

HarperCollins *Publishers* India

First published in 2020

This edition published in India by HarperCollins *Publishers* in 2022
4th Floor, Tower A, Building No. 10, Phase II, DLF Cyber City,
Gurugram, Haryana – 122002
www.harpercollins.co.in

2 4 6 8 10 9 7 5 3 1

Copyright © Ashwin Sanghi 2020, 2022

P-ISBN: 978-93-5629-249-9
E-ISBN: 978-93-5629-254-3

Typeset by Art Works, Chennai

Printed and bound at
Thomson Press (India) Ltd

Disclaimer

This book is a work of fiction. Names, characters, places and events are either the products of the author's imagination or used in a fictitious manner. Any resemblance to actual persons, living or dead, or actual events is purely coincidental. No claim regarding historical or theological accuracy is either made or implied. Historical, religious or mythological characters, events or places, are always used fictitiously and deviations from the accepted record also occur.

Om Chaturmukhaya Vidmahe
Hansa Rudraaya Dhimahi
Tanno Brahma Prachodayat

May we know the god with four faces.
Let us meditate on the god who rides a swan.
We ask Brahma to inspire and illuminate.

Om Narayanaya Vidmahe
Vasudevaya Dhimahi
Tanno Vishnu Prachodayat

May we know the god who rests on water.
Let us meditate on the god who permeates life.
We ask Vishnu to inspire and illuminate.

Om Tat Purushaya Vidhmahe
Mahadevaya Dheemahe
Tanno Rudra Prachodayath.

May we know the most powerful of men.
Let us meditate on the greatest of gods.
We ask Shiva to inspire and illuminate.

Om Aanjaneyay Vidmahe
Maha Balaya Dheemahe
Tanno Hanuman Prachodayat

May we know the son of Anjana.
Let us meditate on the one with the greatest strength.
We ask Hanuman to inspire and illuminate.

Map Showing Xuanzang's Journey
(from 627 to 645 CE)

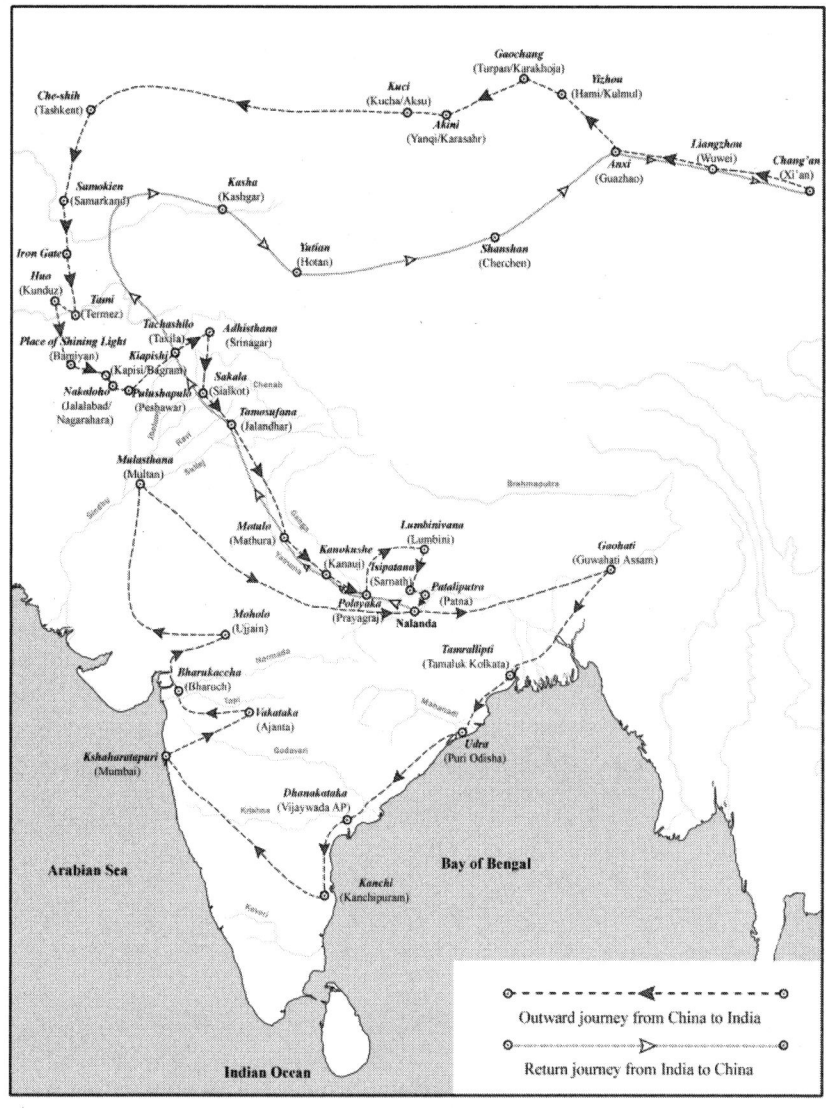

Present-day political boundaries not shown. Map not to scale. Xuanzang's route shown may not be entirely accurate. Ancient names in italics, modern names in parentheses. River names are current.

1

The Indians saw them and were paralysed with fear.

The weather that day had been unforgiving. Icy winds howled in chorus with bursts of thunder and rain. The men of the 17 Mountain Division braced themselves for the worst as sleet hit their faces like bullets.

At a height of 14,000 feet, the plateau of Doklam lay on the border between the Himalayan kingdom of Bhutan and its superpower neighbour China. The loftiest points of the plateau lay on its western shoulder, between Batang La and Mount Gipmochi. From there, the plateau sloped down towards the southeast, eventually meeting the Amo Chu River. The entire expanse of thirty-four-plus square miles between the highest and lowest points was boulder-strewn, hence the name Doklam—'rocky path'.

The Chinese called it by a different name: Donglang. In fact, they claimed it as their own. But their efforts to build a road through the plateau had triggered a flashpoint with India, Bhutan's longstanding friend and ally. India knew that a road through Doklam would give China the ability to enter Indian territory with little effort. Halting the Chinese initiative was not an option—it was an imperative.

The first encounter with the Chinese had been largely peaceful. After weeks of posturing and negotiations, both sides had agreed to withdraw their men and machines beyond the buffer zone. But this latest Chinese move was altogether different. There was no pretence of innocence. The dragon was on the move.

The men from the Indian contingent, supported by the Royal Bhutan Army Corps, cautiously calculated their own strength. There weren't too many of them to defend Doklam. The number of soldiers was limited because of the time it took them to acclimatise. Any soldier coming to the plateau needed at least five days to adjust to the altitude. It was impossible to rush in reinforcements at short notice.

The commander of the Indian side looked through his binoculars with bated breath. All he could see was desolate, rock-covered land. He wondered why they were fighting at all. There seemed so little to be gained by acquiring vast expanses of barren stone. He could not discern any movement through his binoculars. But they were there. Every soldierly instinct told him they were there.

And then he saw them. And found himself utterly and helplessly afraid. *A hero is no braver than an ordinary man, but he is brave five minutes longer*, he reminded himself, not for the first time in his life.

Wave after wave of soldiers streamed into Doklam from the Chinese side. Even steep cliffs and deep ravines could not stop them. They leapt over these effortlessly. Not of the average Chinese build, these soldiers were extraordinarily tall and muscular. Their muscles strained against their armour. Like Greek gods on steroids. The Indians and the Bhutanese trembled as the Chinese troops shouted, 'Sha! Sha! Sha!'

Everyone knew what it meant. *Kill! Kill! Kill!*

The Chinese fighters were also astonishingly outfitted. All of them sported radar-equipped helmets, lightweight yet lethal assault rifles, wrist-mounted computer-navigation systems, night vision goggles and omniphobic full-body armour. The Indian and Bhutanese contingents were in their military fatigues, armed with only standard-issue rifles.

Three field cameras that had been installed on rock surfaces were silently capturing all the action and relaying them via satellite to the Indian control room a few hundred yards away.

The defenders mustered their courage and yelled a war cry of their own. 'Bharat mata ki jai!' *Long live Mother India!* They were no pushovers. The 17 Mountain Division that guarded the area was also known as the Black Cat Division. They had fought in all the battles in which Indians had participated since World War II. They had played an instrumental role in the 1944 Burma Campaign and in the 1961 Liberation of Goa. They usually lived by the words of the American war hero George S. Patton: 'No dumb bastard ever won a war by going out and dying for his country. He won it by making some other dumb bastard die for his country.'

But the odds were stacked against them today.

What followed was brutal.

The first few kills were not by snipers or grenades or shells. The soldiers of the 17 Mountain Division were bludgeoned or stabbed to death. The Chinese soldiers wielded Ka-Bar fighting knives with razor-sharp blades. They had been trained to cut upward. That was the most effective option—to simply drive the point of the blade into a man's lower belly and rip upward. It meant getting soaked in the victim's gore, but that only added to their bloodlust.

The Indo-Bhutanese soldiers pulled together and fought back. Their first ploy was to gun down the Chinese who were suspended from ropes anchored to the cliffs surrounding the plateau. The attackers were leaping from one rope to another like trapeze artists, providing protective fire to their comrades and creating mayhem.

The Indians fired indiscriminately into the spider web of ropes hanging from the cliffs, but to no avail. A few Chinese combatants were injured by Indian fire, but they simply used specialised field tourniquets to stanch the bleeding and carried on as though nothing could come in their way.

The commander of the Indian forces was awestruck by the agility and speed of his opponents but had little time to think about it, as a Chinese soldier swung his Ka-Bar knife at him. The commander deftly sidestepped the arc of his opponent's knife and let loose a volley of fire. His attacker leapt several feet into the air, expertly dodging the stream of bullets. He took aim from an aerial vantage position and fired cleanly into the commander's skull. The Indian fell to the ground, his brain splattered across Doklam's rocky ground.

It was nothing short of a massacre that day. But strangely, the Chinese appeared uninterested in holding the territory they had just captured. Exactly ninety minutes after the attack started, a clarion call announced the cessation of hostilities for the day. Almost as quickly as they had entered Doklam, the Chinese forces exited the plateau, hooting and thumping their chests in caveman-like glee, and stomping their feet in unison. The ground reverberated with their coordinated and sinister exit march.

The surviving Indian and Bhutanese soldiers watched the retreating forces in bewildered frustration. What was the point of killing over a hundred men if there was no intention of acquiring territory? Or was the main attack yet to come? They began collecting the remains of their fallen comrades, their bodies drooping with weariness. It was a day that would go down as one of the worst in the history of the 17 Mountain Division.

Or was it?

2

The meeting at Integrated Defence Staff HQ at Kashmir House, on Rajaji Marg in New Delhi, had lasted several hours. The entire Chiefs of Staff Committee—the COSC—was present in the conference room. General Jai Thakur, the special adviser to the COSC, had personally telephoned each member and curtly said, 'Attendance is compulsory. No excuses for your absence unless you're dead. And even then, try to make it.'

More than an hour had been devoted to sweeping the conference room for listening devices. Members had been asked to deposit their mobile phones outside. The polished teakwood sideboard held bottles of water, flasks of tea and coffee, sandwiches and biscuits, so that no additional personnel would be required inside while the meeting was in progress. The matching art deco conference table was stacked with thick dossiers containing satellite images, ground reports and ordnance survey maps.

The team at Kashmir House bore the primary responsibility of coordinating actions across multiple branches of the Indian armed forces. Its members were drawn from the army, the navy and the air force. In addition, there were delegates from the Defence Research and Development Organisation, commonly known as the DRDO. Representatives from two key ministries, external affairs and defence, completed the assemblage. Inputs from both constituents were critical to the decisions made by the COSC.

Although the chairperson of the COSC was usually the seniormost person, it was widely known that the real power lay with the special adviser, General Jai Thakur; he had the ear of both the prime minister and the minister of defence.

The men in the room viewed the footage of the Doklam attack as the army chief explained his concerns. They were left stunned by the field camera captures of the bulky Chinese fighters ripping their knives through the Indian soldiers with minimal effort, swinging across cliffs using little more than thin ropes and taking massive strides effortlessly.

Having noticed the intense reactions around the room, the army chief quickly switched off the horrendous video. He turned to a slide that showed a map of the area and used a laser pointer to indicate the farthest points that the Chinese troops had reached. 'Frankly, what is most worrying for us is that the Chinese now stand poised to take over the Siliguri Corridor,' he said grimly. 'The only reason they haven't is because of their utterly inexplicable withdrawal.'

More commonly known as Chicken's Neck, the Siliguri Corridor is a narrow strip of land belonging to India that lies between Nepal, Bhutan and Bangladesh. The most tapered point of the corridor is just over 16.7 miles wide, and a Chinese takeover of the region would mean cutting the rest of India from its northeastern states: Sikkim, Assam, Arunachal Pradesh, Nagaland, Manipur, Mizoram, Tripura and Meghalaya. This had actually happened during the 1962 Indo–China War. India did not want to leave any room for a repeat performance.

The men looked at the images of the terrain taken by the Cartosat satellites. The harsh topography of the region made the railway and road networks vulnerable to damage from the frequent landslides and record-breaking levels of rainfall. Men were far better suited to such hostile terrain than machines.

'What do you suggest?' asked General Jai Thakur, patting down his bushy white moustache.

'We cannot fight an enemy we do not know,' replied the army chief softly.

'We know they were Chinese troops,' responded Thakur gruffly. 'What more do you want to know?'

'Yes, we know *who* they are, but *what* are they?' asked the army chief, doing a good job of hiding his impatience. 'Are these regular soldiers? Androids? Martial arts experts? Apes? I for one cannot figure out what they are, by looking at the images. And how are Indian soldiers expected to fight such ghastly odds?'

'Any thoughts, gentlemen?' asked Thakur, looking around the table at the other service chiefs.

'I have an idea that I would like to propose,' replied the army chief carefully, recalling his recent conversation with one of India's highest-level spooks.

'Let's hear it,' said Thakur irritably. Thakur's impatience was telling. He had received an earful from the prime minister's office. General elections were around the corner and decisive action was needed not only for national security but also for political survival.

'Our ability to neutralise the threat will improve if we can understand what we are dealing with,' said the army man in measured tones.

'And how do you propose we go about doing that?' asked Thakur.

'We need to fight smart rather than fight hard,' replied the army chief. 'Let's find out exactly what makes the Chinese forces so potent. Once we have *that* answer, we can fight them better. Identify the malaise and you will find the remedy. I suggest we bring in a young investigator from the DRDO who can help us.'

'What's his name?' asked Thakur.

'Her name,' corrected the army chief, waiting for Thakur's reaction.

Thakur's eyebrows shot up. 'A *woman?*' he asked incredulously. In Thakur's opinion, women took care of husbands, bore children, cooked, cleaned and warmed the bed. Nothing more. Perhaps he had read Chanakya: A good wife is one who serves her husband in the morning like a mother, loves him in the day like a sister, and pleases him at night like a whore. Not that any of it mattered to Thakur, who was a widower, although there were whispers from time to time of a long-running affair.

'I assure you she's the best we have,' said the army chief. 'She's the daughter of the late Colonel Kishan Khurana.'

'The hero of the Indian Peace Keeping Force?' asked Thakur. There was a moment of hesitation, as though he was contemplating a response. But her parentage had seemingly made a difference. In Thakur's scheme of things, no amount of training, education or experience could compensate for a poor bloodline.

The army chief nodded. 'Her name is Paramjit Khurana. Let's get her in here.'

3

Wing Commander Paramjit Khurana paced outside the conference room, waiting to be called in. She shivered. Delhi's winters had grown colder and the summers were blisteringly hot. She rubbed her hands together, then put them into the pockets of her coat. *Damn global warming.*

Her clenched fists inside the coat pockets gave away her nervousness. It wasn't every day that one was included in the deliberations of the COSC. The phone call had been unexpected and brief. 'Drop everything you're doing and get here immediately,' she had been told.

'Where do I come?' she had asked.

'A car and driver are waiting for you outside your house,' came the reply. 'Look outside the window. No need to tell anyone where you're going.'

She had peeped through the curtains and, sure enough, a car and chauffeur were waiting on the street outside her home.

Paramjit—Pam to her friends—worked for the DRDO, an agency of the Indian government. The DRDO operated a network of fifty-two laboratories across India. Each of these was responsible for developing defence technologies in domains as diverse as aeronautics, communication, armaments and life sciences. The DRDO employed 5,000 scientists and 25,000 support personnel. Pam was a shining star in a sky full of soaring minds clouded only by bureaucracy. Like every other government department, the DRDO too was controlled by an army of civil servants. Pam often joked that DRDO bureaucrats were like defective guns: they never worked and could not be fired.

Pam absently scanned the photographs adorning one wall of the waiting room as she paced the Burma teak floor of Kashmir House. Groups of soldiers outfitted in distinctive uniforms were framed in black, white and sepia tones. Photographs of famous regiments held pride of place, including the Sikh Regiment, the Gorkha Rifles and the Maratha Light Infantry. These were men who had tirelessly served the country in troubled times, often sacrificing their own family's security, their happiness and even their lives for the nation.

And then she saw his photograph. Her mother always said that Pam had inherited her dimpled cheeks from her father. Pam had lost him when she was barely seven. He had been part of the Indian Peace Keeping Force— the IPKF—sent by the then prime minister Rajiv Gandhi to Sri Lanka in 1987, purportedly to maintain peace between the warring Sinhalese and Tamil factions. The misadventure had eventually cost Gandhi his life, when a suicide bomber deputed by the Liberation Tigers of Tamil Eelam—the LTTE—had blown herself up with a kilogram of RDX strapped to her waist as she touched his feet before an election rally. The explosion had killed the target, the assassin and twenty-five bystanders. Very little of Gandhi's body had remained for his last rites.

Colonel Kishan Khurana had survived the Lankan civil war but had died an untimely death during the return leg of his tour in 1990, killed by a stray bullet as his boat crossed the choppy Palk Strait between Sri Lanka and India. His death had left Pam devastated. Pam's mother had brought her up singlehandedly, against all odds. A foundation called the Vegavathy Trust had kindly offered her financial assistance in addition to the widow's pension she received from the army. It had been a tough life, but observing her mother's grit and determination at close quarters had been the bedrock of Pam's early education. As she grew older, she realised that she had no alternative but to pick herself up and focus on being the best.

Pam had been one of several female cadets admitted into the Indian Air Force, one of the most female-friendly wings of the armed forces. Women pilots had been inducted from 1994 onwards and had played an important role, initially in support missions and later in combat roles. Pam had flown support sorties in several combat zones and had risen quickly through the ranks. Unfortunately, a last-minute ejection from a Russian MiG aircraft had left her with a flexor-tendon injury in her left hand. While surgical intervention and physiotherapy had restored her hand movements, she no longer met the stringent physical standards required of a combat pilot.

She had eventually been deputed to the DRDO on account of her uncanny ability to interface between the armed forces and civil engineers. A tech-savvy soldier was supposed to be an oxymoron according to most people. Pam, on the other hand, went on to play a pivotal role in developing user-friendly interfaces such as missile guidance menus, drone surveillance dashboards and helmet-mounted navigation control.

Pam spotted her reflection in the glass of her father's photo frame. She was thirty-six but looked younger owing to her short hair, bright brown eyes and warm smile. The smile hid much sadness; in her eyes one could detect the traces of melancholy. Although she had a petite frame, she packed a punch owing to her daily workouts at the gym. She continued staring at the photograph of her father, her own reflection merging with his face. *Why did I lose you so early? Are you looking at me from above, Papa? Are you proud of me?*

She heard footsteps on the teak wood floor. She patted down her hair, straightened her badges and turned around. 'The committee is ready to see you,' said the aide perfunctorily. His face was expressionless, his features frozen like a waxwork in Madame Tussauds. The statue guided her to the heavy door and held it open for her. She took a deep breath and entered the conference room.

She had heard about the eccentricities of General Jai Thakur. It was rumoured that on one occasion he had run after his aide-de-camp with a loaded rifle because his high-gloss leather shoes did not adequately reflect his face.

It was Pam's first ever meeting with the seniormost defence advisory council to the cabinet. And she was the only woman in the room.

4

General Jai Thakur motioned Pam to sit down at the far end of the conference table. She could feel everyone's eyes on her as she took her place and attempted to make herself comfortable in an uncomfortable chair.

Thakur lit a cigarette, ignoring the non-smoking policy in all government offices. No one had the courage to argue with him. He was a grumpy man, old school to the core, and spoke in clipped Oxfordian tones although he hadn't set foot inside that hallowed institution. The joke was that he not only slept with his shoes on but also had his batman polish them before turning in.

Unlike the ex-officio members of the committee who were service chiefs from the armed forces or ministry representatives, Thakur's chair was at the pleasure of the prime minister. Thakur had fought in the Indo-China War of 1962 at the age of twenty-three, been captured as a prisoner of war with 3,900 others, held at a POW camp near the Chongye monastery in Tibet and eventually made it safely back. Not as a war hero, but certainly as one among several brave soldiers who had done their best in spite of the bungling by their political masters.

Given his vast experience and unflinching commitment to the country, no PM ever thought of retiring him from the committee, even though he was in his eighties. The consensus was that there was simply no one more qualified than Thakur to keep the army, the navy and the air force united. Moreover, he was an outspoken critic of China. For many years now, he had been suggesting switching focus from Pakistan to China, but his advice had not been heeded. He had even predicted the cozy relationship between Pakistan and China well before anyone else noticed it.

Thakur kept up the pressure through multiple administrations, constantly cautioning the government against any carelessness along the Indo-China border. He often quoted from Chanakya, the great strategist of the fourth century BCE, who recommended that a debt should be paid to the final penny and an enemy finished to the final trace. He rued the fact that the Chinese had read Chanakya's *Arthashastra*, while the Indians had not bothered reading Sun Tzu's *The Art of War*.

Thakur nodded to the army chief, who replayed the relevant footage for Pam. She felt sick to her stomach as she watched the carnage that had been captured by the field cameras. The enemy forces had not only bulk but also strength, energy, agility, training and equipment. Pam knew that the Indian forces were no match for these elite Chinese commando units. The army chief shut down the video window.

'Wing Commander Khurana,' said Thakur, drawing her attention to himself.

'Yes, sir,' she responded mechanically as she turned towards him.

'We need to know how these men are being trained and equipped,' began Thakur. 'But critically, we need to know their weak spots, if any. We must also examine whether similar technology can be rapidly procured for our own men. The Chinese advantage must be diluted.'

'Can we consider using air power to neutralise their camps beyond the buffer zone?' asked Pam.

'Not an option. The air force of the People's Liberation Army—the PLA—has been acquiring fourth-generation fighters since 1996. Our estimate is that the number of such aircrafts is around 700, including the deadly Su-30 MKK multi-role fighter jets. On the other hand, our IAF continues to be burdened with a significant number of obsolete second- and third-generation aircrafts, like the MiG-21 and -23. China is way ahead of us in air power. If they're avoiding using air power against us, it would be foolhardy to goad them into doing so. We had stronger air power than them in 1962 and unwisely avoided using it. We should not make the opposite mistake this time.'

Thakur's mention of the MiG brought back memories of that fateful day when Pam had been forced to eject because her aircraft was defective.

'While the Indian public knows that there have been clashes at Doklam, no one knows the extent of the carnage,' said Thakur. 'Even the adrenaline-pumped news channels are calling the recent one a skirmish. Luckily for us, the Chinese are downplaying it too. The Chinese president does not seem to be interested in escalation.'

'Why?' asked Pam. 'Why attack in the first place?'

'There are differing camps in China, just like in India,' explained Thakur. 'In any case, if the extent of carnage were made public, it would be demoralising—for our armed forces and the nation too.'

'How can one cover up such a big story?'

'Given the desolate nature of Doklam, we have managed to hide some elements of the battle. Corpses are being returned to families under oath of secrecy, with a substantial payout linked to their silence. But I do hope you realise why time is of the essence. We need you to find out how we can match China's terrestrial power—quickly.'

'I work at the DRDO. You know it's a tech organisation,' replied Pam. 'I have neither the support of the intelligence services nor police resources. At the minimum you will need to provide me with intelligence inputs from other agencies, sir. You can't expect me to fly blind.'

There was an uncomfortable silence. Thakur was unaccustomed to being countered, that too by a female less than half his age. The angry flush on his face said it all, but it only lasted a moment.

'You are being appointed as a temporary officer in the Central Bureau of Investigation. This means you will have police powers of search and arrest during your enquiry. But the matter must necessarily be kept under wraps,' he snapped. 'You may not discuss this with anyone else. We will share any *relevant* intelligence inputs as they reach us, but for the most part you should consider that you are on your own. Treat everyone—and I mean *everyone*—as an informant.' It was an emphatic command, not a suggestion or request.

Pam realised that Thakur was not entirely wrong to be cautious. There had been a wave of intelligence leaks in recent years, and they simply could not afford another, but she wondered whether she could push her luck further.

'I'm no scientist,' she countered. 'I'll need to discuss these issues with relevant technical experts. I can be the one who analyses data that emerges *from* them, but I cannot *become* them. You must allow me to create a team I can work with.'

Thakur nodded. 'Fair enough. Provide us with a list of names in advance—a circle within which this discussion will remain.'

Pam was inclined to argue further about the futility of bureaucracy in an urgent investigation, but she held back. *Use your ammunition wisely and keep your powder dry*, she thought to herself.

5

A giant structure on the east side of Tiananmen Square in downtown Beijing housed China's national police command. Adjacent to that was a building that was protected round the clock by heavily armed police. Any visitor who loitered for more than a few seconds was routinely shooed away or picked up.

Getting inside was an even more arduous task. One needed to clear multiple levels of security checks, including full-body scans, to go in or out. All doors were protected with biometric access that recorded every entry and exit.

At the core of the building, accessed by an elevator that descended five floors into the bowels of the earth, was a high-tech lab that could resist earthquakes, floods and nuclear blasts. The foundations of the structure were built on coil springs so that even the most intense vibrations could be absorbed. The concrete columns, beams and walls were several feet thick, engineered to withstand any natural or man-made calamity. Massive turbo pumps stood silently on standby to instantly pump out water in the event of a flood. The entire structure was layered in one-inch stucco plaster over a frame of metal reinforced mesh, thus adding immense fire-retarding capabilities.

Inside, though, the facility was an ocean of calm. A silent atmosphere-control system regulated the temperature to a comfortable 22° Celsius. The air-circulation system ensured that stale air was flushed out and oxygen levels were kept high. Artificial lighting mimicked the outside environment so that the biorhythms of those who worked there could be kept normal in spite of hours and days without exposure to direct sunlight. In addition to the main laboratory, which was spread over 200,000 square feet, there were sleeping pods, a 24/7 cafeteria, a library, gym, swimming pool, showers and a convenience store. All so that the workers didn't need to step outside for anything.

Inside a glass-walled section, a scientist named Erkin Chong was using touch-sensitive joysticks to manipulate a robot behind an armoured wall. Erkin was in his forties and had a nervous demeanour, fidgeting endlessly with anything within arm's reach. He fit the stereotype of a scrawny nerd with his thick Buddy Holly-style glasses and slicked-back hair. Several coloured pens stuck out of his shirt pocket.

One of the teams that Erkin looked after was known by the acronym ADAM—Adaptable Design Artificial Manpower. Erkin struck off items on a checklist as he put his robot through various drills—left kick, right kick, left jab, right jab, uppercut, back flip, jump, leap, bend, climb, roll … the list was long. He looked at the robot and sighed. His knees shook nervously. Progress was good, but it would be many years before ADAM was perfected.

Some years ago the Chinese president had called for a robot revolution in the manufacturing sector. This had led to a flurry of activity aimed at boosting productivity. China added 87,000 industrial robots within a year, slightly less than the combined figure of Europe and the United States. Foxconn, the primary manufacturer of Apple's iPhone, had consciously dropped its headcount by a third as it employed 'foxbots' that could spray, press, assemble, disassemble, weld, pack and track goods. The hectic pace of robotic development in manufacturing had opened up applications into the world of defence. This had resulted in the subterranean research facility. Robots were slaves and most great civilisations had been developed on the back of slave labour. Robots did not require holidays or hours off; they required no pay and never experienced mood swings. But Erkin knew the harsh truth. Getting a machine to mimic humans was exceptionally difficult. Slightly easier was getting humans to mimic machines.

The research team went about their work, blissfully ignorant of the eyes watching them from the large black bolts that held the columns and beams of the facility in place. If they had looked a little closer, they would have noticed that each bolt contained a microscopic camera.

There were simply no blind spots. Every part of the facility was constantly being surveyed and every activity recorded.

Erkin turned off the joystick controls and activated the body sensors. A young team member stepped forward and Erkin strapped him up with multiple sensors. The man began to perform various routines. The robot faithfully mimicked them, almost simultaneously. From time to time, Erkin would press a 'boost' button on his console, and the robot would amplify the action of the human, much like a video game cheat key that adds a turbo charge to the actions of an avatar.

'Okay, let's try voice mode,' said Erkin, turning off the body sensors. The robot performed equally well, understanding each command perfectly and executing it flawlessly.

Erkin switched to AI mode. The robot went through the first half of the motions perfectly. But then it abruptly stopped its routine. Erkin operated his control unit to send the robot an electronic pulse to bring it back on course. And then the machine went crazy. It was almost like a temper tantrum. It began slamming the wall with its fists, every blow shaking the room. When the blows did not produce the desired outcome, the robot began kicking the electronic door that separated it from Erkin.

Erkin hurriedly deactivated the robot by cutting the power, cursing under his breath. This was the eleventh time the bug had appeared. He had tried every possible fix, including rewriting significant portions of the code, but nothing seemed to work. Head in his hands, he sat in silence, wondering what he would report to the Buzhang. He was already under immense pressure to deliver results. At the last briefing, the Buzhang had even threatened to pack Erkin off to a re-education camp as punishment for his lack of progress. But Erkin knew it was an empty threat. No one else knew as much as he did about their two top secret projects. In the absence of Erkin, what progress would the Buzhang make? Erkin cursed himself for getting entangled in this web.

He stood up and did a couple of Tai chi moves using gentle, flowing motions. His mind automatically focused on his form to bring back a state of clarity. Once he was done, he began methodically reviewing the bugs he had fixed the previous day.

He crossed his fingers and hoped that he could deliver on at least one of the two projects. Maybe EVE, if not ADAM.

6

Pam looked at the footage on her tablet for the hundredth time. Each time she reviewed it, she was convinced that they were not dealing with humans. *Fine, they're not human. But then, what exactly are they?*

Her office was a small one at DRDO Bhawan on Rajaji Marg. She sat at her desk and looked at the pin-up board placed above it. The board held the usual stuff—a time planner, reminder Post-It notes and a few photographs. She looked at a photo showing a group of participants at a seminar in Thailand, standing in front of a Buddhist temple. She was wearing a straw hat and sunglasses. Standing next to her, his arm around her shoulders, was a man in a navy blue T-shirt and a white golf cap. Mark Richards.

Something clicked in Pam's head. *My go-to man is Mark. This investigation could really do with his help.*

Mark headed a company called Centre for Bioengineering, Training and Terrain. CBTT was a joint venture between the DRDO and Israel's AXTech, one of the world's largest defence technology firms, headquartered in Tel Aviv.

The relationship between India and Israel was a sensitive and important one owing to the fact that India was Israel's largest purchaser of military equipment. But the rapport operated under the radar so as to keep India's friendship with the Islamic world intact. CBTT operated silently and never allowed its employees to talk about what they did. Many senior executives had received marching orders when they proved to be indiscreet. 'Even a fish would not get into trouble if it kept its mouth shut,' the chairman of AXTech was known to say. Discretion was key.

Pam and Mark had become friends while attending the same technology seminars and conferences. Both of them were connected, albeit in different ways, to the DRDO. Mark was an ex-Marine, ex-CIA man who had handled assignments in Thailand, Cambodia, China and Vietnam during his stint in the agency. His career had taken a toll on his marriage, which had finally ended in a nasty divorce. And then the final whammy—he had been diagnosed with leukemia.

But Mark was a fighter. Even while undergoing multiple rounds of chemotherapy, he would joke with the nurses. 'How are you today, Mr Richards?' the pretty nurse at Sloan-Kettering would ask him as she opened the curtains.

'I was getting better yesterday,' he would reply, 'but today I've taken a turn for the nurse.' Needless to say, Mark eventually made a full recovery and also earned a date with the pretty nurse.

Some months later, he was headhunted by AXTech to lead a technology company that could improve the odds for armed combatants in the field. Mark was the ideal man for the job because of his engineering degree from West Point, his combat experience and deep understanding of geopolitics.

Mark would never forget that first AXTech interview. The dossier they had compiled on him was two inches thick; there was virtually nothing about him they did not already know. *Why do they even need to interview me?* he had wondered. But he soon realised the interview was a marketing pitch to get him to join AXTech.

Among AXTech's biggest customers were the Indian armed forces, with 1.4 million active personnel and 2.1 million in reserve. The new job would mean relocating to New Delhi, and his doctor was worried about the effects of the city's polluted air on his health. But it was exactly the sort of significant change Mark was looking for. He desperately wanted to put the past behind him, forget just about everything he had done, and all that had happened, even the terrible nightmares that plagued him as he slept. He accepted the offer with alacrity.

Under Mark, CBTT morphed into a behemoth that straddled all spheres of human–machine interaction and predictive analytics and automation. This included products that leveraged artificial intelligence in combat— on land, sea and air. Mark's innate ability to distinguish between technologies that were merely 'sexy' versus those with solid relevance for an emerging power like India made him indispensable at CBTT. He often joked with his colleagues that it was easy to develop artificial intelligence but much more difficult to counter natural human stupidity.

Pam looked at the group snapshot again and hesitantly reached for the phone on her desk. There was no denying that Mark was an attractive man. He was just shy of fifty, with blonde hair and an athletic frame. On the bridge of his nose sat a pair of tortoise shell glasses. He wore one of his many identical navy blue T-shirts, almost like a Steve Jobs uniform.

A year ago Pam and Mark had met at a conference in Goa. The age gap of thirteen years had proved utterly inconsequential because it turned out they connected at every level. The last evening of the conference had resulted in too much booze and a shared bed for one passionate night. Both had agreed to leave that encounter behind them, thus avoiding complications. They both needed to get on with their lives, but a tinge of regret lingered. Whether this was for the time spent together or for the parting of ways that followed was uncertain. Pam wasn't sure if calling Mark was such great idea after all. She held the handset without dialling his number. *Should I?*

Her elbow touched the screen of her tablet. The attack video started playing again. *This carnage could be repeated if I don't figure it out.* She made up her mind. Personal feelings could not get in the way.

She needed Mark's help irrespective of Thakur's approval or disapproval. And irrespective of how it might complicate her life.

7

When Pam reached the building occupied by CBTT in Gurgaon, the lobby was teeming with security guards. She passed through a metal detector and was then frisked with an electronic wand. It was a full ten minutes before she was able to make her way to the elevator.

Stepping out on the fifteenth floor, Pam entered a world of polished concrete tiles, gleaming stainless steel furniture, dark wood and modern art. The opulence was intimidating. *The broom closet here is probably bigger than my office*, she thought.

Mark's secretary was waiting for her near the reception. A plump lady with her hair up in a tight bun, she led Pam through a corridor until they reached a large corner conference room with a magnificent view of the other gleaming towers in the business district. 'He'll be with you in a moment,' she announced as she closed the door behind her.

Mark walked in less than a minute later. Any initial awkwardness quickly dissipated with his affectionate hug and casual demeanour. Pam was relieved. It was good to know that Mark had put that night behind them. They sat down at right angles to each other at the head of the table while the secretary brought them water and coffee.

'My lucky day. What brings you here?' asked Mark, a genuine smile on his face. It was obvious that he was pleased to see her.

'I must tell you that I'm not supposed to be discussing this with you, Mark,' began Pam. 'The matter is top secret. As of now I still do not have the requisite clearance to share information with you.'

'Would you prefer that I left the room?' joked Mark. There was no reaction on Pam's face. 'Ah, serious matter, then,' he said. 'Fine, scout's honour. Information does not leave this room without your approval.'

Pam removed her tablet from its sleeve and ran the video for Mark. 'Where is this happening?' he asked. 'Doklam?' That skirmishes had taken place in Doklam was public knowledge. What was not commonly known was the extent of the carnage.

'I'd rather not confirm or deny,' said Pam. 'All I want is for you to take a look at the attackers. I'm confounded by their bulk, strength and agility. Are these ordinary human soldiers, or could we be dealing with something else?'

Mark ran through the footage a few times. 'Have you heard of motion capture?'

'You mean animated films?' asked Pam.

'Yes,' said Mark. 'It's a method of recording the actions of human actors and using that information to animate digital characters in films. Effectively, the animated figure mimics the actions of a live actor.'

'What does that have to do with the video I just showed you?' asked Pam, confused.

'Here at CBTT, we've found a way to reverse the process. We can look at the actions of an on-screen figure and have those actions performed by life-size dummies. By measuring the actions of the dummy—one that has the physical attributes of a human—we can tell you whether the actions are within the realm of normal human endeavour.'

'Incredible,' murmured Pam. 'So by doing a reverse motion capture of this footage, you could answer my question?'

Mark nodded. 'We've just developed a set of algorithms that can carry out millions of calculations to precisely answer that sort of question. Shall we try it?'

He stood up and held the door open for Pam. They walked back through the corridor to an elevator that took them from the fifteenth floor to the eighteenth. Mark placed his palm on a scanner to open the door to a technology suite that looked like a recording studio. On one wall were banks of screens wired up to a cluster of sleek high-end servers. At the console end were terminals for input and output. Behind the screens was a room that contained a variety of life-size dummies that could be activated from the terminals.

Mark shooed away the sole technician in the room. Pam was relieved that they were not widening the number of people that needed to be brought into the loop. He streamed the video from Pam's tablet on to one of the screens and allowed the moves to be replicated by DB73, one of the closely matching dummies. A parallel screen showed the dummy replicating the reverse motion capture.

On the terminal screen were multiple readings of torque, displacement, velocity, acceleration, power and momentum. It looked like a bunch of garbled numbers to Pam, but Mark was studying them intently. 'I'll call in the technician to make sense of the numbers,' he said, picking up the intercom. 'Luckily we don't have to share the footage with him.'

The techie came back and sat at the terminal, studying the numbers without any reaction. 'Have you ever played video games?' he asked Mark, continuing to stare at the numbers.

'Sure,' replied Mark.

'Fortnite?'

'Heard of it,' said Mark. 'Every kid in town seems to be playing it these days.'

'Within the game, you have something called a "power level" for each player. It determines what type of missions you can undertake, how strong you'll be and even the kind of experience you'll have on different missions. In other combat games you have cheat keys that can deliver greater power from an ordinary kick or punch.'

Pam wondered where he was going with this. 'So?' she asked.

'Let me give you an example,' said the techie. 'When a combatant kicks his opponent, we know that the angular acceleration of the lower leg should be maximum at the instant of contact. If we look at the angular velocity, angular acceleration, mass moment of inertia, angular momentum and plane of motion thrown up by these numbers, they all seem in line with those of humans.'

'So every action of these combatants matches that of humans?' asked Mark.

'Yes, but highly amplified, as though some sort of turbo-boost has been applied,' said the techie. 'The sudden spurt of power in their actions goes way beyond the scope of even experienced martial arts practitioners.'

Pam looked at Mark. He shrugged helplessly. They were no closer to a solution.

8

At the headquarters of India's external intelligence agency, the Research and Analysis Wing, the RAW chief picked up the phone on his desk. 'Jaya, could you please see me?' he said into the handset as he looked out from his window at the treetops of Lodhi Road in central Delhi.

Venkata Thirumala Kumaramangalam was never referred to by his full name because it was such a mouthful. Those in RAW and government and intelligence circles simply called him VTK. In most documents, he was referred to as 'Secretary-R', a title that was utterly understated. The 'R' in the designation simply stood for 'Research', and every chief of RAW had held that odd and rather modest title since the founding of the agency in 1968 by R.N. Kao.

VTK was a veteran in the business, having spent over twenty-one years with the agency. It was possible to walk into a room and completely miss him, but in his line of work, that was an advantage. He had a wiry frame, and his hair had turned salt-and-pepper many years ago, probably from the stress of the job. He always wore khaki trousers and a white bush shirt, even when he dropped in to see the prime minister. Perched on his nose were a pair of thick glasses that ensured nothing escaped his attention.

VTK had been born to a poor farmer in the hamlet of Kodagarai in Tamil Nadu. He walked three hours each day to reach the nearest government school and then three hours back. His determination had come to the notice of the district collector, who stepped in to sponsor his education. VTK had started his career as an officer with the Indian Police Service and then been deputed as a young agent to RAW. During his career he had served in tricky foreign capitals such as Karachi, Beijing and Moscow.

RAW had been established with just 250 people in 1968 but since then had expanded to around 8,000 agents. But its staffing and budget remained a secret. VTK reported directly to the prime minister. In fact, RAW had not been structured as an agency but as a wing of the cabinet secretariat. This meant that RAW was not answerable to parliament and was conveniently out of the purview of the Right to Information Act. Unknown to the public, from its very earliest days, RAW had also nurtured a secret relationship with Mossad—Israel's external intelligence agency. VTK had completed a training stint in Tel Aviv in his early days.

He looked up when he heard a knock on his door. The lady who stepped in, Jaya Roy, was an old hand in RAW. She was in her late fifties but incredibly fit owing to her morning yoga routine followed by an hour's walk at Lodhi Gardens. Her tightly pulled back hair gave her a strict, schoolmarmish look. She sat down on one of the visitors' chairs opposite VTK.

Jaya had been born into an intellectual and academic-minded Bengali family. Her inclination to learn new languages had resulted in her graduating with honours from the School of Language, Literature and Culture Studies at Jawaharlal Nehru University. Two of her research papers in the 1990s had brought her to the attention of the then Indian prime minister, Narasimha Rao, who was multilingual himself. Young Jaya had quickly been inducted into the prime minister's office to assist with work related to drafting agreements, speeches and international treaties. It was while she was working under Rao that VTK had noticed her. He had requested the prime minister to spare her, and Jaya had come to work for RAW. It had been a good decision. Over the past few decades, she had been posted at various Indian embassies around the world as RAW's eyes and ears, now fully trained in the art and science of covert action and intelligence. Presently she headed the China and Southeast Asia desk.

'The prime minister's office has been in touch,' said VTK to Jaya. 'They want you to assist Pam Khurana with investigating the Doklam attack. Please give her whatever help she needs.' He pushed a thin folder towards her.

'Pam Khurana?' asked Jaya as she skimmed through the folder. 'Colonel Kishan Khurana's daughter?'

VTK nodded. 'There are research and technology issues involved, hence the need for a DRDO person to spearhead the effort instead of RAW. She's among the best.'

Jaya nodded in assent, toying with the locket around her neck. She could not understand why the assignment had not been given to her department. RAW's China and Southeast Asia desk was entirely capable of handling it. Jaya believed that intelligence was best left to professionals. Of course, on the opposite side were those who believed that the term 'Indian intelligence' was an oxymoron.

Jaya let go of the locket self-consciously and asked, 'Any specific protocols to be followed?'

'You report only to me,' replied VTK. 'Put nothing in writing. Keep me posted on *everything* that Pam Khurana asks for and *everything* you give her. Remember that this matter is being personally monitored by the PMO. I have that old sod General Jai Thakur breathing down my neck and he throws in references to the prime minister and the minister of defence in every second sentence.'

Jaya laughed uncomfortably, refusing to comment. It was always a good idea to steer clear of politics. She had seen too many good agents sacrificed at the altar of power play. She stood up, gathered her papers and left.

VTK looked down at his desk. Two mobile phones lay on it. One of them had a mobile scrambler plugged into a port. He picked up the scrambler-jacked phone and dialled a number.

'Hello?' he said. 'We need to discuss developments.'

9

Mark and Pam walked over from his office block to the neighbourhood Starbucks. The cold winter air felt refreshing. *This is beginning to feel like a date,* Mark thought, then he banished the thought quickly. Whatever had happened was in the past. Neither of them needed to go back there.

They settled down at a two-seater window table with their food. It felt good to be in the warmth of the restaurant. Pam dug in. She was ravenous. 'Do you think China may have succeeded in engineering droids?' she asked between mouthfuls of her grilled chicken sandwich.

Mark looked at her, a faint smile on his lips. She had breadcrumbs and mayo on her upper lip. There was something so childlike about her. *There's a reason I fell in love with you, Pam Khurana,* he thought.

Mark forced himself to snap back to the question. 'Depends on what your definition of "droid" is,' he replied. 'The word was actually coined for the *Star Wars* franchise and entered scientific vocabulary over a period of time. Assuming you're referring to a robot equipped with some degree of artificial intelligence.'

'Yes, exactly,' said Pam. 'Do you think the Chinese are there yet?'

'It's possible,' replied Mark carefully. 'One of China's most sought-after and highly respected scientists, Erkin Chong—who until recently was conducting pathbreaking research in RAS and AI at Stanford—has been lured back to Beijing by the Chinese authorities.'

'RAS and AI?'

Mark accessed a file on his phone and passed it to Pam. 'Read this,' he said. It was an excerpt from a document drafted by the US Congressional Research Service.

Autonomy: The level of independence that humans grant a system to execute a given task.

Robot: A powered machine capable of executing a set of actions by direct human control, computer control or both.

Robotic and Autonomous Systems (RAS): A framework to describe systems with a robotic element, an autonomous element or both.

Artificial Intelligence (AI): The capability of a computer system to perform tasks that normally require human intelligence, including decision-making.

Pam looked up at Mark. 'Want to tell me why Erkin has gone back to China? Seems strange, given he was at Stanford.'

'The Chinese have their ways,' said Mark. 'If it isn't money, then it's some information that they can leverage. And their agencies know everyone's weak spots. They know how to turn the screws on anyone. It's believed that Erkin has been brought in to accelerate their programmes.'

'Which programmes?'

'Apparently the Chinese have two key programmes,' said Mark, swallowing the buckwheat noodles in his mouth. In comparison to Pam, he was positively elegant in his eating habits. 'ADAM and EVE. The former stands for Adaptable Design Artificial Manpower. The latter for Enzymatic Viability Engineering. Both programmes are geared towards defence, not manufacturing.'

'How exactly do you happen to know all this?'

'Let's just say I may be ex-CIA, but my friends are still around when I need them.' *I wish I could tell you everything, but then I'm not sure you would still want me around*, thought Mark.

'Is the Chinese robot programme like the American one?' asked Pam.

'Not really. When the US military uses the term "robot", they mean everything from self-driving trucks to what one would conventionally think of as a robot. They're more accurately called autonomous systems rather than robots. The Chinese programme is different because it attempts to combine RAS with AI.'

'How?'

'Their aim is to create humanoids that are battle-ready—humanoids that can take lethal combat decisions. But the general consensus within defence circles is that they are many years away from anything like that. They selectively leak misinformation to keep their enemies in constant fear.'

'Why? What's to be gained by revealing what one is up to?'

'Read Sun Tzu's *The Art of War*,' replied Mark. 'One of its lessons: Appear weak when you are strong and strong when you are weak. The supreme art of war is to subdue the enemy without fighting. The Chinese are doing precisely that, fighting a war of perception. Much of the stuff being attributed to Chinese labs is hogwash.'

But can one assume that? Pam wondered as her mind went back to the slaughter at Doklam. She forced herself back to the present. 'Superhuman engineering,' she murmured. 'Who would have ever thought we would be discussing this in the context of India–China.' She paused. 'Mark, who can help me figure this out? I know nothing about human engineering.'

'Have you heard of Dr Raja Rao?' asked Mark.

'Who is he?'

'He's a ninety-year-old recluse. He used to live in an academy near Chennai, but his current whereabouts are not known. I'm not even sure if he's still alive, but it would be worth your while to track him down if he is.'

'Why Rao in particular?' Pam asked.

'He is, simply put, the most knowledgeable man alive on the subject of human engineering. CBTT's parent company, AXTech, and several others tried many times to recruit him, but with no success. He was no longer interested, not even in the capacity of a consultant. Something must have turned him into a recluse, but I don't know what.'

Pam noted Raja Rao's name in one of the back pages of her diary. It was the same diary her father had used for his notes and was among her most prized possessions. Along with his lighter, pen and hip flask, it was the only thing that had survived Colonel Kishan Khurana.

She often wished he could talk to her through that diary. She could do with his advice and direction.

10

I stood resolutely at the gate of the Jing Tu monastery in Dongdu.[1] My feet were numb because I had been standing there for over three days, refusing to take a break. I was on the verge of collapsing from the heat, hunger and dehydration, but there was something that kept me rooted there.

It had recently been announced that the studies of fourteen young men at Jing Tu—or Pure Land—monastery would be fully sponsored by the state.

Located on the north bank of the Luo River, a tributary of the Huang He,[2] the monastery was set in a picturesque region, surrounded by mountains and hills. It was the sort of environment that prompted children to play outdoors all day, but that feeling was alien to me. I was the quiet, indoors sort, the sort that took pleasure in solitude.

I desperately wanted to be among the fourteen chosen ones, but I knew that my age would be a problem. I, Xuanzang, was just

---

1. Modern-day Luoyang in Henan Province, China.
2. Yellow River, the second longest river in China.

thirteen, and the minimum age for acceptance was fifteen. It seemed highly unlikely that the abbot, Zheng Shanguo, would bend the rules for me. For every seat that was available, there were a hundred candidates waiting in line.

Standing outside the gates without food or water had given me plenty of time to take stock of my life so far. I had been born in the year 602 in Chenliu[3] and given the lay name of Chenhui. Chenliu was quite close to this monastery in Dongdu and was located in the province of Henan, often regarded as the cradle of Chinese civilisation. The abundant, fertile plains made this region one of the most prosperous in the land. Of course, prosperity also comes with inherent risks. The Huang He frequently flooded the plains, carrying crops, houses and people with it. That is the binary nature of the world; every positive comes with a negative.

I was the youngest of four sons. My mother passed away when I was only five, and my father died just a few years later. Both my parents gave me an abundance of love during the short time they spent with me. In addition to love, we were surrounded by books. Ours was a family that valued education and wisdom. You see, one of my ancestors had been a minister to a king of the Eastern Han dynasty. My great-grandfather served as the prefect of Shangdang.[4] My grandfather was a professor at the Imperial Academy. My father was a scholarly Confucian who also served as the magistrate of Jiangling.[5] Thus, my family had a long tradition of serving emperors in positions that required education and intellect.

I grew up rather serious and introspective. My favourite activity was reading, typically the writings of ancient sages. I would ignore the voices of my friends playing outside so that I could absorb the wisdom of the written word. Our home was characterised by piety, kindness, culture and gentleness.

---

3. A town in Kaifeng County, Kaifeng, in Henan Province, China.

4. Modern-day Changzhi City in southeast Shanxi Province, China.

5. Modern-day Jingzhou, Hubei, China.

While I was still a baby, my father resigned his magisterial post and decided to stay away from court. Although I knew nothing of this then, I later understood the importance of his action. The political climate of Cina[6] was turbulent at the time. The country was ruled by the Sui dynasty—the successors to the Qin—but it was evident to all that it would be shortlived. The internal and external pressures on the kingdom were simply too great. It necessarily had to make way for another. My father's decision to stay away from the political turmoil proved to be a smart one, because the Sui dynasty was soon overthrown by the Tang. Thanks to my father's farsightedness, our family escaped being branded as enemies of the Tang.

I was desperate to be accepted into Jing Tu. I tried several times to catch the attention of the imperial envoy, who was easily identifiable by his red silken Hanfu. It made him stand out from the multitude dressed in blue or black hemp, a regulation that applied to all of us common folk. But I had no luck. I eventually decided to take matters into my own hands, having stood there for three days. I gave the guards the slip by using a little-known gate in the back alley and wandered in towards the examination hall. I could see hundreds of boys competing to acquire one of the coveted spots, and my heart sank. There was simply no way I would be accepted.

Just as I was about to give up and turn away, the imperial envoy walked up to me. Unbeknownst to me, he had been observing me for the past few days. He asked my age, to which I gave a truthful answer. Then he enquired why I so fervently wanted to be a monk. I did not hesitate. 'I want to be Di San Sou Chuan in the service of our emperor and the Buddha,' I replied, then paused fearfully, I had no clue what I had said and what reaction it would produce. It was just something I had heard my father say often, that Cina needed the next 'Di San Sou Chuan'. He never explained himself.

---

6. China

The imperial envoy smiled at me from behind his horseshoe moustache, adjusting the hair above his lip with his emerald-encrusted ring finger. He remained for a few minutes in contemplation. Apparently no one had ever given him such a clear response till then. I discovered later that he was impressed by my humility, confidence and enthusiasm. He told the monks that they could not exclude me because he saw immense potential in me. He urged them to make an exception in the matter of my candidature.

Eventually, my age was overlooked by the abbot and I was accepted into the order, much to the disappointment of many other qualified candidates. I was ecstatic. My elder brother Chengsu was already a monk at Jing Tu, and I could be now close to him.

I did not know it at the time, but my journey henceforth would be a lonely one, without friends or family by my side. And it had already begun.

11

I was seated in the main hall of the Jing Tu monastery. All you could hear was the low chanting of hundreds of monks like me. The dark interiors were bathed in a soft glow from the oil lanterns that hung from the rafters. A comforting smell of incense pervaded the hall. Time stood still—the past, the present and the future all absorbed into one solitary moment.

Our routine was both monotonous and arduous. We would be up well before dawn to meditate and chant. After a few hours of this, we would walk around the neighbourhood to collect alms from the community. We had been taught that seeking alms was necessary in order to demolish the ego. We would then go back to the monastery, have breakfast and bathe. This was followed by a few more hours of chanting and meditation. Lunch, the last meal for the day, was a silent affair, followed by teachings from the Buddhist scriptures. A few hours in the evening were again devoted to meditation before we turned in for the night. The pattern never varied.

I was blessed with an outstanding memory that allowed me to remember almost everything in a single reading. I had my revered father to thank for that. He had introduced me to books at such an early age that I had quickly learnt how to scan and absorb material almost effortlessly. It was easy for me to remember blocks of text and the specific pages they could be found on.

One day, when I was repeating verses from the Heart Sutra as recited by my master, I began making variations. It was instinctive; to this day, I cannot understand why I did it. The master raised his eyes, questioning my carelessness. Lay monks were meant to be disciplined, not casual, in matters of learning.

Later in the day, the master called me to his chamber. I stood before him nervously, awaiting a reprimand. His expression was sombre. But suddenly a smile appeared on his face. 'I now realise you were reciting the Heart Sutra exactly the way I recited the verses a month ago, although that recitation was from another version. You have an incredible memory, Xuanzang. Nothing seems to escape you.' I bowed before him in gratitude.

As a reward, the master permitted me some time off to visit the White Horse temple in Dongdu. I was overjoyed. The White Horse was no ordinary temple. It had been built more than five centuries ago by Emperor Ming to commemorate the arrival of two eminent monks from Yindu,[7] Kashyapa Matanga and Dharmaraksha, or She Moteng and Zhu Falan, as the Chinese called them. They had brought with them many Buddhist sutras and statues loaded on the back of a white horse. Their arrival marked the first time that Buddhism had made an appearance in Cina. The temple was the very cradle of Buddhism in our land.

But why on earth had the two monks come all the way from Yindu? As the tale goes, Emperor Ming of the Han dynasty

---

7. India

had a dream in which he saw a spirit that had a body of gold and a head that emitted rays of light. The emperor's wise men identified the spirit as the Buddha. The emperor then commanded that a delegation go west, looking for the Buddha's teachings. The envoys eventually brought back these two monks from Yindu, who carried with them various sutras for translation and transmission.

The two monks had remained busy for many years, translating sutras in the temple, with a team to assist them. It is said that they translated six texts, the last of which was the Sutra of Forty-two Chapters, the only one to eventually survive. The sutra made the White Horse temple famous; people from all over the region came there to study, pray, meditate and preach.

I was filled with joy as I walked through the immense, tranquil grounds. A light breeze wafted through the pine trees. Just outside the gate was a languid pool that had fish swimming in it. I crossed the stone bridge over the pool to enter the temple. To the east and west of the gate lay the tombs of She Moteng and Zhu Falan, the two monks from Yindu. From there, I crossed into the Hall of Heavenly Kings, the Hall of the Great Buddha, the Hall of Mahavira and, finally, the Hall of Guidance. In the centre of this hall sat the laughing Buddha of the future, Maitreya.

I noticed an ornate urn lying in front of Maitreya and enquired about its contents. One of the monks, who had taken upon himself the responsibility of giving me a tour, told me that the urn had been brought by the great traveller Faxian many years ago and was soon to be shifted to the Shaolin temple in the forests of Mount Song.[8] He did not know what it contained, but knew that it was revered by all the monks.

I had heard of Faxian, a Buddhist monk who had travelled on foot to Yindu between the years 399 and 412. He had returned to Cina via the sea route and had brought back many Buddhist texts and

8. Mountain in China's Henan Province.

treasures, including the urn that was now at the White Horse temple. I found myself fascinated by the tale. At that moment I made up my mind that I would one day visit Yindu, the land of the Buddha.

One of the older monks at the temple blessed me with a toothless smile. 'What do you wish for, son? Search your heart and tell me,' he said softly.

'I want to be Di San Sou Chuan in the service of our emperor and the Buddha,' I replied.

The gentle monk placed his hand on my head in blessing and whispered, 'May Maitreya make it so. Go in peace, my son.'

12

I spent three satisfying years at Jing Tu, from the year 615 onwards. Unfortunately, civil war broke out in Cina around then. The Sui dynasty was on its last legs, as had been foreseen by my revered father. There were riots in Dongdu, and I fled westwards along with my brother Chensu and other monks.

Eventually Chensu and I sought refuge in the mountains of Si Chuanlu,[9] where I spent the next three years in the monastery of Kong Hui. I immersed myself in the study of texts such as the Abhidharmakosa Sastra and, finally, in the year 622, I was ordained as a monk.

I spent the next few years touring various provinces in quest of Buddhist knowledge. One of the places I visited was the Shaolin temple in Yangcheng.[10] Shaolin derived its name from Shaoshi Mountain, one of the seven peaks of the Song range. It had been made famous a century ago by a monk from Yindu who sat inside a cave, facing the wall in meditation, for many years.

---

9. Modern-day Sichuan Province, China.

10. Modern-day Dengfeng in Henan Province, China.

Special land grants and privileges had been bestowed by the emperor upon the monks of Shaolin. And truth be told, they deserved them all. Life in the temple was gruelling, and they lived in conditions bereft of comfort — pretty much as I had done at the Jing Tu monastery. They awoke several hours before dawn, studied and then followed a rigid routine of physical conditioning. All of this happened even before breakfast. The rest of the day was a cyclical repetition of the morning schedule. Being a monk at Shaolin demanded both mental and physical strength.

In Shaolin, I saw the monks paying their respects to two urns. I was reminded of my visit to the White Horse temple many years ago, where I had seen a similar urn that had been brought by Faxian from Yindu. The monks revealed that one of these was from the earliest days of the founding of Shaolin. The other was the one that had originally been kept in the White Horse temple. It had been shifted to Shaolin a few years ago. When I asked what was special about the urns, they replied that they were called the Kangzhi urns, but only the seniormost masters knew what they contained.

One of the monks turned to me and said, 'You can be Di San Sou Chuan if you try hard enough.' I had heard the term used repeatedly ever since I was a child, but I was surprised to hear the monk mention it so casually to me. I knew by now that the expression had always been used as a mark of great respect and admiration within Cina. But what did it actually mean? What was the significance of Di San Sou Chuan?

In the year 625, I reached Chang'an,[11] *the capital of the Tang empire. Chang'an was one of the greatest medieval cities in the world, occupying an area that was six times the size of Daqin.*[12] *It was a city of over a million people, and there was a substantial foreign population that had migrated from northern Yindu and*

---

11. Modern-day Xi'an in Shaanxi Province, China.
12. Rome

central Yazhou.[13] *Confucianism, Taoism, Buddhism, Nestorian Christianity, Zoroastrianism and Manichaeism jostled for space. With so many fine exponents of music, art, cuisine, metalwork, poetry, mathematics, linguistics and fashion, it was the culture and knowledge capital of the world.*

Chang'an boasted protective walls that were over sixteen feet high. Zones were earmarked for specific activities such as manufacturing, trading, prayer, government, entertainment and ordinary living. The city was laid out on a rectangular grid with 114 individually walled blocks. Its wide avenues and streets numbered eleven from north to south and fourteen from east to west. All the streets were tree-lined and had ditches running alongside for drainage.

Chang'an even had a network of canals to facilitate the movement of goods across the city. This would eventually be copied by many capitals around the world. Government and palace buildings were enclosed in walled compounds and also contained areas for the use of visiting foreign embassies. In the southeast of the city was an extensive pleasure park containing a lake, multiple lotus ponds, flower gardens and pavilions. The city excelled in its many tall buildings—mostly Buddhist temples and pagodas. And its temples not only organised religious services, exhibitions of relics and religious festivities but also carried out substantial public services such as providing food for the poor, public baths and medication for the sick.

It was easy to get distracted by the physical beauty of Chang'an, but I was determined to progress intellectually and spiritually. I immersed myself in endless discussions and debates. There were so many great intellectuals in Chang'an. And then, one day, I met a visiting monk from Yindu who was fluent in Chinese. His name was Prabhakaramitra. I was so very excited to meet someone from the land of the Buddha.

---

13. Asia

Prabhakaramitra was working along with a team of linguists to translate three Buddhist texts into Chinese. Around sixty-five years of age, he had a wealth of knowledge to share. For the first time ever, I was able to get insights into Buddhism from someone who had studied the original texts.

I realised then that I should go to Yindu so that I could arrive at the true essence of Buddhism as well as its source texts. Maybe I could also become Di San Sou Chuan along the way, as the monks of Yangcheng had suggested. Prabhakaramitra recommended I go to Nalanda, the ultimate seat of Buddhist learning, and study under Silabhadra, the greatest Buddhist scholar of the time.

I began learning Sanskrit after my encounter with Prabhakaramitra, so that I could read the scriptures in their original form. I also started visiting the western market of the city in order to learn Tokharian, the language spoken in places to the west of Cina, such as Turfan.[14]

I was preparing myself for the real journey of my life.

13

Just before dawn, in an open yard the size of a football field, hundreds of men wearing little more than jockstraps performed exercises. Their focus was on footwork and hand movements. The sticks they held were fashioned out of reeds hardened by repeated immersions in water and vigorous pounding. While the insides of these sticks were like semi-porous cork, they were capable of becoming lethal weapons by virtue of the speed at which they were wielded.

This secret facility in Dengfeng County, in China's Henan Province, was enclosed within prison-like walls. Located

---

14. Modern-day Turpan in Xinjiang, China.

at the foot of Mount Song, it was surrounded by dense forest. An outer perimeter of barbed wire ensured that approaching the facility's walls was near impossible for anyone without being spotted.

High above the walls were electric wires that could kill intruders instantly. Watchtowers at the four corners of the plot were manned by security guards 24/7. All personnel patrolling the facility had to be vetted by the Ministry of State Security (the MSS). No one could enter or leave the premises without multiple levels of clearance. Massive floodlights illuminated every sector of the complex at all times, and a closed-circuit camera system ensured that every zone of the facility was monitored round the clock. It was impossible to tell whether the intense security was to bar outsiders from getting in or to prevent insiders from getting out.

Each of the participants was an expert in the various movements: leaps, backbends, somersaults, handstands and body rolls. They were strong yet graceful. Seventy per cent of their routine was leg-training and thirty had to do with the use of their fists. Up on a stage in front of the exercising men were three drummers, who varied the tempo of their beat as a signal to slow down or speed up, the sound of their grim percussion punctuated by the whoosh of hundreds of synchronised swinging sticks as they cut through the early morning air. There was a theatrical quality to the spectacle.

To the northern side of the plot was a massive residential block; built above it was a viewing gallery used by teachers to observe the participants. Two senior masters from the nearby Shaolin temple lived here to manage the training and strengthening routine of the young men. The masters could smell the clarified butter that was being heated in a large cauldron in the northwest corner. The aroma wafted towards them, helped by an easterly wind. As soon as the masters raised their hands, the drummers stopped. The exercising men rubbed down their bodies with towels and headed towards the platform bearing the cauldron. Each day, hundreds of pounds of butter, along with an amalgam of herbs, were heated to produce sterilised clarified butter. The men formed a disciplined queue, and each received and downed six ounces of the liquid.

Their routine never varied. They were woken two hours before dawn to perform their exercises, followed by a drink of clarified butter. They then proceeded to the spa block, where they received oil massages and mud packs in addition to a daily physical exam. This was followed by a bath and the only meal of the day, sometime between breakfast and lunch: a porridge of lentils, sprouts and vegetables cooked in clarified butter and some mild spices. After an hour's rest, the men went through an hour of meditation, breathing exercises and routines involving intense concentration, before several hours of training in hand-to-hand combat, artillery usage, knife- and spear-wielding and physical endurance. They slept for less than five hours at night, but they slept deeply.

The two senior masters, dressed in yellow robes draped with vermillion shawls, over which their rosaries hung, looked on from the balcony. They should have been pleased with the results, but they looked worried, the wrinkles on the older master's forehead deepening as he watched the proceedings.

'Shouldn't we say something to the authorities?' asked the younger monk.

'How will it help?' responded his senior. 'They have already made up their mind, and there's no argument that can make them see reason. All that we can hope to achieve is to make these men better equipped to deal with the hazard.'

'How?' asked the younger man, unwilling to allow his words to go unchallenged.

'Six elements will improve the odds—reaction time exercises, technique repetition, enhanced physical endurance, weapon drills, synchronised movements and diet. This will enable them to deal more effectively with the undesired side effects of the programme.'

'But isn't it our job to make better warriors? Why are we allowing this to happen to these innocent boys?'

The young monk was familiar with routines that focused on improving the agility of joints and articulations, strengthening internal organs, consolidating body strength and concentrating energy. *Instead, what are we doing? Compensating for unwanted chemical changes!*

'But we're doing all that we must,' said the senior master. 'Remember, these fighters are in command of unlimited power. Their arms weigh only ten jins but can displace objects weighing 10,000 jins with a single stroke. Each warrior's arm is a head; his legs are a tail. A single movement defines this warrior. He is nothing short of a dragon, capable of striking with all parts of his body.'

'A dragon that will die because we have decided that on his behalf,' said the younger monk with pain in his eyes.

The older monk looked at his colleague with a hint of sadness. *He's only saying what I can't,* he thought.

14

Near Mehrauli lies an area known as Sanjayvan. During the day, Sanjayvan is a pleasant picnic spot, but at night, once the woods go silent, it becomes sinister. Within Sanjayvan are the ruins of Lal Kot, a fort dating back to the Tomar dynasty. Nestled among the ruins is a Muslim burial ground that houses the bodies of children. It is believed that the buried children rise from their graves each night, and their laughter and wails can be heard at great distances. Not surprisingly, very few people venture into these woods at night. It is thus the ideal spot for a secret rendezvous—if one is not fainthearted.

Two pairs of car headlights wound their way up the dirt road to the walls of Lal Kot at midnight and halted at a predetermined spot. Two individuals stepped out of their respective cars and sat on a bench roughly hewn from a boulder that had fallen off the ramparts of the fort many years ago. They had used this spot many times in the past because of the nearby peepal tree. Local lore had it that a ghostly apparition, a woman with long hair and dressed in a white saree, hung by her neck from that tree each night, recreating her violent death many centuries ago. Of course, it was absolute hogwash. Why kill yourself repeatedly if you were already dead?

Both were clad in heavy winter coats. Shengli lit a cigarette and inhaled the smoke deeply. The name 'Shengli' was a nom de guerre, and it was often referred to in hushed tones among intelligence circles. No one knew who Shengli was, but everyone knew that the spy was the best in the business. This was conceded by friends and enemies alike. It had now been several years since Shengli had become a merchant of that extremely valuable commodity pricier than gold, diamonds or oil: information. The life of a spy was always risky, but that did not matter to Shengli. There were those who became spies for money, excitement or ambition, but Shengli did not fall into any of those baskets. Shengli was a spy because of *idealism*. Those with deeply held beliefs are often willing to die for their ideals.

Next to Shengli sat a senior government functionary who had been the spy's handler for many years. 'Keep an eye on Pam Khurana and keep me posted on everything she does,' said the official. 'I also want to know about anything she discovers *before* it reaches me selectively through other sources.'

Shengli nodded, exhaling. The smoke was dense and acrid because of the Camel non-filter cigarettes that the spy always smoked. This combined with Delhi's cold air produced a thicker fume than usual. The chances of developing lung cancer were high, but it was infinitely more probable that Shengli would die in the line of duty well before that. Shengli did not really care. *Count the life in your years, not the years in your life. Who had said that? John Lennon? Muhammad Ali? Abraham Lincoln?* Shengli settled on the last name.

Both ignored the stray noises emanating from the forest. It was foolish to attribute supernatural reasons to ordinary jungle sounds. And they both knew that humans were far more dangerous than ghosts.

'What if she finds out about her father?' asked the spy. 'I mean, the reason he died and the things he knew.'

'Stop worrying about that,' responded the functionary. 'The details died with him. It's also important that we do not allow ourselves to get distracted. We need to be clear regarding our objective: ensuring that the strategic military distance between China and India is maintained. Unfortunately, Pam Khurana can alter that. We must make sure she does not achieve that under any circumstances.'

'How?'

'Let Pam Khurana lead us to the information that India needs. We can then ensure that one of two things happens. One, that it is used to the advantage of our Chinese friends. Two, that the information is destroyed so that it can't be used by India.'

'What about the LLL?' asked Shengli.

The Leninist Liberation League, a far-left radical guerilla outfit, was headquartered in the wild forests of Nagaland. The Naxal organisation was committed to fighting and overthrowing the Indian state. Like many such organisations, it was heavily influenced by Mao Zedong's political ideology.

'We will use them at the right time,' replied the official, thankful to have a resource like Shengli. It was so much easier to deal with people who were of the same ideological disposition.

15

General Jai Thakur alighted from his shiny black Ambassador at the gate of 7 Lok Kalyan Marg, the official residence and principal office of the Indian prime minister. It was six o'clock on a crisp winter morning. The PM was known to begin his meetings at five o'clock in the morning, keeping all his support staff on their toes.

There was only one gate leading to the twelve-acre complex, which comprised five bungalows that housed the PM's residence, an informal meeting room, a conference facility and a guest house. One of the bungalows was occupied by the Special Protection Group (SPG) charged with the PM's security.

Only those who were on the visitors' roster were allowed in. There were no exceptions to that rule unless you were General Jai Thakur. But even Thakur had to park his vehicle at the checkpoint and walk the rest of the way. It was a lovely walk, though, along manicured lawns dotted with arjuna, gulmohar and semal trees, and with peacocks for company.

Thakur was greeted with smart salutes as he walked towards Number Five. This particular bungalow was used by the PM as his residence and informal meeting area. Security was exceptionally tight, with members of the SPG and the Central Reserve Police Force (CRPF) providing cover at every strategic point. The entire complex was a no-fly zone. Thakur's meetings with the PM were always held here rather than in South Block.

On reaching Number Five, Thakur was met by one of the PM's private secretaries, who accompanied him through a small corridor, ignoring the visitors' room. Paintings from the National Gallery of Modern Art adorned the walls. Thakur strode past with barely a glance while the secretary ran ahead and opened the door to a meeting chamber. The PM was already inside. He looked incredibly fit for a man who was just short of seventy.

'Have you initiated the process?' he asked as soon as Thakur was ushered in. There were no greetings, pleasantries or preliminary small talk. Both understood the gravity of the situation.

'Yes, sir,' replied Thakur. 'The assignment has been given to Pam Khurana.' *Someone you wanted. I found out only later that the army chief recommended her because you had already put forward her name.*

'In the meantime, have we called in reinforcements to Chicken's Neck?'

'On their way. The 59th Infantry Division from Panagarh, the 27th Mountain Division from Kalimpong and the 23rd Infantry Division from Ranchi.'

'Equipment and supplies?'

'The very best that we could put together. But if the Chinese use their special forces yet again, we will have a problem,' replied Thakur, unused to mincing his words. It was the reason so many different political dispensations trusted him.

'What do you need from me?'

'Time,' replied Thakur. 'Time to figure out how best to match the power of the Chinese troops. Once we move in a given direction, I do not want to backtrack.'

The PM nodded. 'The moving finger writes; and, having writ, moves on,' he said, quoting Omar Khayyam. The PM's first love was poetry, and it was his incredible oratory that had pulled him into the political arena. By training, he was a medical doctor. But poetry had always been his passion.

Thakur pretended to be appreciative.

'Let's find a way to buy you some time,' said the PM, picking up the phone and calling for his external affairs minister. He motioned for Thakur to leave as the minister walked in.

'I had a fruitful meeting with the president of China only last year,' said the PM to the man who next entered. 'It's unlikely that he is behind this. India and China are emerging superpowers, and it's in our mutual interest to work together.'

The external affairs minister, a Harvard-educated diplomat with two decades of experience in international relations, regarded his boss quizzically. 'China and India are ostensibly different because, unlike India, China is a command–control country where the supreme leader decides everything,' he said. 'But the truth is further away. What happens is not necessarily what the leader wants. It seems that this aggressive posturing is the initiative of the Buzhang, his right-hand man.'

'Have you spoken with the American ambassador about this latest Chinese aggression?'

'The ambassador spoke the usual platitudes but was unwilling to offer anything.'

'What do the Americans want?'

'A deal. They're worried you're veering towards the Russians or the French for the upcoming order of fighter jets.'

'What time is it in Washington DC?' asked the PM suddenly.

The minister looked at his watch. 'They're ten-and-a-half hours behind in winter, so it's 7.30 p.m.,' he replied.

'Let's call him,' said the PM, cutting out the usual protocol of scheduling calls in advance. He asked his private secretary to make the call.

'What will you tell him?'

'That the Americans can have our purchase order for fighter jets provided the technical requirements and commercial terms are in India's best interests.'

'And?'

'The American president must apply pressure on the Chinese to hold their fire and remain at their pre-conflict positions.'

'Why would the Chinese agree?'

'We'll make a fuss about China's one-belt roadway through Pakistan Occupied Kashmir but will allow it to go through anyway,' said the PM. 'We have virtually no control over that region. It's a small concession, but it gives the Americans something to hold out as a carrot to the Chinese.'

The phone rang and the PM answered. 'Nice to talk to you, Mr President,' he said, proceeding to outline his thoughts.

The minister scribbled something on a pad and held it out for the PM's attention. It had a single word. *Intercepts.*

The PM nodded and raised the final issue. He wanted access to American intercepts, particularly those of the National Security Agency. After all, the NSA was the world's largest eavesdropper. Each day, its computers intercepted and stored 1.7 billion e-mails, phone calls and assorted communication.

'I am asking the NSA to keep a tighter vigil on Chinese communications and movements related to India,' assured the American president over the encrypted line, probably one of the few lines that the NSA did not tap. He was delighted that he finally had something his defence lobby would appreciate.

16

While I was in Chang'an I had a vivid dream one night. I had a vision of Mount Sumeru at the centre of the universe, a mountain fashioned from gold, silver, crystal and beryl, and surrounded by a great sea. I saw myself riding on the varnished saddle of a skinny chestnut-coloured horse, inching up the mountainside. The ground was rocky and slippery, so my horse would often lose its footing. But whenever I thought we were about to slip or fall, massive lotus flowers bloomed to support us just in time.

I awoke with a start and realised that the dream was a message: A trip to Yindu would indeed be arduous, but the Buddha would help me get there if I persevered.

I decided to act on the message. I submitted a petition to Emperor Taizong requesting permission to travel to Yindu. I wrote that it was my earnest desire to be Di San Sou Chuan, for which I wished to undertake this trip.

My petition was quickly rejected, without any reason whatsoever. But through my circle of friends and advisers I was told that the Tang empire was still very young and its security was uncertain. Its borders necessarily had to remain sealed. In addition, the empire wanted the civilian population to remain within the city walls in case Chang'an needed to be defended. These were challenging times because of the frequent attacks by the Turks from the north.

To add to my woes, the Tang rulers were suspicious of Buddhists like me. We Buddhists had gained immense power under the previous Sui dynasty—this threatened the Tang monarchs. In fact, the Tangs initially promoted Taoism instead of Buddhism precisely on account of this perceived threat.

But in the autumn of the year 627, there was a poor harvest in the Tang empire when crops failed due to untimely frost. The nine-year-old empire was not adequately prepared to meet the resultant food shortages. The gates of Chang'an were thrown open so that people could make their way to regions of the empire where food was available.

I myself was about to leave, when something unexpected happened. I received an invitation for a personal audience with the emperor. I was completely unprepared for this. Did he wish to dissuade me from my travels? Was he angry with me for having made the request?

I entered the court of the Great Luminous Palace with trepidation. The palace, constructed within the grounds of a great hunting park on the northern edge of the city, was surrounded by extensive flower gardens and water features. No expense had been spared in its construction or appointments. A poor monk like me had never been amidst such opulence.

Walking into the grand hall where the emperor sat, I made my way through the central aisle towards the throne. The emperor was dressed in an exquisite longpao of pale yellow silk embroidered with auspicious animals and dragons. It would have taken four master tailors and embroiderers a full two years to make that single garment; such was the majesty of the emperor.

I got to a circular mark that indicated where I should halt. I knelt before the emperor in the qi-shou position, ensuring that my hands and forehead touched the ground, and stayed there until I was commanded by the monarch to rise. When I did so, he motioned for me to approach him. I paused hesitantly a few feet away, but he beckoned for me to draw closer. Finally, when I stood close beside him, he whispered in my ear: 'The folly of Qin Shi Huang needs a solution.'

I would have liked to probe the meaning of this riddle, but the emperor motioned for me to step back. Once I had retreated, he publicly proclaimed that I had his permission to leave Chang'an but not to leave Cina. My orders were to stay within the borders.

The very next day, I met Prabahakaramitra. I knew he was the only one who could guide me in my secret plans. Prabhakaramitra informed me that there were two routes to Yindu. One was the fairly dangerous sea route from the east. This route had been used by Faxian, at some risk, on his return journey from Yindu.

The other was the land route from the west, which would take me via Xiyu[15] to Yindu. Since silk was the main commodity traded along this route, it was called the Silk Road. It had been used by Faxian on his way to Yindu.

Fifty-four clerics before me had used the Silk Road since the year 260, but most of them had failed to reach their destination. The best example of a successful expedition remained that of Faxian, who went to Yindu in the early fifth century and returned thirteen years later. I was so inspired by his life that I vowed to walk in his footsteps.

I left behind my brother Chengsu and exited the gates of Chang'an a day later.

17

Three large south-facing windows behind the oak desk overlooked the floodlit lawns of the White House. The fireplace at the north end of the office crackled comfortingly.

---

15. Western Regions, the lands beyond Yumen Pass.

The cold wave in Washington DC had turned nasty over the past few weeks, and the toasty interiors of the West Wing were a relief.

The president set down the receiver of the encrypted telephone on his desk and turned to his Director of National Intelligence. 'Are we handling this right?' he asked. 'Why should we even care what happens to India? They still can't get over their ideological hang-ups and will ditch us when it suits them.'

The DNI was used to dealing with the president's impulsiveness. He framed his reply in his mind before responding. 'We must understand that the Chinese are using India as a laboratory experiment. Once they're successful there, they'll apply the strategy to the rest of the world. We need to keep watch. Remember one more thing, Mr President. India can be our primary counterbalance to the Chinese strategy of dominance in Asia.'

'The only difference between China and India is that China actually *has* a strategy,' sneered the president. 'India just lumbers on from one crisis to the next. Then, when China bullies them, they come running to us like tattling schoolkids. And if we don't console them, they run into the arms of Russia.'

'India is a messy democracy, like ours,' said the DNI. 'But we shouldn't forget that China spends four times the amount India spends on defence. China has double the number of aircrafts, three times as many naval ships and twice as many nuclear warheads. An overly aggressive and dominant China will not suit our long-term objectives, Mr President.'

'But India has nukes. And when it comes to nukes, you don't need to be equal. Just a few that sneak through the defence systems of your enemy are enough to bring them to their knees.' He made a grand but farcial gesture with his hands to indicate a massive explosion.

'You can't use nuclear weapons in limited wars because you run the risk of escalation into mutually assured destruction,' replied the DNI. 'The Chinese know that India will not use nuclear weapons in response to conventional warfare. That's why they prefer to engage in salami tactics — slice-by-slice warfare — where they have the edge.'

'By using superhuman robots?' asked the president.

'Difficult to say *what* they are at the present moment. CIA operatives are trying to find out, but the going's been tough.'

'Do we have feet on the ground in India and China?'

The DNI nodded. 'India is relatively easier. Throw a lot of cash and you have a bunch of ministers, bureaucrats, scientists and officers ready to cooperate. But China has been an uphill task.'

'Why?'

'As you know, the Chinese have killed or imprisoned more than thirty of our people in the last two years. Caused by a botched communication system that was easily hacked by the MSS. It took them just twenty-four months to wipe out our most significant assets. The better part of my term as your Director of National Intelligence has been spent patiently rebuilding assets there.'

'What has the progress been like?'

'We've realised that buying existing information sources within China is near impossible. Most people are terrified of being imprisoned or sentenced to death. But planting fresh sources is not so difficult. We're also taking some help from Israel's Mossad, which has better access to China. Some developments are on the cards. We've used the past year to regroup. If we're successful, we may see events unfold rapidly.'

The president nodded. 'Any divide-and-rule at play here?' The president's bumbling exterior concealed a raw intelligence.

'The Chinese leadership consists of two clear groups. One, the idealists committed to the beliefs of Mao Zedong. Two, the reformers committed to the ideals of Deng Xiaoping. We need to play that card. Mossad is in the process of getting to an insider at the Chinese secret prison in Yining in Xinjiang.'

'Why?' asked the president.

'Thousands of people are locked up in gulag-type internment, but some of those prisoners are valuable to us,' replied the DNI.

'Good. I don't really care for the Indians. They're pompous pricks. But I detest the Chinese even more. God alone knows when they'll sneak up and slit your throat with their yellow hands. They seem to reach everywhere.'

The DNI laughed, a tad nervously. He looked around, almost expecting the Oval Office to be bugged. After all, the entire country's eavesdropping network was under his control. He was relieved that the conversation was entirely off the record. It would be a foreign policy disaster if the president's racist remarks were to become public. The man seemed to walk into minefields on purpose. Amazingly, he always emerged unscathed from the explosions he caused.

But the DNI also realised that the president was not entirely mistaken. From time immemorial, the Chinese had managed to get their people to peek into distant territories. The West tom-tommed Marco Polo's trip to China, but that expedition had been six centuries after Xuanzang's journey to India, and ten centuries after Faxian's.

In the early fifteenth century, Chinese emperor Yongle had commissioned the construction of 3,500 ships. Some of these were the largest ships the world had ever known. The fleet's nine-masted flagship measured about 400 feet in length, as compared to the famed explorer Christopher Columbus's Santa Maria, which had measured only eighty-five feet. If subsequent emperors had kept the maritime tradition alive, China, rather than Spain, the Netherlands, England or Portugal would have been considered the greatest seafaring nation in the world.

'Let's keep abreast of what they are both up to because either nation may pull out a rabbit from their hat,' said the president, rising from his chair. He opened the humidor on his desk and carefully picked a cigar from his selection of Cohiba, Gurkha, Arturo Fuente and Regius. He sniffed the chosen cigar appreciatively, then poured himself a shot of bourbon. He gestured for the DNI to join him, knowing full well that the offer would be declined.

'We'll try to ensure that it's our rabbit,' said the DNI cryptically, gathering his papers to leave.

The president walked towards the east door that opened on to the Rose Garden, cigar and glass in hand. He could deal with the cold outside but not with the no-smoking policy of the White House. A peg of Jack Daniels did not taste as good without a Gurkha.

'Make sure it's your rabbit, your hat, your wand and your magician,' he said as he opened the door. 'It's the only way you'll bring the dragon to heel.'

18

Each sector of the Doklam battlefield had been assigned to a different investigator from Mark's forensics team at CBTT. Pam had had no option but to reveal to Mark the exact coordinates of the recorded battle, even though she had held off at first. The objective was to find any biological material—blood, hair, fibre or tissue—that could help identify the enemy soldiers. A secondary objective was to photograph footprints, collect spent casings, discarded ammunition or any other items that could help in assembling a comprehensive profile of the Chinese fighters.

The winds howled as the team painstakingly set up a rope grid to divide the rocky plain into examination sectors. In the distance, the Chinese road that was being extended southwards across the Torsa Nala was visible. If construction had continued, the PLA would have reached Zompelri Ridge, a point that would have given it full access to the Siliguri Corridor, India's northeast jugular.

The investigators were clad in ECWCS—Extreme Cold Weather Clothing System. India used to spend millions acquiring the stuff from foreign suppliers until CBTT developed and started producing the garments within India. Each CBTT examiner was also equipped with a digital camera, a forensic light source, a metal detector, marker flags, evidence bags and a forensic tool kit.

But there was one catch, and the team knew it. General Jai Thakur was still not in the loop. Pam had used the influence of her DRDO boss to get access to a zone entirely cordoned off to outsiders. Pam knew that Thakur would blow a fuse when he got to know, and it was only a matter of time before he did. But she also knew that getting one strong lead could make all the difference.

Pam believed it was easier to beg forgiveness afterwards than to seek permission beforehand. The strategy usually worked, although it came with severe risks of reprisal. Sitting in her office in Delhi, she kept tabs on the team's progress.

All the CBTT examiners were experts at crime scene documentation and capable of reconstructing almost anything, from bullet trajectories to airplane crashes. They were also trained in firearms and trace evidence research and analysis. Mark had insisted on employing an inhouse team at CBTT because the examination of evidence from existing battlegrounds was incredibly useful in developing technology for future application. Trace materials—such as soil, glass, fibres and hair—often contained a wealth of information that could be collected, aggregated and analysed for future use.

But the CBTT investigators were an unhappy lot today.

It seemed that the Chinese had been very careful to sweep the area before withdrawing. In any case, the plot was simply too wide and wild. Whatever remained would have been swept away by nature. No blood, no hair, no tissue, no fibre. The CBTT team was losing hope.

And then, it got worse. The strong winds morphed into a gale. The team ran for cover and took shelter in bunkers built by the Indian Army. They whiled away their time drinking hot tea from tin mugs and cursing the lousy weather. They didn't know it, but the gale was about to reveal itself as a blessing in disguise.

It was a full three hours by the time the gale subsided. The team was able to get back to their assignment, but the strong winds had played havoc with their initial work. Markings had disappeared and bagged samples had been blown away.

The team was unaware that in Delhi, Pam had received an angry phone call from General Thakur. His fury could have melted steel. 'Didn't I tell you that no one was to be involved in this investigation without my prior approval?' he thundered. 'This is complete insubordination. You have accessed a high-security no-go area without seeking permission, then had the temerity to involve a defence contracting firm without my say-so.'

Pam quietly heard out his rant, holding the phone a few inches away from her ear to prevent his rage from frying her brains.

'I apologise, sir,' she said quickly. 'I shall get the team to withdraw immediately.' She cut the line, desperately hoping that her gambit would pay off.

She picked up the satellite phone that would allow her to call off the fact-finding mission in Doklam, but something prevented her from acting. She waited a few minutes more, praying the team would deliver a result that would pacify Thakur sufficiently to overlook her misdemeanour.

Over in Doklam, one of the senior investigators yelped with joy. 'I think I have something, guys!' His colleagues carefully made their way over to him. Sticking out from underneath a rock was a bright blue medical tourniquet. It was routinely used by field soldiers to provide instant compression to an artery or a vein in case of excessive bleeding. This one was clearly stained with blood. The colour and markings on it were not those of the Indian Army.

The tourniquet had not been visible earlier because it lay under a thick layer of soil that had blown over it. The culprit wind had now turned saviour. The senior investigator quickly bagged the bloody tourniquet with gloved hands and placed it in his satchel, preparing to move on to the next search sector.

Just then there was a shout from one of the guards at the bunker. 'General Thakur is on the line. He has instructed us to clear you out immediately. It seems you're officially trespassing.'

19

In a small gatekeeper's cottage set within a large, abandoned complex of buildings on the banks of the Vegavathy River in Kanchipuram, a ninety-year-old man was chewing his food slowly. He belonged to a generation that knew the value of masticating their food with extreme concentration.

Kanchipuram, located in Tamil Nadu, had always been regarded as a place of learning but was more famous for its flowers and handwoven silks. The city had been ruled by various royal dynasties—the Pallavas, the Cholas, the Pandyas, the Vijayanagara kings, the Golconda Sultanate and, finally, the British. Kanchipuram's landscape was dotted with Hindu temples from different eras. For Hindu followers of the god Vishnu, Kanchipuram was one of the seven holiest pilgrimage sites to attain moksha. In fact, of the 108 sacred temples devoted to Vishnu, fifteen were located in Kanchi. And among the followers of god Shiva, too, Kanchipuram constituted a holy site for pilgrimage.

The old man was enjoying a simple meal of idli, sambar and coconut chutney. The meal, as usual, had been cooked with care and served by his daughter, Anu, a sixty-five-year-old spinster. Father and daughter lived in separate houses, a few minutes' walk apart, but they always ate together.

'Why do we continue to stay in Kanchi?' asked Anu. 'The academy shut down many years ago. There is nothing to keep us here.' She knew his reply would be the same as it had always been.

Dr Raja Rao smiled indulgently at his daughter as he dunked an idli into the hot sambar. 'Kanchipuram was never *just* about the academy, Anu. This city links us to one of the greatest dynasties of the south, the Pallavas. We should never forget that.'

'But that was so long ago, Appa,' argued Anu. 'The Pallavas established themselves in the third century and had a glorious reign of 600 years. But that was eleven centuries ago. Why should it be of any relevance to us?'

'Because of Cambodia,' replied Rao.

'Cambodia?'

'Kanchi is a vital link to an ancient global network,' explained Rao. 'The Pallavas ruled not only South India but also Cambodia. Many centuries ago, Khambujaraja, a Pallava king, travelled to the region that is now called Cambodia. He faced opposition from a beautiful lady but eventually defeated and then married her. The country they jointly ruled was called Khambujadesa and their descendants were called the Khmer people. Khambujadesa later came to be known as Kampuchea and then Cambodia. In fact, you can see that every structure in this complex within which our own cottage is set, exhibits some elements of Cambodian architecture, including corbel arches, decorated lintels and bas-reliefs.'

Anu listening quietly, almost indulgently. She knew that he loved telling her the old stories.

'Much later, in the latter part of the sixth century, Bhima, the younger brother of the Pallava king Simha Vishnu, travelled to Cambodia to marry a princess and be crowned the king of Cambodia. He had to overpower many competing claims. The odds were stacked against him, but amazingly, he succeeded! Thereafter, all the kings of Cambodia attached the Pallava suffix, Varman, to their names. The Sanskrit word "varman" means shield. After all, kings were required to defend their people.'

There was a brief pause in the conversation as Anu poured some more sambar into her father's bowl. 'The idlis are perfect today,' said Rao, digressing for a moment to appreciate his daughter's cooking.

'Our batter supplier has outdone himself,' said Anu, smiling. 'Credit goes to him, not to me.' Anu adored her father. He had doubled as her mother and father since they had lost her mother to a brain stroke when Anu was just three.

'And it wasn't a one-way street,' continued Rao absentmindedly, unaware that he was digressing once again. 'In the year 731, the Pallava king of Kanchi, Parameswara Varman II, died without a direct heir. A descendant of Bhima in Cambodia, Nandi Varman II, was brought to Kanchi to ascend the Pallava throne. In that sense, the Pallava kings were Cambodian, just as the Cambodian kings were Pallava.'

'But why should that relationship hold us back here?' persisted Anu. 'Appa, please don't misunderstand. I'm quite happy to live in Kanchi, but I think that living in a big city like Chennai would be more practical at your age. Medical attention for one.'

'Don't talk about age,' scoffed Rao. 'I'm biologically younger than many teenagers!' Anu did not argue. Both father and daughter were healthier and fitter than far younger people.

'Was the India–Cambodia relationship limited to the Pallavas?' asked Anu.

'The friendship continued into the Chola period,' replied Rao. 'In the twelfth century, a Khmer king, Suryavarman II, built the glorious temple city of Angkor Wat. By then, the Pallava territories in India were part of the Chola kingdom. When the Chola king Kulottunga I was constructing the famous Shiva temple at Chidambaram, Suryavarman II sent him highly polished stone all the way from Cambodia. Thus the connection between India and Cambodia flourished even after the Pallavas were long gone.'

'That still does not answer my question. Why are we bound to Kanchi?'

'One day you will understand,' said Rao. 'Kanchi–Kamboja was an axis, an axis for many important ideas. I am the guardian of one of those ideas.'

'But can't you perform that role from Chennai?'

'Every question does not require an immediate answer, my child.' Rao's left hand covered Anu's briefly. 'One day you will understand,' he repeated.

'You never get angry or impatient with me, Appa. No matter how much I badger you.'

Rao quoted his favourite Tamil poet, Thiruvalluvar. 'To use bitter words when kind words are at hand is akin to picking unripe fruit when ripe ones abound.'

20

Having left magnificent Chang'an, I travelled stealthily along the Hexi Zoulang[16] that cuts between the Menggu Land of Grasses[17] and the wild Qinghai Plateau.[18] This corridor eventually reaches the sands of the Takelamagan Shamo.[19] Most of the corridor was controlled by Turks, and there was the everpresent danger of being looted, killed or kidnapped for ransom. By the grace of the Buddha, I reached Liangzhou[20] safely almost a month later.

The Tang empire and the Turkic people were on the verge of war, and Liangzhou was like a heavily guarded fortress. Armed

---

16. The Hexi Corridor in Gansu Province, China.
17. The grasslands of Mongolia.
18. Tibetan Plateau
19. Taklamakan Desert in southwest Xinjiang, China.
20. Modern-day Wuwei in Gansu Province, China.

soldiers patrolled the streets, and all significant entry and exit points were under constant watch. The Tang empire's spy network maintained constant surveillance on residents to report any suspicious activity. My arrival would definitely have been reported.

I knew that I would need to travel on to Anxi[21] from Liangzhou. Anxi was the gateway to the desert and the Silk Route. Unfortunately, no one at Liangzhou was allowed to travel west without official permission; it soon became evident to me that no such permission would be forthcoming from the local administration. Why would any of them be foolish enough to defy orders from Chang'an?

I waited impatiently in Liangzhou, giving lectures and preaching at various temples and public gatherings for a little over a month. One day I noticed a very old monk watching me. His face was wrinkled, and his skin was transluscent and thin, like parchment. He had been tracking me and dropping by to listen wherever and whenever I spoke. I realised that he was Liangzhou's most revered monk and held in high esteem by the locals.

One day he beckoned me to him. I kept a respectful distance, but he signalled me to draw closer. Eventually the old man whispered into my ears, 'You will need to reach Anxi, the last spot at which you may stop for supplies before the desert takes over.' I did not know how to respond. There were spies everywhere and the clergy was no exception; if he was planning to test me, the simple act of expressing my intention could land me in prison.

The old man smiled at me, showing his broken teeth. 'Trust me, son. I know that you are aiming to be Di San Sou Chuan, and I would like your endeavour to bear fruit. Consider me your friend.' Feelings of love, relief and submission overwhelmed me, and I fell at his feet. I knew in my heart that he would not betray me.

---

21. Modern-day Guazhou in Gansu Province, China.

The senior monk then quietly packed me off with two of his disciples to Anxi. We travelled incognito by night and hid by day to avoid detection. Even in darkness we would often stop and take cover behind rocks or inside caves when we saw any guard patrols of the Tang empire. If we were caught, the outcome would be punishment by death for defying the local governor's order not to travel west of Liangzhou.

We finally reached Anxi, the last military post of the Tang empire. I stayed quietly at an inn to avoid being discovered, while my two companions returned to Liangzhou. I was overcome by a feeling of emptiness and melancholy. I missed my dead parents. I missed my elder brother, Chengsu. I felt utterly alone. And then my only companion, my horse, died. Struck by fear and anxiety, I wondered whether I had the mental and physical strength to make the journey.

To make matters worse, spies from Liangzhou had informed the district governor at Anxi of my intention to travel west. One evening there was a loud knock at my door. Before me stood three burly, scowling guards. I was commanded to appear before the district governor. I truly thought it was the end of the road for me.

Luckily, the district governor was a man of piety. When I stood before him, he asked the guards to leave us alone. We stared at each other for a few minutes with scarcely a word exchanged. Then the governor held up the arrest warrant he had received and carefully tore it up. I did not know how to respond. It almost seemed like the Buddha was ensuring that the obstacles in my path were removed. The governor earnestly advised me to leave in haste. He could not assure my freedom if I lost time, he cautioned. He even provided me with a sturdy white horse for my trip so that I could be on my way quickly. I could not believe my good fortune. A divine force was making my journey to Yindu possible.

I promised the governor that I would leave within a day. It was pitch dark when I made my way to the Ta'er complex.[22] *It*

---

22. Ruins of Souyang City in modern-day Guazhou County, China.

contained a temple in honour of King Ashoka, who had helped spread Buddhism far and wide from India. The temple complex was very large, with a massive pagoda surrounded by eleven smaller ones. Towards the periphery were a drum tower, a bell tower and residential quarters for the monks. I sat quietly in contemplation inside the Hall of Heavenly Kings, praying for the Buddha to continue to guide my mission. I did not know that I was being watched by someone.

Someone who could kill me without blinking an eye.

21

Inside the subterranean laboratory in Beijing, a meeting was in progress in one of the conference rooms.

Occupying most of the space in the room was a carved and lacquered conference table that could seat ten. Every seat was occupied. On one of the longer walls was a mural depicting Mao Zedong raising his arm in salute to soldiers against the red backdrop of the Chinese flag. On the wall at the head of the table was a portrait of the current president. The seventy-three-year-old seated at the head of the table was a general of the People's Liberation Army, but most knew him by the honorific 'Buzhang'.

The Buzhang was the right-hand man of the Chinese president and had a reputation as one of the most feared men in the party structure. His appearance enhanced his fearsome reputation; completely bald, his face was close-shaven to the point that it looked waxed. The only hair on his face was courtesy a Fu Manchu moustache and a pair of thin eyebrows. He was always dressed in the crisp olive-green uniform of the Chinese PLA, which included a swagger stick. The stick was made from rattan and had an ornamental metallic head with a five-pointed star engraved on it—the emblem of the PLA. He placed it on the table before him like a strict schoolmaster about to whack a naughty student.

Seated to his immediate right was Erkin, the Stanford-educated engineer who had been brought in to head up the ADAM and EVE programmes. The other eight chairs were taken by members of Erkin's team—software engineers, biotech researchers, robotics specialists and scholars in artificial intelligence and intelligent design.

Erkin controlled two aspects of the programme; each had a different approach. ADAM was attempting to replace men with machines, while EVE was trying to convert men into fighting machines, chemically and technologically.

'What progress do you have to report, Mr Chong? Any at all? Or will your entire project be limited to science fiction?' asked the Buzhang, taking a sip of hot jasmine tea from a red teacup that bore a golden dragon. Erkin took a sip of water from the bottle in front of him. His throat felt parched whenever he sat through one of these meetings. The air control system maintained a comfortable temperature of 22° Celsius and humidity at fifty per cent, but Erkin could feel the sweat build up under his arms. He cursed himself for having got ensnared in the project. But he had had no choice.

'It will be a while on ADAM, Buzhang,' replied Erkin, although his colleagues had advised against providing an honest answer. He fiddled with his pen nervously. 'I do not wish to make promises I cannot keep. We're facing many difficulties getting the system to behave perfectly all the time. There are too many unpredictable bugs. Each time we think we have finally got it solved, another problem manifests. The present ADAM programme needs much more work, and it is in our interest to take the required time to solve these problems. Using the technology in real battle without debugging would be dangerous.'

The Buzhang nearly erupted in fury but calmed himself by taking a few deep breaths. 'What about EVE? Have you filtered the next batch of nanabolics?' Erkin's team was responsible for synthesising advanced formulations of natural anabolics, known in common parlance as nanabolics. In addition, the EVE programme involved equipping soldiers with advanced radar-ready helmets, super-sensitive assault rifles, satellite navigation, infrared vision and ionogel body armour.

'Yes, Buzhang. But we will need more Bamahao and Shipo for the next batch of nanabolics. I'm wondering what will happen once we run out of material. The stock position of both these is currently very low.'

'Did I hire you simply to hear you rattle off problems?' asked the Buzhang, his eyes blazing. 'I was under the impression that you were supposed to find creative solutions. Or is that no longer part of the Stanford curriculum? Did you consider the MCPH1 route?'

'Yes, Buzhang. I mean, no, Buzhang,' Erkin stuttered. Sweat ran down his face. He used a tissue to dab it away, then mustered the courage to speak again. 'The MCPH1 route is not viable. We need to look at the process in reverse. But, as you know, there is a missing piece in the current formulation and its absence means we are playing with lives.'

The Buzhang could control his anger no longer. He slammed his swagger stick down on the conference table. 'You let *me* worry about that,' he shouted as Erkin nervously knocked over the open bottle in front of him. Water splashed across his papers. Erkin hurriedly picked them up and shook them to get the moisture off. The Buzhang followed this comedy of errors with his steely eyes.

'What happens at the border with India is a mere experiment,' he said finally in a lowered voice. 'We need this programme to work to ensure China's global domination. Nuclear weapons, submarines and battleships are no substitute for elite fighting hands. We've seen how ineffective aircrafts and bombs are when fighting guerilla soldiers in deep jungles. Even the new islands created by us in the South China Sea will need elite manpower provided by ADAM and EVE. Is no one on this team aware of the criticality of this project?'

The Buzhang took a deep breath. He placed his swagger stick gently on the table. He wondered if there was any information from Cambodia. Had they found what he needed? If so, it would dramatically change the direction of the entire programme. He made a mental note to speak with the expedition leader, Lee Zhou. Maybe he would have better news than this pessimist.

22

They were in an interrogation centre in some sort of housing complex. Prisoners were routinely brought in, beaten and tortured as preliminaries to the interrogation. Sometimes they were killed when they had served their purpose. Behind the house was a pit in which mutilated corpses were thrown. Reflective mirrors had been installed to scare away vultures that would otherwise circle the pit, but many of them persisted. Maggots and flies in the food were normal. The prisoners would often discard their food, preferring starvation to eating filth. The residual food was instantly snapped up by massive bandicoots that had a free run of the place.

Mark stared at his interrogator blankly through swollen eyelids. *Why don't you kill me? I'm already a corpse fit for the vultures. Why not simply put an end to this? Let my flesh become nourishment for someone.* Never before had death seemed such a beautiful option. His face and limbs were swollen and bruised from the blows he had sustained. He was wearing filthy underwear soaked in urine and caked with faecal matter. Sweat dripped down his face as his interrogator clamped the pliers along the edge of one of his fingernails and began to pull. Mark screamed as the pain ripped through him.

He woke with a start.

With a gasp, Mark attempted to pull himself out of the claws of the nightmare. He felt he was choking, as though his head was being held under water. He coughed violently. A moment later, the spasm subsided. He looked around in fear and was unable to understand why he was in a comfortable bed in a clean room without any rodents for company. His trembling fingers reached out for his glasses on the nightstand, and he looked at the time on the bedside clock. Four in the morning. His body was drenched in sweat.

It was always the same nightmare. He was a young man of twenty-two, bound to a chair inside the house. An interrogator towered over him, holding a pair of pliers. 'Are you willing to honestly answer what I ask?' the man would say, his stinking breath on Mark's face. When Mark refused, the torture tactics would begin. Sleep deprivation, starvation, water-boarding, electric shocks, cigar burns and fingernail removal, amongst many other 'creative' methods to break prisoners. Those who ran the facility were experts in mental and physical terror tactics, having discovered ways to break the will of even the most obstinate. If there was hell on earth, it was right here.

Mark got to his feet, walked over to the bathroom and towelled himself dry. He looked at himself in the mirror, almost embarassed by the fact that he was still trembling from his dream. Would he ever be free of the visions that plagued him?

He pulled on a fresh pair of shorts and a T-shirt and poured himself a glass of water from the refrigerator, gulping it down thirstily. The nightmares had started during a period in his life that he desperately wanted to forget, but couldn't. Some experiences were just too vivid to be erased. He knew he needed to exorcise his nightmares. But how? He had tried everything: meditation, yoga, intense workouts, herbal remedies, psychiatric drugs, expensive weekly sessions with a shrink, even weed, but nothing had worked. Like a morsel of food stuck in the throat, his nightmares could neither be expelled nor swallowed.

Mark walked through his bedroom and into his study. He opened his laptop and logged in via a three-step process, then activated a programme that allowed all communication from his computer to be encrypted. In the background, his operating system was running a crypto-shredding programme, ensuring that no forensic team would ever be able to access his material. Mark Richards was a careful man. Years of training had ensured that.

He began typing an email. The subject line read: 'Re: Pam Khurana'.

23

It was an exceptionally hot day in South India's Cuddalore district. Here stood the exquisite Chidambaram Nataraja temple. Within the temple premises, a group of Japanese tourists were excitedly taking photographs with their Nikon cameras. Most of them sported straw hats and wore cloth masks on their faces for fear of bugs. Some of them were mopping sweat off their faces with handkerchiefs.

The Nataraja temple was a massive structure, with nine intricately carved gateways and five massive halls, including one that had 1,000 pillars. The temple was situated on fifty-five acres of land and contained a massive water reservoir in the third corridor. The awe-inspiring golden roof had been constructed with 21,600 golden tiles fixed in place with 72,000 golden nails. The temple was undoubtedly magnificent, a veritable feast for the eyes.

The group's tour guide, a man who appeared to be in his sixties, was dressed in a khaki bush shirt and trousers. He had a thick salt-and-pepper beard and a bushy moustache, as well as a small ponytail. He wore a cap and dark Ray-Bans. He appeared to be an average tour guide, but there was something compelling about him. With his cap, sunglasses, beard and long hair, there was very little of his face that was actually visible.

'Ancient texts indicate that a temple has stood here for many centuries,' said the guide to his flock. 'Remember that the town of Chidambaram was the early capital of the Chola dynasty, and it's possible that the earliest structures of this complex are from that period. The temple is dedicated to the dancing form of Shiva, called Nataraja.'

The guide paused before the flawless statue of Nataraja. 'Nataraja is encircled by a ring of fire, which symbolises the cyclical cosmos. In his upper right hand, he holds an hourglass-shaped drum—time. His upper left hand holds fire, which signifies creation and destruction. A cobra is coiled around his lower right forearm, while his palm remains in a relaxed posture. This indicates the god's invitation to approach him without fear. The third eye on his forehead urges devotees to perceive with inner wisdom rather than mere sight. His right leg is placed on a demon, thus suggesting the end of the demon of ignorance.'

In his enthusiasm, the guide had instinctively adopted a posture similar to the statue's. There were murmurs of approval from the group, who were obviously fascinated by his knowledge. A few fanned themselves. The weather in this part of South India was always hot and humid.

'Do you know what else is fascinating about this temple?' asked the guide, abandoning his dancing Shiva pose and standing upright. 'Within the inner courtyard are shrines with statues of both, the creator god, Brahma, and the preserver god, Vishnu. In that sense, Chidambaram is one of the very few temples where the Hindu trinity of Brahma, Vishnu and Shiva are worshipped together.

'Have any of you been to Angkor Wat in Cambodia?' he then asked. A few hands shot up; they were like students eager to please their teacher. 'Well, this temple was significantly expanded by the Chola king Kulottunga I in the eleventh century. While the expansion work was still in progress, the king of Cambodia, Suryavarman II, the king who built Angkor Wat, sent over something strange on one of his naval vessels.'

'What?' asked one of the tourists.

'It was an ordinary block of stone that the Cambodian king wanted incorporated into the construction of the Nataraja temple,' replied the guide. 'Kulottunga's ministers were puzzled. It seemed rather odd that a single block of stone should be sent as a gift. Nonetheless, they happily incorporated it into the upper front row of the stone wall of the shrine. In fact, they even carved an inscription indicating its origin.'

He translated the Tamil inscription into English: 'This stone, presented to our king by the king of Kamboja, was placed as per the instructions of our king in the front portion of the temple and subsequently fixed in the upper front row of the stone wall of the shrine.'

The guide pointed out the stone to the tourists, who excitedly clicked more pictures.

24

I sat in contemplation inside the hall of the Ta'er temple, seeking guidance from the Buddha. I did not realise I was being watched. The stranger who was closely observing me turned out to be a traveller called Bandha. He was dressed in flowing black robes, capped by a matching turban. His eyes were shifty, always darting from side to side. A long beard reached his chest and was knotted into a little tuft towards its end.

He approached me hesitantly. When I asked what he wanted from me, he bowed low and said he wanted to take the vows of a lay Buddhist. I first attempted to understand his motivations for taking the vows. 'I am tired, O learned master,' he said. 'I have lived my life as a consummate traveller and merchant. But along the way, I have also wronged many. Please set me on the right path.' I was not entirely convinced of his motivations but decided to give him the benefit of the doubt.

I sat with him for some time and instructed him in the five vows before he took them. 'One, I shall refrain from killing,' repeated Bandha after me. 'Two, I shall refrain from stealing. Three, I shall refrain from lying. Four, I shall refrain from sexual misconduct. Five, I shall refrain from using intoxicants.'

I blessed him. Bandha looked pleased. But he seemed unsure whether he would be able to scrupulously follow the five vows. His eyes continued darting all over the place, almost as though he expected someone to be spying on us.

Bandha thanked me for administering the vows to him and asked if he could repay the favour. I told him of my desire to travel west. After all, Bandha was a veteran merchant who was probably familiar with all the major trade routes. He would undoubtedly be an asset during the initial part of my expedition. He agreed to take me past the Yumen Guan[23] and the five signal towers of the desert.

---

23. Yumen Pass or Jade Gate, west of Dunhuang in Gansu Province, China.

Next morning, I awaited his arrival on the road that led to the Yumen Guan. He eventually appeared with a skinny chestnut horse. Walking alongside the horse was a very old man who had apparently made the journey across the desert more than thirty times. The old man offered me his malnourished horse with a tarnished saddle in exchange for my white steed. His horse allegedly knew the route and was capable of sniffing out water sources.

I recalled my dream of Mount Sumeru, in which I had seen myself reaching the sacred mountain on a skinny chestnut horse. I traded my well-fed horse for the skinny one. The old man hurried off, having got himself an amazing deal. I had a feeling I had been swindled, but I was not bothered. The Buddha would protect me.

Bandha and I immediately left on our journey. We soon reached the Yumen Guan, the gateway from the Tang empire to Xiyu, which lay outside the empire's borders. It was heavily guarded, with every person, animal and cart being stopped and checked, irrespective of whether they were coming in or going out. 'Yumen' means 'jade'; the gate derived its name from the numerous jade-laden caravans that passed through it. The Yumen Guan opened onto the sands of the Takelamagan Shamo. Nephrite jade was brought in from mines located in Xiyu, to be crafted within the empire, and silk was traded out. This particular route had been used for many hundreds of years.

At the gate was a long line of camel trains loaded with goods waiting to be cleared in or out. Bandha diverted the attention of the guards by pretending to be sick. A consummate actor, he lay on the ground as though he had passed out from the heat and dehydration. The guards focused their energies on reviving him, and this diversion gave me the much needed opportunity to slip past on foot.

Bandha met me on the other side of the pass, having appropriately 'recovered' a couple of hours later. We decided to rest for a while *before moving on. I sat deep in prayer, when from the corner of my eye I saw Bandha creeping up on me, dagger drawn.*

I was dismayed. Why had he bothered taking the vows of Buddhism if he had no intention of changing his ways? Or had that been a ruse to gain my confidence? I mustered my courage and boldly turned to face him. 'Why do you wish to spill my blood? I have no valuables and there is nothing to be gained from killing me. If you want the horse, you may have it.'

'Because I now realise you may inform the authorities that I assisted you. If that happens, I will be arrested and put to death, while you as a holy man might still be spared,' replied Bandha. I could see a swirl of sand rising in the west and knew that I needed to buy time. Bandha's eyes were darting around, closely following my own, so I avoided staring at the developments in the west.

'I can take you to a spot where there are untold riches,' I said to him. 'All you need to do is guide me past the five towers.'

His eyes glinted. Behind him, the sands began rolling in from the west. 'You're just saying that,' he said. 'You want to trick me into believing your story.'

'Not at all,' I said. 'When the word of the Buddha was brought to this land, many riches were dispersed along the way. Being a monk, I have read all the scriptures and am aware of the treasures that they refer to.' I was not lying. I was referring to spiritual treasures, knowing full well that Bandha was interested in the more earthly variety.

Bandha was listening intently. I could almost see the scales in his brain weighing his options. I mentally counted down to the moment when I could take him by surprise. It came soon enough.

As soon as the storm hit us, I leapt on the horse and headed to the first beacon tower, leaving Bandha with no alternative but to make his way back on foot to Yumen Guan. I did not bother to look back.

I knew there was a possibility that Bandha would snitch on me, but that would involve implicating himself too. My instincts told me that he would cut his losses. Of course, if he decided to complain about me, there was nothing I could do. The emperor had a wide network of informants and spies even outside the kingdom, and there was no guarantee that I would not be hauled back to Cina.

I would have to take my chances. I prayed to the Buddha for his help to make my mission successful.

25

Pam sat in her cubicle with her legs propped up on her desk. Her tablet lay on her lap. On her desk were three half-consumed cups of canteen tea, the dregs having coagulated. The Doklam footage on her tablet was playing on a loop. She had lost count of the number of times she had reviewed it, searching for clues that would reveal the nature of the enemy. She was exhausted but pushed herself to stay focussed.

She remembered a song that her father used to amuse her with when she was little. He would place her on his lap, settle her head against his shoulder and sing:

Baa-maa-ko-ki-joo-ka-lo
Wee-noo-ko-ki-moo-pa-lo
See-waa-ko-ki-soo-pa-lo
Haa-noo-ko-ki-poo-da-jo

She would laugh and laugh at the gibberish song. Sometimes he would lift her up and swing her in sync with the words. It was their private joke, one that her mother was never part of. Pam was passionately possessive of their secret ritual. Once, when her father had attempted to include her mother in the game, she had sulked the entire day. Gibberish though it was, the words never changed from one day to the next. Eventually, Pam also learnt the words and began to sing along.

She hummed the song now as she sat deep in thought. What was it that looked familiar about those Chinese soldiers? She couldn't place her finger on it, but felt a strong sense of déjà vu. She had seen them before, but where? A movie? An ad? A web series? On television? During her travels? Her brain struggled with the memory and sadistically pushed it further away from her consciousness.

A conference was taking place at DRDO Bhawan, and the din of visitors in the corridors outside was distracting. Pam plugged in her earphones. And then she saw her father's diary lying on her desk. She picked it up, running her fingers over the worn leather, paying special attention to the gold-embossed initials. 'K.K.' Kishan Khurana. Whenever she placed her fingers there, she felt that she was somehow connected with her father. It was as though she were back in time, reaching out with her baby fingers to caress his cheeks, rough like sandpaper.

She opened the diary and flipped through it. One page had fragments of a letter that he had begun writing to his daughter, who was then all of seven. 'Even if I am not physically with you, my little angel, remember that I am always with you. I am always watching over you.' Pam had read that line a million times over.

Pam's father had been a consummate note-taker, scribbling thoughts, observations and plans meticulously with a Waterman fountain pen. He had been a good-looking man, she knew. She had seen a photograph of him stylishly lighting his favourite Four Square cigarette with an olive-green Zippo lighter. In another one, he was pouring himself a shot of Old Monk rum from his hip flask. But his diary was a revelation. There were notations on plants, the weather and terrain; there were observations on military tactics, firing distances of guns and quick sketch maps of terrain. Some of the pages even contained Urdu couplets and poetry he had written when stationed far away from Pam's mother. Page after page contained neatly presented notes and sketches in his trademark royal-blue ink.

The déjà vu Pam was experiencing was connected to something she had seen within the pages. Something had triggered a memory. She frantically flipped through the diary. *C'mon, think, woman! Think!*

She was halfway through the pages when she saw it. The sketch of a very tall, muscular man with facial features that were monkey-like. It was one among her father's several sketches, but Pam had no idea where he had been when he made them and whether they were based on someone real. Maybe he had doodled imaginary superheroes.

On the page opposite the sketch was written:

Selaginella bryopteris
78% protection against oxidative stress
Hexoses and proteins
Nessus effect

Was the sketch connected to the notations? Or was the fact that they were side by side a mere coincidence? What the hell was the Nessus effect? She ran a search on Google, only to find pages relating to an antivirus product. She only vaguely knew of one other Nessus, and he was from Greek mythology. It was said that Nessus had attempted to rape Deianeira, the wife of Heracles. Heracles had shot a Hydra-poisoned arrow to kill Nessus and had succeeded. But the infected blood of Nessus had eventually found its way to Heracles and killed him.

Below the *Nessus Effect* was a rhyme that made no sense.

Virile above
and plus below
the three monkeys
and the centre aglow.

On another page was a version of the Gayatri mantra that paid obeisance to various deities.

Om Chaturmukhaya Vidmahe
Hansa Rudraaya Dhimahi
Tanno Brahma Prachodayat

Om Narayanaya Vidmahe
Vasudevaya Dhimahi
Tanno Vishnu Prachodayat

Om Tat Purushaya Vidhmahe
Mahadevaya Dheemahe
Tanno Rudra Prachodayath.

Om Aanjaneyay Vidmahe
Maha balaya Dheemahe
Tanno Hanuman Prachodayat

Pam ran the footage again. She had become almost immune to the sight of the Chinese soldiers slicing their razor-edged knives up through the bellies of the Indian soldiers. She forced herself to ignore the blood spouting from the soldiers' bodies, the anguish on their faces. Instead she concentrated on the Chinese attackers and their build, features and movements.

There was no doubt. When the attackers smiled in vicious glee, their mouths remained open with only the lower teeth exposed. When they killed, their lips instinctively pulled back to expose both the lower and upper teeth and gums, much like monkeys or apes. There were definite similarities between the Chinese soldiers and the figures in the sketches.

26

Mark and Pam were inside the CBTT conference room used by the research team. It felt ridiculous for just three people to be using a room built for a hundred. But the technology backup that was available here made presentations far more effective.

One of Mark's vice-presidents, a young man in his thirties, was making a presentation about the future of the Indian soldier. He had made the presentation to the senior management team of CBTT a month ago, but Mark wanted him to repeat it for Pam's benefit. It would be the quickest way of bringing her up to speed with the technological possibilities in the world of warfare.

The initial part of the presentation focused on products such as smart clothing that could reduce the soldier's visual, radar and infrared signature; an enhanced sighting system mounted on the helmet to shoot at targets around corners or in trenches; encrypted radio that allowed members of a unit to be in hands-free communication; and special coverings and applications to protect combatants in the event of nuclear, biological or chemical warfare.

Pam was still thinking about the Chinese fighters from the footage. They had radar-equipped helmets, lightweight but lethal assault rifles, wrist-worn navigation systems, night-vision goggles and omniphobic armour. If India had any hope of succeeding in this fight, it would need to give its men the best tools to fight with.

The VP moved into the second part of his presentation. It focused on thermal sensing helmets that could monitor for concussion while transmitting the soldier's vital medical signs to a control centre. In fact, it could automatically detect threats through inertial and visual navigation sensors coupled with advanced algorithms. It could also provide soldiers with 3D navigation even where mobile networks were weak or unavailable.

Next came a magnetic flux generator to fire projectiles without the use of chemical explosives. Once perfected, the projectile would be capable of penetrating armoured vehicles too. But the topper was a machine-gun-equipped robot that could shoot based on commands received from the control centre.

Pam listened patiently. In spite of being an employee of the DRDO, she had no idea of these cutting-edge technologies being developed by CBTT. She was particularly fascinated by a hydraulic-powered exoskeleton that would allow combat troops to transport heavy loads without tiring.

She interjected, 'What's stopping us? If we have all this technology, why aren't we giving it to our soldiers?'

Mark and his VP looked at each other sheepishly. 'Good old Indian bureaucracy,' Mark replied. 'Each time we submit proposals, they are held up in paperwork on account of trivial issues.'

'What sort of trivial issues?' asked Pam. She was familiar with the methods used by bureacrats to put up a pile of rules, regulations, forms, files and procedures to the point where nothing moved at all.

'Ridiculous stuff,' replied Mark. 'For example, why not mount regular combat rifles on a robot? Why not seek permission from the Medical Council of India for earpieces that monitor body temperature? Why not ensure that autonomous vehicles meet fuel-emission norms? Somone at the very top is doing everything possible to keep us in the Dark Ages. In the meantime, the Chinese continue running circles around us.'

27

Pam returned to the DRDO and decided to try her luck at tracking down Dr Raja Rao. She jotted down a list of people who could possibly have been involved in a high-level project involving combat training. She was not surprised when that proved to be a dead end. No one seemed to even know of Rao. If they did, they were maintaining a strict code of silence. *What is so secretive about Rao's work?* she wondered. She phoned Mark to find out whether he had any links to Rao.

'When CBTT was interested in collaborating with Rao, our access to him was his deputy, someone called Dev,' replied Mark.

'Dev?' asked Pam. 'No surname?'

'Just Dev, I'm afraid. Let me see if I have any coordinates for him.' Pam heard Mark typing on his keyboard. 'I have a landline number, but I'm not sure if it's still valid.'

'I'll take anything,' replied Pam, writing down the number. She quickly did a reverse number lookup and found a Delhi address in Connaught Place. After dumping her stuff in a satchel, she stepped out to check the address. It turned out to be a small café, bustling at that time of the day. She walked over to the counter and asked someone who looked like a manager about Dev.

'No one by that name works here,' came the reply. The manager was busy counting the change in the till.

'Maybe the landlord of this place would know?' said Pam.

'Wait a minute,' said the manager. 'This place used to be a gym before it became a coffee shop, and we retained his landline. The guy who ran the gym was called Dev. The board outside used to read DG. Dev's Gym.'

'Any idea how I can reach him?'

'I don't have any details, but I know he shifted to a cheaper locality.'

Pam sat on a bench outside and googled 'Dev's Gym'. She added Delhi to the keywords so as to eliminate anything outside the city. The guru of search spat out five possible locations.

Two of them were in neighbourhoods that were pricier than Connaught Place, so she eliminated them. The other three were in different parts of the National Capital Region. Pam knew that the rest of her day would be consumed by travel. She decided to ditch her car and use the metro instead. It would be quicker.

She headed to Rajiv Chowk station and waited for the Blue Line. When the train whooshed in, she entered one of the first compartments and settled down. She did not notice the person who had entered the metro along with her and detrained with her at Noida City Centre.

It took less than ten minutes to eliminate this Dev's Gym from her shortlist. Its name came from its location in the basement of Hotel Devlok, with nobody named Dev in the establishment. She sighed as she headed back to the metro. Her next stop would be HUDA City Centre in Gurgaon.

This gym was far more luxurious than the previous one and was located in a smart residential area. The receptionist, sporting a tight black T-shirt and streaked hair, smiled at Pam, getting ready to sell her a membership.

'May I speak to Dev?' asked Pam. The receptionist seemed disappointed as she picked up the intercom to buzz her boss.

He walked out of his office and into the reception area a few minutes later with a fierce-looking Rottweiler on a leash. The dog looked at Pam suspiciously and growled, but to his credit, did not touch her. 'Down, Sultan,' Dev commanded, and the dog obediently lay down on his tummy.

Dev was in his mid-fifties but had the appearance of a bodybuilder. Pam quickly rechecked that he was indeed the Dev who had a gym with the phone number she had been tracking down. He was a tad cagey. 'Why have you been trying to find me?' he asked warily. 'Who are you?'

She did not give her full name. 'You can call me Pam,' she said with a bright smile. 'I *really* need your help, Dev.' *Am I laying it on too thick?* she wondered. 'I've been given an assignment by my editor to track down Dr Rao. If I don't succeed, that's the end of my job.'

She explained that her magazine was attempting to locate Dr Rao to do a feature on martial arts training. She turned on the charm, hoping to get Dev to open up to her. There was an appreciable softening in his attitude. Even the dog seemed to be less suspicious of her.

Dev led her to his office and offered her green tea. He chatted with her amiably while firmly instructing his Rottweiler to sit still. The opulence of the gym made Pam wonder how Dev supported the bloated overheads.

'I was once a student of Rao,' said Dev. 'He used to run an academy in Kanchi for the Indian Army some decades back, and I eventually became his deputy. I was in my mid-twenties then, and had spent my teens training under him. The academy's objective was to enhance the combat prowess of Indian special forces.'

'Is the academy still in operation?' asked Pam. She saw Dev hesitate. 'I would have suggested having dinner to chat about this, but I'm travelling for the next few days,' she said hastily. She wrote her mobile number on a slip of paper and handed it to Dev. 'Call me. But I really do need your help.'

Dev took the slip and smiled. It was tough leading a lonely life, exiled to a gym. Dinner with a female companion would be nice. He thought wistfully of Anu. Those had been wonderful days.

'My magazine would also like to do a photo shoot with you for a future issue,' said Pam. 'It could substantially increase your business here, not that I'm suggesting you need it.' Pam smiled again, but she could see that Dev was already hooked.

'There was a change of government,' Dev began. 'The new government was politically dependent for its survival on the support of leftist parties. Subtle Chinese pressure was brought to bear via the leftists to shut down the facility, helped along by Chinese sympathisers in the government. Rao was mistreated by the Indian bureaucracy and his funding was choked. The academy has been lying closed ever since.'

'Does he still live there?' asked Pam. 'Will he meet me?'

'Knowing him, I imagine he still lives on the grounds of the academy,' said Dev. 'But he stopped meeting anyone years ago. Except for his daughter—her name is Anu. Frankly, I've been out of touch for a long time and have no idea whether he is alive or dead.'

'The daughter, Anu, lives with him?'

'Unlikely,' answered Dev. 'But their houses were close to each other's. She too would be getting on in age—around sixty-five, I think. She used to bring him food every day, but other than that, Rao led the life of a recluse, post-retirement. That's assuming he's still alive.' Dev's thoughts went back to Anu. An age difference of ten years had not prevented them from falling in love.

There was a pause. Dev seemed to be unsure whether to say something or not. Pam smiled at him encouragingly.

He gulped nervously. 'There's something else you should know about Rao.'

28

I was now entirely alone. I moved on, mounted on my scrawny horse. I had been told that after crossing Yumen Guan, I would see five signal towers located next to water springs. The towers lay along the road leading to the sands of Takelamagan Shamo. I would need to stop at each of them to replenish my supply of water, but any halt would also expose me to the risk of being arrested or killed by the guards.

Searing heat radiated not only from the sun above but also from the sand and gravel that I traversed. You could cook an egg on it. Very little life could survive the extreme weather. Even experienced travellers could lose their way in this vast desert, and I came across many skeletons of humans and animals, picked clean by scavengers and the dry heat.

I was suddenly terrified by the sight of thousands of ferocious warriors streaming towards me. They were galloping on their sweating steeds, their swords and spears glinting in the blazing sun. But just as they were about to attack me, they vanished, disappearing as quickly as they had appeared. I squinted my eyes to look for them, but they had dissipated into thin air.

I then saw a caravan, camels piled high with goods and horses carrying finely attired merchants. I tried to attract their attention as they drew closer, but they too diffused into the atmosphere. Exhausted and thirsty, I had begun hallucinating in the desert sun. It had become impossible to distinguish the real from the unreal. Almost like the journey of one's life.

I fought my mental demons as best I could. After about twenty-five miles, I reached the first beacon tower. Although my throat was parched, I waited for darkness to descend before fetching water from the spring. I drank like I had never drunk before, the water seeping into every dry crevice. My body sucked up every drop like oil on cloth. I then washed my hands and face, enjoying the refreshing caress of the water on my skin.

Just as I was filling my water bag, arrows begin whistling past me. I had been discovered! I shouted that I was a monk on a mission to bring back the word of the Buddha, but another arrow grazed my knee, drawing blood. I could hear commands being shouted, followed by the sounds of running feet and clanging metal. Torches were lit and there was a flurry of activity. I was too exhausted to even consider running. A moment later, I was surrounded by a contingent of soldiers, their weapons pointed at me.

I tried explaining that I was a monk, not an enemy warrior, but I was arrested and taken to the commander of the signal tower. I stood before him, wet and bloodied, trembling from fear and the cold night air. He drew closer and inspected me. Miraculously, there was a sudden change in his demeanour.

Apparently the commander of the watch tower, Wangsiang, was a Buddhist. He had already heard of me and my mission. He even knew of my intention to journey west and to become Di San Sou Chuan. The Buddhist information network was no ordinary one, it seemed. Talk about the Buddha's blessings!

Surprisingly, Wangsiang tried his best to dissuade me from crossing the desert, suggesting that I go to the monastery at Shazhou[24] instead. He argued that it would be a 300-mile journey to the oasis of Yizhou,[25] one that would involve travel through a scorching desert with very poor odds of survival. He reminded me of all the corpses and skeletons I had seen en route. He warned

---

24. Modern-day Dunhuang in Gansu Province, China.
25. Modern-day Hami in Xinjiang, China.

that my scrawny horse and I could end up like them. On the other hand, Shazhou was at the convergence of the northern and southern silk roads and could be reached in a few days.

Shazhou was an important centre of Buddhism where over a thousand caves served as temples, meditation halls, libraries and residences for a flourishing community of monks. Some of the caves were exquisitely painted and were points of pilgrimage. Some were even sponsored by kings and rich merchants. I could see why Wangsiang was prompting me to go there. It was out of genuine concern for my wellbeing. I knelt down and offered my neck to him. 'Please kill me instead,' I said. 'I would rather die than give up on my plan.'

Wangsiang realised that there was no point in trying to alter my course. He pulled me to my feet. He then knelt before me to apologise for having tried to break my resolve. Rising, he instructed his soldiers to provide me with food and water. He personally tended to my wounds and then arranged a spot for me to rest for the night. The next morning, he gave me a parcel of food, and water in an extra-large leather container. He then personally conducted me to the appropriate point from where I could resume my journey into the desert.

Wangsiang told me to avoid stopping at the fifth watch tower because the officer commanding it was not a good man and would be very pleased to capture and pack me off to the emperor. 'Do not go there under any circumstances,' he warned, as my little horse and I left on our adventure.

29

Five miles north of the Cambodian city of Siem Reap lies a huge temple complex. Angkor Wat is the world's largest religious monument and was built in the twelfth century by King Suryavarman II in honour of the Hindu god Vishnu. It is one of the most incredible human endeavours in the world.

Within the massive Angkor Wat complex, a group of Chinese researchers and scholars were busy carrying out LiDAR (Light Detection and Ranging) mapping. It was no easy task. Angkor Wat was spread over 400 acres — more a city than a temple. The very name 'Angkor Wat' translated from Khmer to 'temple city'. The team had to contend with not only the sheer size of the complex but also the fact that over 50,000 tourists visited each day, very often trampling over their markers, barriers and equipment.

Although built in honour of Vishnu, the massive architectural marvel had not remained a Hindu place of worship for long. By the end of the century, the rise of Buddhism and the corresponding decline of Hinduism had resulted in Angkor Wat becoming a Buddhist centre, and a new set of myths developed around the wondrous complex. The Buddhists believed that Angkor Wat had been constructed on the instructions of the god Indra in one single night. But anyone looking at the temple would know that it probably took several decades to build. By the nineteenth century, Angkor Wat became an almost abandoned site, decaying from neglect and covered with weeds. It was 'rediscovered' around 1860 by the French explorer Henri Mouhot, who served as the inspiration for many Hollywood movies, *Indiana Jones* and *Tomb Raider* included.

The Chinese team was using far better technology than Indiana Jones, though. They had employed a helicopter equipped with LiDAR lasers to carry out the initial mapping. LiDAR worked much like radar or sonar but used coherent light waves from a laser source instead of radio or sound waves. Flying with a programmed schedule that determined flight path, altitude and airspeed, the helicopter sent out a million pulses per second. The Chinese used as many as sixteen laser beams per ten feet of survey area. Their LiDAR system calculated the time it took for light to hit part of the construction and be reflected back. Each of these readings was then aggregated into a 3D visualisation of the entire complex. It was undoubtedly cutting-edge technology.

But LiDAR had limitations when it came to subterranean details. The team was now supplementing their 3D map with images gathered via robotic equipment sent into shafts, tunnels and sealed chambers. They talked excitedly as their robot made its way inside the western edge of the temple. But excitement turned to disappointment when it was found to be empty. The previous day, the robot had explored a chamber that contained some materials, but it had turned out to be a dead end. Their problems were exacerbated by the fact that parts of Angkor Wat had been damaged during the Khmer Rouge rule of the 1970s, resulting in rubble-filled cavities that were difficult to navigate. Sometimes it was like searching for a needle in a haystack.

Initially, the obvious choice for a possible secret chamber had been the temple itself. Their team leader, Lee Zhou, a grey-haired scholar, had spent several days scanning the five primary towers. Angkor Wat had been built to represent Mount Meru, the abode of the gods, and its five towers were a human rendering of the five peaks of Meru. The walls and the moat around the temple represented the mountain ranges and lakes surrounding Meru. Lee's detailed surveys had produced a wealth of hitherto unknown information that could possibly fuel several research papers, but that was not why his team had been sent here by the Buzhang.

Why do you play hide-and-seek with me? wondered Lee. *At any other time I would have been so excited about the discoveries that we've made.* During their research, they had found that the lost cities of Mahendraparvata, Beng Mealea, Koh Ker and Angkor had all been connected via advanced waterways and roads. The Khmer empire would have been one of the world's largest urban centres of the time, with one of the most sophisticated water management systems ever. But the Buzhang couldn't care less. As far as he was concerned, Lee's search had been in vain so far.

Lee sat with his team inside an air-conditioned tent full of computers on the fringes of Angkor Wat. One of the team members made a presentation about the spaces that had already been examined. There were accompanying photographs—pictures of the fifteen-foot high wall, the moat, the sandstone causeway, the seventy-foot primary tower.

'The Pallava connection is apparent,' said the presenter. 'The bas-reliefs are very similar to those in the Pallava temples. We have attempted to scan them and even search behind them and within their crevices.'

Lee cut their discussion short. He had just received a dressing-down from the Buzhang on the phone. 'The Buzhang has asked me to ensure that we complete our mission within four weeks. We have no time to marvel at the wonders of Angkor.'

There was a collective gasp from the rest of the team. 'Searching 400 acres will take years, not weeks or months,' said one of the researchers nervously. 'It simply cannot be done. We are familiar with the painstaking work involved in trying to send robots to spots that cannot be LiDAR-mapped. It's impossible! And we're assuming that we only look at Angkor Wat, not the hundreds of other temples in Angkor. We have not even considered temples like Phnom Krom, Phnom Bakheng or Phnom Bok.'

'Let's not complain,' replied Lee. 'We must deliver results. Let's work on the key target areas rather than the entire stretch. Which specific areas do we wish to focus on?'

Lee sounded assertive, but he was a worried man. He knew that his life was on the line.

30

Deep in the forests between Kanchi and Sathyamangalam was a settlement. The people who inhabited it lived in mud huts and caves dug into the hillsides. Their huts had no walls and the floors were fashioned from palm leaves. The caves were painted with red ochre and were used for community festivals.

Members of this tribe were hunter-gatherers, and the forest was their source of sustenance. They prided themselves on the fact that they had very little contact with the outside world. Which was just as well. They were one of the last remaining pre-Neolithic tribes in the world, and sustained contact would have brought innumerable problems.

Rather than humans, their friends were animals— elephants, tigers, leopards, antelope, blackbuck, deer, wild buffalo, sloth bears and hyenas that roamed the forest. There were also the birds: treepies, bulbuls, babblers, mynahs, crows and even vultures. The tribe detected the presence of each animal by its droppings, sounds and smells. They were trained to remain intimately aware of the habits of the flora and fauna that surrounded them. It was almost as though nothing separated them from the world they inhabited. They were one with the forest.

Their food consisted of all that the forest could offer them— nuts, fish, berries, wild honey, edible bark, coconuts, wild plants and game. They used bow-like harpoons to fish and fishnets woven from vines. Although isolated from the world, the tribespeople were excellent warriors. Their weapons consisted of bows, arrows, slingshots, flatbows, clubs and javelins fashioned from hardened wood.

Nothing about them had changed over thousands of years. This was despite the ruthless development that the region around the forest had been subjected to. Their saviour in this regard had been Sathyamangalam's tigers. Concern for the survival of these majestic beasts had prompted the government to declare the entire area a protected forest reserve. The result was that very few outsiders were allowed inside it, and the forest continued to flourish. From time to time, forest officials would report having seen strange ape-like creatures, but they would quickly be reprimanded for drinking on duty.

What was common to each member of the tribe was their physique. All of them had broad shoulders and chests, rippling biceps and muscular thighs. They sported long hair held in place by headbands made from dried vines. They wore no clothes except for the occasional animal skin or vine skirt around the waist. Their faces were coloured red using red ochre pigment from minerals rich in ferric oxide. The pigment served to highlight their bulky brow ridges, long, protruding faces, and large teeth and jaws.

Ikoalikum was the tribe's chief. He was undoubtedly the best-looking and best-built among them and wore a vine like a crown around his head. In the traditions of the tribe, the chief's post was not hereditary. He had fought his way to the top using a mixture of alliances and aggression. His position now guaranteed that he had the final say in matters of territory, patrol duty, mating rights and division of spoils. Below him in the hierarchy were several other males who constituted his coterie and enabled him to retain power. But he always remained alert for the next challenger.

Ikoalikum spoke to his tribe in a language that had only ten phonemes—seven consonants and three vowels. It was a simple, guttural language unspoken outside the tribe.

He raised his palms in prayer now, his face radiant in the morning light. As his hands inched towards the sky, he leapt upwards, his broad shoulders flexing and the muscles on his back rippling as he zoomed several feet into the air. It was an effortless flight, and he came to rest gracefully on the branch of a tall tree. The tribe people followed him one by one. Once they were all off the ground and on the treetops, they looked at each other and then at Ikoalikum for his signal.

Upon his nod, they began singing.

31

In one of the less-frequented lanes of Sadar Bazar stood a shop that could very easily be missed. It was an oddity in this market because the proprietor dealt in antiquities, not something one would expect here. His name had been given to Pam by a common friend who vouched for his reliability. The board outside had decayed to the point that it was barely readable. As Pam walked in, a little bell tinkled, informing the shopkeeper of the arrival of a customer. She announced her name and the man smiled, showing his paan-stained teeth.

Sadar Bazaar was one of the largest wholesale markets in India. It was made up of many smaller markets, each specialising in a particular commodity. If one wanted to buy household goods, electronics, toys, imitation jewellery, clothing, leather articles, stationery, plasticware, furniture or timber, one could buy them all at Sadar Bazar. It was also a haven for knock-offs, its narrow and congested lanes hogged by hawkers attempting to sell fake luxury brands produced in its numerous sweatshops. There was never a dull moment in Sadar Bazar, the multiple food-vendors providing a full-frontal sensory attack of sweets and savouries deep-fried in ghee or some dubious oils.

The proprietor seated her on a rickety stool and opened a leather folder, inside the plastic sleeves of which were various ancient and medieval coins. He flipped the pages to show her a breathtaking variety. One of his prized possessions was a British India Twin Currency coin, minted to pay Indian soldiers who fought in World War II. He then showed her a one-rupee coin from 1939. 'The last pure silver coin minted in India,' he said with pride. He flipped the page to show her a gold mohur from the era of Queen Victoria.

'I need something older than these,' said Pam a little impatiently. *Why is he wasting my time when he knows what I want?*

The proprietor nodded. 'Patience, memsa'ab,' he said. 'I will ensure that you get what you want. Trust me; I have it all.' It was evident that this was not a mere business for him. Numismatics was his passion. He enjoyed explaining the provenance of each coin and talking about the nuggets of history that went with it.

He turned to another page to reveal a Mughal era zodiacal mohur. On the opposite page, he delicately ran his fingers over rare coins issued in the names of Razia Sultan, Noorjehan and Naganika. 'Not too many coins were issued in the names of women,' he murmured. 'That's what makes them so rare. Men hogged most of the space.'

Not much has changed, thought Pam.

They moved on to octagonal coins issued by the Shahs of Malwa, Shakya punch-marked coins, Gandhara silver *satamanas* and Mauryan coins with five punches. There were Panchala, Indo-Scythian, Pandya and Bactrian coins.

And then she saw what she was looking for. She heaved a sigh of relief.

There was an entire section devoted to them. Minted in lead, copper and bronze, they were in round and square shapes. They varied in size, from four-tenths of an inch to one inch at the widest point. 'The smallest one weighs around half a gram, while the largest is around ten grams,' the proprietor said, noting the glint of excitement in her eyes. The coins were embossed with various emblems: bulls, lions, swastikas, elephants, ships. 'You will not find these anywhere, online or otherwise. Even the world's biggest collectors do not have them.'

'How come *you* have them?' she asked.

He laughed. 'Nothing is impossible if one has the will to go after it. Every important museum curator, collector and archaeologist knows that I will pay the right price for the right coin.'

'How do I know they aren't fake?' she asked, then bit her tongue. The proprietor looked genuinely hurt. He quickly closed the leather folder and indicated that she could leave. In all these decades, no one had ever questioned his integrity or the provenance of his coins.

Pam apologised profusely. It took another few minutes to get him to relent and reopen the folder. She looked through all the coins on offer and selected one. She negotiated hard on the price. It would have seemed suspicious if she hadn't.

Finally, a deal was struck. 'You're hurting me with that price,' said the proprietor. 'But you're a nice person, and I want you to come back for more purchases.' Pam did not have the heart to tell him this would probably be her first and last visit.

Pam paid cash and pocketed the coin. She then returned to Mark's office. She made a very specific request to him, unsure if he could get his team to do it.

But she was in luck.

'Sure,' said Mark, looking at the coin. 'It's precision work, but I think I can get my guys to do that for you.' He smiled at her. She knew that smile because it wasn't just *any* smile. There was a twinkle in his eyes and Pam knew exactly what it meant. She looked away. She was not going to fall for that again. No further complications were needed in their relationship. The past was done and laid to rest.

As Pam left Mark's office, her phone began to ring. It was General Jai Thakur. She stood quietly and listened to his angry outburst as he questioned why she had discussed the case with Mark without first seeking his consent. She heard him out without argument. It was better to lose the battle in order to win the war. *Crotchety old sod*, she thought.

32

I bypassed the fifth tower upon the advice of Wangsiang, the commander of the first watch tower. Instead, I headed thirty miles into Gashun Gobi Shamo,[26] the River of Sand. I was hoping to reach the Spring of Wild Horses,[27] an oasis at the edge of the desert, within a day. But I was foolish and did not realise that desert sands could disrupt the best of intentions.

Not a blade of grass grew in this desolate area. There were no shrubs, animals or birds. There seemed to be no life at all. And I ended up losing my way. Every dune looked like the next. The intense heat and harsh sunlight made it almost impossible to concentrate. I covered my head, nose and mouth with a scarf to protect myself from the heat, sun and whirling sands, but nothing seemed to help.

To add to my woes, my goatskin bag fell to the ground. My water supply of several days was drained in the blink of an eye. All I could do was gather up the empty bag in the hope of finding water to replenish it with. I was hopelessly lost. The warnings

---

26. Gobi Desert in China and Mongolia.

27. Modern-day oasis of Nanhu in the Gobi Desert.

of Wangsiang and so many others came back to haunt me. Why had I been so stubborn? Why had I not heeded their advice? Why had I not gone to Shazhou instead of embarking on this fanciful endeavour?

I turned back towards the signal towers, realising that I now had no real alternatives. But then an immense feeling of guilt washed over me. I remembered my mission to become Di San Sou Chuan. My head told me to retrace my footsteps in the direction of the watch towers, but my heart told me the exact opposite.

Eventually, I listened to my heart.

I can't remember exactly how many days I wandered in the desert. It was probably five, but could have been more. Or less. I had very little to go on, to calculate the passage of time. I was in a vast desert, my throat was parched and my belly was on fire. My skin felt as though it had been roasted crisp under the sun. At night, I was terrified by tongues of fire rushing out of the sands. I would only later learn that they were fires from gases produced by rotting corpses under the sands. They were called corpse candles, I was told.

On the fifth day I fell to the ground, unable to walk farther, praying to the Buddha for deliverance. My muscles felt paralysed. The pounding in my head was so severe that every step felt like a hammer to my skull. I lay on the desert sands leached of life, slipping in and out of consciousness, praying to the Buddha to let me die.

Suddenly, a cool breeze touched my skin. Like a gentle caress. I staggered to my feet and felt the cold air on my face. I felt revived, enough to take a few more steps. I set off again, but my horse wandered off in a different direction. I had no option but to follow him.

In my helplessness, I allowed myself to be guided by that scrawny runt of a horse. It turned out to be the best thing I ever did. Soon before me lay a tiny green oasis with shimmering water at its centre. I wondered whether it was another mirage. What if I tried to drink, only to discover I'd imagined it all? But then I saw my horse drinking and I knew it wasn't a mirage after all.

My horse and I drank long and deep. We drank as though we had never tasted water before. And the water was the sweetest I'd ever had. I replenished my water bag. We rested briefly and were soon on our way again. I laughed; the unassuming horse had saved my life, something my white steed would have been unable to do. Sometimes the most unlikely acquaintance can turn out to be your saviour.

Two days later, we reached the oasis of Yizhou, the first of a string of oases along the foothills of the snow-capped Heavenly Mountains.[28] *The glacial waters of these mountains rushed down the slopes and eventually into the dunes of Takelamagan Shamo. In the ordinary course, the water would have been lost to the desert sands, but the dwellers of Yizhou had developed an ingenious system of underground channels and wells that allowed them to store and utilise it. This system helped them grow an abundance of millets, rice, wheat, beans, hemp, melons, grapes, and even mulberry trees. It was an absolute miracle of nature to see this agricultural paradise in the midst of nothingness.*

In Yizhou, I stayed at a temple where three Chinese monks lived, to recuperate from the long journey. They were overjoyed and shed tears of happiness to see someone from their homeland. It was from transit monasteries, such as this one, that the teachings of the Buddha had found their way into Cina. The monks looked after me as though I were a long-lost family member. They used herbs and medications to treat my wounds and heal the blisters on my feet. They fed me the sweetest melons I had ever tasted. I was grateful for their hospitality and rested with them for a while.

But the route to Yindu beckoned.

I planned to take the northern route to Yindu because it passed through grassland. The middle and southern routes passed

---

28. Tian Shan mountains in Xinjiang, China.

through desert regions. I began my preparations for the next step of the journey, but my plans were upset by a message from Gaochang.[29]

Gaochang was a kingdom that lay along the middle route. The king of Gaochang wanted the priests of Yizhou to ensure that I appeared before him. The message sounded ominous, and I had no idea what awaited me. The king had sent horses to bring me from Yizhou.

I suddenly found myself surrounded by a battalion of soldiers, and wondered whether I was the king's guest or prisoner.

33

Pam went home to pack a bag. Booked for a flight to Chennai early next morning, she quickly shoved a few clothes and essentials into her military holdall while her mother watched and fussed.

'What is so urgent that you must leave immediately?' asked her mother, eyeing the open diary on the bed. Pam had been flipping through the pages repeatedly, revisiting her father's sketches.

'There's someone I need to track down,' replied Pam. 'His last known address is in Kanchi, and the closest airport is Chennai. A car will take me there from Chennai. It's about two hours away.'

'I worry about you, beta,' said Pam's mother distractedly. 'I lost the man I loved, and now you are all I have. I can't afford to lose you too. But you are just like him. Brave, strong and reckless.'

Pam stopped what she was doing. She walked over to her mother and enveloped her in a hug. 'Nothing is going to

---

29. Modern-day Karakhoja in Xinjiang, China.

happen to me, Mom. You're stuck with me for the rest of your life.'

Her mother smiled. Tragedy had aged her, but she remained a very elegant woman at fifty-five. Her trim figure, unblemished complexion and silken hair gave her an air of nobility. Most of his friends had been jealous of Colonel Kishan Khurana because he had landed the best-looking wife among them. He was regularly ribbed about being a cradle-snatcher since she was nine years younger than him.

'I find it hard to believe even after all these years that he's no longer with me,' said Pam's mother. 'I had spoken to him just that morning before he boarded the boat from Mannar and headed for Rameswaram.'

'What was the state of his mind then?' asked Pam. She had had this conversation with her mother many times but never tired of it. She discovered a few additional details each time her mother narrated the events of that fateful day.

'He was very worried about something. There was something he wanted to say, but he held himself back. I asked him why he wasn't flying and was taking the boat instead. He said he wanted to stop for a few days in the south before returning to Delhi. I was about to ask where exactly he was planning to halt, but the phone lines were terrible in those days and we got cut off. That was the last time I heard his voice. He was only thirty-five.'

Pam's mother gulped. Talking about that last conversation always caused her eyes to well up, even after so many years.

'What actually happened to him?' asked Pam. 'You never share the details.'

'That's because what I've been told is also sketchy. The naval boat had just left the docks, heading into the Palk

Strait. Your father was on the deck, smoking. There were several ships of the Indian Navy on that stretch, but the weather was rough and cloudy. There were also some fishing trawlers around. It's possible that one of them may have been under the command of the LTTE. A bullet hit your father out of the blue. We still have no idea where it came from. All we know is that it was fatal. He was moved into the doctor's cabin, where medical attention was provided, but he was dead within a few minutes.'

Pam could see that her mother's tears were about to overflow. 'When did you find out?' she persisted.

'The next day. They refused to send his body to Delhi and instead flew me to Chennai, where the cremation was done almost immediately upon my arrival. It was a closed casket placed in an electric crematorium, so I couldn't even see him. I only received his ashes.'

'Why the hurry? Did they carry out an autopsy?'

'Usually the Armed Forces Medical Examiner does that, but the findings were never shared with me,' said Pam's mother, her cheeks wet with fresh tears. 'They didn't even bother to share his personal effects with me. Luckily, he had given a manila envelope containing his diary, lighter, pen and hip flask to one of his friends, telling him to pass them on to me should anything happen to him. That was also strange, as if he had a premonition of sorts.'

Pam thought back to the many occasions she had touched her father's things just to feel connected to him. She was grateful that those items had been preserved and were with her. The diary especially.

'Why do you think everything was done so secretively?' she asked.

'A conspiracy,' replied her mother with conviction. 'A very big one. I don't know *what* your father knew, but my heart tells me that it got him killed.'

Pam never knew how to respond to her mother's suspicions. She desperately wanted to believe that it was a stray bullet in a very busy war corridor that had killed her father. But there was something about her mother's words that rang true. She tried to make sense of the conflict in her head. *What could that secret have been?*

Almost as though reading her mind, her mother answered, 'I have no clue what the big secret was. Your father was a disciplined soldier and never shared anything he wasn't supposed to. He had this incredible ability to compartmentalise everything. I can't ever recall him sharing anything about work with me, nor did he ever talk about family to his colleagues. He was like that in financial matters too. If it hadn't been for the army pension and assistance from the Vegavathy Trust, I don't know how we would have managed.'

Pam nodded as she thought about the sketches in her dad's diary. Who was the man with the monkey-like features? Was it a man, woman or animal? Why had her father sketched that particular figure? And what were those random jottings alongside it? She hummed her dad's nonsense verse under her breath.

Baa-maa-ko-ki-joo-ka-lo
Wee-noo-ko-ki-moo-pa-lo
See-waa-ko-ki-soo-pa-lo
Haa-noo-ko-ki-poo-da-jo

'Please be careful, beta,' said her mother. 'I'm terrified that something will happen to you too. Please don't take any unnecessary risks.'

34

Pam flew to Chennai and proceeded to Kanchi by cab. The amiable driver ensured that she was comfortable, keeping the air conditioning at just the right temperature and thoughtfully leaving a bottle of chilled mineral water for her on the rear seat. She noticed that he was dressed in a khaki uniform, the outfit favoured by cabbies, and had a bushy beard. He wore sunglasses to shield himself from the glare while driving.

It was a significant weather change from freezing Delhi. Mercifully, the driver was not talkative, which suited Pam just fine. He looked at her reflection in his rear-view mirror rather too often, though. Pam ignored him.

Once they were in Kanchi, they took the road to the academy located on the banks of the river Vegavathy. They followed the road that ran parallel to the river and eventually turned off into a private lane. The lane had remained unused for many years, and there were more potholes than surfaced road. What should have been a drive of a few minutes took close to an hour. Pam thought she would slip a disc from the juddering of the car. But they did eventually reach.

It was in a state of utter disrepair. There was only one gate and it was locked. A faded 'No Trespassing' sign hung on a chain from the gate, warning would-be intruders to stay out. A thick growth of wild grass and weeds at the foot of the gate indicated that it had not been opened in a very long time. Pam asked the driver to park the car in a side lane and wait for her.

She strolled around the area, looking out for cameras. Once she was convinced there were none, she made her way to the gate and nimbly clambered over it. She feared it would collapse under her weight, creaky as it was, but it did not.

It was painfully evident that the plot had been abandoned several years, possibly decades, ago. She was tense as she walked along the dirt track. Desolate and deserted properties always spooked her. All around her, the grounds were covered by a thick growth of waist-high weeds. She wondered how many snakes wriggled underfoot, and wished she had brought back-up.

It was a huge complex. Classrooms, kitchens, dormitories, pools and gymnasia that would once have been bustling with activity now lay utterly silent and empty, deserted and dusty. Up ahead, Pam could see a crumbling grey building, looming like a hideous monster. It was the main residential block.

Her feet squelched through mud as she headed towards it. As she approached, she saw that the roof had caved in. The building seemed to have survived a fire; some of the walls were still blackened and cracked. The windows were either broken or coated with a thick layer of dust and grime. Behind those windows lay utter darkness. She shuddered involuntarily.

As she arrived at the porch leading to the primary entrance, she encountered a solid wooden door 'that had been subjected to layers of adolescent graffiti. A rusted padlock held the door shut, and a couple of plump lizards sat guard on the brickwork around the door. She wondered whether there would be anything worth examining here. Rao was hardly likely to be living in this ramshackle place.

Except for the chirping of crickets, there was no sound to be heard. The nearest habitation was over a mile away. Trash lay everywhere—wrappers, used condoms, cigarettes and broken bottles. The place was probably a haven for teenagers looking to experiment with sex and drugs. Pam spun around quickly when she heard a clanging noise. It was a bandicoot, as big as a dog, knocking over an empty metal can. She exhaled in relief.

She did not have a warrant from the CBI to enter the place, but the urgency of the situation demanded that rules be broken. She picked up a smooth rock and struck it against the rusting padlock. The blows reverberated in the stillness, shattering the calm. With just a layer of rust holding the padlock together, it required virtually no effort to force it open. She kicked in the door and gingerly made her way into the forbidding interiors. *Why do I feel like I'm not alone?*

Decades of abandonment had deposited a heavy layer of dust everywhere. Pam brought a handkerchief to her face as she looked around. She walked through the entrance lobby. To her right was a doorway leading to smaller office rooms. To her left was a wall pockmarked with hooks that must have borne the weight of several paintings or commendations. In front of her was a wide staircase leading to the floor above. She headed towards it and halted in her tracks as a group of pigeons suddenly took to the air, the flapping of their wings startling her.

She took a deep breath and gathered her wits as she carefully negotiated the steps, hoping they would not give way under her. She reached the first floor and walked into a large room filled with corroded bedframes. At the farther end of the room was a platform with an old cauldron that would have been used to serve the candidates their prescribed rations.

The entire building must have consisted of dormitories bustling with trainees. Pam felt her hair stand on end as she felt the menacing forces still trapped within. She could hear her own breath. Every sound within the large room seemed to reverberate. She felt her stomach tighten.

Sensing a sudden movement behind her, Pam spun around. But her response was a fraction of a second too late.

The blow to her left jaw felled her, and she passed out, dropping to the ground with a thud.

35

Pam opened her eyes slowly and tried to recall where she was. The dull pain in her head was a reminder of the blow she had received. She was still inside the abandoned dormitory but on a clean sheet placed on the floor.

Above her she could see a high ceiling crisscrossed by rafters of rusting metal. The dirty, corroded concrete floor she lay on met exposed brick walls and broken or grime-covered windows that she had observed from outside. Huge ducts and exposed pipes ran overhead. They had probably been installed to maintain high oxygen levels for the cadets in training. A single naked bulb hung on a wire from an ancient beam above her.

Pam cursed herself for not being alert. She turned her head to look around and found a tall woman towering over her. Incredibly fit and muscular, the woman would have effortlessly won in straight combat with Pam. But there was also a strange meditative peace that emanated from her.

'My apologies for knocking you down,' said the woman softly, 'but you were intruding. It's only after you passed out that I saw the DRDO and CBI identification cards in your pocket. Also that coin.'

'I should be the one apologising,' said Pam. 'I had no business breaking in. I was trying to trace the whereabouts of Dr Raja Rao and was told that this was his last known address.'

'I'm Dr Rao's daughter, Anu,' said the woman. She was surprisingly athletic, lithe and powerful in spite of her greying hair. She offered her hand to Pam, who gratefully took it to get herself off the ground. The grasp was vise-like. 'Let's go outside,' said Anu. 'It's more pleasant there.'

As they made their way out, Anu asked, 'Why are you looking for my father? You're probably aware that he sees no one. I haven't seen him make an exception in years.'

Good, he's alive, thought Pam.

Pam ran a hand over her injury to soothe the area. Anu smiled sheepishly. 'It was a carotid strike that caused you to pass out,' she explained. 'It's delivered to the carotid sinus, located on either side of your neck, slightly behind your jaw. The strike causes a sudden loss of oxygen to the brain, followed by a black out. The swelling will subside in a few minutes. Apologies, once again.'

'Where did you learn that?' asked Pam, making an effort to smile.

'My father taught me everything I know,' said Anu simply. They began walking to the main gate, their eyes taking a moment to adjust to the harsh sunlight. They passed the crumbling Olympic-sized swimming pool, now an abandoned crater overrun with weeds and with most of the tiles missing. To one side lay a rusted machine with massive pipes running into the sides of the pool.

'Wave machine,' explained Anu. 'The training included resisting various types of forces, including aquatic force.'

They walked along a muddy path that cut through a bamboo grove. 'We used to maintain our own bamboo farm because sticks were needed for the cadets' training. Of course, now we permit local farmers to harvest them.'

'What's that?' asked Pam, pointing to massive parallel stone blocks with rusty faucets above.

'The sticks used in our form of fighting are usually bamboo, but sometimes we also use teak or rose chestnut wood. Irrespective of the material, it needs to be immersed in water repeatedly, then beaten against stone to strengthen it. The strengthening was done on these stone blocks.'

Pam was genuinely curious. 'Bamboo is adequate defence?'

'Well, the length of the bamboo depends on the height of the person wielding it,' replied Anu. 'Ideally, it should touch the practitioner's forehead. With the right height and in the right hands, the staff can be absolutely deadly. The technique is known as silambam, an ancient martial art that originated in this region that we now call Tamil Nadu. But enough about this place. Do you mind telling me what made you break in?'

Pam explained her predicament. 'Indian soldiers are dying at the border at the hands of Chinese attackers. We have no clue what gives the attackers their strength, size or skill. The only person who can help me with this absolutely critical issue is your father. Please give me just a few minutes with him.' She knew she was pleading. 'If he still wishes me to go away, I will respect that.' They reached the main gate that she had clambered over earlier, and paused briefly.

Anu looked directly into Pam's eyes. 'All I can promise you is that I will *try* to get Appa to meet you. I cannot guarantee that he will. Follow me.'

They walked twenty-five paces to the right of the main gate until they reached a thick hedge. Within the hedge was a small wicket gate that Anu now pushed open. Pam wondered how she had missed it on her way in. Then she realised that the gate was angled into the hedge such that it remained invisible from the main road and gate.

Soon, they were standing on a reasonably well-maintained lawn, to the right of which was a small cottage made of teak wood in the Chettinad style, with a pillared verandah. The front door was intricately carved, but it was evident that the home was missing care and attention.

Anu walked up to the door and knocked, Pam by her side.

36

After a trek of six days, I reached Gaochang. It was a tiring journey, back on dry and hot desert paths, but this time my chestnut runt and I had enough food, water and company.

By the time we reached Gaochang on the sixth day, it was dark. But King Kuwentai had arranged for hundreds of torchbearers to illuminate my path to the beautiful pavilion, where he awaited my arrival. He met me like I was a respected guest and guided me to a seat of honour. Gaochang had the largest population of ethnic Chinese in Xiyu — the western regions — and the king was a devout Buddhist. It was a prosperous kingdom because the silk and tea of Cina and the spices and jewels of Yindu were all traded and transported through it. This ensured buoyant tax revenues for the king. The king was equally generous, receiving over 9,000 state guests each year and bearing all their costs.

The king sat next to me; then his queen, a beautiful and elegantly dressed lady, came before me to pay her respects. Following her were a trail of ladies-in-waiting who had been assigned the task of ensuring I ate well. Aware of the fact that I was a vegetarian, the queen had thoughtfully arranged for milk, rice, honey, nuts, fruits, vegetables and millet bread.

After I had eaten, the king guided me to a couch and sat down next to me. I was very tired after the long journey, but he was in no mood to let me retire to my sleeping quarters. He kept me up into the wee hours of the morning, discussing the teachings of the Buddha. Finally, the queen managed to get him to understand that I needed rest. I was led by four eunuchs to a beautifully appointed bedchamber, where I fell into deep slumber.

The next morning, when I stepped out of my room, I had a breathtaking view of the city. Spread over two square miles, it was divided into three parts — an outer city, an inner city and, within that, the royal palace. The layout was very similar to that of Chang'an, because the young Kuwentai had spent time in that city and had been tremendously influenced by its beauty. In fact, he had presented himself to the emperor in the Chinese court and had paid him rich tributes. The city walls of Gaochang were thirty feet high and the landscape was dotted with stupas, temples, monasteries, gardens and neatly planned homesteads. The king requested me to deliver a sermon to 300 guests at a specially constructed pavilion. I obliged.

The next day, I thanked the monarch for his hospitality and expressed my desire to proceed on my journey to Yindu, but he insisted that I stay on for a few days as his guest. I was unable to refuse, fearing he would take it amiss.

Ten days elapsed and I was getting restless. I broached the topic gently, but the king had different ideas for me. He wanted me to give up my plans to proceed to Yindu and instead join his court as his trusted adviser. I respectfully declined. After all, my mission could not be compromised. He offered me vast riches and treasures to stay, but I was resolute. He even offered his seniormost concubine's daughter in marriage if I gave up my monk's habit and habits, but I did not budge. Unused to being disobeyed, the king grew livid and ordered that I be forcibly restrained in Gaochang. He even threatened to return me as a prisoner to Emperor Taizong.

I decided to go on a fast, refusing all food and water. The monarch had not expected such a reaction from me. Each day he and the queen would personally bring me food and try to convince me to eat or drink, but I would decline. Finally, after three days, my breath became very feeble, and the king relented, realising that keeping me back would bring upon him my death. Upon his assurance, I took a sip of water and ate a small meal. Relief washed over the king's face.

The next day, the king and I sat before a glorious statue of the Buddha inside a massive square hall and took vows as sworn brothers in the presence of his trusted courtiers. The oath meant that we were now responsible for protecting each other throughout our lives. I also agreed to stay on for a few more days to preach to his subjects.

The king pledged his support for my pilgrimage and selected four able monks to accompany me as my disciples. He provided me with gloves, leather boots, face coverings, thirty horses and twenty-four servants to ensure that I was comfortable during my journey. In addition, he gave me one hundred taels of gold, 30,000 silver pieces and 500 rolls of silk, satin and taffeta. I wondered why I was being showered with expensive gifts. After all, I was merely a humble monk.

I asked him why he was being so generous. He replied that he wanted me to be able to travel for the next twenty years without having to seek alms. The gold and silver were meant to ensure that. He also wanted that other monarchs on my route should cooperate with me. The satin, silk and taffeta were tributes for those kings. My new brother also wrote twenty-four letters, one for each kingdom that I would pass through, requesting safe passage and horse relays for me. In addition, he commissioned one of his senior officers to guide me to the court of the Great Khan of the Western Turks.

The royal family, monks and citizens of Gaochang saw me off with what appeared to be genuine regret. I too was sad to leave them, but my mission called. Before I left, I promised the king that I would stop at Gaochang on my return journey. Little did I know that I was seeing him for the very last time.

37

Mark leaned forward in his chair and looked at the insulated box on his desk. It had arrived a few minutes earlier, brought by his forensics team on a special aircraft from Doklam. He had hastily cleared his desk of his coffee cup and water bottle for fear of messing up.

His phone began to flash; it was Pam. 'Yes, the sample has arrived,' he reassured her. 'I'll put my best guy on the job. Let me get back to you once I have some preliminary results.' Mark picked up the intercom and called the lab to summon one of his best forensic pathologists.

'I need you to do something very important,' he said as he handed the box to him. 'See if there's any chance of getting a DNA profile from the blood on this.' If there was anyone whose lab work he could trust, it was this man. The pathologist had helped him on several occasions, particularly when they were testing the stress levels of Indian soldiers in border areas. CBTT had gone on to devise an experimental technology to lower blood cortisol levels when soldiers were in high-stress situations.

The pathologist opened the insulated cooler box. Inside was a paper bag. He lifted the bag, opened it and looked inside. It was evident that the tourniquet had been placed in a paper bag—as was standard practice—so that the blood would not dry.

'The blood looks relatively fresh,' he observed. 'In which case, the cells will not have dehydrated as yet. I don't think they will have ruptured either. Assuming I'm right, microscopic tests in addition to serological and molecular tests should be possible. Give me some time to come back to you.'

Mark nodded.

The pathologist carried the box back to his lab. The concrete interiors had been given a new skin built of channel glass, metal panels and perforated metal screens. Clever angling of mirrors bathed the rows of gleaming laboratory tables and equipment in sunlight. A long, white, illuminated table ran along the entire length of the lab on one side. Along the other wall lay cutting-edge equipment—spectrometers, microscopes, DNA sequencers, thermal cyclers, centrifuges, incubators, rotary evaporators and lyophilisers.

Using artery forceps, he carefully extracted the tourniquet from the specimen bag and placed it on a large single-use dish. Starting a video recording using the camera attached to his forehead, he snipped off small potions of stained and unstained material for testing, placing the rest in a sealed and labelled envelope. He sprayed the smaller part of the snipped portion with luminol, turned off the laboratory lights and lowered the blackout drapes. Once the lab was entirely dark, throwing UV light on the tourniquet caused a fluorescent glow. He was reasonably sure that it was blood, but luminol was known for giving false positives. He would need to confirm.

He placed another small blood-stained snipping on an examination slide and added one drop of phenolphthalein, followed by a drop of hydrogen peroxide. And there it was, pink! But this was CBTT, and Mark would erupt unless the most exhaustive procedures were followed.

He prepared a sample for a Takayama crystal test. He carefully added Takayama reagent to a fresh slide with the bloodied sample and dried it at 115° Celsius. He looked at the result through his microscope. Sure enough, he could clearly discern dark red, feathery crystals. There was no doubt that this was a blood stain. The bigger question now was the source of the blood.

DNA is located within cell nuclei. His first step would involve breaking open the nucleus and releasing DNA molecules into a solution. Then he would try to separate the molecules he wanted from other cellular material and debris. He chose an automated system called Maxwell 16 that would do the job in around two hours. He took a coffee break while waiting for the system to do its thing.

Several hours later, the sample was ready for molecular duplication. The system would create millions of copies of the sample DNA sequence through polymerase chain reaction. Then, using capillary electrophoresis, he would develop a DNA profile for the sample.

But as the DNA results began showing up, the pathologist wondered whether he had made an error. He rechecked all his notes, mentally retraced his steps and checked the video recording. All protocols had been followed in the right sequence, with no chance of contamination. Yet the number of chromosomes in the sample was off. How could that be? He decided to repeat the entire procedure on a new sample from the tourniquet using a manual process. He snipped off another part and immersed it in a chemical solution. He thought through the steps as he proceeded.

It would be a long night.

38

The black Hongqi limousine pulled up at the entrance of the hospital in Dengfeng County, Henan. The car had been customised for the Buzhang with plush leather upholstery and polished wood trimmings. The hospital was located less than thirty minutes away from the training facility. Like other rural Chinese hospitals, this one too was crowded. It was also poorly maintained, with inadequate maintenance services and rundown equipment.

The Buzhang pulled out a small platinum jar from the leather recesses of the armrest, opened it and dabbed a touch of camphor balm under his nose with his manicured fingers before getting out of the vehicle, to ward off any unpleasant smells. He grasped his swagger stick firmly in one hand.

He was accompanied by Erkin. Together they crossed the vast lobby and reception before they reached a locked gate. The staff stood ramroad straight at attention whenever the Buzhang passed but did not accompany him. The Buzhang placed his thumb on a scanner and the gate rolled open. They entered a secret ward that could only be accessed by staff with security clearance. Even the president of China could not enter this place without the Buzhang accompanying him.

The secret ward was a gloomy place. The walls were painted a dreary grey and the harsh ceiling lights were the kind you might expect to find inside a prison. The floors were equally monotonous: long stretches of unimaginative, speckled tiles. Nurses and orderlies went about their business impersonally, carrying samples, transporting medicines and handling patients. On one side of the long corridor that led to the ward were steel benches used by patients to take a break from their hospital beds. The other side was occupied by gown-clad patients in wheelchairs.

The Buzhang crossed the corridor and entered the ward, the clicking of his polished leather shoes echoing through the dreary place. Erkin consciously remained a couple of feet behind. The common ward was a large room with a hundred beds. It was just as stark and miserable as the rest of the hospital. Its only redeeming quality was that it was spotlessly clean and the equipment was newer. But the smell! Buzhang hated the smell of disinfectants in hospitals.

He swept his eyes across the ward. There were rows and rows of steel-framed beds containing frail old men wearing striped hospital gowns. The ones who were not lying down were attempting to stroll, their IV drips following them like obedient puppies. A hunchback was trying to get up from his bed, but his spine was bent at an angle that made it difficult. One man was coughing violently, another was staring blankly into space, a third was twitching uncontrollably, and yet another was retching violently. What was common to all of them was that they looked very old and decrepit.

A dedicated team of doctors had been attempting to develop medical solutions using a mixture of modern medicine, hormonal boosters, antibiotics and traditional Chinese remedies, but nothing had worked so far. A team of doctors, nurses and orderlies were attempting to take care of the men, but they seemed weary.

One of the doctors had a thick and shiny pen in his coat pocket. He never wrote any notes or instructions with that pen. Instead, its silent eye took photos of the ward at regular intervals.

The Buzhang took in the scene with steely eyes. Erkin, though, had tears in his.

'What is the actual age of these men?' asked the Buzhang.

'Eighteen to twenty-two,' replied Erkin, trying hard to mask the emotion in his voice. *All this could have been avoided if you had not been in such a damn hurry.* This ward was no longer a treatment centre. It had become the equivalent of an end-of-life care centre, a hospice where healthy young men were being sent to die.

The Buzhang motioned for the senior doctor to approach. 'What is the prognosis?' he asked.

The doctor shook his head. 'All that we are trying to do is to keep them pain-free and as comfortable as possible. We have lost count of the number that we have already lost.'

The Buzhang waved his stick arrogantly, gesturing to the doctor to move away and carry on with his work.

'I hate to say it, but we are sending these men to their death by not finding Pishinou,' said Erkin.

The Buzhang scowled as he smashed his swagger stick against an empty metal gurney in anger. The sound woke some of the sleeping patients. The nurses would have liked to reprimand the Buzhang but they were quiet. None of them wanted to see the insides of a labour camp.

'I'm surrounded by hopeless people who lack the talent to find creative solutions,' he snapped. 'Why can't I have problem solvers rather than whiners?'

Erkin shut up, but his mind continued running frantically. He was mentally reciting a prayer. *Allahumma inni a'udhu bika min zawali...*

39

The door opened. At the entrance stood a barefoot nonagenarian whose back was surprisingly straight. He had a full head of black hair, and the skin on his face had the tautness of youth. He wore a simple white shirt with a pale cream veshti. On his forehead was a sandalwood paste mark that indicated he had performed his morning prayers. Despite his age, he wore no glasses. This was a man who had succeeded in keeping himself perfectly preserved.

Rao's eyes went directly to Pam. He then turned to his daughter with a strange expression. It was as though she had betrayed his trust by inviting a stranger to his home.

Silently, he turned around and walked back inside the living room that doubled as his study. Anu and Pam followed him hesitantly. It was a dark and musty space, overrun by books, lab equipment and document binders. A faint smell of sandalwood paste and jasmine incense hung in the air. Two old fans creaked on the ceiling. A windowed wall overlooked the garden, while the remaining three bore shelves that groaned with books on almost every conceivable subject—science, medicine, religion, spirituality, history, mythology, ayurveda, philosophy, yoga, archaeology and linguistics. The desk near the window was also covered with books and numerous notepads—but no computer. A fountain pen and an old-fashioned ink bottle had pride of place on the desk.

The old man was clearly upset that Anu had brought a stranger home, but was too dignified to say so in Pam's presence. Anu motioned Pam towards a well-worn couch. Father and daughter left the living room and disappeared into the adjoining pantry. Pam looked around and noticed there were absolutely no photographs in the house. *What was Rao hiding? Or was it that he was trying to forget?*

Pam could only hear snippets of the conversation, a mixture of Tamil and English, but she picked up enough to understand that Anu was receiving a lecture from her father. In turn, she was attempting to pacify him by saying that Pam was worth talking to, for the sake of the country, if not for any other reason. 'What has the country ever done for me?' retorted the old man bitterly.

That particular outburst was loud enough to be heard by Pam. There was no doubt in her mind that Rao had been mistreated. *Even if he agrees to talk to me, how cooperative will he be? And why did Dev send me here? Has this been a wasted trip?*

There were a few more words exchanged before the duo emerged. Anu brought a glass of water from the kitchen as her father sat down facing Pam. 'I have no idea why my daughter has brought you here,' he said. 'She knows my policy of not meeting anyone. I haven't broken that rule in many years. But I trust her judgment. She believes you. So speak, child. Tell me what you want from me.'

Pam got up from the couch wordlessly and knelt on the floor before Rao in supplication. She then extracted the bronze coin she had bought in Sadar Bazaar, now attached to a chain. The coin was ancient Pallavan, with the emblem of a twin-masted ship. She offered it to Rao, keeping her head bowed with her gaze to the floor.

Rao took the coin from her and examined it. He turned it over a few times, squinting a little to discern the contours. 'The early Pallava coins depict single-masted ships, but their later coins depict double masts. Tells you how much their shipbuilding technology had progressed. That's why their ships dominated the ocean trade between the Coromandel Coast and Southeast Asia,' said Rao. 'Pallava coins like this one have been found in the countries they traded with.'

Pam knew that the old man was moved but was trying to mask his emotions by talking about the coin. 'What is your name?' he asked in a quavering voice. He was barely audible.

'Pam Khurana.'

'Related to the late Colonel Kishan Khurana? Who was part of the IPKF?'

'He is … *was* my father,' replied Pam with pride.

Rao instantly softened. He placed his hand on her head in a gesture of blessing and asked her to rise.

'Why didn't you tell me earlier?' He smiled for the very first time since he had met her. 'Your father was a dear friend. We met very often. Around twenty-five years separated us, but we had this incredible bond. He often spoke about you. You were the love of his life. And your dear mother, of course.'

The smile on his face was genuine, yet there was a sadness in his eyes when he mentioned Pam's father.

'He never mentioned you to me or to my mother,' said Pam wistfully.

'He knew better than to do that,' replied Rao. 'He would have been endangering your lives.'

40

My entourage and I traversed the desolate hills of the Huoyanshan.[30] These were barren, red sandstone hills that lay on the northern rim of the desert. The deep gullies gave the mountains the appearance of reddish flames at certain times of the day.

I stopped there, dismounted and took in the wonder of the mountains. I then carefully made my way to a gorge under the cliffs of the Huoyanshan. It was a short but treacherous walk towards the deep ravine, but once I was there, I beheld the most amazing sight. There were hundreds of monks' cells cut into the vertical rock face. A river gushed far beneath. This was one of the most incredible monasteries I had seen. It was called the Thousand Buddha Caves.[31]

Hundreds of monks were chanting in hushed tones from inside their caves. I sat at the mouth of one of the caves to chant along with them. The peace that washed over me was truly wondrous. Sitting on the narrow ledge with an incredible view of the majestic river below was an exhilarating experience.

The monks wanted me to stay on with them, but I knew that I had to proceed with my journey and my all-important mission to become Di San Sou Chuan. But before I left them, they gave me a tour of the caves. They were rectangular in shape, with rounded and arched ceilings that blazed with exquiste murals of the Buddha, depicting different scenes from his life. Each one was a masterpiece.

---

30. Flaming Mountains, sandstone hills in the Tian Shan mountains of Xinjiang, China.

31. Modern-day Bezeklik Caves in Xinjiang, China.

I took leave of my brother monks and walked back to where my party awaited me. We decided to rest for a brief while before proceeding, because our guides wanted to avoid the heavy winds that had been forecast. They did not need any equipment to make meteorogical observations and were mostly self-taught, but skilled in leveraging their immense knowledge of landmarks, wind directions, desert conditions and astronomical positions.

I could hear the sound of wolves in the distance, but I was assured by the monks that they were harmless. Just then, another caravan laden with goods passed by. I advised them to stop and travel with us. Their leader thanked me for my concern but expressed his inability to halt. Apparently their caravan contained silk, ivory, jade, perfumes, spices, cotton, olive oil and wine, all of which had to reach the Great Khan for an important event. Reaching in time was critical.

'Son, not every caravan is the same,' I advised. 'Caravans of monks have the Buddha to protect them. Caravans of diplomats have kings as their lord protectors. But merchants have neither. Bandits will not hesitate to rob you. Stay with us because we have the protection of the king of Gaochang. Our guides are telling us that the heavy winds will die down in a while. Better safe than sorry.'

The merchant leader smiled at me. 'I have made over a hundred trips in my life. I have been robbed seven times. On each occasion, God has protected me. The greatest quality of any traveller is to have no fear. My grateful thanks to you for your offer, revered monk, but I must carry on.' Saying this, his group passed us by and continued on their long journey.

After having refreshed ourselves, our caravan began the 200-mile journey towards our next destination. To do this, we had to ascend a range of mountains known for their silver deposits—the Silver Mountains.[32] It was a difficult trek because mining had reduced the strength of the pathways. One careless move was

---

32. Argu Tagh Range in Xinjiang, China.

all that was required for any of us to plunge to certain death. Vultures circled overhead, picking flesh off the corpses of men who had fallen to an untimely end.

Just as we crossed Silver Mountains, we came upon a ghastly sight. Tens of slaughtered bodies lay in our path. Their belongings had been picked clean and their pack animals were nowhere in sight. Not a single man had been left alive. I recognised the merchant I had met at the Flaming Mountains of Huoyanshan. I bent over his corpse and mouthed a silent prayer for him. I wished that he had taken my advice, but his time had probably come. One cannot avoid death unless one is already dead. And even then, one cannot avoid the endless cycle that follows.

Suddenly, we heard hooves in the distance. Clouds of dust formed as a large contingent of bandits charged towards us, their swords raised and glimmering in the harsh sunlight. Evil smiles played on their faces as they anticipated the bloodbath and plunder that was about to follow. In all probability, they were the very ones who had killed the people in the caravan before us. They were now returning for more.

The senior officer who accompanied us took matters into his own hands. He stood on a rock and shouted, 'If you touch a single man in this party, you will be declaring war on the king of Gaochang! This party is headed by the king's adopted brother, Xuanzang. Think very carefully if you wish to incur his wrath. On the other hand, if you show compassion towards the members of this group, I shall arrange for each one of you to receive a handsome reward.'

The bandits understood that there was nothing to be gained by having the king as an enemy. They also probably knew that the king's sister was married to the son of the Great Khan. No one wished to get on the wrong side of the Great Khan, whose influence stretched over vast swathes of territory. The king of Gaochang was himself a vassal of the Great Khan and entitled to his protection. The code between kings was taken seriously by bandits too.

They accepted the purses that the king's officer handed out and fled with their bribe, grateful to be spared the wrath of the king. The goods meant for the Khan were gathered up by us so that they could reach him safely.

41

Rao cleaned the coin carefully with a handkerchief. He then put the chain around his neck so that the coin hugged his chest.

'I'm grateful for this,' he said to Pam, smiling. He was truly touched by her gesture. He walked over to one of the bookshelves and rummaged around. He pulled out books and put them back, he opened the drawers of the antique chest that sat below the window, he took out folders and mulled over them, he opened a trunk that lay on the floor, he even stood on a chair to access some of the higher bookshelves. Eventually he let out a little shout of joy as he found what he was looking for.

It was a bundle of maroon cloth. White cotton shoelaces held the fabric in place, much like files in Indian government departments. A thin film of dust had settled on the fabric. He carefully opened the bundle to reveal a manuscript. The pages had been sewn together on one side; the cover was unmarked and yellowed with age.

Rao wordlessly handed the manuscript to Pam. She flipped through it, attempting to make sense of what the old man was trying to convey. She couldn't understand what lay within the pages, because the paragraphs alternated between Mandarin and Tamil, and neither language was known to her. Pam was bewildered. *Doesn't he realise that both these languages are alien to me? I wonder if he is slightly senile.* 'May I ask you some questions about the work you were doing here?' she asked him.

'Come back to me when you are done reading this document. I'll be happy to answer any questions you have for me. But not before you make an effort first. Also, please read a work called *Rasavinoda* by the Odiya poet Dinakrishnadasa. Many of your questions will have been answered by the time you finish perusing these two documents. Treat this with the care and respect it deserves. The only reason I am even willing to share it with you is because you are the daughter of my dear friend.'

Pam knew she had no choice but to do what Rao commanded. She would need assistance from a translator. *Won't Jaya have all the resources of RAW to get it done?* Any input from Rao was precious and could not be lost. She tucked the document under her arm, thanked the old man and headed to the exit.

As she was leaving, she noticed a little sculpure on Rao's desk. It depicted the three wise monkeys that represented the principle of 'see no evil, hear no evil and speak no evil'. When she asked about it, Rao explained that the three figures were from Japan. 'The idea was popularised by a seventeenth-century carving over the door of a Toshogu shrine in Nikko, but was inspired by Confucius's Code of Conduct from China. I even have names for each of them—Bok, Bakheng and Krom. Think about it. True power comes from following the code of the three monkeys. And in India we have always considered the rhesus species to be sacred.'

Anu accompanied Pam outside. 'I hope you didn't mind my father's blunt ways in the beginning. Appa is still hurting from the way he was treated by the government. They ended his lifetime's work abruptly, without assigning any reason. He felt betrayed by the powers that ruin rather than run the country. But I know he genuinely liked your father, so I'm quite certain he'll help you.'

'I understand,' replied Pam. 'Thank you for convincing him to meet me. I know you took a risk. Why did you stick your neck out for me?'

'Instinct combined with a lucky guess. The Pallava coin tumbled out of your pocket. While putting it back, I saw your identification papers indicating your last name. It was too much of a coincidence.' Anu smiled.

'You are amazingly fit and youthful for your age,' said Pam admiringly. 'I would never have imagined you're sixty-five. You don't look a day over forty.'

'How do you know my age?' asked Anu astutely.

Pam bit her tongue. She had unwittingly let on more than she needed to. 'Must have been Dev,' Anu said thoughtfully. 'It's fine. You don't need to confirm or deny anything. Dev too was forced out by the bureaucracy and was put to devious use to discredit Father's initiatives. But that doesn't dilute the fact that he cares about my father.' *And that I cared about him once. A long time ago. Before he betrayed Appa.*

'In what way did he discredit your father's work?' asked Pam.

'Let's not go there. It just seemed as though there was an invisible hand manipulating Dev.'

There was an uncomfortable pause. 'But seriously,' said Pam, changing the subject, 'what *is* the secret of your youth?'

'My father's training. I used to be the drill sergeant for the men who came in. They would think of me as just another woman but were always surprised when I would effortlessly pin them to the ground in combat. We women always have to work far harder to prove ourselves to be better than our male counterparts.'

Pam nodded. It was easy to empathise with Anu. They were both strong-willed women who had fought hard for their respective positions. Pam too had fought misogyny and the male-dominated security establishment to get where she was.

Pam took Anu's leave, carrying with her the binder that Rao had given her.

Anu made her way back inside the house. Father and daughter exchanged furtive looks. 'Why didn't you tell her, Appa?' asked Anu. 'She should know. Her own life could be in danger.'

'Why should I tell her that my ancestors were fools?' replied Rao. 'And how do I explain his absence to her? You want me to tell her that I was weak and caved in to pressure?'

Rao took a gulp of water and sat at his desk, looking out of the window. Anu let him be. She knew that his brain was working overtime.

42

Pam returned to Delhi that same day by an evening flight. On landing, she phoned Jaya, her contact at RAW. Jaya had been expecting the call ever since her boss, VTK, had requested her to render all possible assistance to Pam.

Pam headed directly from the airport to the DRDO office, having agreed to meet Jaya there at eight o'clock. She used her access card to reach her cubicle, sat at her desk and opened the drawer with her key. Inside it were notepads, files and USB drives spanning many projects and cases. But something felt odd; she always kept the files below the notepads and the USB drives in the right-hand corner. The arrangement had changed.

She got down on her knees to examine the lock on her drawer, using the flashlight function of her phone to give the bolt a closer look. Sure enough, there were scuffmarks indicating that the lock had been picked. *Who has been through my stuff?* she wondered. She looked around at the empty office. *Am I under surveillance?* Nothing seemed to have gone missing though.

The DRDO was deserted by the time Jaya got there. Indian bureaucrats are famous for getting into work late and leaving early. The heating had been switched off, so Pam had covered herself with a shawl. She poured two cups of tea from a thermos flask that the canteen had helpfully supplied and handed one to Jaya, who accepted it gratefully.

Pam got down to the issue at hand without wasting time on preliminaries. 'I've been given this document. It's in languages I cannot understand. Can you help me?'

'Let's have a look,' said Jaya, putting on a pair of reading glasses. She took the bound papers from Pam and began reading. Her hands toyed with the locket around her neck as she read. 'Who gave this to you?' she asked as she turned the pages.

'An old friend,' replied Pam vaguely. She did not feel comfortable sharing information regarding her meeting with Rao with anyone else. Not yet, anyway. Jaya did not seem to take it amiss. In her line of work, being secretive was par for the course.

A slight smile played on Jaya's lips as she continued to read. By the time she had finished a few pages, she was laughing. 'This manuscript contains a Chinese classic from the sixteenth century,' she explained. 'It's called *Journey to the West* and was first printed during the time of the Ming dynasty. The novel is usually attributed to a writer called Wu Cheng'en.'

Why did Rao give me this novel? How can a sixteenth-century story answer my questions about superhuman engineering?

'What's it about?' asked Pam.

Jaya continued, obviously in her element. 'This is one of the four great classical novels of Chinese literature,' she explained. 'It's a fictionalised account of the travels of the Buddhist monk Xuanzang to India.'

'Shian ...' began Pam.

'His name is pronounced "shian-zan" but is written X-U-A-N-Z-A-N-G,' explained Jaya patiently. 'We spelt his name as Hiuen Tsang in our schooldays. He was a monk at the Jing Tu monastery in Luoyang during the late Sui and early Tang dynasties. He left the capital, Chang'an—present-day Xi'an—and crossed what now constitute Xinjiang, Kyrgyzstan, Uzbekistan, Tajikistan, Afghanistan, Pakistan, Kashmir and the Punjab to reach the Gangetic plains sometime in the year 630. He remained in the Indian subcontinent for thirteen years, studying at Nalanda and travelling the length and breadth of the country before returning to Chang'an in the year 646 with several treasures and Buddhist texts.'

'So this novel is an account of that journey?'

'The actual journey was recorded by Xuanzang's disciple Bianji upon the monk's return. It was called *Great Tang Records on the Western Regions*. This particular novel that you've been given is inspired by that journey but isn't really an account of it. It's an adventure, a comedy, a parable, a folk tale and a mythological narrative, all rolled into one. And in any case, the primary character of the novel isn't Xuanzang.'

'Then who?'

'A monkey who accompanies Xuanzang. His name is Sun Wukong. There's also a pig called Zhu Bajie and a sand demon called Sha Wujing. The team undergoes eighty-one trials but is eventually successful in its mission to bring back sacred documents.'

What is it with monkeys? wondered Pam. *They keep popping up everywhere!*

Jaya explained to Pam that the story had been presented parallely in Mandarin and Tamil. 'The good thing is that I may not need to translate it for you at all. There are several existing English translations from various periods: 1942, 1977 and 1982, to be precise.'

'How do I get one of those?' asked Pam.

'Let me source one for you. Arthur Waley's translation, *Monkey*, is popular in the Western world. I'll email a PDF to you. In the meantime, I'll take a photocopy of this document so that I can ensure that the content is in conformity with the translation I give you. Might take me a couple of days to review, though.'

Pam stood up to signal the end of the meeting, but Jaya remained seated. 'I suggest you don't share this document with anyone else,' she said.

'Why?' asked Pam. 'If it's a novel that is already in the public domain, why should sharing it be a problem?'

'Until we've gone through the entire document, we cannot be sure that it is entirely that. In addition, there are the Tamil lines that may or may not be exact translations of the text. Also …'

'Yes?' asked Pam curiously.

'Also, it's possible that some of the lines in either or both languages constitute a code,' said Jaya. 'We must get our cryptanalysts to look at it and see if there are hidden meanings that may emerge on closer examination. Until then, it's best that it remains between the two of us.'

43

The two senior masters from the training facility in Dengfeng County made their way towards the temple. They did not usually leave the training centre, but the instructions were clear and necessitated a visit to the temple. The snaking pathway was rocky and steep. A single misstep would mean a precipitous fall several hundred feet below. But the monks had walked this route many times. Once the two men reached the gates of Shaolin, they walked towards the Shadow Cave in complete silence.

Like most ancient monuments, the Shaolin temple too had its secret rooms, passages and exits. Not just the tourists, even the teachers and students did not know the layout in its entirety. Many of the spaces were hidden away, well beyond prying eyes. Shaolin was actually far bigger than the eye could discern. One among its numerous secrets was a room that could only be accessed through a 'shadow wall'. This particular wall had an important history and was integral to the very existence of Shaolin.

The origins of Shaolin could be traced back to a monk who arrived in the court of Emperor Xiaowen in the year 495. He was provided with a grant of land to build a temple on Mount Song. The grant resulted in the establishment of Shaolin.

But thirty years later, another monk reached the temple from a distant land in the west and asked for admission. He claimed to have a deep understanding of yogic meditation, a practice that would, centuries later, be known around the world as Zen Buddhism. The abbot of Shaolin, Fang Chang, denied him admission. The monk tried every trick in the book, but to no avail.

The rebuffed yet stubborn monk retreated into a cave near the temple. He would continue to remain there for the next nine years, not emerging even once for light or fresh air. He sat for extended hours in intense meditation, facing one wall of the cave; this eventually resulted in his shadow getting imprinted on the wall. It came to be known as the shadow wall.

Finally, the abbot was left with no alternative but to grant the adamant monk admission into Shaolin. During his nine-year-long meditation, the monk had developed an exercise routine to keep his limbs, joints and blood circulation in top condition. The aim of his workouts was to neutralise the prolonged physical inactivity during his spells of intense meditation. He combined these physical workouts with combat moves that he had brought with him from his homeland, along with a herbal potion. Once he was accepted into the Shaolin brotherhood, these exercises became common practice at the temple and evolved into kung fu, the martial art that Shaolin eventually became famous for.

The senior masters entered the temple through Shanmen Hall, ignoring the two crouching stone lions crafted during the time of the Ming dynasty. They passed into the Hall of Heavenly Kings, its entrance guarded by several Buddhist warriors, each figure intricately carved from stone. They briefly murmured something before the statues of the four kings who were ostensibly responsible for human behaviour, and crossed into the Mahavira Hall, surrounded by sculptures of stone lions. They did not stop to admire the beauty of the hall but walked through it into a graveyard known as the Pagoda Forest, the resting place for important Buddhist monks through the ages. Then they crossed the graveyard to reach the Shadow Cave. This was the very spot where their obstinate forebear had sat for nine years, awaiting admission to the temple.

From some distance away, they could hear the short whooshing sounds made by the warrior monks practising their routines at the Wushu Training Centre, one of the most idyllic and scenic spots within the estate. Unlike ordinary combatants, warrior monks were bound by a Buddhist code, a set of ethics called 'wude'. Among the many principles enshrined in the code were the need to remain loyal to teachers, to never fight for frivolous reasons and to never injure an opponent beyond the bare minimum that was required to subdue him.

The Shadow Cave was not very big, just around twenty-three feet deep and ten feet high. The two senior masters walked to the wall where the shadow had once been imprinted. There was no shadow to be seen now because the entire wall had been carefully dismantled many years ago. It had been moved to a museum for viewing by unending streams of tourists.

One of the masters inserted his fingers into a crevice in the upper right corner, deep in the recesses of the stone wall. He pressed a switch, and a section of the wall swung open. It was incongruous, the technology a little too modern for the traditional monastic surroundings of Shaolin. The opening wall had been around for hundreds of years but was originally operated by a hand crank.

The two monks entered the chamber with measured steps, almost deferentially. The only light inside the room came from oil lamps, although ducting for fresh air had been installed. The door closed behind them and the masters knelt before three jade platforms placed side by side, each supporting an urn, with a bundle of smoking incense sticks in front. In the hazy light of the room, it was difficult to tell the condition of the urns, but they were obviously valuable possessions of the temple. The flickering oil lamps created a pattern of dancing shadows on the walls as the two men knelt before the urns. In front of the platforms lay a fine silk carpet; placed on it was a manuscript. On its cover were calligraphed painstakingly in gold embroidery the words 'Yu-Jin Xi-Sui'.

'Shall we do what has been asked of us?' enquired the younger master. His voice quavered. He felt conflicted, and now the pressure was getting the better of him.

The old master nodded slowly with a look of resigned acceptance. He said sombrely, 'I wish it had never come to this.'

44

I finally reached the kingdom of Akini.[33] Apparently the name 'Akini' was derived from the Sanskrit word 'agni' that meant 'fire'. The people of Akini wrote in a script that was modelled after one used in Yindu. They wore clothes of felt and coarse wool. The king of Akini extended his hospitality to me, but I found him to be vain and egotistical. He thought of himself as an equal of Emperor Taizong, and I shuddered to think what would happen if the two ever met face to face. I stayed in Yanqi for less than a day before setting out for Kuci[34] because there was far too much ground to cover.

The king of Kuci was a friend of my newly adopted brother, the king of Gaochang. When word reached him of my imminent arrival, he waited outside the gates to greet me along with the senior officers of his court. Hundreds of monks escorted the king. Kuci was famous for its musical instruments, both wind and stringed. Accompanying the king was an entire Kuci orchestra that had been trained to play songs that were popular in Chang'an. I could recognise some of the more famous ones such as 'The Jade Woman Hands the Cup Around' and 'Meeting on the Seventh Evening'. Little did I know that the orchestra was being trained so that the musicians and their instruments could be gifted to Emperor Taizong.

33. Yanqi, coinciding with modern-day Karasahr in Xinjiang, China.

34. Also called Kucha (or Kushan), modern-day region of Aksu, Xinjiang, China.

Although an avowed Buddhist, the king was not of Chinese descent. In fact, he had red hair, blue eyes and pale skin, evidence of the fact that he was of mixed descent. But that was of little relevance when it came to political alliances. He had successfully sent a tribute of fine horses to Emperor Taizong, and, in return, the emperor had made him an important ally.

I was surprised to find that the Buddhist monks of Kuci consumed what they called 'pure flesh'. This was the meat of animals that they had not seen being slain on their account. Pure flesh was thus unseen, unheard and unsuspect, much like the monkeys of Confucius that saw no evil, heard no evil and spoke no evil. It was a ridiculous concept; we Buddhists should never partake of flesh.

The king of Kuci oversaw one of the most prosperous kingdoms of the region. He sat on a golden throne and on his head was an exquisite turban with a long sash hanging from it. Kuci produced pomegranates, grapes, pears, plums, peaches and apricots, as well as gold, silver, copper, iron, lead and tin. The kingdom was known for its great artists, sculptors, musicians and writers. It was a land that was not only prosperous but also fostered creative and artistic expression. Unfortunately, their artistry included pressing the heads of babies into flattened shapes using planks, ostensibly in order to improve the aesthetics of the human form. They too wrote in a script that was based on one from Yindu.

It turned out to be a longer stay than I expected. I remained stuck for two months owing to exceptionally heavy snow blocking my route. I used my time efficiently because the kingdom had twelve monasteries and over 5,000 monks. It was an important place on the Buddhist circuit, and to each side of the western gate of Kuci were exquisite statues of the Buddha. My visit coincided with a great festival in which the monasteries took out processions of ornate statues and images of the Buddha accompanied by music. I was invited to deliver a few sermons, which I willingly did. The citizens of Kuci made me feel welcome, and I was happy to spend some extra days in their company.

Kuci practised an older form of Buddhism known as Hinayana. My studies, on the other hand, were in Mahayana, the newer vehicle. During one of my sermons, I reminded the listeners that Kuci was an important link between Hinayana and Mahayana. 'Kumarajiva, one of the greatest translators of Mahayana texts was from Kuci, and he spent ten years in Chang'an supervising a team of translators towards this effort,' I told them. My audience grew excited upon hearing this and hung on to my words with greater interest after this little-known fact was revealed to them.

West of Kuci was Congling,[35] the plateau where the Kunlun Shan[36] and Heavenly Mountains met. Despite the treacherous weather, I decided that we should continue on our journey. The king's councillors advised against it, but I was adamant. I had not set out on this trip to remain rooted in any place other than my destination. My satisfaction was linked to reaching Nalanda.

Against the advice of everyone, we eventually decided to cross through Congling Pass[37] at 14,000 feet at the northern end of the plateau. The pass was steep and covered with snow throughout the year, with tall sheets of ice blocking the pathways. In biting blizzards, even the heavy coats provided by the king of Gaochang were not much help as we trekked up the rugged path. Howling winds, thin air and avalanches were our constant companions. It was impossible to keep our eyes fully open owing to the cold air and the glare of the sun reflecting off the ice sheets.

I lost track of time. I even lost consciousness at times, and it was my disciples who took turns propping me up and ensuring that I was revived. There were numerous occasions when intense snow showers separated some of us from the rest of the group. It took hours, sometimes even days, to regroup. By the time we found each other, we would have lost yet more team members.

---

35. Pamir Mountains, located at the junction of the Himalayas with the Tian Shan, Karakoram, Kunlun, Hindu Kush, Suleman and Hindu Raj ranges.

36. Kunlun Mountains on the northern edge of the Tibetan Plateau.

37. Bedal Pass, between Kyrgyzstan and Xinjiang, China.

I realised the grievous mistake I had made in pushing forward when I began to lose my men and animals to fatigue, starvation and frostbite. Half of the twenty-eight men accompanying me had died by the time our group passed Hantenggeli Feng.[38] Most of the thirty pack animals also died. Of the four disciples deputed by the king of Gaochang, I lost two. We were nowhere close to our destination and I had lost many valuable companions. It was a heavy price that I paid for my obstinacy.

The stubborn Buddhist monk who meditated in the Shadow Cave of Shaolin had got what he wanted, but there was no certainty as to whether my own stubbornness would get me to my destination.

I prayed every moment for the Great Pure Lake[39] to appear. It was said that this lake never froze—its water was salty and warm. Because of its warmth, the Great Khan of the Western Turks had made his winter capital on its shores, transferring himself each year with his entire retinue from Che-shih,[40] his summer capital. In the desert I had had hallucinations from the heat; now I had delusions from the cold. Sometimes I couldn't stop thinking of how good a full belly and a warm bed would feel.

Such thoughts would quickly be followed by guilt. After all, as a Buddhist, am I not supposed to remain unaffected by pleasure and pain?

45

Kanchipuram was quiet at that early morning hour. Dawn was still an hour away. A mild breeze spread the aroma of incense through the air. In the distance, the morning chants from numerous temples had already begun.

A few minutes away from the cottage occupied by Dr Raja Rao, just down the private lane that touched the river, stood

---

38. Mount Khan Tengri, part of the Tian Shan Range.

39. Modern-day Lake Issyk Kul in eastern Kyrgyzstan.

40. Modern-day Tashkent, Uzbekistan.

a simple house; its external walls were rendered in lime plaster and the structure was supported by heavy wooden beams. As with all traditional structures in the area, the central part of the house was an open-to-sky courtyard. It was here that the lone figure of Anu was performing a set of well-rehearsed routines.

In the southwest corner of the courtyard stood a small statue of Hanuman, who symbolised flexibility and strength. In front of it were fresh flowers, a smouldering incense stick and a small pot of water. Anu's morning exercises always began with a brief prayer to the deity, the very source of her strength. *Never forget that you are simply channelling his energy. You can never be the source.* Anu would perpetually remind herself of that ultimate truth.

The floor of the courtyard had been plastered with red clay. Anu would sprinkle water on the clay from time to time to soften it. The clay provided a natural cushion for her complex routines, far better than any sports rubber, synthetic foam or AstroTurf. She was dressed in a simple white saree, tied in a *panchagacham* style so that the movements of her legs and arms remained entirely unrestricted, almost as though she was wearing a tracksuit.

The perimeter of the courtyard had racks containing assorted weapons, including staffs of varying lengths, metal whips known as *surul vaals*, blackbuck horns, *velkambu* spears and large *vaal veechu* swords. Anu would sometimes switch from sticks to weapons, although the rules for a student demanded that only one weapon be used at a time. In her hands, even an ordinary stick was a deadly weapon that could be used to devastating effect.

The routine never varied. She would wake up at four in the morning, drink a glass of warm water with lemon and honey, bathe, say her prayers, meditate and then spend two hours performing her exercises, which were a combination of two ancient forms of south Indian martial arts: silambam and kalaripayattu. Silambam had originated in Tamil Nadu a few thousand years ago as a form of bamboo-fighting, whereas kalaripayattu had emerged in Kerala some centuries later as a method of combat using different types of weapons.

Folklore, however, held that silambam was engineered by the sage Agastya, who honed the skill of fighting without weapons, while kalaripayattu was birthed by the sage Parashurama, who perfected the art of combat with weapons.

Even at her advanced age, Anu was lithe and strong. Placed in the centre of the courtyard was a scarecrow-like dummy wrapped in several yards of cloth. At lightning speed, Anu leaped into the air and struck it from different angles with graceful, yet powerful moves. The strokes required intense mental concentration, rigorous fitness and regular application. Each motion was geared towards enhancing several key attributes: flexibility, power, speed, agility, balance, hand-eye synchronisation, kinaesthetic awareness, stamina, muscular endurance and cardiovascular capacity.

Every now and then, she would fling her staff up in the air and leap up to catch it midair. She twirled it with such force that it resembled the propeller of an aircraft. Her mental alertness and muscular coordination were flawless. A thin film of sweat on her face was the only indication that she was performing an intense workout; otherwise she was utterly calm and composed. To the uninitiated, each of her moves seemed different, but that was not the case.

'Remember the classical ragas,' her father would tell her. 'Each composition sounds different even though a limited set of notes is used for a given raga. Similarly, the same set of ingredients can be combined differently in various recipes. The same applies to your moves. There are only seven basic moves and four fundamental stick rotations. It's the unlimited permutations and combinations that make each action look different.'

Each step enabled her to effectively use her entire body to generate power. Every move combined attack with retreat in order to get within range of an opponent without compromising one's own defence. Her legs and arms moved like those of a ballet dancer. For most moves she employed a hammer grip, with her weaker hand being used only to guide the movement of the stick. Years of training had made her ambidextrous, and it was difficult to distinguish the dominant hand from the more passive one. Each blow derived speed from her wrist and power from her entire body.

Her attacks were aimed at very specific points of the dummy. The ancient physician Sushruta had identified and described 107 vital points of the human body in his treatise, *Sushruta Samhita*. Of these, sixty-four were considered to be lethal if struck with a fist, a stick or another weapon. Anu not only knew each of those points but had also studied Ayurveda and *uzhichil*, the ancient herbal remedies of medicine and massage. She led an extremely disciplined life, abstaining from drinking, smoking and eating meat. Daily meditation had trained her mind to stay calm in even the most trying of circumstances. She ended her routine with a short prayer thanking Hanuman for her strength.

Perched on the roof of a neighbouring house, a stocky man was observing her intently. He had paid a premium to rent the house near hers. Unlike Anu's single-storeyed structure, the adjacent house was two floors high, and the terrace offered a view into Anu's courtyard. Unknown to her, the man had been tracking her for weeks—taking pictures, noting time and routines, and following her every move.

46

In Cambodia, the exploration team was racing against time to deliver results to the Buzhang. They had employed every trick, technology and technique in the book to widen their search in Angkor Wat but had found nothing.

They had evaluated the entire layout, in particular the east-west orientation of the temple that was in stark contrast to most temples in the region. Even the bas reliefs were in a counter-clockwise direction. What could explain it?

It was team leader Lee who had stumbled upon the answer. 'Hindu funeral services take place in reverse order of ordinary rituals. If the original design of the complex was not only to honour Vishnu but also to serve as a funerary complex, it would follow that everything is the opposite of ordinary. The creator of this monument, Suryavarman II, was on a quest to be immortal, much like the great Qin Shi Huang. We must keep looking. All signals are favourable.'

Lee's team members understood. All great kings longed for immortality, and the Chinese rulers had been no exception. The powerful Qin Shi Huang had pumped millions into creating a terracotta army to fight his battles long after he was dead. As many as 8,000 clay soldiers, 130 chariots and 670 horses executed in stunning detail had been buried along with him. And Qin Shi Huang's quest had not just been about the afterlife. He genuinely wanted to live forever. Having conquered all six warring states in China, he was undoubtedly the most powerful emperor the land had seen, but could he also be eternal?

'Qin Shi Huang issued a formal edict that required the people of China to search for an elixir that would give him eternal life,' said the deputy team leader. 'Ironically, he continued consuming cinnabar, or mercury sulphide, in the belief that it would make him immortal. Instead, it poisoned him to an early death by the age of thirty-nine!'

Another team member took up the story. 'He even sent his personal sorcerer, Xu Fu, to the eastern seas, searching for the elixir of immortality. He was given sixty ships, 5,000 crew members and 3,000 support staff to find and bring back the potion. Instead, Xu Fu discovered Japan and declared himself king of the region, refusing to return. Wise man. He would probably have been put to death by his boss if he had returned empty-handed.'

Lee cut in. 'All the signs indicate that Angkor Wat was designed as a funerary complex for the great Suryavarman II to continue to rule even after his death. Last time, we had decided on seven focus areas that held promise and allocated our resources accordingly, but each of these has turned out to be a dud. Do we have any fresh ideas?'

There was pin-drop silence. Every night, they collapsed into bed, only to commence once again before sunrise. It was an impossible task that would have daunted the toughest of men, even with all the technological support and resources that the Buzhang had thrown at them.

The researchers huddled in their control room and nervously discussed the way forward. 'Should we consider the temples outside Angkor Wat?' suggested one of them. 'The Angkor Park has many temples that are not part of Angkor Wat.'

'But who will inform the Buzhang that scanning Angkor, even just the shortlisted areas, could take years?' asked Lee's deputy despairingly. None of them wanted to be the bearer of bad news.

The Buzhang had been aggressively following up for a breakthrough and was hoping that their discovery would be a game changer. While success meant promotions, public recognition and massive financial rewards, failure meant being thrown into hell on earth. The Buzhang had personally overseen the creation of a secret prison in Changsha in Hunan Province. Inmates there underwent a programme called *laojiao*. The literal translation of the term was 're-education through labour', which was just a face-saving term for a cruel internment. While some of the camps that had been set up immediately after the Revolution had eventually closed, this one was meant for those who did not fall in line with the Buzhang's agenda. It was unclear whether the president of China even knew about the Buzhang's secret prison.

Lee looked anxious. He knew he would have to take the final responsibility for failure. He felt a chill run up his spine as he imagined how that particular conversation with the Buzhang would play out. 'Leave it to me,' he said, putting up a brave front. But the sweat on his forehead was proof of the terror that plagued him.

The next day, he set out on a journey by himself, leaving his mobile and satellite phones behind. He told his team to continue the search whilst he visited secondary spots that had not received adequate attention.

Lee drove one of the team's jeeps to Siem Reap, the town where most tourists visiting Angkor stay. He parked near the airport and got into a tuk-tuk. He instructed the driver to take him to Mango Cuisine, a fine-dining restaurant famous for its European menu. From time to time, Lee would look into the driver's side-view mirror or cautiously peer outside to ensure that no one was following them. He got off near the restaurant, paid the fare, waited for the vehicle to leave and then walked to a public telephone booth nearby. From there he dialled a number and hung up after a single ring.

He waited near the phone and picked it up the moment it rang. 'Hello?' he said. 'By when do you think I should come around to Sangkat Wat Phnom?'

47

Pam immediately got down to reading the English translation of *Journey to the West*. It was late at night, and the DRDO office was deserted. Just a single table lamp illuminated the small office where she sat. She munched on a Snickers bar to keep up her energy. Sometimes she wished she were a smoker like her father. People who smoked needed only a shot of nicotine to keep them recharged for a few more hours.

The novel was a fascinating account of the travels of the Chinese monk Xuanzang to India in the seventh century, undertaken with the intention of accessing the original sacred texts of Buddhism. According to this fictional, almost mythical retelling, Xuanzang was accompanied on his trip by Sun Wukong, a powerful monkey who caused many hilarious situations. In fact, many of the problems that Xuanzang encountered were created by the mistakes of Sun Wukong, but to his credit, the monkey also got him out of several jams.

The novel had first been published in the sixteenth century during the rule of the Ming dynasty. It retained the broad outline of Xuanzang's own account, *The Great Tang Records on the Western Regions*, but added jazzed up details from folk tales and myths, and Confucian, Taoist and Buddhist philosophy.

It was also long—a little over 1,43,000 words. The text was divided into a hundred chapters and organised in four unequal parts. The first dealt with the backstory of Sun Wukong, who was a master of Tao in addition to the martial arts, bodily transformation and the secrets to immortality. Part two introduced the character of Xuanzang, referred to by a changed name, and talked about Xuanzang's early life, his monkhood and the reasons that prompted him to undertake his monumental journey. The third dealt with the actual journey and the many travails of the monk and the monkey as they made their way to their destination, despite flaming mountains, deep gorges, extreme weather, evil magicians and bandits. The last part described Xuanzang's efforts to return home.

Pam was only a few chapters into the book when her phone rang. It was Mark. 'You're up late,' said Pam, stifling a yawn.

'I could say the same of you,' came the reply. 'Where are you?'

'Office.'

'Wait there. I'm coming over. There's something I need to show you. Leave a message with the security officer to let me in.'

'Are you sure, Mark?' Pam looked at her watch. It was past one in the morning. It felt like she hadn't slept in days.

But Mark was insistent. 'It's very important. And I can't tell you over the phone.'

He arrived fifteen minutes later and was shown in by the security guard. He looked fresh and wide awake. A hint of aftershave indicated that he had spruced himself up before coming to meet her, even at that odd hour.

Mark got to the matter at hand without preliminaries. 'My team has carried out a full analysis of the blood on the tourniquet. The results are astounding.' He placed a thin folder on her desk. Inside was a single-page report with CBTT's logo stamped on the top. Pam scanned it but was unsure what the numbers meant.

'The blood and tissue samples showed similarities with the rhesus macaque,' explained Mark as she continued looking at the report.

'Rhesus?' Pam recalled having heard the term before but was unsure where.

'The sandy-furred, pink-faced monkey species found in China, Afghanistan and India,' replied Mark. 'Nowadays, villagers associate them with the havoc that they cause by raiding crops. Not their fault that we took over their land for agriculture.'

She suddenly remembered where she had heard that word. From Rao, when he had been explaining the three Confucian monkeys that saw no evil, heard no evil and spoke no evil. *Think about it. True power comes from following the code of the three monkeys. And in India we have always considered the rhesus species to be sacred.* Pam's heart raced. *What is this whole monkey puzzle?*

She put down the report and riffled back to the foreword of *Journey to the West*. It explained that in the original journey of Xuanzang, he had initially been accompanied by a merchant called Bandha.

Bandha? Was that name inspired by "bandar", the Hindi word for monkey?

'There are forty-six chromosomes in the human blood but forty-eight in rhesus blood,' explained Mark.

'And this sample?' asked Pam.

'Forty-seven. Somewhere between the two species. This is quite incredible.' The excitement in Mark's voice was infectious.

Pam looked at him, confused at first, then with a dawning understanding. He smiled back at her gleefully. And suddenly, without warning, the air between them was charged with anticipation.

They sat facing each other, their eyes locked. Then, slowly, almost reverentially, Mark bent down and brought his face close to hers. Pam sat still, her eyes wide open and watchful. Their lips touched.

They both knew there was no going back.

48

A year after setting out, my sadly diminished party and I crossed the mountains into the steppes controlled by the Great Khan, leaving the western regions of Xiyu behind. We soon reached the Great Pure Lake that was also known as 'the hot sea'. I was told that this was purportedly the second-largest saline lake in the world. It had warm blackish-blue water that was bitter on the tongue and it was rumoured that sea monsters and demons inhabited the lake, hence the higher temperature.

The Great Khan's winter capital was at Suiye,[41] along the northwestern side of the Great Pure Lake. His summer capital was the famous Che-shih. The Great Khan's empire, which later came to be known as the Western Turkic Khaganate,[42] was at its peak. The word 'Khan' was simply a contracted form of 'Khagan', which meant chief or ruler in some Turkic languages.

I made my way to his abode with a mixture of eagerness and trepidation. He was, after all, the most powerful ruler beyond the western regions of Xiyu. He had a reputation for having a ferocious temper but also a legendary friendship with Emperor Taizong. He was said to have sent several exquisite belts in solid gold embedded with precious stones for the Chinese emperor. This was in addition to 5,000 sturdy horses from the steppes.

---

41. Modern-day Tokmok in Kyrgyzstan.

42. Modern-day Kazakhstan, Uzbekistan and parts of Kyrgyzstan, Tajikistan, Turkmenistan, China and Russia.

The Khan and his people were worshippers of a god called Ahura Mazda, who had supposedly created spirits known as yazatas to help him in his fight against evil. It was the sacred duty of worshippers to aid Mazda in this struggle of good against evil. I tried to understand this faith in the context of the Buddha's teachings and hoped that I would someday be able to bring the Khan and his followers to the true path. But this was not the time for it.

While I rested inside a tent, I heard the thunderous sound of hooves. I rushed out to see a dust storm kicked up by hundreds of animals and their riders heading directly towards us with lances firmly in hand.

As it turned out, my fears were misplaced. The Great Khan was returning after hunting in a dense forest called the Thousand Springs. He gave me a warm welcome, dismounting from his horse to embrace me. He was very happy that I had brought the goods meant for him, which the bandits had attempted to steal. He was impressive looking, dressed in a robe of green satin. His hair was bound by a ten-foot silken band that twirled around his head and fell behind him. He was surrounded by 200 officers dressed in fine brocade and furs. Around them stood thousands of men carrying lances, bows and standards and mounted on wonderfully bedecked camels and horses. It was impossible to count the multitude.

A grand feast was held in my honour in the Khan's opulent yurt, a massive round tent covered with fur and skins to protect its occupants from the harsh cold. The interiors were bedecked with flowers of gold, sparkling in the light of the oil lamps. Quarters of mutton and boiled veal were piled high in front of the guests, who sat on two long rows of mats. The food was served with copious quantities of wine. The merriment was aided by an orchestra that produced a variety of chords—they sounded alien to my ears. There was very little that seemed delicate or refined about the Great Khan and his followers. He exuded raw power.

The Great Khan had asked his cooks to arrange a special meal for me, having been informed in advance that Buddhist monks were vegetarian. Special rice cakes, cream, mare's milk, crystallised sugar, honey and raisins were placed before me along with grape syrup. The Khan asked me to deliver a short sermon, and I acceded to his request, ensuring that my talk was only about love and mutual respect. I touched upon the Ten Virtues of Buddhism, which included non-violence, generosity, truthfulness, honesty, renouncing sexual misconduct, helping others, praying, avoiding foul language, letting go of anger and abandoning heretical views. I kept my discourse short because I did not want the Khan to think I was an evangelist.

I noticed that an emissary from the Tang empire was present at the banquet. He kept eyeing me suspiciously throughout the meal. I was worried. I had left Cina against the will of the emperor. Emperor Taizong would soon know of my 'disobedience' through his ambassador, if he did not already. After the banquet, the envoy sidled up to me and told me that the emperor would not be happy. His small, sly eyes observed me closely for a reaction.

'Please inform his majesty that I shall return as soon as I become Di San Sou Chuan in the service of our emperor and the Buddha,' I whispered into his ear as calmly as I could. The envoy immediately shut up. I did not know what message he would eventually convey, but I suspected that he wanted to hedge his bets. He did not seem to know whether I had the sanction of the emperor or not. My instincts told me that he would play safe and avoid bringing up the matter with his master.

The Great Khan tried to dissuade me from going to Yindu, calling it a 'land of barbarians'. But seeing my determination, he gave me letters of introduction to the princes of Gandhara,[43] *who were his vassals. He presented me with fifty pieces of silk and a set of clothes in crimson satin. He then ordered some of his officers to accompany me for part of the journey into Yindu.*

---

43. Modern-day Peshawar Valley, Kabul Valley, Swat and Chitral.

I thanked the Great Khan profusely. Then I thanked the Buddha for opening up my path to his spiritual home. I felt refreshed and enthused. I looked forward to my onward march with a newfound spring in my step.

49

Inside one of the offices at the Lodhi Road HQ of RAW, Jaya was personally scanning and printing Rao's document. It was a tedious process; she wanted to preserve the binding, so she had to open each page on a flatbed scanner rather than load a bunch of pages into the feeder.

There was no signboard outside to indicate that the building was occupied by the Research and Analysis Wing. The eleven-storey structure stood on prime real estate, a mere stone's throw away from the famous Lodhi Gardens, where Delhi's rich and powerful took their morning walks. The building housed all of RAW's divisions under one roof, including a communication interception unit, counter-intelligence division, special operations department, country desks, an electronic signals intelligence section, secret divisions like the Special Frontier Force and divisions maintaining the more ordinary and mundane functions, such as accounts.

As each of the pages was scanned, Jaya reviewed the uploaded image to check for resolution and completeness. She then marked the Chinese and Tamil portions, numbering them sequentially to ensure that the engine maintained the original sequence. She was using a proprietary software created by linguists at RAW that could watch for incoming scans in multiple formats and languages. It could then translate and collate these. The usual Optical Character Recognition software was designed to recognise machine-printed text, not handwriting or cursive scripts or calligraphy; these were invariably roadblocks. The RAW system could handle them far better. Technological advances aside, though Jaya made it look effortless, it was hard, painstaking work.

Jaya added her own notes and observations into the software periodically so that she would eventually have a consolidated document that would contain not only the original texts provided by Pam but also her own reminder margin memos relating to specific passages. She looked at one of the pages in front of her and smiled at the poetic narration. Her hands toyed with the locket around her neck, an old habit that always reassured her.

One hundred two thousand six hundred years ago, heaven and earth made love and everything was born, virile above and plus below, the three monkeys and the centre aglow. Humans and beasts and birds came into being and the world was divided into four great continents. The East continent and the West, the North continent and the South.

VTK peeped in. 'Any progress?' he asked, looking at the heap of printed papers on her desk.

She looked up from the documents and smiled. 'Prima facie many passages seem like a simple translation of *Journey to the West*. Let me finish going through the entire document before I report to you.'

VTK nodded and left. He had found that Jaya worked best when she was left to do her own thing.

50

VTK stood in his overcoat, watching the flames. It was five in the morning; save for the occasional enthusiastic jogger, the area was deserted. Some minutes later, a man in a leather jacket and a woollen cap walked up and stood next to him. They didn't look at each other. They merely stood like two tourists interested in the memorial, their breath fogging the cold air.

India Gate, which resembled the Arc de Triomphe in Paris, contained a black marble plinth underneath its arch. The plinth supported a sculpture of a reversed rifle capped by a war helmet, four gas torches surrounding it. This structure, known as Amar Jawan Jyoti, or the Flame of the Immortal Soldier, served as India's memorial to the soldiers it had lost in its war with Pakistan in 1971.

'Are we on track?' asked VTK without turning his head.

'Yes,' replied the man, continuing to stare at the flame. 'We have established contact and now it's just a matter of time.'

VTK remained quiet, deep in thought. It was a murky world that he inhabited, one in which it was impossible to tell the motivations or loyalties of another. A Hollywood actor had once said that men were only as loyal as their options. He had been speaking in a different context, of course, but VTK's take was similar. *Everyone is loyal but to whom, or what, varies from time to time.*

'The outcome, if successful, will be good for both you and me,' said VTK eventually. 'We cannot afford to screw up now. Is the conduit holding up? Confident?'

The man nodded. 'The wild card is Pam Khurana. We must keep her in check so that the final outcome is not endangered.'

'What have her activities been?' asked VTK. The two men spent the next few minutes discussing her.

'We're getting two birds with one stone,' said the man. 'Actually three, if we count the mother.'

'I wonder what the reaction will be,' said VTK.

'Every action has a reaction. We'll deal with it as it comes. We need to be careful, though. Eyes and ears everywhere. Particularly after Doklam.'

VTK read the words 'Amar Jawan' engraved on all four sides of the cenotaph. He laughed inwardly. The words translated to 'immortal soldier', but the truth was that soldiers were soldiers because they were willing to die. What was immortal about that? And this entire episode? This frenzied quest for power, strength and immortality? What drove it? Thousands of years had not changed anything. The same desire had impelled emperors and rulers down the ages, and modern governments were no different. Nation-states spent billions on espionage, covert actions and information-gathering, just to get an edge over their competitors.

VTK looked at the four urns placed along the corners of the cenotaph. Only one burnt continuously. The other three were lit only on Independence Day and Republic Day. Why? If thousands had died for their country, couldn't the country keep all four flames burning continuously?

He forced himself out of his reverie and focused on what his companion was saying. Then he concluded their meeting with the words: 'All further communication between us should be only on scrambled phones. No need to meet until the final result is achieved.'

51

When the Buzhang was shown into the office of the president, he was busy signing orders and letters. A secretary stood by his chair, helpfully placing the right papers before him. The president looked over the top of his glasses and motioned for the Buzhang to sit down while he finished signing the last of the documents. Once done, he smiled at his friend. The secretary quietly withdrew, leaving them together.

Zhongnanhai was quiet at this hour. The former imperial garden adjacent to the Forbidden City served as the central headquarters of the Communist Party of China and the central government of China. It contained the office of the general secretary of the party—who was also the president—as well as the offices of the premier and most of the Chinese leadership. It was an odd blend of grey brick office blocks and Qing dynasty palaces standing side by side on the banks of two large artificial lakes. Zhongnanhai was China's Kremlin, and security here was all-pervasive.

'You seem preoccupied these days,' said the president, looking directly into the eyes of his general.

'Nothing like that,' said the Buzhang casually. 'It's just that many of our initiatives are taking more of my time and attention than originally anticipated.'

'I hope that you are not proceeding with those ridiculous experiments?' asked the president. 'We are already the third-largest military power after the US and Russia. That fear in itself is sufficient to subdue our foes. Let's not waste our time on the unnecessary.'

'Of course,' said the Buzhang. 'No experiments. Just ordinary matters like allocations, training and equipment upgrades. China must forge ahead.' *Even though you give up territory acquired by me.* The Buzhang had never been happy about the president withdrawing to pre-attack positions in Doklam.

The president nodded. 'And what is this I hear about labour camps? I thought we had taken a collective decision to scale those down.'

'And so we have,' replied the Buzhang. 'In some instances we've moved inmates and consolidated multiple camps into a single one. Increased numbers owing to consolidation may have conveyed the false impression that we're expanding.'

The president eyed the Buzhang suspiciously. Something did not ring true. Despite their closeness over many years, the president had the uncomfortable feeling that his friend was keeping secrets from him.

The Buzhang had supported his leader through his most troubled years, and the president had never forgotten that, bestowing immense powers on the man he saw as his most trusted ally. Neither was unaware of the persistent rumours that they did not see eye to eye on many matters.

The president believed that China deserved pride of place in the global order and that it could easily achieve this through diplomacy, economic strength, international trade, financial aid, soft cultural power, a network of allies and the omnipresent fear of its military capacity. The Buzhang believed that there was no substitute for brute strength. In his view, Genghis Khan had not stitched together the massive Mongol empire through love and friendship.

The strange equation between the two men was rooted in China's history. In 1958, Mao Zedong, the then chairman of the Communist Party of China, launched what came to be known as the Great Leap Forward. This involved the mass mobilisation of the Chinese people into collectives that were given the task of producing steel. Most of it was low-grade and unusable, owing to the pathetic conditions in which it was produced. In that mad quest, farm output crashed. It was an economic disaster that led to terrible famines in China and resulted in millions of deaths.

Eventually, Mao was forced to take a backseat and allow more pragmatic members of the party to take up the reins. But by 1966, Mao bounced back and launched a movement called the Cultural Revolution, aimed at purging the country of what he believed were bourgeoisie elements that wanted China to return to capitalism. The Cultural Revolution lasted from 1966 to 1976 and was controlled by four individuals who were considered close to Mao. They came to be known as the Gang of Four. It was a period marked by excesses, and the Gang of Four ruthlessly oversaw the death of over a million people.

After Mao's death, it was the ascendance of Deng Xiaoping, who had always been seen as a reformer, that opened China to market forces and kick-started the process of economic reform.

The current president had served as an aide to Deng Xiaoping. In fact, much of his training and grooming in his twenties had happened under the watchful eyes of Xiaoping. The young man had been exiled in his teens to Yanchuan County during the years of the Cultural Revolution, owing to his father being on the wrong side, but had been called back after Xiaoping assumed control. From then on, he had worked his way up through several posts, including provincial party secretary, district governor and member of the Politburo Standing Committee.

The Buzhang's trajectory had been altogether different. During the Cultural Revolution, power was concentrated in the hands of the Gang of Four. One of them was Zhang Chunqiao. The Buzhang was just a young member of the Red Guards during those years but his ruthlessness and ability to get things done came to the attention of Zhang Chunqiao, who ensured his progress up the ranks.

Although the president and the Buzhang stood on opposite sides of the ideological fence, a twist of fate had brought them together. That twist was called Tiananmen Square. In 1989, student protests erupted at the square. The demonstrations were sparked by the death of pro-reform Communist leader Hu Yaobang.

Deng Xiaoping's reforms had led to a thriving market economy that came at the cost of political freedom, followed by rampant corruption, inflation and power imbalances. The students were demanding more political accountability, constitutional reforms, democracy and freedom of speech.

Although the two men had differing views on how the protests should be handled, they both agreed that China's economic progress depended on the stability of one-party rule. Both men valued order over chaos and were willing to do whatever it took to restore normalcy. Their reasons for doing so were different, but the destination was the same.

The Buzhang shifted uncomfortably in his chair. 'There are some things that you are better off not knowing,' he said to his boss. 'India is a minor irritant from time to time, a fly that makes one's meal less enjoyable. America is a bee whose sting could be painful. All that I'm doing is ensuring you are not bothered by flies or stung by bees.'

The president pondered over the Buzhang's words. He said, 'We share much in common with India. We would never have gained knowledge of Buddhism had it not been for India. The sweetness of sugar came to us from India and went back from us to India many centuries later. We share geography and a long border. We both have very large populations and are both attempting to improve the economic and social lot of our people. Yes, there are disputes, but we're also dealing with common problems. There is no reason two countries cannot compete and cooperate in parallel.'

'India is a pain,' argued the Buzhang. 'Their democracy, free press, freedom of opinion and judicial system have got them nothing. Our centralised control got us growth, development and prosperity. Their freedom is worth nothing. We should remember Chairman Mao each day for setting us on the right path.'

'Mao had wonderful ideals, but it needed Deng Xiaoping to set us on the path to progress,' said the president emphatically. 'Let's never forget that, my friend.'

After the Buzhang left, the president called in his aide. 'How are we doing on those three dossiers? And what about the photographs from Dengfeng County?'

52

From Che-shih, I crossed the She River,[44] which was mostly still and muddy, but turbulent in places. From here, I entered the Desert of Red Sands,[45] where there was neither water nor grass. The road was lost in the barren wilderness, and I had to use the guidance of bones that lay scattered about to determine which way to go. We traversed the sands to reach Samokien,[46] the westernmost point on my journey.

Samokien had been continuously inhabited since the past 800 years and was renowned for its arts, crafts and culture. It had once been been considered one of the greatest cities of the world and still had the finest craftsmen, weavers and artisans along the Silk Route. Located in a river valley fed by melting snow, it enjoyed abundant natural resources and a temperate climate.

The rulers of Samokien had wisely invested in a complex network of irrigation canals, thus ensuring that Samokien and its surroundings were always lush green. Everywhere you looked were picturesque mountains, verdant fields, generous

44. Syr Darya River, known by the Greeks as Jaxartes River, flowing through modern-day Uzbekistan and Kazakhstan.

45. Kyzylkum Desert, in modern-day Kazakhstan, Uzbekistan and Turkmenistan.

46. Modern-day Samarkand in Uzbekistan.

pasturelands, babbling brooks, gardens, reservoirs, flowers and fruit trees.

The city of Samokien was an overload for the senses in every possible way. Rich traders dressed in fine silks walked the same streets as sweaty coppersmiths, potters and paper-makers. Trotting horses, camel bells, creaking wagons, squelching mud and the cries of merchants mixed together to form a continuous daytime narrative. The smells of incense, cloves, boiling lamb, cinnamon and curry spices jostled for dominance in the bazaar.

Samokien opened its gates to all who were willing to obey the laws of trade. It was a paradise for commerce. Its market provided the widest variety of goods you could imagine. These included rare manuscripts, language and translation guides and even slaves to cater to strange human fetishes. It was often said that when the traders of Samokien gave birth to a son, they put honey on his lips and placed glue in his palms. This was to ensure that when he grew up, he would speak only sweet words while holding tight to his wealth.

The traders here were legendary for their skill in crafting profit out of thin air. Many of them had settled in other cities around the world and carried on a flourishing global trade from their new homes. You could recognise them instantly by their distinctive features — hawk nose, a bushy beard that covered most of the face and eyes that were blue, green or grey.

The commodities traded in the bazaar included cotton, spices and gems from Yindu; tea, jade work and ironware from Cina; and fur, minerals, cattle and hides from Xiyu. You may wonder why I didn't mention silk. Silk was indeed a major commodity from Cina but it was used more as currency. People were often paid in bolts of silk, and traders found it easier to carry rolls of soft fabric than the very heavy coins that were in use. Among the most valuable items traded were living beings — horses and slaves. The Chinese were willing to pay a premium for the muscular Shen steeds reared in the grasslands, and these were bought and sold in lots in Samokien. Unceasing battles between warring groups also ensured a steady supply of slaves.

Like the Great Khan, the people of Samokien were worshippers of Ahura Mazda. Two Buddhist monasteries lay in ruins, having been abandoned many years ago. Samokien was a cultured kingdom, but its people were fiercely protective of their religion. Two of my disciples naively visited the Buddhist ruins to pray in them. The local residents thought they were on a mission to promote Buddhist worship and attacked them, brandishing flaming torches. They had to flee for their lives and only succeeded in saving themselves by running into the palace grounds. Luckily, the king of Samokien was a vassal of the Great Khan, and I was treated with respect and care. He was also a fair man and was furious when the incident was brought to his attention. He immediately summoned the palace guards and commanded that the attackers' hands be amputated. The ringleader was to be put to death.

I felt responsible for the fate of these men. I should have warned my disciples about the dangers of visiting the monasteries. Had they not prayed at the ruins, none of this would have happened. I pleaded with the king to show restraint and mercy. He finally relented and let them off with a warning.

But the mere act of imploring the king for mercy towards our attackers had a profound effect on the monarch. He invited me to deliver a sermon to an assembly on the palace grounds. He listened to my discourse and then pestered me with questions late into the night. With the first rays of the sun, he decided to embrace Buddhism.

After I left, the king acted upon my advice and sought to become a vassal of Emperor Taizong. The emperor declined the request, but the two countries established diplomatic relations. I was happy that my travels were proving to be of some use to the Tang empire. It would, I hoped, help my cause when I stood before the emperor upon my return to Cina.

53

Not far from where Anu and her father lived, on the road from Kanchi to Vandavasi and on the banks of the river Palar, stood the Sanjeeviraya Hanuman temple. Unlike other temples in which the monkey god Hanuman was worshipped as an accessory to Vishnu or Rama, the primary focus here was Hanuman himself.

In the great Indian epic Ramayana, it is said that Hanuman had plucked and transported special herbs to Lanka to revive Lakshmana, who had been injured in battle. Apparently, Hanuman had been uncertain about the specific herbs that were needed, so he had decided to bring the entire mountain on which they grew. Folklore held that part of his cargo fell to the ground near Kanchi.

Many millennia later, in the sixteenth century, Tatacharya, the chief minister of the Vijayanagara empire in South India, was on his way to Kanchi to deliver gold donated by his king, Venkataraya II, for a temple in the city. When the group broke their journey for the night, Tatacharya and his entourage fell asleep under the trees after assigning guard duty to a few of their men. Unfortunately, later that night, they were attacked by bandits, who had got a whiff of the immense treasure that was being transported.

When all seemed lost, a group of human-sized monkeys swooped down on the bandits and saved the chief minister, his retinue, as well as the treasure. The bandits were forced to flee in absolute terror. Tatacharya was convinced that Hanuman himself had come to the spot to save him, his people and his gold. Overwhelmed, he sang a few verses in praise of Hanuman. Then he vowed to build a temple there. He built not only the beautiful Sanjeeviraya Hanuman temple but also, facing it, a massive tank stretching over 150 acres. It would serve as a water source for the local wildlife, including monkeys. A magnificent enclosure of twenty-four pillars on the banks of the pond depicted various forms of Hanuman.

A separate cottage on the banks had been constructed for the priest who would take care of the temple. It was a dark, moonless night when Anu reached there. The priest was fast asleep, snoring loudly. His slumber was interrupted by the persistent knocking on the door. He awoke with a start and stumbled out of bed to see who it was. He opened the door angrily but softened on seeing Anu.

'Why have you come here so late at night, child?' he asked after inviting her in and offering her a chair.

'There have been some unexpected developments,' replied Anu. 'Appa is very worried that something untoward may happen. Suddenly, there's too much interest in the past. He specifically asked me to check on you and the deity.'

'Everything is fine,' said the priest, wrapping a shawl around his shoulders. 'But why did you come at this odd hour? You could have spoken to me on the phone.'

'I'm being watched,' said Anu. 'So is Appa. We're not sure whether our phone lines have been compromised. Neither do we have any clue as to who is watching us. That's why I had to come here in the dead of night.'

'What does your father want me to do?' The priest had known Anu's father since childhood. They had studied together, played together and eaten their meals together. Rao's destiny had taken him towards science, while his friend had veered towards spirituality. Rao always joked that a good scientist had to be spiritual at heart and a good spiritualist had to be a scientist at heart. The two concepts of science and spirituality were not incompatible.

'Please ensure that the deity is not disturbed under any circumstances,' said Anu. 'If you wish, we can send you some people from Kanchi so that you are not entirely alone in this huge complex.'

'Hanuman is the most powerful protector of this temple. No additional manpower is needed. We would be drawing attention to ourselves by bringing in reinforcements. In any case, the sanctum sanctorum remains locked after the daytime visitors have left, and I am the only one who has the key. Please assure your father that I shall guard the deity with my life. He need not worry.'

Anu smiled. 'Thank you. Now I must go.'

'Take some puliyodharai for your father,' said the priest. 'I know he loves it.' The special tamarind-flavoured rice was cooked in the madappalli, the kitchen of the temple. 'I shall write a small note to reassure him that all is well. Will you take the prasadam and note to him?'

Anu nodded. 'You know your friend. Appa never refuses good food. Particularly when it comes from Hanuman's kitchen.'

54

Heavily armed policemen protected the unassuming compound located along Route 332 of the public bus service. To the west of the Beijing Chinese Medicine Hospital in Xiyuan stood scores of policemen, who ensured that no vehicles were parked there, nor could visitors loiter in the area. Cameras were confiscated immediately. This secret compound was the nerve centre of the MSS, China's security agency. The Xiyuan facility was located next to the Summer Palace, while an adjacent compound called Yidongyuan provided housing to the MSS personnel who worked at Xiyuan.

The MSS was a behemoth headed by the minister of state security, who reported to the Central Committee; its divisions were manned by bureau chiefs, all veterans who were powerful in their own right. The MSS was meant to keep tabs not only on countries that were militarily, politically or economically relevant to China, including the US, Taiwan, South Korea and Japan, but also on regional powers with which China shared borders, like Russia, India and Vietnam.

Inside the compound were structures built along the cardinal points with a large open courtyard in the centre. Inside one of the conference rooms, the Buzhang was meeting with the bureau chief for India. It was an undocumented meeting, with the Buzhang's visit having been kept off the entry log records maintained at the gate.

The India bureau chief was a thin man who wore wire-framed glasses. He was so fragile that he looked like he would collapse if someone exhaled in his direction. But the petite exterior contained an exceptionally intelligent and politically astute man who often knew about happenings in India before they took place.

The bureau chief and the Buzhang had been classmates at Tsinghua University, and their friendship had endured. The Buzhang knew that his friend would talk openly without allowing the matter to reach the president.

'There is a development in India,' said the bureau chief. 'You may want to know about it.'

'What?' asked the Buzhang.

'Someone new has been given the task of investigating what happened at Doklam. This is not one of the usual operatives of RAW but a young woman from DRDO. Her name is Pam Khurana. Her single-point agenda is to find out the secret of our special forces.'

'Why does that name sound familiar?' asked the Buzhang, stroking his Fu Manchu moustache thoughtfully.

'We share a history with her father,' said the bureau chief. 'Remember Kishan Khurana?'

'Ah, yes, now I remember. What does Shengli say?'

'Shengli says we should not worry too much and that Pam Khurana's digging will lead her nowhere.'

'I worry when people tell me not to worry,' said the Buzhang.

His friend smiled because he shared the feeling. 'We have eyes and ears everywhere in India,' he said. 'Over the years we have recruited politicians, bureaucrats, military personnel, journalists, diplomats, scientists, businessmen and even academics to funnel information that is relevant. But this time there is silence. Khurana is working on her own. She only uses the services of people who are immediately necessary to her.'

'Has she met Rao?' asked the Buzhang.

The bureau chief nodded. 'Yes. We've had the father, daughter and that assistant, Dev, under surveillance for a long while now.'

'Do you think she can be bought?' Years of experience had taught the Buzhang that everyone had a price. Those who said they couldn't be bought were simply holding out for a better deal.

The bureau chief shook his head. 'She's exceptionally honest. Like her father. A real pain in the ass.'

'What does she know about her father?'

'Only that a stray bullet killed him on board a ship. But given her new assignment, she could end up finding out about our interest in the matter.'

'We can't kill her,' said the Buzhang. 'Correction, we *can* kill her but we *should* not. She's possibly our best hope for discovering the missing piece in our puzzle. I'm tired of that pathetic Erkin whining about it.'

His friend nodded in agreement. 'It means we need Shengli more than ever. Shengli will have to ensure that Khurana's discoveries are used to our advantage.'

'Correct,' said the Buzhang. 'Please do whatever is necessary. Use both Humint and Sigint. The Khurana information could alter geopolitical equations.' The Buzhang was referring to human intelligence and signals intelligence. The former used the Chinese network of spies and sources; the latter was focused on communications, cyber snooping, electronics and satellites.

The bureau chief was in agreement with his friend. Knowledge dominance was critical. Twenty-five centuries ago, the military strategist Sun Tzu had said, 'Know thyself, know thy enemy.' Over the years, the MSS had made this their guiding principle and ensured that the world's secrets were laid bare before them.

'Should we consider using LLL?' asked the bureau chief. He was referring to the Leninist Liberation League, the Maoist guerrilla group in Northeast India.

'Let's review the situation from time to time and then decide,' said the Buzhang. 'But now that you mention it ...'

55

Mark Richards left his office and used the Delhi Metro to reach Janpath. He avoided using the company car and chauffeur on such trips. It was a journey that he made every once in a while, leaving his mobile phone behind so that his position could not be traced. He was quite certain that his secretary thought he was having an affair that necessitated such odd behaviour. She always gave him a strange look when he walked back in. Which suited him just fine. He was like a magician who drew his audience's attention to one thing to distract it from another.

Exiting the Janpath metro station, he walked through the lane alongside the station. On either side were little shops that sold paintings, tapestries, jewellery, furniture and antiques. Several tourists could be seen, being herded around like cattle by their guides.

Mark walked briskly, zipping up his goatskin jacket to protect himself from the winter chill. He ignored the first few shops, but once he was halfway down the lane, he slowed down. He finally stopped when he saw the red signboard with golden lettering. He felt slightly anxious, but years of training had taught him to channel stress productively. He used the tension to go on full alert. Every clandestine meeting was a risk, no matter how prepared one was.

He walked inside, nodding to the proprietor, a man of Chinese descent, who smiled at him with nicotine-stained teeth. *He always smiles that sugary smile. Not surprising that the Hindi word for refined sugar is 'cheeni', meaning 'from China'.* Mark remembered reading somewhere that the first Chinese immigrant to Bengal in the late eighteenth century was someone called Tong Achew, who had established a sugar cane plantation and a sugar refinery in a region that continued to be called Achipur thereafter. Funnily enough, when the Chinese traveller Xuanzang had visited India several centuries earlier, he had discovered sugar and candies and taken some back for the emperor.

The shop's proprietor hurried to the entrance, flipped over the 'open' sign to 'closed' and locked the door. His family had migrated to India in 1837, and his Hakka-descended great-grandfather had successfully established a carpentry business in the Bow Bazaar Street of Calcutta. Over the years, successive generations of shoemakers, carpenters, tannery owners, restaurateurs, dentists and beauticians had flourished here. He had moved to Delhi a decade ago because his best customers seemed to be increasingly concentrated in the north. Also, collectors in America, Europe and Japan were easier to access from Delhi. He had, in addition, developed a very nice little side hustle with Mark. It was risky work but the payoffs were immense.

The store had a dark and musty feel, partly owing to stale cigarette smoke, but there was something else in the air. Opium? Mark knew that many old-timers still added the stuff to their tobacco, a habit that the British had inculcated in the Chinese. There was no end to British deviousness. They had forced the Indians to grow opium, shipped it to China, ensured that the Chinese got addicted and then used the money to buy tea, which fetched them hefty margins in India and Britain. Many of the greatest wealth-creation stories of that era were actually narratives of drug-dealing. They were simply given the respectable veneer of international shipping and trade. Not much had changed since then. The most profitable business in the world continued to be drugs.

Thick, reinforced wooden shelves on three walls of the shop displayed artefacts. It was evident that these were not the usual brass or copper trinkets that the average shop passed off as antiques. These were stone carvings, busts, contraband ivory, carpets and jade idols. Ivory trade was banned in India, as was trade in the wool of Tibetan antelopes. Yet, this shop seemed to stock everything in full public view. No policemen ever bothered the shopkeeper. His clout was truly remarkable.

There was no way to tell whether the material in the shop had been procured legally or stolen from temples and museums in India, Cambodia, Sri Lanka, Thailand or Vietnam. It was more likely the latter. There were hundreds of collectors around the world who paid hefty prices to source items for private collections. They were not concerned with how the objects had been acquired, because they had no intention of ever selling them.

'What should we discuss today?' asked the proprietor slyly, pouring two cups of jasmine tea from a thermos.

'There have been many developments. Lots of activity. Messages back and forth,' said Mark in fluent Mandarin. 'Why don't we discuss how we can make my bosses happy? Obviously there's something in it for you. I'm always generous.'

'Making your bosses happy often means unhappiness elsewhere,' said the proprietor. 'But who am I to argue? You're the one calling the shots. Me? I simply go where the money is. You and I both know that what I can give you is priceless.'

'One or two?' asked Mark. The Buzhang was on his mind.

'Three,' answered the proprietor. 'Exactly what you wanted.'

Mark pondered over the proprietor's words. 'I've discussed the matter,' he said cautiously. 'And obviously we've agreed to the terms …'

56

I turned south and kept going until I reached Pu-ho[47] and thence to the famous Iron Gate.[48] This was a pass created by two vertical faces of natural ferrous rock. Between these two sheer walls was a narrow road blocked by massive wooden double doors that were reinforced by iron plates and fitted with bells. On either side of the gates were smooth reddish walls that marked the boundary of the lands controlled by the Western Turks.

Hundreds of people had formed a queue on both sides of the pass, wishing to go through, but the vast majority was being turned back. The fortress above the pass was controlled by a

---

47. Modern-day Bukhara in Uzbekistan.
48. Iron Gate, a narrow pass between Samarkand and Balkh.

Turkic chieftain, who used the pass to extort duties and fees from travellers. However, the letter from the Great Khan worked miracles. Not only was my entourage allowed to pass through, but the chieftain insisted that I partake of his hospitality.

The chieftain's daughter was an exceedingly beautiful young lady, who ensured that I was well looked after. It is impossible to describe how lovely she was. Flawless skin, sparkling blue eyes, long hair, a petite figure, and dimples when she smiled. She was also gentle and caring, and had a sweet disposition. She made sure that I was offered food that was in conformity with my beliefs and also saw to it that my resting quarters were comfortable. She also instructed her servants to take care of the other members of my party and to provide food and water for our pack animals. Her attention to detail was impressive.

The young lady's father was in the process of finding a suitable match for her, and he offered her hand in marriage to me. I humbly refused, owing to my vows of celibacy, but I promised to find a good match for her. The next day I made my way to Huo[49] after crossing the river Po-tsu.[50] I was happy to note that Buddhism was flourishing in Huo and that there were over a thousand Buddhist monks living there. I came across a stunning sculpture at one of the monasteries. It depicted the Buddha lying in a parinirvana position, surrounded by disciples.

The ruler of Huo, Prince Tardu, was the son of the Great Khan. He welcomed me warmly. Tardu had been married to the sister of the king of Gaochang; she had died recently. Given that I had letters from both rulers, I was treated as an extraordinarily important guest. The prince hosted me for several days even though the kingdom was in mourning.

Tardu suggested that I spend some time visiting the monasteries in the region. Unfortunately, a royal conspiracy was brewing

---

49. Modern-day Kunduz, Afghanistan.

50. Amu Darya River (or Oxus River), which flows through Afghanistan, Tajikistan, Turkmenistan and Uzbekistan.

in Huo while I was busy with my monastic tours. Even before the official mourning period had ended, Tardu began a torrid romance with his wife's younger sister. This in itself would not have been a problem, but the scheming younger sister was also having an affair with Tardu's son. It was evident that the people of Huo were unhappy with these developments, but Prince Tardu seemed oblivious to the conspiracies that were being hatched. One evening, I tried to warn him about the rumblings, but he was besotted with the woman and unwilling to see reason.

My worst fears soon came true. The scheming woman poisoned Tardu's wine. Tardu was found dead in his bedchamber the next morning. Before anyone could react, the woman ensured that Tardu's son ascended the throne. I knew what would come next. She would marry the young man—technically her nephew—and become queen. While I did not wish to involve myself in local politics, I realised that she would have to be neutralised. I owed it to the Great Khan. Ironically, it meant going against the younger sister of the king of Gaochang, but I knew he would not have approved of what his sibling had done.

I set about trying to win the young ruler's trust. We had several conversations over the next few days, and I avoided saying anything negative about his scheming aunt. It was many days later that I casually let slip that I had met the most beautiful woman on earth during my journey through the Iron Gate. He was immediately curious. Who was she? I described her in great detail. The young man had a notorious reputation when it came to women, and I knew that he would be intrigued. He requested me to talk to the chief of the Iron Gate. I agreed to do so, provided he keep the matter completely secret.

I retraced my steps to the Iron Gate, a journey of several days, to broach the subject of a matrimonial alliance on behalf of the prince. The Iron Gate chief was only too glad to oblige. It was a powerful match. When I returned with the beautiful young lady, Tardu fell in love with her at first sight, much to the horror of his aunt, who had had every intention of becoming his queen. The nuptials were organised before my departure.

I knew that I must leave Huo immediately because my life could be in danger. I had created a powerful enemy by upsetting her well-laid plans. I blessed the young couple, then took leave of them. I also discreetly suggested to Tardu that he should consider sending his aunt back to Gaochang.

57

At the underground headquarters of the National Security Agency, one of the specialists at the S2A—the South Asia Section—reported that several calls between Beijing and Kohima in Nagaland, India, seemed to be referring to someone or something called 'Shengli'. The same calls also mentioned the words 'mission', 'liberation', 'revolution' and 'assassination'.

The headquarters of the NSA were located in two high-rise buildings off the Patuxent Freeway, skirting Fort Meade and fifteen miles southwest of Baltimore. They looked like, expressionless office blocks.

As with all things involving the NSA, what one didn't see was more important than what one did. The two modest-sized buildings were located on a massive plot of land that boasted a mammoth ten acres of underground work space that accommodated over 20,000 employees of the NSA. The NSA was not only one of the largest employers of Maryland but also the world's largest employer of mathematicians. It was expected that within a few years the number of employees at HQ would cross the 40,000 mark.

Within the workspace of the NSA stood one of the world's most powerful supercomputers. The information that the agency collected—not only at headquarters but also from the other computer labs, regional centres and satellite interception posts around the world—was eventually funnelled through it. The NSA was focused on one, and only one, activity: signals intelligence. This effectively meant snooping on every piece of communication even before it could be established that it carried any sort of risk. A single NSA station collected over one trillion metadata records and greedily gobbled up a billion cell phone calls a day.

The Beijing–Kohima calls had popped up due to an NSA programme called PRISM. One part of the NSA collected and stored emails, videos, photos, text files, voice chats, voice-over-IP calls, file transfers and social networking communications. Virtually all telephone networks, social media platforms, email servers and undersea cables were snooped on. But PRISM was about analysis, not snooping. It ran complicated algorithms to take in billions of these data points and sifted out the few actionable ones based on terms that were deemed relevant.

The S2A specialist alerted the chief of the Operations Directorate, who escalated the matter to the director of the NSA, who recalled the briefing received from the White House. *Keep us informed of any communication chatter that could have a bearing on the China–India conflict.* He immediately sought an appointment with the director of national intelligence. The DNI was the cabinet-rank official responsible for coordinating intelligence from multiple agencies and was answerable to the president.

Within a few hours, the two men were meeting at 1,500 Tysons McLean Drive, the office of the DNI in McLean, Virginia. It was located adjacent to the Terrorist Threat Integration Center and was often referred to as Liberty Crossing. Save the security gates and a barrier at the entrance, it was impossible to tell from outside that the building housed the office of America's chief spook. An aerial view, however, revealed that the structure was shaped like an X, symbolic, perhaps, of the elusive and enigmatic nature of the job.

Each part of the complex was designed like a vault with a coded lock. The external windows were bulletproof and blast proof; the interiors resembled a James Bond filmset. The director was shown in immediately and sat opposite the DNI at a desk shaped like an amoeba. He wondered how people figured out their usual seating positions at the table.

The DNI looked at the transcripts, while the director waited for his reaction. 'Maybe it's something that should be shared with the Indians?' asked the director. 'It's my understanding that we are committed to assisting them with any relevant chatter, right?'

'The keyword is "relevant",' replied the DNI. His face was expressionless. 'Let's not bother with this until we have greater clarity.'

'That might be too late,' argued the director. He stopped himself. It was foolish to get into a spat with the DNI.

The DNI remained very quiet, but it was evident that his brain was buzzing. Finally he said, 'Let's keep it to ourselves for the moment. If the Chinese are so interested in this Shengli, it is possible that something important is on offer. Let's figure out whether we can have a piece of what Shengli has.'

58

Dev was working out. His routine never varied. The alarm would sound at 5.30 a.m. and Dev would walk to his gym that was ten minutes away, to get warmed up, accompanied by his Rottweiler on a leash. Sultan was well-trained and could actually be kept off the leash, except it seemed to terrify most passersby.

On reaching the gym, he would change in the locker room, meeting up with the diehard members who started their days early. Then he would proceed to do a warm-up that included running on the treadmill. Warm-up over, Dev would move on to circuit weights that pushed him to the limit, followed by cone hops, barbell bench presses, dumbbell squats, pull-ups and planks. His workout was aimed at inducing a hormonal spike so that his body was geared to building muscle and burning fat all day on account of a higher resting metabolic rate.

Dev's knowledge of bodybuilding stemmed from all that he had learnt under Rao. He had been one of Rao's best students. To this day, he considered him his guru. He hated that he had been forced out by groups that were antagonistic to Rao. It had cost him the love of his life.

There wasn't an ounce of extra fat on Dev's body, and his thin T-shirt, drenched in sweat, splendidly displayed his rippling torso muscles. One would imagine that with a physique like that, Dev would have no problem in getting female attention, but that was not the case. His life had turned topsy-turvy after Rao's academy shut down. He had been forced to relocate and to cut off contact with friends, relatives and colleagues. Anu had refused to see him again. She saw his act as the ultimate betrayal. After that, Dev had found it safer not to get too close to anyone.

Done with his workout two hours later, he consumed a dose of whey protein powder to keep his catabolic hormones in check, then showered vigorously and slipped on some comfortable clothes. He then headed to the neighbourhood café for breakfast. On the way he passed a seedy shop that was known for taking unofficial bets on everything from cricket to politics. The proprietor nodded at Dev, but Dev did not stop. He knew what his betting habit had done to him. He refused to go down that road again.

He entered the café and nodded to the waitress. Breakfast was always king-sized for Dev, and the waitress knew his order by heart. High on protein and good fats, low on carbs, his breakfast was often recommended by the restaurant owner to aspiring athletes and fitness buffs. They called it 'Dev's Breakfast of Champions' on their menu.

Dev was about to sit down when his phone rang. It was an unknown number—probably a spam caller trying to sell him insurance. He picked up the call nonetheless. Secretly, he was hoping that it was Pam. She had come across as attractive, and chatty in a dignified way.

'Who asked you to direct Pam to Rao?' asked the muffled voice. 'Do you realise the mess you've just caused?'

'I ... I only gave her the address of the ac ... academy,' Dev stammered. 'She could have found that out from anywhere else. It's even on Google Maps.'

'You moron. You could have nipped the matter in the bud by not talking to her. Do you know who she is?'

'Sh ... she said she was from a sports magazine. She even gave me her mobile number.'

'Congratulations on having managed a date with such speed,' said the voice caustically. 'Did it even strike you to find out her full name? Or were you too bowled over by her looks?'

'I remember asking her for her full name but can't seem to remember it,' said Dev. He had not bothered to find out her full name. He had been too taken in by her.

'She is Pam Khurana, daughter of Colonel Kishan Khurana. Now do you understand what a fucking mess you've made?'

Dev mumbled an apology. He knew he had screwed up. Pam Khurana had led him on. He was a lonely man leading a loveless life owing to continuous surveillance and backseat driving of his actions. He couldn't even take a dump without those bastards knowing, much less have an affair. Ever since Rao's academy shut shop, he had been dependent on them. The slightest attention from the opposite sex made him do foolish things.

'I wasn't thinking,' he replied. 'Please excuse the lapse.'

'Remember what happened to Rao's elaborate plans? Remember what happened to Colonel Kishan Khurana?'

'Yes ... yes ... I do remember all that,' said Dev, sweat trickling down his face. These were not people to be messed with. They knew everything, they saw and heard everything, they controlled everything.

'You were lucky that we rehabilitated you after the mountain of gambling debts you accumulated. We established you in Delhi with a regular source of income, a car and a house. You now seem to be outliving your use.' *I was Judas Iscariot and I received my thirty pieces of silver,* thought Dev miserably. *And lost the only person I cared about, Anu.*

'I pr ... promise I'll be m ... more careful ...' began Dev, but the caller had already disconnected.

Dev hurriedly put down the phone and used a napkin to mop the sweat from his face. He cursed himself for having even spoken to Pam. He would have been better off relying on the affections of Sultan.

59

On the border of India and Myanmar was a complex network of hills usually shrouded by clouds. The highest of these peaks was Mount Saramati, reaching an elevation of 12,552 feet. Within one of the valleys of this densely wooded region, a group of young men underwent a harsh drill that resembled a modified triathlon. All of them were dressed in military fatigues, red bandanas tied around their heads.

Their ages varied from fourteen to twenty-five. Each of them had been fully indoctrinated with the notion that the Indian state was their greatest enemy; the only way to preserve their own order of things was to overthrow the ruling elite. All of them fervently believed that Mao's philosophy was the only one that could better their lives and that an armed struggle was justified when dealing with a heartless state. Most importantly, they were certain that their ends justified their means.

This was densely wooded territory bounded by the Doyang and Diphu rivers to the north and the Barak River in the southwest. Strong northwesterly winds at this time of the year ensured freezing temperatures and a thick layer of frost on the ground. The dense cover of timber and mahogany forests often made it impossible to get from one point to another without a machete. Neither the terrain nor the weather were for the fainthearted.

The state of Nagaland had joined India as recently as 1963, over sixteen years after India's independence from British rule. Since then, insurgency had plagued the state, with some groups demanding secession of Naga territories from India. While most of these groups were home-grown, a few derived sustenance from Myanmar or China. In fact, one particular group had managed to travel to the Yunnan province of China to receive training. Some of these men were considered the very best in jungle warfare owing to their finely honed fighting skills and survival tactics. Even the British had never been able to conquer the Nagas and had been forced to satisfy themselves with a small slice of their territory.

The cadets cut through several miles of rough terrain, swinging their machetes to clear a path through scrub forests, high grass and reeds. Then they swam through ice-cold swollen rivers, combating the strong currents with ease. They had no time to recover, because the moment they reached the opposite bank, there was another group of combatants waiting to wrestle with them while their instructors fired pellets from the treetops. After they were done with that ordeal, they had to climb a sheer vertical rock face using little more than their hands and feet to reach the end of the challenge. The first one to the top would be declared the winner.

It was a routine that pushed human endurance to the very limit. But endurance was precisely what these young men were made for. The Naga people were made up of around sixty-six tribes, the majority of whom had originally been head-hunters. Headhunting was no longer practised, but even two decades ago, there had been a tribal conflict in which men from one village had hacked the heads off twenty-eight members of an enemy village and brought them home as trophies. Some villages even boasted community relic houses where the skulls that had been won were displayed. The law of the jungle prevailed.

Living conditions were equally demanding. Cadets lived in bamboo huts with thatched roofs that afforded little protection from rain or cold. The camp was guarded by ditches, roughly hewn stone walls and deep pits. While rice rations were provided daily, the cadets had to supplement these by hunting and gathering. Their diet included worms, snakes, snails, rats, squirrels, and even spiders and ants. There was nothing they did not eat.

Fluttering in the centre of their camp was a red flag that read 'LLL'. Leninist Liberation League. The group received ideological inspiration, arms training and financial assistance from private groups in China, many of these being outfits created by the Buzhang or the MSS.

An intense-looking young man with a deep scar on his cheek was going through all the routines expected of him. He was the first to reach the top of the cliff. Sweating profusely and with aching limbs from the excruciating sequence, he did not sit down like his comrades. He remained standing at attention, his back ramrod straight, awaiting further instructions from his commanding officer, who was busy talking on a mobile phone. The only indication that he was tired was his rapid breathing, which he took pains to hide.

After a few minutes, his commander called him aside. 'Tomorrow you leave for Delhi, as per the instructions we've received,' he said. 'Are you confident and committed to your mission?'

The young man nodded vigorously. He had been waiting for an opportunity like this for a long time. It was about time he was allowed to prove himself. He recited a short prayer to Rutzeh, the giver of sudden death. Most Nagas had converted to Christianity over the years under the influence of American Baptist missionaries, but many of the tribes' cultural beliefs were deeply ingrained, including the belief in Rutzeh.

'Do not let us down,' said his commander. 'You will be met at the airport with the required arms and ammunition. This mission is important to our Chinese friends. Long live the glorious revolution!'

The young cadet saluted smartly. 'Long live the glorious revolution!'

60

No one knew exactly when the city of Ta-mi[51] was founded. There are records of it having existed for at least a thousand years, because it was occupied by the Great Conqueror from the West[52] around then. The region around the city was known to these invaders as Bactria.

On my way to a monastery, I chanced to meet a monk called Dharmasimha. He had visited Yindu, and I utilised the time I spent with him to gain a better understanding of the land and its people. He described Kasmira,[53] the fertile plains of Jalandhara[54] and the mighty roar of the Fu-shui.[55] He told me about the rich kingdoms that stretched seamlessly across the land. But I was disappointed to hear that the way of the Buddha was in decline and that the older faiths of Yindu were once again becoming the norm.

South of the river Po-tsu were fertile plains and valleys. There were more than 3,000 Hinayana monks in the area, and the region was dotted with stupas that had been erected to preserve the relics of the Buddha. The most precious ones were usually kept in containers of crystal or gold and the less valuable ones in wood or stone.

Among the hundreds of monasteries in the region was Navavihara in Foho.[56] It was the largest and had had an unbroken succession of masters. I was welcomed by the head monk, Prajnakara. I was stunned by the opulence of Navavihara. Cave temples, stupas, courtyards, sculptures, elaborate wooden roofs, ornate columns

---

51. Termez in Uzbekistan near the Hairatan border crossing of Afghanistan.
52. Alexander the Great
53. Modern-day Kashmir, India.
54. Modern-day Jalandhar, Punjab, India.
55. Ganga River, India
56. Velayat-e-Balkh in Afghanistan.

and gilded stone umbrellas bestowed on the entire complex an aura of magnificence. There were several images of the Buddha, studded with precious stones, and the abbey's halls were adorned with costly rarities shimmering in the light of oil lamps that were constantly refreshed. There was no shortage of food owing to the vast agricultural tracts under the monastery's control.

I stayed there for almost a month and became friends with Prajnakara. I asked him why the stupas in this region had a specific shape. Prajnakara smiled and told me a story. It seems that two rich traders had met the Buddha on a journey and had shared with him their meagre food of parched grain and honey. In return, the Buddha had spent some time teaching them the Five Commandments and Ten Virtues. After the traders had learnt the core of the Buddha's teachings, they requested the master for something to remember him by. The Buddha reiterated that he was not to be worshipped, but gave them a lock of his hair to remember his teachings by. The traders then asked him how best to preserve that lock of hair. The Buddha folded his three garments and piled them up with the largest at the base and the smallest at the top. Then the master took his begging bowl and inverted it on top of his folded garments. Finally, he placed his staff on top and that became the design for the stupas that would contain his relics in the future. I found the story fascinating and entirely believable.

I used my visit as an opportunity to learn more about the Hinayana belief system. Prajnakara introduced me to scriptures I had not read before. He even shared with me an important text, the Mahavibhasa, that I took with me for future translation. Prajnakara told me to spend time not only in Nalanda but also in Kasmira, which was where many of the old texts had been codified.

When it was time for me to leave, Prajnakara kindly accompanied me through the Snowy Mountains[57] to the Place of Shining

---

57. Hindu Kush Mountains that stretch through Afghanistan to northern Pakistan and into Tajikistan and China.

Light,[58] *famed for its massive statues of the Buddha that were covered with gold sheets.*

The trek across the Snowy Mountains was treacherous because of the permanently snow-covered peaks and the blizzards. Along the way, Prajnakara, two of my disciples and I were separated from the rest of the group. This was a dangerous development, because the area was known to be home to looters, wild animals and evil spirits. We were stuck. After several days, we were saved by a leopard hunter, who guided us through and reunited us with the rest of our group. I thanked the Buddha for sending us a saviour in the shape of the hunter. It felt odd advising him to give up his profession and adopt the path of ahimsa. Had it not been for his hunting expedition, we would never have been saved!

We finally approached the Place of Shining Light, an oasis town that lay in a valley of the Snowy Mountains. The mere sight of it took my breath away—two gigantic statues within gargantuan niches. I could feel my heart beat faster, but I knew that it would be several days before we reached the statues.

By now, I shared a strong rapport with Prajnakara. I revealed to him that I wanted not only to source the original texts from Nalanda but also to return to Cina as Di San Sou Chuan. Prajnakara then told me to visit 'the Fragrant Land' if I was serious about becoming Di San Sou Chuan. I asked him where the Fragrant Land was located, but he had no idea. It had been mentioned in several writings, but Prajnakara had never visited the place. I wondered how I would ever find it.

As usual, I placed my trust in the Buddha.

61

The little shop was located close to Anu's house, and the Iyengar owner knew each customer by name. Anu was a

---

58. Modern-day Bamiyan, Afghanistan.

regular at the shop, and many of the meals she shared with her father were prepared using the batter procured from here. It was, hands down, the best batter on earth, and she refused to cook without it.

The shop was extremely modest, to the point that one could miss it entirely. A wooden signboard outside bore the family name in Tamil. A rusty rolling shutter was brought down on the premises at night but was rarely locked. Inside, grey ceramic tiles lined the floors and walls, ready to be washed with steaming hot water at the end of the work day. Cleanliness was next to godliness here. On one wall was a photograph of the deity at Sri Varadarajaperumal temple, with a little shelf on which a single incense stick was lit each morning. A wooden counter towards the front of the shop was where the day's quota of food was sold from. The shop's inventory was usually exhausted by 10 a.m., and regular customers knew they would return empty-handed if they reached later than that. Preparing limited quantities ensured that leftovers were minimal and that the batter sold each day was absolutely fresh.

At heart, Kanchi was still a small town, where shopkeepers and customers knew each other over generations. The shop owner's father had built a reputation by selling the famous Kanchipuram idlis, having worked his way up from the madappalli of the Sri Varadarajaperumal temple that was dedicated to Lord Vishnu. The dish had to be perfect because it was served to the deity and was made with a recipe that could not be varied even slightly. The son had continued the tradition but had expanded his offerings to include traditional idli and dosa batter. He was a thin, dark man, almost always dressed in a white bush shirt and a white veshti with a prominent sandalwood mark on his forehead. His thick white eyebrows seemed colour-coordinated with his clothes.

Families from across Kanchi would descend on his little shop to partake of the Kanchipuram idlis and purchase batter for their own kitchens. Perfection did not come easy. The shopkeeper personally soaked the parboiled rice, split black gram and fenugreek seeds in his secret proportion before grinding them to a smooth paste every evening.

By 4 a.m., he was already hard at it, preparing for the first batch of breakfast seekers and housewives, stacking banana leaves at the counter, his traditional, environmentally friendly alternative to paper and plastic plates. Stacking done, he turned his attention to the large brass vessels in which he prepared his signature idlis. The chutney and sambar were still to be prepared.

The shopkeeper was no mere trader; he was an artist. He was passionate about what he did, and that passion reflected in the quality of his food. He hummed to himself as he worked.

Once the shop opened, the humming would stop. No sooner did the customers start walking in than he would get busy greeting them by name and asking after their families. To the odd customer who asked for instructions on how to use the batter, he would provide more details than a cookbook could.

But before the buzz of daily routine began, he was the only one inside the store. Or so he thought. He had failed to observe the stranger who was already inside, a thickset man with his hands in his pockets.

He looked at him now, running a hand over the counter to check that there was no dust. 'We've not yet opened for business, brother,' he said. 'Come back after an hour.' The burly man did not budge. The shopkeeper wondered whether he had understood him; then he saw it. The man's right hand gripped a gun whose shape was visible even through his pocket.

The shopkeeper panicked. He had never seen a gun, except in the Tamil movies he watched with his family on TV. His life was a simple and modest one. What could the thug possibly want from him? 'You can open the cash drawer and take whatever is there,' he said nervously. 'It's not much. There is very little to steal inside this shop.'

'I don't want your money,' said the intruder, 'nor do I want to hurt you. Do as I say and you will be fine.'

'What exactly do you want?' asked the shopkeeper cautiously.

The man fished out a vial containing a white granular powder. 'I need you to add this to a specific batch of batter.'

62

It was around 11 p.m. when Pam finished reading *Journey to the West*. She sat on the floor of the living room, the sofa supporting her back. The book had turned out to be fascinating, although a little tedious at times. *A better title would have been 'The Monk and the Monkey'*, she thought. On the one hand, the monkey thought that by taking a bite of the monk's flesh, he could become immortal; on the other hand, the monk needed the monkey—who had powers to fly, become invisible and transform into other shapes—to fight dragons, looters, spirits and evil wizards that could sabotage their quest. *But what's the great lesson in it? And why this obsession with immortality? Why would a great monk need a supernatural monkey on his journey? What's the deeper secret the book is preserving?*

She did a quick Google search for the author, Wu Cheng-en. Very little was known about him. He had lived sometime in the sixteenth century and shared an interest in literature with his father. He sat for the Imperial University examinations on several occasions but was unsuccessful in getting admission. By the time he finally succeeded, he was middle-aged. He took up official postings in Beijing and Changxing, but found the work boring. He spent the rest of his days writing stories and poems. His best-known work, *Journey to the West*, was published under a pseudonym. *Why is that? What revelation within this novel of fantasy and adventure demanded that the author keep himself anonymous?*

Pam's greatest confusion lay in Rao's request to her to read the work. *Has the old man lost his marbles? How is the novel related to the present happenings in Doklam? What was the need for me to wade through thousands of words? Just to garner an appreciation of the Chinese classics?*

Pam was oblivious to her mother, who was seated on the sofa, watching a TV serial with the volume set to near mute so that Pam would not be disturbed. She noticed her smart phone screen lighting up. Mark was calling. She put away the computer and took his call. Mark asked if she would like to meet. She looked at her watch. It was late, but not *that* late. They agreed to meet at an all-night street eatery, one of many that Delhi was famous for.

Her mother had taken off her glasses and was staring at Pam. There was a moment of uncomfortable silence. 'If he's nice, why don't you invite him over?' asked her mother, suddenly full of hope for her daughter's marital prospects. Pam sighed. It was impossible to have these discussions with her mother. Every conversation seemed to lead to the topic of marriage.

'He is a scarred man, Mom,' said Pam.

'You mean from his divorce?'

'I mean from his years leading a life diametrically different from the one he now leads. I'm not sure whether some scars ever heal. There is a darkness that hangs over him. I don't think I'm ready to share that.'

Her mother harrumphed. She had heard it all before from her stubborn daughter.

Pam quickly got ready, stepped into her car and drove towards AIIMS—the All India Institute of Medical Sciences. Just opposite AIIMS was the Safdarjung Hospital gate; outside it was an all-night dhaba that served parathas and tea 24/7. Getting there from her house in Dwarka at this time of night would take less than twenty minutes, although would have taken over an hour during the day in Delhi's notorious traffic snarls. The monotony of the sodium streetlamps she drove past had a strangely calming effect on her. She pushed a button on the car's stereo and allowed the music from her phone to stream via Bluetooth. The haunting Dire Straits track *Water of Love* began playing. She sang along with Mark Knopfler as she drove. It was Mark Knopfler on her lips but Mark Richards on her mind.

Memories came flooding back as she drove. The conference in Goa and the constant merrymaking; the seafood joint run by a third-generation owner; the hippies who were happy to share their Malana Cream joints with them; the smell of weed hanging in the air; the overdose of strawberry daiquiris and feni; the late-night dancing on the beach; and that shared bed in the beachfront suite. The next morning they had skipped the morning session. Instead, they had ordered breakfast in bed, and fed each other waffles with extra maple syrup.

They had talked incessantly until it was time to get back to the conference. In that one morning, Mark had told her about how he had survived his years in Cambodia, China and Vietnam; how he had been captured by the Khmer Rouge exiles in Thailand and tortured; how his marriage had broken up; how he had fought cancer.

Mark had been through a lot. He was nothing if not scarred, and Pam knew it. But there were gaps in his stories, things she knew he was holding back. She wondered whether she would ever be able to trust him fully. Her rational mind had several questions for him, about him.

But she also knew she was falling in love with the man. And love was rarely about rationality.

63

Pam pulled up at the eatery. Several cars were already parked outside, the place being the preferred haunt for those who needed hot, spicy soul food even at odd hours. Carhops took orders from patrons, who remained seated in their cars, and delivered their food to them in minutes. One oversized tava and two frying pans up front were the centre of action. The shop's owner turned out hundreds of parathas every night from these pans, with different fillings as per the choice of his customers.

Mark reached the spot a few minutes later. He parked his car some distance away, walked over to Pam's and settled into the passenger seat. He reached over, kissed Pam on her cheek and then craftily edged towards her lips. Pam smiled but pulled away.

'Business first,' she said firmly.

'Aww, party pooper,' said Mark, disappointed. 'Shoot.'

A carhop dressed in a black T-shirt and jeans and with a pencil tucked behind his ear knocked on Mark's window. Mark ordered chai and parathas for both of them. The man made a note of their order and disappeared. Business was rocking, and none of the staff seemed to have an extra minute to spare. Staff and patrons had to be quick in placing orders, the cooks had to be swift in turning out those orders, the carhops had to be efficient in reaching orders to the waiting cars and customers knew they had to speedily vacate parking spots for the next car once they were done eating. It was a well-oiled operation, and yes, time was money.

'The document Rao gave me was actually a version of the Chinese novel *Journey to the West*,' explained Pam. 'In the story, the Chinese monk Xuanzang makes his way to India to source the original Buddhist scriptures, accompanied by a monkey-king character, Sun Wukong.'

'Why should that excite you?' asked Mark. 'How can a novel be of significance to your immediate goals?'

'Because the Chinese attackers at Doklam had monkeyish features. Even the blood analysis done by your team indicated something between humans and the rhesus.'

'That could be a mere coincidence.'

'The number of coincidences is just too high. We know that *Journey to the West* was inspired by an earlier work, *The Great Tang Records on the Western Regions*, written by Xuanzang's disciple Bianji. In that account, Xuanzang found a merchant to help him cross the desert beyond the Jade Gate. The merchant's name was Bandha.'

'So?' asked Mark. He couldn't understand what Pam was going on about.

'"Bandha" sounds suspiciously like "bandar", the Hindi word for monkey,' replied Pam. 'Was the name simply a corruption of that original word? But there's something else too. It concerns my father.'

'What?' asked Mark, screwing up his eyes.

Pam opened her father's notebook and held it up under the light. She flipped through the pages towards the end and showed Mark the sketches. 'Why did my father sketch these figures? Who are they? Whom do they represent? And where were these done?'

Mark looked at the pictures carefully. The figures clearly indicated ape-like features. But wasn't it possible that Colonel Khurana had just been doodling?

'When I was leaving Rao's house, I saw a little sculpture on his desk,' continued Pam, oblivious of the thoughts running through Mark's head. 'The three wise monkeys symbolising the principle of see no evil, hear no evil and speak no evil. We think of them as Japanese characters, but their origin lies in China, in Confucius's Code of Conduct, according to Rao. So many connections, all leading back to monkeys!'

'If you examine any subject deeply enough, you will always find lots of connections,' argued Mark. 'Those connections could be random occurrences and may mean absolutely nothing. Remember also that Rao is an old man. He could be going senile.'

Pam nodded. There was some truth in Mark's view, but she still needed to think this through. 'Rao said something else when I was leaving. That true power comes from following the code of the three monkeys—monkeys that he had assigned names to—and that in India we have always considered the rhesus species to be sacred. And he's right. Hanuman was possibly the first superhero to be worshipped. Much before Superman or Spiderman. And then you tell me that we found forty-seven chromosomes in the blood on the tourniquet blood, something between human and rhesus.'

Mark remained silent. He was attempting to absorb all the information Pam had thrown at him. Pam was on her smart phone, searching for something. 'What are you looking for?' asked Mark.

'This,' she said, passing the phone to Mark. It was an article from Beijing's *National Science Review*. Mark looked at the summary on top. Chinese researchers had taken human copies of the MCPH1 gene, considered to play a critical role in human brain development, and had introduced it into monkey embryos by means of a virus that carried the gene.

'Could it be that we're dealing with modified monkeys?' asked Pam as Mark scanned the article, the light from the phone's screen casting a glow on his incredulous face.

His reverie was interrupted by the carhop's knock. Their parathas and tea had arrived. Mark rolled down his window to accept the two small trays of food, passing one to Pam. The food smelled wonderful.

Suddenly, there was a deafening noise, and Pam's window shattered. She screamed as she realised that a bullet had narrowly missed her. The carhop held a handgun tightly and aimed yet again at Pam, but this time Mark threw his cup of scalding tea at the man's face. He let out an anguished scream as the tea seared his face and his gun fell to the ground. He recovered quickly but Mark was out of the car by then and knocking him to the ground.

Pam recovered from her initial shock and pushed open her door. Getting out of the car, she ran over to Mark's side of the vehicle. Mark was raining blows on the carhop, who was matching him blow for blow. Other customers from nearby cars had seen the commotion, heard the gunshots and slunk away to a safe distance.

Mark attempted to pick up the carhop's gun, but before his hand could grasp it, the young LLL revolutionary had wrested it away. Another shot rang out, and Pam saw Mark fall to the ground, having taken a bullet in his stomach. Pam skidded along the slippery road and her feet hit the carhop like a projectile. He fell, losing his grasp of the weapon. The gun flew from his hand; Pam reached for it with her right hand. Her fingers caught it midair and pulled the trigger without any conscious thought. It was as though her brain had too much data to process and her subconscious was guiding her.

The bullet caught her would-be murderer square in the chest. He lay on the road in a pool of blood. Pam dropped the gun and knelt next to Mark, who was bleeding profusely. She cradled his head in her lap and used her scarf to stanch the blood. 'Call an ambulance,' she yelled. 'Someone please get help!'

The tears came unbidden as she held Mark in her arms, praying she would not lose him like she had lost her father.

64

Coming down the slopes of the Snowy Mountains, we approached the Place of Shining Light. Each step brought us closer to the two massive statues that had been carved into the sheer cliffs. The Place of Shining Light was a verdant valley that seemed very prosperous. The land evidently produced a variety of cereals, fruits and flowers. In addition, there was abundant pastureland for cattle, sheep and horses. The people were well-attired, dressed in garments of fur and wool. I could feel my heart beating faster as we approached the statues. Never in my life had I seen a sight so incredible.

Immense cliffs of soft earthen colour had been painstakingly chiselled to create two massive niches, and two enormous statues of the Buddha stood within them. As we drew closer, we noticed that the statues were brightly coloured, one in blue and the other in red. They dazzled the eyes because of the gilded ornaments they wore and the precious and semi-precious stones embedded in them. Even their faces and hands were covered with gold. It was no wonder the site was called the Place of Shining Light. I stood transfixed, staring at the glorious statues, wondering if they had been built by men or a greater divine power. I wondered whether the people of this land, who saw these statues every day, would ever be able to appreciate the monumentality of what stood in their midst. How would future generations treat these great undertakings? I whispered a prayer to the Buddha to protect them.

The king had been informed of my arrival and was already at the foot of the statues. After greeting me warmly, he personally escorted me to the monastery, which was carved into the caves behind these two gigantic south-facing statues. I now noticed that they were of different sizes. One was around 175 feet high and the other around 125 feet. Between them were monks' cells, as well as halls for meditation and prayer. Each of these was richly decorated with intricate paintings depicting the life of the Buddha. Four miles east of the two Buddhas was reported to be a third statue, a glorious Parinirvana Buddha. I hoped to catch a glimpse of it on my return journey.

From the Place of Shining Light, I travelled east, climbing the Sigh Koh[59] at over 9,000 feet. This pass gave us access to a valley where the mountains miraculously parted and the beautiful kingdom of Kiapishi[60] revealed itself. The resplendent valley was surrounded by snow-capped mountains on three sides and was fragrant with fruit trees, saffron, walnut and mulberry. I spent six months here, among the monks from over a hundred monasteries, sharing views and exchanging stories. Besides the monasteries and stupas, there were ten massive temples dedicated to the ancient gods of Yindu. The king was a Kshatriya from the Suli tribe, and every year he got his craftsmen to make an eighteen-foot silver statue of the Buddha.

The king was a generous man, who looked after me well. He lorded over the erstwhile Kushan empire from Kiapishi. That was the true crossroad of the Silk Road, being halfway between Daqin and Chang'an on the East-West Road and midway on the North-South Road between Samokien and Yindu. All over the kingdom, one could see beautiful examples of Gandhara art, a mixture of Western styles with Eastern philosophy. I was told that even the creases and folds in the clothes of the Buddha were inspired from the art of Daqin and Xila.[61] The

---

59. Shibar Pass, connecting Parwan Province to Bamiyan Province.

60. Ancient Kapisi, modern-day Bagram in Afghanistan.

61. Greece

people spoke fondly of the great monarch Kanishka, who had lived several hundred years ago and had ensured the stability and prosperity of the nomadic tribes that called themselves Kushans.

Near Kiapishi was a large monastery known by a strange name: the Monastery of Hostages.[62] I wondered about this name. It was one of the king's councillors who told me the story of a prince from Cina who had been taken hostage by Kanishka. He had been held prisoner at the monastery, but the king had requested the monks to treat him as an honoured guest. The prince had learnt many things from the monks from Yindu, relating to their physical, spiritual and dietary routines. When he was finally released and returned home, he sent a treasure chest back for the monks. It was to be buried at the feet of the primary deity and was to be dug up only by someone from Cina, if the monastery ever fell on hard times.

The monks were overjoyed to see me. They saw my arrival as a good omen to dig for the treasure. I was happy to assist them. We dug about eight feet before we discovered a copper chest covered by a rich tapestry and bearing a sword on top. The chest was filled to the brim with pearls and gold, enough to sustain the monastery for another hundred years. Engraved on the sword were two simple Chinese letters.

I made a sketch of the engravings just in case I needed to remember them later. My memory was usually razor-sharp, but the fatigue of incessant travel often came in the way.

The king of Kiapishi was delighted to hear that I had assisted the monks and invited me to be part of a five-day religious congress.

---

62. Shotorak Monastery, north of Kabul, Afghanistan.

This included several debates that I was happy to participate in. I believe I demonstrated my mastery over several streams of philosophical thought, and the king was happy to shower me with gifts that would help me on my journey.

By now I had been on the road for more than a year. My physical, mental and emotional reserves had been tested to the extreme. I had crossed several deserts, mountain ranges, rivers and forests. I had met with so many different people from varied walks of life—kings, merchants, monks, artists, bandits, priests and soldiers. I murmured a silent prayer to the Buddha for having seen me through the difficult journey and for bringing me close to the very gate of the land I sought: Yindu.

65

It was an absolute miracle that the eatery Pam and Mark had chosen for their late-night rendezvous was located close to two of the best hospitals in New Delhi.

An ambulance from Safdarjung Hospital happened to be parked a short distance away; its driver, on a smoke break, had been having a cup of tea at the dhaba. Hearing the commotion and observing Mark with his head in Pam's lap, he pulled out his ambulance from the parking slot and raced towards them. Bystanders helped the driver load Mark into the ambulance, and Pam got in with him. They were at the emergency block of the hospital within a few minutes.

Hospitals in Delhi were notorious for delays in treating accident or crime victims in the absence of police procedures. This often meant that critical moments would be lost when medical intervention was most needed. Pam knew the drill and prepared for it accordingly. Delhi was a city that ran on connections. Press the right buttons and anything could get done. For the vast majority, though, those buttons were inaccessible. Pam phoned her boss at the DRDO from the ambulance. He immediately called his friend, the Delhi police commissioner, who called the hospital so that there would be no delays in Mark's treatment. He also despatched a police team to the spot of the shooting. 'I'm putting my best men on the job,' he told Pam's boss.

Upon arrival at the hospital, Mark's stretcher was transferred to a gurney, and the doctor on duty immediately radioed his team. The nurses running alongside the gurney attempted to examine the location and extent of the wound. Once inside the ER, they placed IVs and began drawing blood for tests. At Mark's head stood an anaesthesiologist, who inserted a breathing tube. The primary surgeon stood at the foot, attempting to log all possible wounds, including shrapnel, while determining the level of patient stability and the pre-surgery routines needed.

Waiting outside the ER, Pam heard the doctor yelling instructions to his team, getting the nurses to record vital signs: pulse, blood pressure, respiration and oxygen saturation. 'I want two large-bore IV lines with crystalloid infusion. Hundred per cent oxygen by face mask. Use O-negative blood till we can get a cross-match. Blood pressure is erratic. Fluid resuscitation please. Naso-gastric tube needed. Decompress stomach and initiate haemorrhage protocol.'

Pam could hear everything but nothing was registering.She had tuned out. All she could think of was a world without Mark. She had tried so very hard not to get involved with him, but it was impossible. She knew that there was a side of him she hardly knew, and his unknown dimensions presented a danger, but she couldn't think of that now. Her thoughts flashed back to her father, who had always hidden things from her. He had probably been under an oath of secrecy.

The new emergency block at Safdarjung Hospital was colossal, accommodating 260 beds, thirty-seven ICUs and six operation theatres. The corridors were long and wide, and Pam plopped into one of the visitors' chairs, awaiting more information from the duty doctor. Her clothes were bloodstained from cradling Mark. She stared blankly into space, clutching her mobile phone. A kind nurse brought her a cup of coffee, but she refused it. She didn't want anything. Just for Mark to be well again.

Safdarjung was familiar to her for all the wrong reasons. Her grandmother had breathed her last here. So had Pam's maternal uncle. Pam associated Safdarjung with death. And now Mark was a patient within.

A few feet away, the elderly duty nurse who had brought Pam coffee was staring at her. She was dressed in the usual nurse's uniform of white pants, smock and shoes. Her hair was tightly tied in a bun, and she wore thick spectacles. She walked over to the nurses' station and casually picked up the folder in which Mark's admittance details had been noted. She quickly scanned through the few pages.

She put the folder back on the desk and walked further down the corridor before fishing out a mobile phone enclosed in its original plastic wrapping. She opened it and powered on the phone, which had a pre-installed SIM card. The phone and the SIM would be used only once before being discarded. Intelligence agencies around the world supplied their agents and informants with these burner phones that were extremely difficult to trace.

'Hello,' she whispered into the phone. 'I have information that is important. You may wish to pass this on. Shengli …'

Pam did not see or hear the nurse. She was busy staring at a man who seemed strangely familiar. It took her a moment to realise that he had been almost in step with her from the moment she entered the hospital. She had just been too distracted to notice him. *Is he shadowing me?* she wondered.

66

The antiques dealer from Janpath had taken a Korean Air flight from New Delhi to Seoul. From Seoul he had hopped on to a train that dropped him at Jangseong Station. From there, he took a taxi to Daesan Hotel, his only lodging option in the vicinity of the port. He tipped the driver, smiling through his nicotine-stained teeth, and checked in.

The port of Daesan was located by a town called Seosan. Seosan was small. Very small. It was located in the South Chungcheong Province of South Korea, around seventy-eight miles south of Seoul. The only visitors to the city were those who had family or business interests in Seosan. The only tourists were the birds. Thousands of ducks, geese and cranes came at this time of the year. In fact, the city dedicated a bird-watching festival to them every year, but the humans who attended were locals. Even touristy places such as the Haemieup-seong fortress were only frequented by locals. Nothing much ever happened in Seosan, and the residents seemed to like it that way.

But there was a part of Seosan that was always busy, night or day: the port of Daesan. Located just 273 miles from the fishing port of Yantai in mainland China, Daesan was not only a port but also a significant petrochemicals hub for companies that finished the refining process here before shipping finished goods to the rest of the world. Daesan was thus a focal point for logistics along the Yellow Sea.

The antiques dealer quickly grabbed a bite to eat, freshened up and then left on foot for his meeting, wearing a face mask. Strong winds bearing dust from the polluted Chinese mainland were a problem in Daesan. The locals called it *hwanga* or Asian Dust. There was no way to avoid it except by wearing a mask. He laughed softly to himself. The actual hwanga in his life was Mark Richards. And Richards could not be avoided with a mere mask.

Daesan was cold. The first snows of winter had already fallen. The dealer pulled up the zipper of his parka, adjusting the hood around his head as he walked towards the rendezvous point. It was an office marked by a board that read 'Yantai Fisheries'.

He walked into the very ordinary but warm interiors. Many overburdened desks were crammed into a tight space, and metal racks with bulging files looked down on the mess. Employees somehow managed to work in the midst of the chaos while still retaining a smile for their boss, a businessman in his sixties, who monitored everything they did. He occupied a corner office and motioned for his international visitor to cross the corridor and enter his cabin.

The boss, dressed in a polyester office shirt that had seen better days, was sucking on a new nicotine vape that kept his urge for cigarettes at bay. His hair was slicked back with gel, and a cheap plastic pen peeped out from his shirt pocket. Looking at him, it was impossible to tell that he had made a small fortune over the years by allowing his fishing trawlers to 'accidentally' stray and fish in international waters. Sometimes he also allowed smuggled items—including people—to be stowed on board.

He usually remained a step ahead of the coastguard by hacking into maritime communications. Ever since the creation of internet-based navigation systems that could track the real-time locations of boats around the globe, the Korean had been able to outmanoeuvre the authorities. Some of the ships were foolish enough to use public IPv4 addresses without any firewalls.

The two men were an odd pair, with little in common. They had done lots of business deals over the years, but this would be the biggest of them all. The dealer knew that the Korean would quote a price higher than anyone else but would get the job done efficiently and quietly. The Korean knew there would be no backtracking or payment hassles with the Delhi man. There was a quiet confidence in their dealings that only came from mutual trust built up over several successful transactions.

They sipped tea as they discussed the plan that needed execution. Both would get into trouble if anything went wrong. Ships from China, North Korea and South Korea plied the waters of the Yellow Sea. No mercy would be shown to the Korean ship-owner if the plan went south. In such an event, both the Korean and the Chinese-Indian would have no protection from their bosses and would be disowned entirely. In fact, they would be conveniently made scapegoats, sacrificed at the altar of international relations.

'How will the goods reach Yantai?' asked the Korean.

'That is not your problem,' replied the Indian. 'Once we have a deal, your responsibility starts from Yantai. You tell me which vessels are available and when. I will look at which option works best for cargo movement into Yantai.'

The Korean looked at his computer screen. He pressed a few keys to check the projected positions of various ships in the Yellow Sea. There was always some risk in such movements, but one could minimise it through planning. Having examined the data, he nodded, exhaling a plume of water vapour from his e-cigarette. After some negotiation, a deal was struck; date, time, location and password were agreed upon.

The goods would be transferred from Yantai to Daesan as per the contract, but movement up to Yantai and from Daesan were not in the Korean's scope of work.

67

The doctors at Safdarjung Hospital did a CT scan with a triple contrast enhancement of Mark's chest, abdomen and pelvis. It showed a bullet in the left upper quadrant of the abdomen. They also found air bubbles, possibly secondary to his intestinal injury. The long surgical procedure lasting several hours involved removing the bullet, lavage, and repairing the gastrointestinal perforation. Mark was then placed on a very strong dose of intravenous antibiotics to prevent any possible infection and wheeled into the ICU.

Pam continued to pace up and down the corridor outside the ICU when she saw familiar faces from Mark's team at CBTT. His secretary, the plump woman with a tight bun, spotted Pam first. Along with her were Mark's deputy, who had made the presentation on Indian defence technology, the engineer who ran the motion-capture lab at CBTT, and the pathologist, who had performed the forensic tests on the tourniquet.

Their arrival coincided with the surgeon popping out to meet Pam. He smiled at her and advised her to stop worrying. 'We've removed the bullet and sealed the perforation,' he explained. 'But he was very lucky that you could get him here so quickly. A little delay and the complications would have been far more severe. We will need to monitor him carefully over the next few days, but I have no doubt he will make it.'

Pam exhaled. A deep sigh of relief. Inexplicably, she felt tears welling up in her eyes. She had no clue why she was crying in the face of good news.

Mark's secretary placed a hand on Pam's shoulder. Pam looked up and the lady smiled. 'Mark will be in for a long stay at the hospital,' she said. 'I suggest you go home and get some rest. The CBTT team will take turns to be here. Don't worry. Mark is family for each one of us.' Pam nodded gratefully and got up.

She was walking towards the elevators when she saw the man who had been shadowing her for the past few hours. And then the penny dropped. Although he was in plain clothes, his sombre expression, the threadbare blue blazer, slicked back hair, handlebar moustache and worn-out shoes suggested police.

'I'm Kumar from the CBI,' he said, showing his ID. The Central Bureau of Investigation. 'Technically you work for us, given you are a temporary employee of the CBI, at least on paper.'

'I thought the Delhi Police was handling the investigation,' said Pam curiously.

'They were meant to. But because the case involved a DRDO employee and a foreign national and an assassin with possible terror links, we had to take over the case. We've already placed round-the-clock security for Mr Richards at the hospital, but I need a detailed statement from you whenever you're ready.'

Ordinary mortals would have delayed the statement after such an exhausting ordeal, but not Pam. 'Now is a good time,' she said. 'Let's do it in your car.'

'Why the car?' asked Kumar.

'Because you're taking me to the crime scene,' said Pam nonchalantly. She realised she had no authority to order Kumar to take her there, so she played a different card. 'It'll be easier to tell you what happened if we are at the spot.'

Kumar smiled. He knew she was playing him, but he went along. They took the elevator to the car park and got into Kumar's unmarked SUV.

The crime scene had been cordoned off with tape, and police officers stood guard to prevent anyone from encroaching on the spot. A police photographer and crime scene examiner were already at work. Pam's car was being studied, as were the blood spills on the road. The carhop's body had already been inspected, photographed and packed off to the mortuary. Mark's car, which stood several yards away and was not part of the crime scene, was nevertheless being checked.

Kumar began making notes based on Pam's answers. *At what time did you arrive? Who decided the place to meet? Did you discuss where you were meeting on the phone? When did the shooting start? How did each of you get here?*

Pam paused when he asked about her relationship with Mark. 'It was professional,' she said briefly. 'We were working on some new technologies. Mark's company, CBTT, is partially owned by the DRDO.'

Kumar made a note but did not seem entirely convinced. He had seen her state of disarray at the hospital. It did not seem like a purely professional relationship. The forensic examiner took Pam's fingerprints for elimination as they talked.

Suddenly Pam's phone began buzzing. It was an encrypted call on the Signal app installed on her phone. The app was a free open-source software that employed end-to-end encryption of messages and calls. The call was from VTK. Kumar noticed who was calling and gestured for her to take it.

VTK seemed truly concerned about her and Mark. He suggested that Pam be placed under police protection with a couple of bodyguards on shifts, but she was emphatically against the idea.

'Give the phone to Kumar,' said VTK. Kumar spoke respectfully to the intelligence chief. RAW and CBI were not always compatible, but Kumar was appropriately deferential to VTK, the country's chief snoop.

'Yes, sir,' he said into the phone. 'We've mapped bullet trajectories. It's very possible that Ms Khurana was the intended target, but we can't be certain as yet.'

There was a pause. 'I understand, sir,' said Kumar. 'The carhop's prints match someone in the Aadhar database. The original address is shown as Nagaland. His family may have registered in order to claim financial subsidies from the government. No ID papers were on his person, though. The gun was a Chinese-made QSZ-92.' He paused as VTK spoke again.

'Sure, sir,' said Kumar finally. 'I'll check that angle too. Yes, I'm giving the phone back to her.'

Pam put some distance between herself and Kumar so that she could chat privately with VTK. He had news for her. 'After the shooting incident, there was a call from the American director of national intelligence. Had they informed me earlier, we may have taken precautions. There were several calls between Nagaland and Beijing. It's possible that you are a target for elimination. I insist that you allow me to give you security cover.'

Pam was equally adamant that she would not have bodyguards tailing her. She explained that she would be unable to do her undercover job with a security detail hovering around her.

Realising that she would not yield, VTK said that he was sending her a Glock-17 handgun. 'Your firearms licence is still valid, I presume?'

Pam said it was, just to get him off her back. Then she changed the subject. 'Is there a mole in the system? How do the Chinese know that I'm the one handling this sensitive assignment?'

There was an extra-long pause. 'Sir?' Pam wondered if the call had dropped. 'Are you there?'

'We're working on it,' replied VTK with a sigh. 'We have suspicions about someone referred to as Shengli, but at this stage we have no clue who that is. Leave it to me. Be careful what you say to Kumar.' He sounded eager to cut the line.

Pam hung up reluctantly, but her head was spinning. *Who is this mole that the Chinese call Shengli? Am I being unwise to forego security? What have I discovered that's causing discomfort to the Chinese authorities?*

Pam concluded that the informant would have to wait. Her first priority had to be getting back to Rao and finding out about superhuman engineering. How did it relate to the documents given by him earlier? Rao's explanations could help bridge the military gap on the Indo-China border.

She returned home and had a shower before talking to her mother. She put her bloodstained clothes into a shopping bag that she would junk on her way out. The last thing she needed was her mother bouncing off the walls with anxiety.

She waited for VTK's man to deliver the Glock. The moment it arrived, she locked it away in her cupboard. It would only get in the way. Carrying arms on flights was a tedious process involving lots of paperwork.

She wondered whether she ought to take the late night flight to Chennai but decided against it. Her mother would worry about her sudden change of programme. In any case, what would she achieve by reaching Chennai at an unearthly hour? It wasn't as if she could just drop in and ring Rao's doorbell in the middle of the night. She made a booking for an early morning flight.

68

I finally reached Nakaloho,[63] which lay between the river Kubha[64] and the river Yindu.[65] I was told that the Kubha derived its name from the Sanskrit word for water vessel, kumbha, which was mentioned in one of the oldest texts of the Fei Tuo[66] of the Polomenkuo.[67] Over the years, though, the local population had begun calling the region around it Kabul instead of Kubha. I was excited to be nearing the river Yindu, which was considered to be the gateway to the land of the Buddha.

While in Nakaloho, I came across many Brahmins and Jains. I even saw ascetics who worshipped a god called Shipo. They smeared their naked bodies with ash and garlanded themselves with skulls. They looked very fierce and intimidating. I also came across many Jain monks who followed the Digambara—or sky-clad—tradition of roaming the earth naked. In addition, there were white-robed non-Buddhists who called themselves Svetambaras. I felt disheartened to see that the Sakyamuni's path was yielding way to other paths. There were eighteen sects in Buddhism, and they always seemed to be quarrelling with one another.

I decided to make extensive notes on all that I saw or heard. One of the people I met told me that Yindu was much larger than I could imagine. 'How big is it?' I asked. I was told that it was around 270,000 miles along the perimeter, with the Snowy Mountains to the north and oceans along the other sides. I wondered whether I would be able to see even a fraction of it during my travels.

---

63. Nagarahara, modern-day Jalalabad in Afghanistan.

64. Kabul River in Afghanistan.

65. Indus River, which runs through Ladakh, Gilgit-Baltistan, Kashmir and Pakistan.

66. *Rig Veda*

67. Land of the Brahmins.

A trader who regularly made trips into Yindu told me that the land was politically divided into seventy kingdoms that were often at war with one another. In fact, the region that I called Yindu was not a single entity. In some texts it was called Jambudvipa, some portions were called Aryadesa and Madhyadesa, but even those terms did not apply politically. The rulers here identified themselves by the kingdoms that they ruled over, for example, Magadha, Kasmira, Andhradesa, Kosala or Dravida.

The quality of soil varied across the land, which meant that the crops grown in different parts of Yindu also varied, as did the food habits. Measurement was very precise in matters of distance and time. The idea of stitched garments was alien to the people here. They preferred wrapping themselves in flowing fabric instead. Their personal hygiene standards were high, with strict rules about bathing, washing and eating. I discovered that the people of Yindu had a caste system that divided them into four major groupings. And they lived in separate, demarcated parts of the city or village. The cities themselves were splendid, with high, broad quadrangular walls, though the thoroughfares were narrow and crowded.

I was unable to understand the language spoken by the common people. A learned Brahmin told me that the languages of Yindu were based on polysyllabic scripts. This was a far better system than the alphabets of Cina. I was hungry for more information about Yindu, so the Brahmin spent the next few days telling me about the kingdoms, their kings, laws, armies, justice, governance and traditions.

Education, it appeared, was revered in Yindu. When children were seven years of age, the great treatises of the Five Sciences were shared with them. The first science was grammar, which explained words and their usage. The second was that of the skilled professions, such as arts, crafts or astrology. The third was the science of medicine. The fourth was the science of reasoning. And the fifth was the science of self, which investigated and taught the five degrees of religious attainment and the doctrine of karma.

Just as I was about to progress on my travels, I was told that many centuries ago, the Buddha had left his shadow in a hollow known as the Shadow Grotto.[68] Most people avoided going there because of bandits and dacoits in the area. I made up my mind that I would visit. My travel companions accompanied me for part of the way, but held back as we drew closer. I could sense their fear, and I permitted them to return. I proceeded for the rest of the journey on my own.

It was late at night by the time the cave came into sight. And almost immediately, I was intercepted by bandits. Worse, they were cannibals, who saw me as their next meal. I thought furiously about how I could extricate myself from this mess. In front of me lay the entrance to the Shadow Grotto, and I suddenly realised that I had a way out.

I struck a wager with the cannibals. They could come with me to the cave and watch me pray. If my prayers made the Buddha appear, they would spare me and promise to reform. If not, I would become their breakfast.

When we reached the cave, it was pitch dark. I sat down to pray, but could feel a draft from a thin angular shaft in the rock. It was related to what I had observed earlier: a small aperture high above the entrance. I recited prayers through the night, patiently awaiting the precise moment when the sun's rays would enter the cave through the shaft. The cannibals waited impatiently, their leader often having to quell the unruly lot who wanted to immediately devour me. But the Buddha saved me. At a certain point of time in the sun's trajectory, the rays hit the angular shaft for a few minutes. This instantly illuminated a pitch-black Buddha statue inside the cave, giving it the appearance of a shadow.

The cannibals saw this miracle and fell at my feet. They repented the error of their ways and took Buddhist vows to reform, then helped me back to the city. My gamble had paid off. I hoped I would continue to have luck on my side during the rest of my trip too.

---

68. Near the village of Charar Bagh, Afghanistan.

69

Dev was in his study, the Rottweiler on the floor next to his feet. He stroked the dog's head absentmindedly as he looked at the old photographs on his desk yet again. Many of them were faded or frayed, but that didn't matter. The memories were beautiful. There was one photograph of Dev standing next to Rao with an entire class of cadets. Another showed Dev adopting a martial arts stance opposite Anu. One captured a fun moment showing Dev, Anu and Rao eating idlis while seated on the grass. Yet another showed him and Colonel Khurana soaking bamboos for strengthening into combat sticks. He looked at the photographs wistfully, a smile on his lips, then snapped back to reality when the dog barked.

'What is it, Sultan?' he asked. He knew that he should check. Sultan never barked unless there was something odd. Dev stood up and pulled on a hoodie. The winter chill demanded an extra layer. He opened one of the glass doors that separated his study from the backyard lawn and peered outside. There was nothing. False alarm. He found the crisp air rather refreshing. He left the door open, returned to his desk and sat down.

Dev stared at the photos again. His eyes moistened as he remembered how he had been compelled to write a letter stating that Rao's programme was a sham and that nothing worthwhile would emerge from it. He remembered the pained look on Rao's face when Dev had stood before the special investigation team to repeat the contents of that letter. His testimony had ensured that Rao's funding was choked and the academy was closed down. He had been the final nail in the coffin. But what option did he have? Dev's terrible gambling habit had resulted in massive debts, and those bastards had used that as leverage to get him to sing their tune. Each time he saw Anu, he only remembered how he had betrayed Rao's trust. How on earth could he ever face her again? And why would she ever accept him?

The Rottweiler sniffed the air and ran out of the room, straight into the garden. He was delighted to find company. He sniffed the puddle of urine on the ground. It was loaded with pheromones that immediately aroused his sexual instincts. He sniffed the bitch's body. The two danced around for a while in a pre-mating ritual. The Rottweiler was entirely caught up in the act of mounting the bitch when an intruder dressed entirely in black dropped over the wall and slipped quietly into Dev's study.

Dev's head was suddenly yanked back and a rope wound its way around his neck. He gasped for breath. The noose was tightened. The killer could not see Dev's face but could sense his fear.

'You never thought it would end this way, did you?' a voice whispered in his ear as Dev struggled to free himself from the grip of death. Dev brought up his hands to the garrotte and furiously tried to loosen the rope choking him, but he had no strength left. His fingers were unable to wedge themselves between the tightening rope and his neck.

He felt darkness descending. It enveloped him as he gasped for breath. 'How do you feel, Dev? Are your lungs on fire yet? Don't worry. You'll soon be unconscious and, following that, brain-dead,' the attacker whispered. 'You had the chance to remake your life, but you blew it.'

Dev went limp. The restricted blood supply to his brain and the pressure on his windpipe had taken their toll. He blacked out, but his assailant kept tightening the grip until the hyoid bone snapped. Dev's body slumped to the floor, his eyes lifeless. The killer then tied the rope to the ceiling fan and suspended Dev's body from it. A murder had just been miraculously transformed into a suicide.

The intruder left by the same route that was taken to enter. The Rottweiler remained busy humping the bitch. Love conquers all.

70

That morning had been like any other. Anu had picked up the batter, steamed idlis for breakfast and dropped in early at her father's house. She had then brewed coffee the traditional way, mixing frothy milk with the decoction obtained by percolating finely ground coffee in a filter. Father and daughter had eaten their breakfast together, sipping the coffee from little brass tumblers.

The old man read the newspaper as he ate, often harrumphing at the state of affairs in India. As always, Anu kept quiet, allowing him to ramble on.

Fifteen minutes later, they were done with breakfast. No sooner did Anu leave the dining table and start washing the dishes than she began feeling woozy. The kitchen spun around her. She grasped the countertop for support. Had it been the food? She dropped the plate she had been washing and picked up the tiffin box in which the remaining batter was kept. She attempted to smell it, but it fell from her hands, spreading messily on the floor. She picked up the plate she had been washing with her other hand, but that too crashed to the ground. She was losing motor control.

By the time she stumbled into the living room, her father was already lying comatose on the couch. The newspaper he had held in his hand lay under his head. She tried calling out to him. 'Appa … Appa …' But the words came out slurred, almost elongated.

A few seconds later, Anu slumped to the floor, her head narrowly missing the corner of the study desk.

The stocky man and his colleague, who had been keeping watch on them, followed the happenings inside the house on their phones. The Flunitrazepam, also known as Rohypnol, the date-rape drug, had done its job. They broke into the house.

The two men efficiently bound the nonagenarian's hands and legs with nylon rope and then did the same to his daughter. They were blindfolded and gagged. They remained unconscious even when lifted like sacks of potatoes and loaded into a waiting vehicle. By the time they woke, they found themselves captive in a moving SUV.

After what seemed like an interminable journey, the vehicle stopped. Rao and Anu were carried out and dumped unceremoniously on what felt like an earthen floor. Their blindfolds and gags were removed, and they saw that they were in some sort of disused shed. Rusting machinery was stacked in one corner. The roof had given way in many places. Their abductors towered over them, their hands crossed over their chests, making it clear that they had the upper hand.

Anu struggled to free herself from the ropes that bound her limbs without comprehending why she felt so weak. She had always been the strong one, the self-reliant one, the determined one. Her terrified eyes looked at her father, then darted to her abductors before taking in the surroundings. She desperately hoped that Appa was fine. Rao lay still, too groggy and muddled to respond.

Anu tried to open her mouth and scream for help. But the sound that emerged was a strangled yelp.

'Scream all you like,' said the stocky one. 'No one will hear you for miles. There's only one way you can get out of here—tell us the location we seek. You know what it is and where it is.'

71

Pam dozed intermittently on the flight from Delhi to Chennai. Her thoughts kept returning to Mark. It had not been easy seeing him in an ICU bed with all those tubes and sensors. The CBTT team were at the hospital in full force. He would be safe with them. Mark's surgeon had also confirmed he was stable. 'We simply need to allow him to rest and for the wound to heal,' he had said.

Should I be leaving Mark in this state? Pam had wondered. 'Don't worry,' Mark's secretary told her. 'I'll keep you informed on his progress.' There was a knowing look in her eyes, the sort of look that indicated that she knew something was brewing between the two of them. But it was an approving look, like that of an indulgent parent.

She found the same car and driver that had transported her earlier from the airport. The bushy-bearded driver smiled and greeted her warmly. There was something about him that felt odd. She couldn't put her finger on it. Like the last time, she caught him looking at her frequently in the rear-view mirror.

She reached Rao's house in Kanchi two hours later. She sensed that something was wrong the moment the car pulled up. For one, the main gate to the academy that was usually shut with a rusty padlock now lay wide open. The weeds below the gate had been disturbed, clearly indicating that it had been opened after a substantial interval of time. The 'No Trespassing' sign lay on the ground.

Pam cautiously followed the winding side path to Rao's cottage. She approached the house slowly, her senses alert to possible danger. The main door was ajar. *Most unlike Rao or Anu; they value their privacy.* She tiptoed inside, almost expecting to be attacked, but there was pin-drop silence. She cursed herself for having taken the early morning flight instead of the previous night's. *Maybe I could have prevented this.*

In the kitchen, she found the plate and tiffin box on the floor. She knelt down to smell the remnants of breakfast. She couldn't discern anything odd. But she knew that some drugs did not leave any traces of smell.

Near the sofa in the living room was a spool of blue nylon rope. *Were they tied up with that?* She examined the main door to see if it had been broken open. The lock had probably been picked because the door was undamaged. She looked around the living room to see if anything could have been taken, but given the haphazard mess that Rao kept his books, manuscripts and papers in, it was impossible to tell.

She stepped outside and took a quick walk around the house. She stopped near the window that looked out into the garden. There were clear treads in the soft soil leading up to it. Pam spotted something in the corner. She climbed the window ledge and touched it. *I knew it. A surveillance camera.* Someone had been watching Rao and Anu. *But why? And who?* Pam activated an app on her phone and brought her phone close to the camera. The app lit up and gently buzzed. The camera was connected to a network. Whoever had hooked it up already knew that she was inside. There was no time to waste.

She wondered how the abductors had managed to overpower Anu, who was so strong and agile.

Pam activated yet another app on her phone. She fervently hoped that Rao had retained the bronze Pallava coin on his person, the one she had bought from Sadar Bazar. Built into it was a GPS tracker that had been installed by Mark's team upon her request. The app suddenly came to life, showing a location somewhere between Kanchi and Vandavasi. She was in luck.

Google Maps indicated that she would make it within forty-six minutes if she left immediately. She quickly took a few photographs of the inside of the house, the camera and the tread marks and sent them to VTK. She would need a crime scene specialist to examine the house. Within a minute VTK messaged back on the Signal app that he would get RAW's Chennai field office to have a look and report. 'Sending police backup too—keep your live location active,' he said. 'Thank god for the GPS tracker on that coin.'

Pam explained to her driver where they needed to go. He laughed when she told him the estimated time. 'That map of yours has no clue how fast I can drive when I need to, madam,' he said as he fired up the engine. 'Fasten your seat belt and don't tell me to slow down. That's all I ask.'

72

I crossed from Nakaloho into the region known as Kantolo.[69] *This place was yet another instance of nature's bounty and was home to many flowering species and shrubs. There was always a pleasing scent in the air, and this gave the region its local name—'Gandhara', or fragrance. I wondered whether this was the 'Fragrant Land' that Prajnakara had mentioned. But most of this region was in ruins, so how could it be?*

---

69. Part of Gandhara, an ancient state in the northwest part of the Indian subcontinent; modern-day Afghanistan and Pakistan.

I made my way to Pulushapulo[70] via the Yindu Pass,[71] which was regarded as the gateway to Yindu. I was sad to see so many monasteries and stupas in a dilapidated state. The old faiths of Yindu were back in vogue, and the way of the Buddha was evidently no longer clear. This was despite the endeavours of the great king Kanishka, who had built one of the finest stupas dedicated to the Buddha in this region many hundreds of years ago.

As the story goes, the king had been out hunting when he was approached by a white hare. The hare led him to a shepherd boy, who was making a small stupa out of clay. The boy told Kanishka that the Buddha had prophesied that a great king would one day make a stupa like this one. Kanishka became a Buddhist and immediately set about constructing the glorious stupa. I looked at the ruins of the stupa with sorrow. It lay abandoned and unkempt, the result of vicious Hun attacks 200 years ago. It was 400 feet high and 185 feet wide. The original would have had a superstructure of copper discs that would have shone brightly in the sunlight.

I walked towards an old house nearby. A tablet had been set into the ground to commemorate the fact that Vasubandhu—someone whose writings I had spent years studying in Cina—used to live here. To my great disappointment, the once-inhabited towns and villages of Gandhara were almost deserted. Most of the monasteries were in ruins, overgrown with wild shrubs. There was only one functioning monastery, with around fifty Mahayana monks staying there. The ruination was attributed to the white Huns, a nomadic marauding group that left death and destruction wherever they went.

One of the most interesting things I discovered was a crop called sugar cane. The people made it into a sweet juice. Then they dried the juice and made it into hard sugar candy. I made a note

---

70. Peshawar, derived from Sanskrit 'Purushapura' or 'City of Men', in Pakistan.
71. Khyber Pass in Pakistan.

to obtain some on my return journey because I knew that Cina did not have anything similar. It would, I hoped, sweeten my meeting with Emperor Taizong.

I left the City of Men and followed the river Yindu to Udakakhanda,[72] where there were no roads, only beaten paths through deep gorges, many of them treacherous. My travel companions who had been with me from Gaochang now left me. Many of them knew they would not be welcome in these lands. Only my two disciples remained with me because they were now bound to me for life.

We trudged on and crossed several shaky bridges made of rope or iron chains over the river Supofastu.[73] Many of these were truly frightening because of the ferocious, roaring rivers below and the jagged rocks easily visible under the water.

We climbed hills that had shaky pegs for steps. It would be so easy for a man to lose his footing and plunge to his death hundreds of feet below. In the upper reaches of the river Yindu lay a monastery perched precariously on a cliff. The monks specifically requested that I do them the honour of visiting and paying my respects to a massive hundred-foot statue of Maitreya, the future Buddha, carved in wood and treated to give off a golden hue.

I made my way up to the monastery, cautiously placing my feet on the pegs that led up to the imposing structure. Unfortunately, one of the pegs was loose. I fell, and my journey would have come to an ignominious end had I not been able to hang on for dear life by grasping a peg above me. Again, I understood that Maitreya was saving me every step of the way. It was an absolute miracle that I was able to catch hold of that peg while falling. I was eventually pulled up by the monks, who sent one of their brothers down to tie a rope around my waist. I felt far more secure now and was easily able to navigate the remaining pegs without thinking about the drop to the frothing river below.

---

72. Muzaffarabad in Pakistan Occupied Kashmir.
73. Subhavastu, modern-day Swat River.

I finally crossed the river Yindu at Utokiahancha.[74] It was a massive, roaring river, and the boat that transported me seemed ready to capsize every few minutes, but I made it safely to the valley of Tachashilo.[75] Tachashilo used to be a great monastery and university several hundred years ago, but most of it had been destroyed by the Huns. I'd learned that students from all over the world used to come here to study over sixty subjects, including Sanskrit grammar, law, military science and medicine. Some of its greatest students and faculty included the Great Statesman,[76] who created the empire that Ashoka eventually ruled; the Great Linguist,[77] who established many of the rules for Sanskrit grammar; and the Father of Yindu Medicine.[78] I was sad to see Tachashilo's state of disrepair, knowing of the heights it had once commanded in prestige and excellence.

I then visited the Seat of Saints,[79] one of the very few surviving monasteries of Tachashilo, with its many Buddhas. I didn't stop there but headed to the northeast, climbing more mountains and traversing even more rope bridges to reach Kasmira through a deep gorge of the river Vitasta.[80] I was received by the maternal uncle of the king of Kasmira. He had been sent with horses to escort me.

Kasmira derived its name from Yindu's mother goddess Parvati, who had several names including Kasmira. It was now a Buddhist paradise and one of the few remaining hubs of Buddhism. This

---

74. Modern-day Hund, a small village in Swabi district of the Khyber Pakhtunkhwa Province, Pakistan.

75. Takkasila, modern-day Taxila near Rawalpindi in Punjab Province, Pakistan.

76. Chanakya, author of the *Arthashastra*.

77. Panini, author of the *Ashtadhyayi*.

78. Charaka, the father of Ayurveda.

79. Jaulian monastery in Haripur district of Khyber Pakhtunkhwa Province, Pakistan.

80. Jhelum River, which flows through northern India and eastern Pakistan.

was owing to the fact that around 500 years previously, the great monarch Kanishka had gathered 500 Buddhist scholars in Kasmira to review and consolidate the Buddhist scriptures during the fourth Buddhist council. I felt exhilarated and blessed to have reached there.

Kasmira was breathtaking in its beauty. I found myself in the midst of verdant valleys, surrounded by snow-covered mountains, babbling brooks, fragrant orchards and lush meadows. If there was a paradise on earth, it was right here.

I spent the night at Husekialo,[81] a monastery near Varahamula.[82] The name 'Varahamula' came from two words: varaha and mul, meaning 'boar' and 'molar'. The people here believed that God had manifested as a boar to defeat a demon. The boar's tooth had created an opening in the mountain, thus allowing the formation of a lake in the heart of the valley.

The next day, I travelled on elephant to Adhisthana[83] and was graciously received by the king, his ministers and over a thousand monks. The king provided me with twenty clerks to assist in translating texts that I wanted to carry back with me to Cina.

I had planned to spend just a few weeks in Kasmira, but the land was so alluring that I stayed on for two years.

73

Pam's driver got her there in thirty-two minutes—not forty-six—although it meant a hair-raising journey that included several near accidents, frequent lane changes, overtaking from the wrong side and persistent honking. As promised,

---

81. Hushkara Monastery. The village still exists as Uskar on the banks of Behat River, two miles to the southeast of Baramula.

82. Baramula town along Jhelum River, downstream from Srinagar, Kashmir, India.

83. Sri Nagara, modern-day Srinagar, Kashmir, India.

she did not complain and allowed him to do whatever he needed to. The only time she felt like admonishing him was when he caused a cyclist with a bundle of hay to lose his balance and fall to the side of the road. Throughout the trip, Pam remained in touch with VTK, whose Chennai team had already begun combing Rao's house.

They crossed many small villages and towns with names that Pam found difficult to pronounce, tongue-twisters like Ayyangarkulam, Mahajanambakkam and Thennangur. She saw people going about their daily lives—drinking coffee at the roadside stalls, setting up their wares or cleaning up. There was an ordinariness to their lives that Pam found calming after the violence she had witnessed over the past couple of days. Somewhere between Kanchi and Vadamangalam, the GPS tracker app began buzzing—a clear signal that they needed to turn off the main road. After several lefts and rights, they reached a deserted shed in the middle of what seemed like an abandoned pumpkin field.

The shed's corrugated roof was entirely rusted and had fallen through, creating gaping holes. Through these holes, the wooden beams that supported the metal sheets were visible, some of them having fallen down. The brickwork of the side walls had collapsed into heaps of rubble, and the only thing holding up the structure seemed to be temporary bamboo scaffolding. *This would be the ideal location to hold someone captive*, thought Pam. She asked her driver to stop the car some distance away and jogged forward, noticing the tyre tracks on her way. There were two sets of tracks. *Could the vehicle that brought them here have already left?*

She made her way into the shed, shoving aside some rusted metal sheets that were arranged near the entry point as barriers. She wondered whether she had been wise in leaving behind the gun VTK had sent her. She walked in cautiously, but the place seemed empty. She checked every corner and looked behind every piece of junk. She even made a quick round outside, ensuring that there was no possibility of an ambush.

She began looking for signs of Rao and Anu's presence. The clues were in plain sight. There were two clear spots on the earthen floor. There were several footprints leading up to and away from there. She bent down to examine the ground closely.

She looked at the app on her phone, which was buzzing furiously. Where was that goddamn coin? She ran her hands over the thick layer of dry mud that lined the floor and found it, half buried. The chain was broken—probably while Rao was being dumped there or lifted back up. But where was he? Where was Anu? Had they been killed? How would she track them without the GPS?

She tried calling Dev. After all, he was the one who had initially pointed her to the Kanchi academy. But his phone was either switched off or outside network coverage. Just when she was about to message him, another call flashed on her screen. It was VTK.

'I think I have an idea where they could be,' said VTK.

'Where?' asked Pam, continuing to look at the coin in her palm.

'Our agents found a letter written by the priest of a Hanuman temple that is not far from where you are. The Sanjeeviraya Hanuman temple. The priest had written to Rao asking him not to worry and telling him that his "offerings" were safe. The temple seems to be a place Rao and his daughter frequented. There could be a connection. You should get there. I'm rerouting the police backup to meet you there.'

'How do I get there?' asked Pam.

'You'll need to turn around and head back towards Kanchi on the same road. You'll see the temple just before you reach Palar Bridge. I'm sending you the coordinates, given that the GPS coin is of no use.' Pam hung up and rushed to her car, explaining the route as she got in.

Once she was settled inside, she paused. *How did VTK know that there's a GPS tracker in the coin I gave Rao? I never mentioned it to him. And how does he know that it's no longer useful?*

74

Pam was on her way to the temple when Mark's secretary called. 'He's doing fine. The doctors think they may be able to shift him out of the ICU and into a private room within a couple of days. I'll keep you informed.' Pam breathed a sigh of relief.

Her driver had been to the temple before. 'Very famous place, madam,' he said. 'Unfortunately, not too many people go there. It looks abandoned, but it is one of the nicest Hanuman temples in India. Eighty-five different forms of Hanuman on the pillars!'

Pam listened absentmindedly, but her thoughts were with Rao and Anu. She kept her fingers crossed that the father and daughter were safe. The Hanuman temple could also turn out to be a dead end. After all, they were basing their actions entirely on a letter from a priest. What if it had nothing to do with their abduction? And what were the so-called 'offerings' that Rao had left with the priest?

VTK's knowledge of her chip-enabled coin was also nagging at her. Was there a leak in Mark's team? Could the technician who installed the GPS microchip be passing on information? And could she trust VTK? He had wanted to put a security detail around her. Had that been his way of attempting to keep tabs on her?

Her mobile beeped yet again. It was an encrypted message from General Jai Thakur. 'You need to see this,' said the text. A few seconds later came another message containing a single photograph. The picture, taken with a high-definition zoom lens, showed surveillance photographs of Mark meeting with the proprietor of an antiquities shop in Janpath. It was evident that the photograph had been taken through the glass door of the shop. But there was no doubt that the person in the photo was Mark. The two men could be seen shaking hands.

'What is this about?' she texted back.

'The proprietor of the shop was kept under surveillance by the CBI on account of a smuggling racket,' replied Thakur.

'What sort of smuggling racket?'

Thakur called her. Without pleasantries, he said, 'Mostly antiquities from India, Cambodia, Thailand and Vietnam. Mark was found meeting this man. The connection only cropped up owing to the shooting incident. The CBI investigator, Kumar, noticed that the victim—Mark—looked like the man in this photo.'

'So what?' asked Pam. 'He may have just been buying something at the shop. It doesn't prove that Mark is involved in anything dodgy.' Something was niggling at her, but she did not want to acknowledge it. She forced herself to discard any doubts about Mark.

'There is some suspicion that the Chinese-origin proprietor could have links to foreign intelligence agencies. He disappeared a few days ago. Investigations show that he was booked on a flight to Seoul. Frankly, I can't be certain that there *is* a problem regarding Mark but neither can I tell you that there isn't. And that's precisely why I'm concerned. For all our sakes, be careful of him.'

'How?'

'Put some distance between you and do not share any new information with him. In any case, he's in hospital at the moment, so your absence will not be suspicious.'

He hung up. Pam was taken aback by the revelation. She knew she had to take the warning seriously. Mark had a chequered past, and she could not ignore that. *How did the shooter know where Mark and I would be that night? Was I under surveillance, or had Mark tipped someone off? Didn't the CBI say that I may have been the intended target? Could it be that Mark cosied up to me with a sinister objective?* She hated the direction her thoughts were taking.

For a moment, she felt utterly alone and helpless. She turned her attention to the driver and the road ahead. As usual, he had one eye on the road and one eye on her in the rear-view mirror.

'How far away are we?' she asked.

'Up ahead is Palar Bridge,' said the driver, slamming the brakes to avoid a cow. 'We'll see the temple before we reach the bridge. Can't miss it because it's the tallest structure in this area. We should be getting there any moment.'

75

Way above the atmosphere, a lone satellite, the RISAT-2, snapped pictures of the Indo-China border. It transmitted them in real time to a monitoring station on earth. The RISAT-2 was no ordinary satellite. The X-band Synthetic Aperture Radar on this particular machine had been obtained from Israel in return for launch services provided by India for the Israeli TecSAR. This very sophisticated aperture enabled the RISAT-2 to relay images at night and even in the most terrible weather conditions. In that sense, it was an all-weather friend.

The Indian Space Research Organisation had its Master Control Facility at Hassan in South India. Images from the RISAT-2 were only transmitted through Hassan. They then travelled through an encrypted network belonging to the Ministry of Defence to reach a control room in a building on Rajaji Marg in New Delhi. This was the Integrated Defence Staff HQ, the very same building where General Jai Thakur and his COSC had met Pam for the initial briefing after the Doklam fiasco.

Both of India's immediate concerns — Pakistan and China — had their own satellites for monitoring the borders. In fact, Pakistan's PRSS-1 had been bought from China so that it could snoop on India. China too had several satellites watching India and was way ahead in the space game. It was reported to have about 280 satellites in space compared to India's 106. The Chinese had multiple eyes and ears, not only on the ground but also in space.

The control room at Kashmir House was state-of-the-art, with large LED screens placed in a semicircular arrangement along a curved wall. Each screen offered a different feed from satellites that kept watch on India's sensitive borders with Pakistan, China, Bangladesh and Myanmar, in addition to the coastal waters shared with Sri Lanka.

In the middle of the room were ten sophisticated workstations, each equipped with encrypted phone lines used to convey important information to key defence personnel. The wall displays were visible from all the workstations. In addition, oversized monitors sat on every desk, providing close-up views of areas that individual operators wished to zoom in on. Thirty observers, ten per eight-hour shift, manned these workstations around the clock, 365 days of the year. That added up to a staggering 87,600 man hours of monitoring per year.

The Indian control room not only received, monitored and analysed the information that came in but also disseminated high-resolution imagery from the borders to help military personnel who were guarding the borders. Of special interest was the China-Pakistan Economic Corridor—or CPEC—a part of which ran through Gilgit-Baltistan in Pakistan Occupied Kashmir. Another focus was Aksai Chin, the disputed territory between India and China. The control room also kept watch over Naxal-dominated areas, or the so-called Red Corridor, for any suspicious activity.

One of the observers looked at the picture on his terminal more closely. He called one of his colleagues to have a second look. 'What are those?' he asked, pointing to the upper left quadrant of his screen. Several little rectangular and circular formations had appeared on it, as though from nowhere.

His colleague screwed up his eyes. He knew he was looking at the YaTong and Tsona sectors on the Chinese side of Doklam. But how had storage structures and a heliport emerged so suddenly? He could also discern what seemed like helicopter hangars.

'There are several semi-permanent structures that have appeared overnight,' he observed. 'Obviously to accommodate troops and equipment. Incredible. None of this was there a few days ago, except for the road constructed to the west of the Torsa River. We know the Chinese have the capacity to build overnight using advanced construction methods, but why didn't we pick up the construction activity over the last few days?'

'There is only one possibility,' said the other man. 'They've mapped out exact viewing and overfly routines of RISAT-2 and worked only during those hours when our bird was looking elsewhere.'

The two men zoomed in on the plateau. At least a hundred vehicles were on the rear slope, just a mile away from the Doklam plateau. 'Are those what I think they are?' asked the first.

The second man nodded. 'Tents under camouflage nets. And the vehicles are armoured personnel carriers. Like those used by the People's Armed Police. They are far more efficient than standard army trucks.'

No one could wish away the fact that the Indians had once again been caught napping while the Chinese advanced. The prime minister would have to be informed immediately. The problem was that they would first need to inform General Jai Thakur.

76

My entourage and I descended from the mountains of Kasmira, crossed the river Chandrabhaga[84] and entered the plains of Sakala.[85] With me were not only my two disciples but also attendants provided by the king of Kasmira. The beauty and serenity of Kasmira was now just a memory. Having spent two years in this picturesque land that was home to 5,000 Buddhist monks and more than a hundred monasteries, I was sad to leave.

My great takeaways from Kasmira were the treatises of Kanishka and the modified new system of logic built upon the old foundations of Vasubandhu and Asanga. I had also been fortunate to spend many hours discussing intellectualism and metaphysics. Kasmira had been a treat not only for the senses but also for the mind. But I knew that duty awaited.

---

84. Chenab River, one of the major rivers of the Punjab, in Pakistan and India.

85. Modern-day Sialkot, Pakistan.

We soon reached a dense forest near Sakala. The ancient invaders from Xila called this place Sagala. The king of Sakala had embraced Buddhism several hundred years ago after losing a debate to a Buddhist monk. Sakala was a major trading hub that was also beautifully planned. It had many parks, gardens and tanks. Its streets were well planned, with squares and crossroads, and the markets were bursting with expensive wares. The city was surrounded by mountains, rivers and woods. It was also well defended with ramparts, towers, walls and moats. Beautiful mansions dotted the landscape, and the streets rang to the sounds of countless horses, palanquins and elephants. But this was precisely why Sakala attracted many criminals. There were rich pickings to be had.

My little group was unaware that bandits lay in wait for us as we trod the forest path. They must have been following us since we left the city. Possibly, our attackers had seen us spending money on the wares on display in the bazaar and realised that we had possessions that were eminently worth stealing.

We had broken our journey for a short rest under the canopy of a giant banyan tree and were dozing off when we heard bloodcurdling screams. The bandits swung down at us from the tree and ambushed us. We were no match for them. Their leader was a ferocious giant of a man with red eyes and long hair, who sported a necklace of human bone fragments. 'Kill them,' he roared as his men attacked us. We ran for our lives, too scared to look back for even a moment. We reached a dried marsh, which must have originally been a lake. It was surrounded by a wall of thorny vines, and running through that barrier was impossible. We were trapped.

My men begged for their lives. 'You already have all of our possessions. You can even have our clothes,' they wailed. 'Please spare our lives.' But the bandits were in no mood to listen. They began tying two of my men to stakes as they chased down the others. At that moment, one of the younger monks in my party pulled me away, towards the eastern boundary of the marsh. I *wondered why he was nudging me there. It was only when we reached the edge that I saw what the younger man had already observed. It was a dried-out hollow that would once have been a water channel connecting the lake to other areas. My young companion pulled me into the tunnel, ignoring its stagnant, mosquito-ridden waters. We could hear the cries of our group, but we knew that we did not have the ability to go back and save them without outside help. We waded through the dark tunnel, allowing the thick sludge to envelop us almost up to our necks. We had no clue where the tunnel went. All we knew was that there would probably be an exit somewhere.*

After what seemed like a very long time, we crept out of the tunnel and into sunlight. The tunnel opened into a hamlet a mile away from the marsh. The villagers saw us emerge and were initially scared because of the thick black sludge that covered us from head to foot. They thought we were strange beasts of the jungle. Luckily, my companion was fluent in their language and explained what had happened. Almost immediately, the villagers organised a fighting contingent and accompanied us back to the marsh.

The sight that greeted us was horrific. Virtually every member of our group had been captured and tied to a stake. One of them lay dead, his skull split wide open. The others had been beaten mercilessly. The bandits seemed to be deriving great pleasure from the torment they were inflicting. Luckily, the sight enraged the villagers and they acted swiftly. They yelled chants to their gods and swooped down on the bandits, outnumbering them. The thugs were forced to flee. The villagers then took us to their hamlet where they allowed us to wash, eat and rest before going farther. Most of our possessions were also restored. The loot that the bandits had collected from earlier encounters was shared among our rescuers.

I was shaken by these events but tried my best to remain calm and detached. I journeyed onward to Chinabhukti,[86] a place which

---

86. Modern-day Firozpur in Punjab, India.

owed its name to the fact that Kanishka had kept several captured soldiers from Cina here. I was lucky to meet the monk-prince Vinitaprabha. I spent several days discussing his treatises before I made my way to Jallandhara via Tamosufana.[87] *By now the rains had set in, and I camped in Jallandhara for several months, waiting for the torrential downpour to end. No sooner had the rain abated than my group navigated thin mountain paths and shaky vine bridges to reach the fir-covered region of Kulu-to.*[88] *The name literally meant 'end of the habitable world'. It was a broad open valley formed by the river Vipasa,*[89] *surrounded by mountains, with rich vegetation, fruits and flowers. Kulu-to also had resources of valuable medicinal herbs, gold, silver, red copper and crystal. The region had twenty Mahayana monasteries and several Deva temples. I would have loved to stay on in Kulu-to, but I knew there was no time for that. So I began the journey south, along the river Yenmouna,*[90] *until I reached Motulo.*[91]

77

The Chinese man left his office on Friday afternoon and walked to the Tiananmen East subway station. He took a Line One train to Xidan, where he switched to Line Four. Six stops later, he emerged into the Beijing South railway station. He went to the counter and bought a ticket for the high-speed G475 train that would leave Beijing at 3.36 p.m. and get him to Yantai by 9.13 p.m.

Once settled into his seat, he began listening to *The Yellow River Cantata* performed by the Shanghai Symphony Orchestra. He looked out of the window, counting the

---

87. Tamasavana monastery near Jullunder.

88. Kulant Peeth, or modern-day Kulu-Manali in Himachal Pradesh, India.

89. Beas River in Punjab, India.

90. Yamuna River in North India.

91. Modern-day Mathura in Uttar Pradesh, India.

stops—Canghzhou West, Dezhou East, Jinan West, Zibo, Weifang ... Train journeys usually made him nod off, but he was too tense for that right now. He knew he had embarked on a journey that could go wrong only too easily. He looked at his fellow passengers uneasily. In China, one simply never knew who was watching whom.

His thoughts wandered to his family and his home in Shihezi. His father and mother had followed the one-child policy of the party. In those days, it was unthinkable for average citizens to disobey government rules. For his parents, it had turned out to be both a blessing and a curse. A blessing because their limited resources could just about sustain their family of three, and a curse because their son remained weak and sickly throughout his growing years and his parents lived in constant terror of losing their only child.

His mother had showered all her love and affection on the boy, but then his father had died, leaving her to fend for both of them. Mother and son had managed to get permission to relocate to Urumqi, the most prosperous town of Xinjiang Province, where she had secured a job at a garment factory. She had singlehandedly seen to it that he received the best education, often depriving herself in order to meet his needs. His brains and her untiring efforts had ensured a college scholarship. There was no one he loved more than her, and he had nightmares at the thought of anything untoward happening to her.

He sat quietly through the journey and spoke to no one. Upon reaching Yantai, the largest fishing seaport in Shandong Province, he took a taxi to Yantai South station. From there he caught a local train to the Weihai bus station, then a bus to Zhifu Island. Zhifu had once been a separate island, but sand deposits over many years had created a wide natural pathway to the island. It was now more of a peninsula. The bus dropped him off at the end of Public

Road 26 at the base of Laoye Mountain. It was the last bus for the night, and he was the only passenger on board when they reached their destination.

He sat on a bench facing the Bohai Sea and waited patiently. There was no one around. The island was a tourist attraction that brought in fishing enthusiasts interested in clams and abalones, but at this time of the year there were no tourists. He pulled up his collar and tucked his hands into the pockets of his heavy jacket to protect himself from the strong wind. Funny that he was embarking on such a momentous journey from Zhifu. China's first emperor and builder of the terracotta army, Qin Shi Huang, had travelled to the island three times while personally searching for the elixir of immortality. It was only after he failed to find the elixir that he dispatched the court magician, Xu Fu, to find it. Of course, Xu Fu had sailed away to Japan, thus avoiding the emperor's wrath. He too felt like sailing away. Maybe to a different destination, but for a similar reason.

It was sometime between eleven and midnight that he saw the five flashes of light from a boat. They were coordinated flashes—short-long-short-long-short, then a pause, then the signal was repeated. The man stood up and flashed his own flashlight, making his way to the pier as he did so.

A few minutes later, the fishing boat drew near. It was a trawler with a superstructure towards the rear. An outrigger boom on each side could haul in the catch while still maintaining a speed of eight knots. The man noticed the name painted on the side of the trawler, *FV Haesbich*. It matched the name that had been conveyed to him. The letters were faded on a peeling black background and the interiors were dirty, but to him the boat looked like a slice of heaven. The vessel was owned by Yantai Fisheries, a company that had earned a small fortune by fishing in international waters.

The ship's captain, a grubby man with crooked teeth, welcomed him on board with a handshake and a burp. After passwords had been exchanged, he walked down a narrow staircase to a bunk bed he would occupy for the 273-mile journey of thirty hours. His destination was Port Daesan, Seosan, South Korea. He looked at his watch. He had very little time. His absence would be noticed by Monday morning, if not earlier.

78

Inside the sanctum sanctorum of the Sanjeeviraya Hanuman temple, the Hanuman idol was no longer in its usual place. The priest had been forced to shift the deity to one side. Then the thugs who had brought Rao and Anu there had forced him to dig a hole under the idol's original position.

Rao and Anu watched helplessly from their crumpled positions in one corner of the sanctum sanctorum. The effect of the Rohypnol had worn off; both father and daughter were now acutely aware of what was happening around them. They couldn't move, though. Their limbs were still tied, and their abductors stood over them. One had his gun pointed at the priest, the other at Rao and Anu.

Anu had never felt so helpless. One of the men had started punching and kicking her father to get him to reveal the location, but the old man had not budged. Eventually Anu had crumbled. She had been unable to take what they were doing to her father.

'Hurry up, pandit!' said one of the kidnappers, looking at his watch. 'We don't have all day. Work faster!' The priest, who was sweating profusely, dug faster in panic. The earth beneath the idol was hard, not having been touched in a very long time. It was difficult to get the shovel in. But his efforts paid off eventually and the shovel clanged against metal.

'Get down on your hands and knees and pull it out,' said the kidnapper who had his gun pointed at him. The priest used his hands to brush away the debris that covered a metal trunk. He reached in to grasp the ornate handles on either side and pulled out the trunk with a mighty heave.

It was a bronze trunk that had turned blue-green with the build-up of a copper patina. On the lid were etchings of the Hindu trinity of Brahma, Vishnu and Shiva. The lid was held in place by an ancient latch.

'Open it,' instructed the stocky man. But in spite of his best efforts, the priest was unable to get the latch to open. It was jammed shut. After years of neglect, the components of the latch had fused together.

In no mood to wait, the man pointed his gun at the latch and shot at it. It fell apart, metal debris flying like shrapnel from the impact. The priest recoiled from the shock of the blast. Rao and Anu looked on despairingly.

The man bent and pried open the lid of the trunk with a crowbar. He gasped in excitement when he saw what lay within. On a bed of fine pebbles nestled three urns. On top of the urns lay a palm-leaf binder. On the cover page of the binder were inscribed some words in the Grantha script.

'What does it say?' asked one of the thugs.

Rao was quiet. The thug raised his gun to bring it down like a club, but the priest spoke before Rao was hurt.

'*Tacai tacainar marram majjai cuttikaripu,*' he said. 'Please don't hurt him.'

'*Muscle Tendon Change and Marrow Purification,*' translated Rao. 'In Chinese it's known as *Yu-Jin Xi-Sui*. It's the ultimate manual on human re-engineering. How a body can be given superhuman strength through a combination of herbs, diet and exercise.'

The criminals laughed gleefully. They had found exactly what their masters were looking for. They lifted the palm-leaf binder and had a quick look at the urns. They seemed intact.

Suddenly there were bloodcurdling screeches from outside. High-pitched screams, howls and guttural sounds. The goons clutched their guns tightly, ready for a possible attack from what sounded like a group of wolves.

But the attack that followed was unlike any other. Rao, Anu and the priest were left dumbfounded as tens of monkeys, almost human in size, descended upon the temple. The gunmen fired wildly at them, but the monkeys were too nimble for them. Being fired upon only made them angrier. They fell upon the kidnappers with a vengeance.

One of the monkeys stood out. He was tall, broad-shouldered and extraordinarily muscular. He was undoubtedly the best-looking and best-built among them and wore a vine like a crown around his head. He bent before Anu and cut open her ropes with a sharp stone knife. Meanwhile, his coterie was busy attacking the kidnappers. The sounds they made were deafening within the limited confines of the sanctum sanctorum.

As soon as the ropes were cut, Anu broke free, leaping into the air like a coiled spring that had been released. She knocked out one of the abductors with an uppercut to his jaw. He fell to the ground, unconscious. The other man shot at her, but she jumped into the air, avoiding the bullet, and landed a direct open-finger punch to his throat. Blood spurted from his throat as he fell to the ground, dead from Anu's knife-like finger stab. His gun clattered noisily on the metal trunk as it fell.

Anu set her father free, quickly untying the multiple knots that bound the ropes around his ankles and wrists. She turned to thank the monkey leader but there was no one there. They had left just as quickly as they had come. Anu heard voices from outside calling for her. It was Pam, accompanied by the local police reinforcements arranged by VTK.

'Are you both all right?' asked Pam anxiously. She cursed herself for not having reached them sooner.

'Don't worry about us,' replied Anu. 'Those monkeys saved us. They also saved these urns and that manuscript from getting into the wrong hands.' She pointed at the trunk.

Pam surveyed the scene: a small room with the idol obviously displaced, a gaping hole, a metal trunk, one man dead with blood pouring out from his throat and another lying dazed on the floor. Pam nodded to one of the police officers, who immediately handcuffed the man and dragged him to a waiting police vehicle. 'I will need to interrogate him later,' said Pam. 'Get his medical checks completed before I visit him in the lock-up.' The rest of the cops cordoned off the temple with a security perimeter while despatching the corpse of the second thug in another vehicle.

Pam, Rao and Anu took the trunk to the priest's quarters, assisted by Pam's driver. Pam didn't notice the silent signal that passed between him and Rao.

'I think you need to tell me everything,' Pam said to Rao gently. The priest hurried into the kitchen to brew some coffee.

Rao nodded wearily. 'So here's the story,' he began.

79

The two Shaolin masters left the secret room behind the cave and settled down in an outer chamber for *Chan Chadao*, the tea ceremony. Something as simple as making and consuming tea was often used by the monks as a path to transformation and awakening. The ceremony forced one to observe the mutual interdependence of wood, fire, water, tea, metal and earth, all perfectly balanced and in harmony. Strength—mental and physical—was an outcome of such balance. The older master addressed the questions of the younger about the urns that lay inside the secret chamber as they sipped.

'Some time in the early fifth century, a Buddhist monk named Faxian travelled to India along the Silk Road. He also spent two years in Sri Lanka. Thereafter, he returned to China, bringing with him an urn given to him by the Pallava king of South India. He called it Bamahao.'

'How did the urn reach Shaolin?' asked the junior.

'Faxian presented it to the monarch, of the later Qin dynasty. The emperor donated the urn to the White Horse temple, which was the very place where two Indian monks had first introduced Buddhism to China, several centuries earlier. Some years later, the urn was shifted from the White Horse temple to Shaolin for safekeeping.'

'But there's more than one urn. How did those come to Shaolin?'

'Sometime in the late fifth century, a Pallava prince travelled to China via the sea route from India to Sumatra, Java, Bali, then Malaysia, and entered China through Vietnam.'

'Who was he?'

'Accounts in Shaolin say he was the third son of a Brahmin king in India. His name was Bodhidharma. He was a yogi who was accomplished in the Indian martial arts known as silambam and kalaripayattu.' He struggled to get the alien words off his tongue but did a remarkably accurate job of it.

'Bodhidharma arrived in Shaolin almost thirty years after its founding in the year 495,' he continued, pausing to sip his tea. 'He claimed to intimately understand yogic concentration, what is now known as Zen Buddhism. Unfortunately the abbot, Fang Chang, denied him admission. Rather than leave, Bodhidharma retreated into this cave—the same one we are now in—and sat here for the next nine years in meditation.'

'What happened next?'

'Well, eventually the abbot was left with no option but to admit the stubborn monk. It turned out that, during his nine-year retreat, the monk had improvised a fitness routine to keep his limbs, joints and blood circulation in order. His practice included a mixture of silambam, kalaripayattu, yoga and breath-and-mind control. Once he was accepted into the Shaolin brotherhood, these exercises became routine and evolved into kung fu, which Shaolin eventually became famous for.'

'But that doesn't explain how one urn became three,' said the junior.

'Bodhidharma had brought an urn from South India. It was called Shipo. Shaolin now had two urns, Bamahao and Shipo. In addition, Bodhidharma wrote a treatise on the regimen called *Muscle Tendon Change and Marrow Purification* in his native tongue, Tamil. It was later translated into Mandarin and was called *Yu-Jin Xi-Sui*. You can see it lying near the urns inside. Bodhidharma took upon himself the task of training monks at the Shaolin temple to defend themselves and the temple from the attacks of barbarians. Thus, he inadvertently became the founder of Shaolin kung fu and the sect of the warrior monks of Shaolin.'

'What was inside those two urns?' asked the junior. They had been extracting the contents regularly for the special forces of the Buzhang, but still did not know what they were composed of.

'The two potions had to be mixed together in order to bestow strength to the recipients,' replied the senior. 'This was in addition to the specified set of routines written by Bodhidharma in the manual.'

'Which part of India was Bodhidharma from?' asked the junior.

The senior drew two characters with his fingers on the earth before them.

'What does this say?' asked the senior.

'Kang-zhi,' replied the junior.

'And you know what Kang-zhi means?' It was a rhetorical question and he did not wait for an answer. 'The land of fragrance.'

'Where is that?'

'In South India is a temple town. Because of the abundance of temple flowers and incense, it is called the land of fragrance. Its real name is Kanchipuram. Kanchi or Kang-zhi in short. This is where Bodhidharma came from.'

'Can we be certain of this?'

'More than 300 years before Bodhidharma, a Chinese prince was captured by King Kanishka and was held at a monastery in Kapisi—a city in today's Afghanistan. There, he had the opportunity to observe the special powers of the monks from Kang-zhi. The warrior monks even gifted him a sword with "Kang-zhi" engraved on it. When the prince returned home, he sent a treasure chest for the Kapisi monks who had taken good care of him while he was captive. On the chest he placed the sword that the warrior monks had gifted him. He had been unable to go there himself, but knew that another Chinese traveller may do so in the future.'

'What eventually became of Bodhidharma?'

'When he died, Bodhidharma was supposedly buried on a hill behind the Shaolin temple. He left instructions that we monks were not to use the herbal potions except in the case of an external attack that demanded a sudden burst of power. Regular use would have terrible consequences for those consuming it. And we can see now what the regular use of these potions has done to the men who are training under us.'

'What about the third urn? The broken one?'

'That was shattered during the Red Turban Rebellion in the fourteenth century. It was an uprising that targeted the ruling Yuan dynasty. Shaolin was attacked and the contents of the urn were lost. We have never been able to replace it.'

'But where did it come from?' asked the younger man, persisting with his interrogation.

The older monk smiled. 'That is yet another story.'

80

I followed the river Yenmouna into Motulo, which was a predominantly Brahmin town and cultural centre. It was home to 2,000 Buddhist monks who lived alongside the Brahmins. This city was believed to be the birthplace of Krishna, the Deva god of the people of Yindu. Buddhism was in decline, and the older Krishna worship was reasserting itself.

Not far from Motulo was a large dried-up pond beside which was a stupa. The stupa marked the spot where a monkey had offered the Buddha some honey. The Buddha had poured the honey into the lake and its water had turned sweet. The monkey was delighted, but in his frolic he fell into the water and died. Owing to his good karmic merit, he was reborn as a human. An example of the intrinsic connect between monkeys and humans.

From Motulo, I now headed towards the Fu-shui. This was one of the mightiest rivers of Yindu, and the local people worshipped it as a goddess they called Ganga. Its waters varied in colour and great waves arose in it. The river had many marvellous creatures in it, but they never injured anyone. Its water had a pleasantly sweet taste. That's why it was called 'Fu-shui' or 'the happiness waters'. Accumulated sins could be washed away by a bath in it.

My next stop was at Kanokushe.[92] It was a fabulously wealthy city and the best of wares from all over the world were traded in the market. Families with great wealth lived here, and the city was home to artificial lakes, gardens, pavilions, lofty walls and glorious mansions. Kanokushe was no less than Chang'an. It was evident that the ruler, Emperor Harsha, gave equal importance to the religion of the Devas and Buddhism, and several temples and monasteries dotted the landscape. There were a hundred monasteries and over 200 Deva temples. Whenever he was in his capital, he fed thousands of Buddhist monks and Brahmin priests daily. He had constructed hundreds of rest houses that were entirely free for travellers. He was also one of the greatest benefactors of Nalanda.

The monarch was a pious man and had stopped the slaughter of animals in his kingdom. I was unable to meet him because he was away on an extended military campaign. Apparently the slaughter of men was acceptable in his book.

---

92. Kanyakubj, modern-day Kannauj in Uttar Pradesh, India.

Harsha had not been the official heir apparent to the throne. An enemy king had murdered his elder brother and taken his sister captive. What had started out as a quest to liberate his sister and avenge his brother's death had turned into a conquest of the whole of northern Yindu.

After several months in Kanokushe, I decided to leave for the Buddha circuit. These were the four great destinations associated with the life of the Buddha: Lumbinivana,[93] the Buddha's birthplace; Urubela,[94] the place of his enlightenment; Isipatana,[95] where he preached his first sermon; and Kusavati,[96] where he died. My party of eighty set off from Ayute,[97] the capital of the solar dynasty of the ancient king Rama, on a boat on the mighty Fu-shui, a river no less incredible than the Yellow River. But before I could even reach the first location, our boat was captured by a flotilla of ten pirate boats. They surrounded us and boarded our ship. My hands and feet were bound and I was brought ashore to a deserted bank.

The pirate captain did not allow his men to beat me. He saw me as a perfect human specimen that could be sacrificed to the goddess Durga, who they believed should be propitiated with blood. They tied me to a stake and prepared for the ritual sacrifice. Just then, a storm arose. The pirates feared that Durga was expressing her anger with them for planning to sacrifice me. Instead of killing me, they fell at my feet. They freed my men and me, returned our possessions and promised to reform. The Buddha had saved me yet again. I had lost count of the number of times that Maitreya had intervened. This time, by his grace, I reached Poloyaka.[98]

---

93. Lumbini, Nepal.

94. Bodh Gaya, Bihar, India.

95. Sarnath Deer Park, Varanasi, Uttar Pradesh, India.

96. Kushinagar, Uttar Pradesh, India.

97. Ayodhya, Uttar Pradesh, India.

98. Prayaga, modern-day Allahabad, Uttar Pradesh.

Poloyaka had very few Buddhist establishments. Hundreds of Deva temples were to be found everywhere. I visited the eastern bank, which was covered with white sand. This area was known as the Grand Arena of Largesse, and it was from here that the emperor periodically donated riches from his treasury.

From Poloyaka, I travelled to Kiaoshangmi[99] through dense forests that were inhabited by wild elephants. The Hinayana monasteries here were in ruins, but the Deva temples were flourishing. The people appeared to be highly educated and cultured.

Leaving Kiaoshangmi, I travelled to Sravasti,[100] which used to be the capital of King Prasenajit during the time of the Buddha. I visited the Angulimala stupa, built by the wicked man who had killed many, cutting a finger off each corpse to string into a necklace. When Angulimala was about to kill the Buddha's mother, the Buddha took her place and eventually convinced him to repent and become a monk.

I then visited all the sites associated with the Buddha. I walked through the gardens of Lumbinivana, where he was born; I visited the site at Kapilavastu[101] where the young prince had seen the four signs—an old man, a sick person, a corpse and a monk—which had set him on his spiritual path; I sat under the four trees of Kusavati, where the Buddha breathed his last; and I meditated in the deer park of Isipatana where the master had preached his first sermon.

Urubela was barely five miles from Kashi,[102] but the contrast could not be more stark. Kashi was the City of Lights and home to over a hundred Deva temples. A giant hundred-foot statue of the Yindu god of destruction reared over the city. He was worshipped by naked, ash-smeared ascetics, who performed the most rigorous

---

99. Kausambi, modern-day Manjhanpur, Uttar Pradesh, India.
100. Modern-day Bhinga in Shravasti district of Uttar Pradesh, India.
101. Tilaurakot in the Lumbini zone of Nepal.
102. Varanasi, Uttar Pradesh, India.

of penances. Isipatana, on the other hand, was peaceful, quiet and simple. I could feel the presence of the Buddha there.

I travelled through Vaisali,[103] where Vimalakirti, a lay follower of the Buddha, had defeated Manjusri, the bodhisatva of wisdom, in debate; then Pataliputra,[104] which had been the capital of the kingdom of Ashoka. It had been gloriously described by Faxian, but none of that glory remained.

When I finally reached Urubela, I could not believe that I was in the very land where the Buddha had received enlightenment. I visited the Stupa of the Five Ascetics, the sages who had believed that the only path to truth was starvation. I prayed on the bank of the river Niranjana,[105] where the Buddha had bathed. I stopped in contemplation at the spot marking the house of two maidens who had offered the Buddha a bowl of boiled milk before his enlightenment. I circumambulated the Mahabodhi temple, where people were lighting lamps and incense and offering flowers. I bowed before the bodhi tree under which the Buddha had arrived upon the Four Noble Truths and the Eightfold Path to Salvation.

I was overcome with emotion and fell to the ground before the tree. My tears were for two completely different reasons. I was now at the very place where the Buddha had received the light of knowledge. But I felt a sense of deep regret that I had arrived in Yindu, not in the time of the Buddha, but when Buddhism was already in decline.

81

'What were those monkey-like creatures?' asked Anu excitedly.

Rao smiled but did not reply. 'Patience, child,' he gently admonished the sixty-five-year-old.

103. Tirhut division of Bihar, India.
104. Adjacent to modern-day Patna, Bihar, India.
105. Phalgu River in Bihar and Uttar Pradesh.

'I am a direct descendant of the Pallava kings who ruled over most of South India from the third to the ninth centuries,' he continued, looking at Pam. 'You knew that, right? That's why you knew that prostrating before me with a Pallava coin in your hand would establish a bond of mutual trust.'

Pam nodded sheepishly. 'Dev told me about the Pallava connection and I needed your support. I also thought that for your own safety I should keep track of you through the coin.'

'I understand. You played your cards well. But now let me explain to you how the Pallava urns of Kanchi ended up with the Chinese and are being used in modern warfare.

'We know that the first urn called Bamahao was presented to the Chinese traveller Faxian by the Pallava king Skandavarman III. Sixty years later, the second urn was taken by Bodhidharma, himself a Pallava prince, to China. Bodhidharma bartered the urn for his admittance into Shaolin nine years later. The urn was called Shipo.'

'But there are three urns in the chest we just uncovered,' argued Pam.

Rao looked at her indulgently. 'There was yet another great traveller. His name, as you know, was Xuanzang. The stated purpose of his journey to India was a desire to visit the land of the Buddha and to carry back manuscripts that could clarify misinterpretations that had crept into Chinese Buddhism. But the secret purpose was to travel to Kanchi and bring back Pishinhou, the third urn.'

'And did he succeed?'

'Xuanzang returned to China in the year 645, a full 233 years after Faxian and 170 years after Bodhidharma. In the spirit of friendship, the Pallava king Narasimhan I gifted him with a herbal potion that would assist the Chinese emperor Taizong in beating back the barbarian hordes that threatened his land. The urn containing this potion was among the various treasures that Xuanzang carried back to China. The subsequent tales and myths, such as *Journey to the West*, about Xuanzang's travels with a monkey, supported the fact that he came to be associated with "monkey strength". After all, he had brought back the third urn, whose contents could now be used in combination with the first two.'

'But what exactly are the formulations in these urns?' asked Pam. 'And if the Chinese have them, then why are they here, hidden in this temple?'

'To answer your question, we must go back to the time of the Ramayana, around 7,000 years ago. We know that in the final battle between the forces of Rama and Ravana, Rama's brother Lakshmana was grievously injured. The physician Sushena told Hanuman to go to the Drongiri Range of the Himalayas and obtain several herbs with which Lakshmana could be restored to health.'

'Yes, we've grown up listening to that myth from our parents and grandparents.'

'It's not a myth,' scoffed Rao. 'In the present-day village of Drongiri in the Uttarakhand Himalayas, there is a mountain that is revered by the locals. The village is located at an altitude of around 12,000 feet and is difficult to access. Even today the villagers have not forgiven Hanuman for defacing their mountain.'

'Is this a class in science or mythology?' asked Pam cheekily.

'The three most important herbs were vishalyakarani, santhanakarani and sanjeevani, and each was required for a different purpose,' said Rao, ignoring the jibe. 'The three herbs together had the power of the Hindu trinity of Brahma, Shiva and Vishnu. The creator, the destroyer and the preserver.

'Faxian's potion was derived from vishalyakarani, *Eupatorium Ayapana*. It is capable of increasing muscle strength and creating bone marrow, thus it is the creator potion. The Chinese called it Bamahao instead of Brahma.

'Bodhidharma's potion was derived from Santhanakarani, *Sonerila Tinnevelliensis*. It has the capacity to produce the burst of strength needed to kill one's enemy; thus, it is the destroyer potion. The Chinese called it Shipo instead of Shiva.'

'What was Xuanzang's potion for?' asked Pam.

'Have you heard of the Nessus effect?'

Pam racked her brains. She had heard the term before. And then she remembered. *The notations made by Papa in his diary! One of the scribbles had been about the Nessus effect.*

She nodded to Rao to indicate she had heard the term before.

'The name comes from Greek mythology,' said Rao. 'Heracles had shot a Hydra-poisoned arrow to kill the malicious centaur, Nessus, and had succeeded in killing him. But the infected blood of Nessus eventually found its way to Heracles through his wife, Deianeira, and it killed him too. The Nessus effect refers to the toxicity produced by what would otherwise be helpful drugs.'

'I am aware of that,' said Pam. 'But how does the Nessus effect come into play in this case?'

'When one mixes Bamahao and Shipo, one gets not only super strength and power but also toxicity,' said Rao. 'It's a side-effect of the mixture. And the only counter is a third potion derived from sanjeevani. *Selaginella Bryopeteris*, the "preserver" potion. It can fight oxidative stress in mammals seventy-eight per cent of the time due to the high content of hexoses and proteins.'

Pam remembered her father's notes. *Selaginella Bryopeteris* had been mentioned. So had oxidative stress, hexoses and proteins.

'The Chinese called it Pishinou instead of Vishnu,' continued Rao. 'It was Pishinou that had the ability to fight the toxins produced by Bamahao and Shipo, thus preserving the life of the user.'

'Why are the Chinese interested in having these three herbs?' asked Anu. She had been listening patiently to the exchange between her father and Pam.

'You need to remember that the three herbs are mentioned not only in the Ramayana but also in the Mahabharata. In the Mahabharata we are told that the Asura guru Shukracharya used them to bring back to life those Asuras who had been killed by the Devas. Combinations of these herbs had also helped an ancestor of the Pandavas, Yayati, to reverse the ageing of his body. As it happened, the Chinese emperors had long been looking for the elixir of immortality. They had sent many expeditions to find it.'

'What did the three potions combined together bring about?' asked Pam. 'A cure? Superhuman strength? Or immortality? I mean, Lakshmana was not immortal.'

'Used as a one-time remedy, the combination of Bamahao-Shipo-Pishinou is a curative drug. That's how it worked for Lakshmana. Used moderately and accompanied by appropriate exercises over a short period of time, the combination has the ability to provide incredible Hanuman-like strength. Used in infinitesimally small doses over an extended period of time, it can reverse ageing, but there is no guarantee that it can produce immortality. Medium-term and long-term usage could actually bring about a transformation in blood chromosomes.'

That's why the blood sample from the tourniquet had forty-seven chromosomes—exactly between the human forty-six and rhesus forty-eight, thought Pam.

Rao quickly made notes on a piece of paper supplied by the priest.

Curative > High dose > Only once
Strength > Moderate dose > Once daily for a month
Longevity > Infinitesimally small dose > Once daily over several years

'Sounds incredible. But how does this tie up with the monkey tribe that just saved you?' Pam asked.

'While Hanuman was on his way to Lanka with the herbs, he inadvertently dropped some of them in the thick forest between Kanchi and Sathyamangalam. The creatures that rescued us today belong to a tribe that consumes those herbs. There is a particular season when the herbs grow, and their usage is limited to that time of the year. But that's enough to bestow the strength and agility of the rhesus on those that feed on them.'

'How do you know that?' asked Pam.

'Because of your father.'

82

'My father?' asked Pam. 'He was a colonel in the army! How did he get mixed up in all this?'

Rao answered her question with one of his own. 'Did your father ever recite a weird song to you? One that sounded like gibberish?'

'Yes, often,' said Pam, wondering how Rao knew about the private joke she had enjoyed with her father.

'Did it go something like *baa-maa-ko-ki-joo-ka-lo*?'

'Yes, yes!' said Pam excitedly. 'I always thought he made it up!'

'He didn't make it up and it wasn't gibberish. Let's take a step back. Your father, Colonel Kishan Khurana, was a hero of the Indian Army. Shortly before he was deputed to Sri Lanka, he had undergone advanced combat training in the forests of South India. The army needed to ensure that their personnel were prepared for the ruthless guerrilla jungle warfare practised by the LTTE.'

'Yes, I remember my mother telling me about the tough training regimen my father underwent. I was scared just hearing about it.'

'On one particular occasion, your father got lost in the jungle. He went missing for almost a week. Where do you think he was all that time?'

'I have no clue,' said Pam, shrugging. 'My mother and I had no idea about this. If she did, she never told me.'

'He had stumbled upon an ancient tribe that lived deep in the forests between Kanchi and Sathyamangalam. They had had no contact with civilisation and had remained isolated since pre-Neolithic times. To this day, the tribe has a very simple language that consists of only seven consonants and three vowels. There's a prayer they recite regularly; it's those words that your father sang to you.'

'Why would Father reveal all this to you?' Pam asked suspiciously.

'We were both very fond of poetry,' said Rao. 'There was a club where we met regularly to enjoy each other's compositions. Your father and I would attend, but so did a third person, a doctor who was a mutual friend. In fact, your father and I got to know each other because of him.

'It was through a series of conversations that we came to know that the herbs referred to in the Pallava texts and those used by the tribe were the same.'

Pam tried to absorb all that Rao had just said. 'What else did my father tell you about the tribe?' she asked.

'He was probably the only person whom the tribe allowed into their village. Your father had a way with people. The tribe's chief was someone they called Ikoalikum, and your father became friends with him.'

'Ikoalikum?'

'The Tamil word *iko* means ego,' explained Rao. 'The other half, *alikum*, means destroyer. So Ikoalikum is "the destroyer of ego". Who else is a destroyer of the ego, Pam?'

Pam had no idea. She shrugged.

'The word Hanuman is made up of two parts. *Han* is destroyer and *maan* is ego. Thus, Hanuman is also a destroyer of the ego. Ikoalikum would have been named after Hanuman.'

'Why? After all, Hanuman only brought the herbs *to* Lakshmana. His strength wasn't derived *from* them.'

'Did you read the *Rasavinoda*, the work that I recommended to you?' asked Rao.

'Not yet. I haven't had the time. What is it?'

'It's a seventeenth-century work by the Odiya poet Dinakrishnadasa. It talks about Hanuman's qualities and the source from which those qualities were derived. Read the relevant extracts.'

'Fine, but why was Ikoalikum thus named?'

'The monkey tribe had once protected Tatacharya, the chief minister of the Vijayanagara empire, in the sixteenth century. It is possible that Ikoalikum is not a name but a title. The title was bestowed by Tatacharya on the tribal leader of that time. He probably considered the tribe to be descendants or avatars of Hanuman. In fact, he went on to build this temple in honour of Hanuman.'

'So my father collaborated with you?' asked Pam.

'Yes. Except for small samples of the three herbs and a tiny amount of the potion used by the tribe, your father was unable to get much from Ikoalikum. But when I ran tests on the potions, they matched those referenced in the ancient Pallava writings of Bodhidharma. The tribe's strength was evidence that they worked. That's when we began work on re-creating the potions and using them along with the training techniques of Bodhidharma. Those methods would have assisted in creating special military forces for India. I even gave some of our test doses to my own daughter. Hence her remarkable strength.'

'But where did you get the herbs from?'

'Good question. Obviously we could not procure them from the monkey tribe, which would not part with them. We could also not risk sourcing them from Drongiri. It would have been like looking for needles in a haystack. So we chose to multiply the samples that we had by tissue culture. It was adequate to begin our program.'

Anu spoke up. 'I'm still unable to understand why such an important initiative was shut down. It could have been a game changer for India.'

'There was someone in the power structure who was close to the Chinese,' said Rao with a hint of melancholy. 'We would have succeeded in substantially enhancing Indian military prowess had we not been shut down by the bureaucrats. It was sabotage executed at the very highest level.'

Who could it have been? wondered Pam. The knowledge that Mark had been meeting a Chinese-origin shopkeeper with possible links to foreign intelligence agencies kept preying on her mind. And that VTK had known about the GPS coin without her ever mentioning it to him. Also, if the prime minister had been so supportive of a collaboration between Rao and her father, why was the programme not revived after he became PM? *Who decided that I was needed for this investigation? Was it done to have me eliminated?*

'Did you never consider reviving the programme independently?' asked Pam.

'I knew I would be eliminated if I did,' said Rao. 'Look what happened to your father.'

'What happened to him?' asked Pam. 'Do you know?'

'That stray bullet was just too convenient. Your father was one of the most ardent and outspoken supporters of my programme, and I loved him for it. My best memories are associated with him. I removed all the photographs in my house because most of them had him in the frame. Maybe that's why…'

Pam could feel a lump in her throat. Even after so many years, the thought of her father struck deep. She quickly changed the subject. 'How did you get custody of the three urns we just pulled out?'

'The urns had been lost to history,' explained Rao. 'Yes, portions of the mixtures were shared out of generosity of spirit with Faxian, Bodhidharma and Xuanzang, but vast quantities remained with the Pallava rulers. When I looked at the ancient writings, I concluded that there were several sets of urns buried in various locations for reasons of security; this set was only one of them. Some of them were red herrings meant to mislead. Needless to say, several urns remained in the safekeeping of successive South Indian dynasties down the ages, but the primary set was in the safekeeping of the three monkeys.'

'The three monkeys?'

'I'm surprised you did not come to the same conclusion after reading the document I gave you. It contained brief travelogues of the three men who took the potions to China, relevant extracts from *Yu-Jin Xi-Sui*, which described the methods of usage and training, the possible location of the urns, and the means to overcome the Nessus effect.'

'Wait, all this was mentioned in the document you gave me? I was told that it was simply a Tamil-Mandarin version of *Journey to the West*!'

'Nonsense,' said Rao. 'Some lines from *Journey to the West* were referenced to explain the monkey connections, but that's all.'

Pam's brain was in overdrive. Why had Jaya misled her? *Is it possible that Jaya is ... a mole?*

'Since you know the language,' she said to Rao, 'how would one translate the word "jaya" into Mandarin?'

'Simple,' said Rao. 'Jaya means victory. And the word for victory in Mandarin is Shengli.'

83

Looking at the buiding that was aesthetically built into the fold of a scenic hillside in Xinjiang, it was impossible to tell that it was a re-education camp. The state, of course, preferred to call it a vocational training centre.

There was a giant, curved fascia of classical columns built on either side of the main gate. The façade gave the impression of a public library rather than a camp. But behind it were several buildings, all gleaming white and six floors high. They overlooked vegetable gardens and a parade ground. The entire complex was cordoned off by high walls, security fences, watchtowers, guard rooms and surveillance systems.

Only people in the know recognised it for the sophisticated prison it was—and they weren't telling.

At one time, there used to be several such camps located at various spots in China. But those were cruel gulag-type labour camps. These were far more refined. People weren't brought here to be worked to death. They were brought here to have their thoughts rewired. It was ideological brainwashing.

Ironically, the camp was located in Xinjiang. The region that the great traveller Xuanzang had passed through after leaving the Jade Gate of the Tang empire. Xinjiang had then been the thoroughfare of ideas along the Silk Road. Xuanzang had overcome his thirst in the desert, fended off arrows from the desert watchtowers and fought captivity at the hands of the king of Gaochang, all in his quest for the original ideas of the Buddha. All of Xinjiang had once been Buddhist, but it had been Islamicised in the eighth and ninth centuries after Turkic Muslims established political power over the region. A call for independence and terror attacks by a group calling itself the East Turkestan Islamic Movement had finally resulted in a massive Chinese clampdown.

Under the Buzhang, many camps had been consolidated into a few. It was not done out of a desire to reduce internment but to humour his boss, the president. There was also the need to keep the camps away from the public eye. Internment had been a tactic for maintaining public control during the 1950s and '60s. Massive prison farms, or prison factories, had incarcerated thousands who were deemed to be politically troublesome during the days of the Great Leap Forward and the Cultural Revolution. But the new camps were primarily aimed at containing the Uighurs, the Muslims of Xinjiang.

The clampdown was typically ruthless and efficient. More than a million Muslims were detained in re-education camps without legal process and with no avenue for seeking redress. Within the camps, inmates were forced to pledge their absolute loyalty to the Communist Party and renounce those aspects of Islam that could be viewed as fundamentalist. They were required to extol the virtues of communism and learn Mandarin, besides learning a vocational skill.

Outside the camps, the eleven million Uighurs living in Xinjiang suddenly found that even the most innocent actions such as visiting a mosque or sending text messages with Quranic verses could land them in a camp. New rules prevented them from growing long beards, wearing veils in public, fasting during Ramadan, selling halal meat, abstaining from alcohol and giving children overtly Islamic names. Ironically, hardly any Muslim nation bothered to fight for the rights of the Uighurs, while waxing eloquent about the violence and perceived injustices in Palestine, Kashmir and Bosnia. None of them had the gumption to take on the might of China.

Xinjiang itself was under constant surveillance. The region was locked into a grid with each square containing around 500 people. Each had a police station that routinely surveyed inhabitants through facial recognition cameras, fingerprinting and checking of identity cards.

Inside the camp, among several thousand others, a woman in her sixties went through the chores that had been assigned to her for the day. The alarm had gone off, as usual, at five in the morning. She had been allocated a few minutes to wash in the bathroom before dressing in the thin blue uniform that was provided to all the inmates. Breakfast was tea and a single steamed bun. For the rest of the day, she planted and tended vegetables, painted walls, cleaned toilets and washed dishes. Her free time was spent singing patriotic songs, memorising Communist Party ideology and learning Mandarin.

She looked at the cell warden warily. The warden was a taskmaster but never cruel. She had allowed her to write to her son, although the letter had to necessarily extol the virtues of the communist system. In her letter she had written, 'The dormitories are in good condition and hot water runs twenty-four hours. We have clean bathrooms, heated floors and even air-conditioning. We are provided with food, clothing, shelter and other articles of personal use. The teaching materials are free. I do not want you to worry about me because I am well. Based on my past mistakes, I could quite easily have been given a sentence of five or ten years. Instead, the authorities merely sent me for vocational training. I am lucky.' It was obvious to any neutral observer that the contents of the letter had been dictated to her.

The warden looked at the lady. 'Your letter helped,' she explained. 'I have managed to convince the authorities that you should be sent home for a week.' The lady was dumbstruck with astonishment. She had thought she would never get parole. What she did not know was that she was the unexpected beneficiary of foreign intelligence agencies infiltrating the camps.

The warden motioned the lady to one side, a blind zone for the surveillance cameras. 'You will be sent home tomorrow for a week. Return to your home in Urumqi. The next day you will receive a call from the Aksu prefecture for a routine police visit. Go to Urumqi's Diwopu International Airport to fly to Aksu as requested by the police and check in for the flight. Take a photograph of your boarding pass and send it to the Aksu police so that they know you are on the way. But do not board that flight. Exactly at that time, there is a flight to Istanbul via Astana in Kazakhstan. Board it. Visa on arrival is available at Istanbul. You will be taken care of thereafter.'

'Why are you helping me?' asked the inmate. The warden did not reply.

She wondered whether it was a trap to get her to do something that would extend her detention. Was she being tested? But she knew she had no option. Life was all about managing risks. This was one risk that she would have to take. In her mind she recited a prayer. *Allahumma inni a'udhu bika min zawali...*

84

From sixty miles away, four monks came to Urubela to escort me to Nalanda. Nalanda was a massive and fabulously wealthy university where students came from far-flung countries such as Goguryeo,[106] Daxia,[107] the Western Turkic Khaganate, Menggu,[108] Tubo[109] and, of course, my own Cina. The faculty of Nalanda had already heard of my impending arrival, hence the escort of four monks that had been sent for me. I accompanied them back to the university. As we approached, another hundred monks and a thousand lay followers joined us with banners, parasols, flowers and incense. I was overwhelmed by the warmth and affection that they showed me.

At the gates of Nalanda, a crowd of some 10,000 students and their teachers awaited me, and the ceremonial gong was sounded. I was to meet the Venerable One, Silabhadra. Silabhadra was the great master Prabhakaramitra had mentioned to me. He was the reason I had travelled so far across the world. But one could not merely present oneself to the Venerable One. There were traditions to be followed. Twenty monks taught me how to approach the great master.

Based on their training, I crawled on my hands and feet towards Silabhadra, kissed his feet and touched my head to the ground before him. 'What is your purpose?' asked Silabhadra softly.

'To learn the stages of yoga practice from you,' I replied. I could not lie to the Venerable One, so I added, 'Along the way I

---

106. Korea
107. Tokhara—parts of Afghanistan, Tajikistan and Uzbekistan.
108. Mongolia
109. Tibet

also hope to be Di San Sou Chuan.' I was surprised to see that Silabhadra was moved to tears. He told me then that he was ill with a painful ailment and had wanted to give up his earthly body. But one night, he had a dream in which he was told that a monk from Cina would come to learn under him. He had delayed his own death and now graciously accepted me as his student.

By now, I had been travelling for eight years. After meeting with the Venerable One, I was shown to my quarters, where I would stay as a guest of his nephew. The quarters were on the fourth floor of a convent built by the emperor and had a direct view of the vast grounds of Nalanda, which were covered with trees, shrubs, lotus ponds, temples and lakes. A massive brick wall surrounded the entire perimeter, thus cutting off Nalanda from the outside world. Some of the buildings here were so high that one could be looking out above the clouds.

Nalanda was exceedingly generous to me. Each day, I would receive 120 betel leaves, twenty areca nuts, twenty cardamoms, an ounce of camphor, one and a half pounds of Mahasali rice, ghee and other staples. Water clocks were used to keep track of time. The gong would sound each morning to remind monks to bathe, and thousands would descend into the ten bathing ponds of Nalanda.

The university was massive, composed of eight halls, countless temples, stupas, libraries, gardens, and 300 residential apartments. The revenue from a hundred villages was directed towards its upkeep. The students learned multiple subjects including Mahayana and Hinayana Buddhism, ancient Brahminical knowledge from the Vedas, Sanskrit grammar, logic, philosophy, law, literature, medicine, mathematics and astronomy.

I was offered the services of two servants, a palanquin and an elephant for my excursions. I made use of these facilities to visit Rajagaha,[110] which was King Bimbisara's capital during the time

---

110. Rajgriha, modern-day Rajgir in Bihar, India.

of the Buddha. Also located in the area was Vulture Peak, where the Buddha had given many sermons. I also saw the spot where the Buddha had tamed a wild elephant that had been fed wine with the intention of maddening it and causing it to trample and kill him. I was simply retracing the footsteps of Faxian, who had visited this place before me.

Over the next few years, I not only studied under Silabhadra but also perfected my logic and Sanskrit grammar. I was truly blessed to be learning Yogacara in its unadulterated form from Silabhadra, who had received it from a long chain of previous masters, including Asanga, Vasubandhu, Dignaga and Dharmapala. I also befriended a Jain soothsayer called Vajra. He was viewed suspiciously by many, but I found my discussions with him to be insightful. Vajra was well connected to many royal households, and he told me that I could count on him for assistance whenever I needed something. He also helped me figure out a riddle that had remained unanswered.

But all along, I was conscious that the second, and equally important, part of my mission remained to be fulfilled.

85

Pam was in the car on her way to Puzhal Central Prison, Chennai, where the captured man had been sent. En route, she had accessed an online translation of *Rasavinoda*. Within a few minutes she found what Rao had told her about. According to Dinakrishnadasa, the trinity of Hindu gods—Brahma, Vishnu and Shiva—had combined to take the form of Hanuman. *That's what Rao was trying to tell me all along! That the Hanuman-like strength came from three separate potions.*

And that's why her father had made notes of the Gayatri mantra, dedicated to the Trinity but ending with the mantra dedicated to Hanuman:

Om Chaturmukhaya Vidmahe
Hansa Rudraaya Dhimahi
Tanno Brahma Prachodayat

Om Narayanaya Vidmahe
Vasudevaya Dhimahi
Tanno Vishnu Prachodayat

Om Tat Purushaya Vidhmahe
Mahadevaya Dheemahe
Tanno Rudra Prachodayath.

Om Aanjaneyay Vidmahe
Maha Balaya Dheemahe
Tanno Hanuman Prachodayat

Several miles ahead of them, the police van made its way to Chennai. In the back of the vehicle was a man who was handcuffed. Around his feet were shackles. He did not seem worried about his captivity. On the contrary, he had the quiet confidence of someone who knew that his masters could get him out of any jam.

Two police jeeps, one in front and the other at the rear, accompanied the van. Instructions had come from the very top that the prisoner had to be safely conveyed to Chennai. It was meant to be a trip of an hour and forty minutes. Getting to the sub-jail in Kanchi would have been a lot quicker, but there was no arguing with the bosses.

The driver made steady progress. As the convoy reached the outskirts of Chennai, it paused at a police checkpoint in Mamallapuram. The guard on duty waved them on when he saw that the orders were from the very highest level. The driver of the van attempted to restart the vehicle, but the engine refused to respond. It was only on the third attempt that he heard the comforting sound of the old engine cranking. By then the pilot jeep in front had already crossed the checkpoint gates. The van driver depressed the clutch and moved the vehicle into first gear. He began manoeuvring through the gates.

Just then, his access was cut off by a shiny black motorbike. The driver was dressed entirely in black, including a black helmet and gloves. The biker paused briefly in front of the police van and then pulled the pin off a grenade. The driver desperately tried to jump out of the van but overstayed a fraction of a second. The grenade rolled under the van and exploded four seconds later, throwing the van and its occupants into the air.

The biker had zoomed off before the actual explosion. The blast was heard for miles. Mangled corpses lay around. By the time rescue teams arrived, they could only save two policemen, who had been some distance away. One of them had had his arm blown off while another was bleeding from shrapnel in his torso. Six men were dead, including the prisoner and the personnel in the truck and the rear pilot jeep.

Pam had been mulling over the revelation of *Rasavinoda* when she received a call from VTK. 'Bad news. There was an attack on the convoy and our prisoner is dead.'

Pam sucked in her breath sharply. *Damn!* She had been hoping she would be able to expose Jaya by interrogating the prisoner. She wondered whether she ought to share her doubts about Jaya with VTK, then remembered that he had known about the GPS coin without her having mentioned it to him.

Who is with me and who is against me? If I can't trust Mark, if I can't trust VTK, if I can't trust Jaya ... whom can I trust? That pompous and arrogant Thakur? But if Jaya is the mole, then Mark can't be, right? But what if he's working with her? How did Papa die? Who was trying to ensure that I did not interrogate the captured man?

She caught the driver staring at her again. There were paid Chinese agents everywhere. *Could he also be one? Why is he always staring at me?* She was beginning to suspect everyone.

'Forget about the prison,' she said to him. 'Take me to the airport instead.'

86

Pam felt like she was back where she had started. Life had come full circle.

They were back in the stuffy conference room of the Integrated Defence Staff HQ at Kashmir House. But this time, the participants were different. Thakur was present, but so were VTK, Rao and Anu. Sitting atop the conference table was the chest that had been dug up from the Sanjeeviraya Hanuman temple.

'Let me start by apologising to Professor Rao for the manner in which he has been treated by this country,' said Thakur. 'I am an army man who has devoted his entire life to the service of the nation, and I know how valuable your project would have been had it progressed to fruition.'

Pam was taken aback. Thakur never apologised to anybody. Even if he made a blunder, he found someone else to be the fall guy. It was quite something, to watch a man with such an inflated ego apologising.

'It's water under the bridge, General,' Rao said sadly. 'All that concerns me now is how we can protect our ancient secrets. We had knowledge and technology that was way ahead of the world in its time. Possibly even today.'

'We are fortunate that events have led to the rediscovery of this chest,' said Thakur. 'We must not lose time. We should quickly formulate our own nanabolics and get our contingent ready to ward off any threats.'

Rao shook his head in disagreement. 'These formulations should never be used casually. When Bodhidharma recommended their usage, it was with a detailed set of instructions concerning diet, exercise, meditation and precautionary procedures. The dosage also affects the outcomes. It would be dangerous to simply feed our men these mixtures, for we are not adequately prepared to deal with their adverse effects. This was the very reason we established the academy—to ensure that all necessary conditions were scrupulously met and precautions taken.'

Thakur's face flushed red. He was unused to being opposed. 'I must strongly object,' he said. 'This is no time for treading with caution. We must immediately utilise these herbs and create a viable deterrent to the Chinese, who, even as we speak, are regrouping at the border.'

Rao murmured a few more words of dissent, but they were drowned by Thakur's proclamations. Rao had dealt with the Indian establishment before and was utterly distrustful of them. He knew that they would eventually do whatever they thought they needed to. He did not put up much of a fight.

'I really do not care what anyone else thinks,' said Thakur eventually. 'My first loyalty must be to my soldiers who are at the border. We have the ability to overcome the Nessus effect by using all three elements. Let's do that immediately.'

Thakur pulled the chest towards him on the tabletop, flipped open the lid and took out one of the urns. He ripped off the ancient jar's seal, fashioned from clay and straw. He had a crazed look on his face. No one dared argue with him.

Once he had pulled off the seal, Thakur peered inside the urn. 'It's empty!' he thundered, his face turning dark red. He turned to Rao. 'Have you emptied these urns?' he demanded accusingly.

'The urns have been in the custody of your personnel ever since they were dug up,' replied Rao tersely. 'Please do not make unsubstantiated allegations. But to answer your question, we know that several sets of urns were buried in different places. Many of them were empty; they were red herrings meant to mislead potential thieves. No one knew where the real set was located except the king and his prime minister.'

'Why are we even bothered about the urns then?' asked Thakur. 'We know that the same mixture is used by the monkey tribe. Let's just snatch it from them.'

'Good luck trying to get it. They've used those potions every season over many generations. They are invincible. It's unlikely that you would be able to get them to capitulate.'

'If you knew that these urns were empty, why were you watching over them?'

'To mislead people,' said Rao simply. 'I knew I was being watched, but I didn't know who was tracking me. India's security establishment? Intelligence agencies? Foreign powers? All I knew was that I needed to throw people off the scent. In hindsight, it was a very good decision.'

'Where are the real ones?' asked Thakur. The words seemed more of a command than a question.

'The mistake people make is to think of the Pallavas as a South Indian dynasty,' said Rao to Thakur. 'What do you think, General?'

'I have no time for riddles, Professor Rao. We must find the real urns—and quickly.'

'It's not a riddle. Khamburaja, the founder of Cambodia, was a Pallava. Many years later, Bhima, the younger brother of the Pallava king Simha Vishnu, was crowned king of Cambodia. In the eighth century, a descendant of Bhima, Nandi Varman II, was brought back to Kanchi to ascend the Pallava throne.'

'What are you getting at?' asked Thakur impatiently.

'The Pallava empire and the Khmer empire were joined at the hip,' said Rao. 'Think carefully. Why was the glorious temple city of Angkor created in the first place?'

87

In Beijing, the Buzhang strutted around his office, on the speakerphone to Lee, the head of the Cambodia exploration team. He was furious. The team kept coming up with excuses. The Buzhang had a good mind to haul them back and line them up in front of a firing squad.

'I'm certain that the potions are in Angkor,' he thundered into the phone. 'Don't give me excuses, give me results!'

Lee did not attempt explaining to the Buzhang that *angkor* was the vernacular form of the word 'nokor', which was derived from the Sanskrit word *nagar*, for 'city'. It was impossible to search an entire city in the time frame that was being discussed.

'We fully understand the urgency, Buzhang,' said Lee cautiously. 'Please trust me, we haven't even slept for several nights now. There is virtually no part of the complex that has not been LiDAR-mapped. The most probable sites have been physically examined, but we're unable to find anything. Isn't it possible that our assumption is flawed? That Bamahao, Shipo and Pishinou do not lie buried here?'

'I'm certain that they are there,' said the Buzhang, barely controlling his rage. 'The only problem is that I sent a team of idiots to find them.'

Lee let the insult slide. Instead, he asked calmly, 'How can we be certain that the potions are in Angkor?'

'Shengli has shared with us a flash drive containing a document authored by Professor Rao when he was in the process of establishing his academy,' replied the Buzhang.

'And?'

'In that document he mentioned how the potions were originally dropped by Hanuman and how the Pallavas came to use them,' said the Buzhang. 'He also wrote about multiple urns being buried at various locations and how a part of these stockpiles was shared with our emperors.'

'But, Buzhang—'

'Rao talks of how Bodhidharma's *Yu-Jin Xi-Sui* treatise could be used in conjunction with the potions and how the Pishinou potion could overcome the toxicity of the first two. Most importantly, he quotes the opening lines from *Journey to the West* but makes a slight variation from the original.'

'How so?' asked Lee.

The Buzhang read from a copy of the document. '*One hundred two thousand six hundred years ago...* blah blah blah... *virile above and plus below, the three monkeys and the centre aglow.*'

The Buzhang took a deep breath.

'Those words, "*virile above and plus below, the three monkeys and the centre aglow*", were not in the original novel,' he said.

And that was when something clicked in Lee's mind. 'Those urns were never at Angkor Wat. But they were at Angkor!' he exclaimed.

'What do you mean?' barked the Buzhang.

'There are three temples near Angkor Wat and they lie in a triangle,' explained Lee, the excitement in his voice palpable. 'Phnom Bok, Phnom Bakheng and Phnom Krom. They were constructed centuries before Angkor Wat and are located on three separate hills.'

'But what is the connection of these temples to the urns?' asked the Buzhang.

'The word *Bok* means plus,' said Lee. 'And *Bakheng* means virile. *Krom* means below. The three temples were in honour of the Hindu trinity—Brahma, Shiva and Vishnu. At the apex was Bakheng while Bok and Krom constituted the base. *Virile above and plus below, the three monkeys and the centre aglow.* Given that the strength potions are derived from these three aspects of the trinity, we simply need to locate the centroid of this triangle and that's where we can find an elixir that is aglow!'

There was a sigh of relief from the Buzhang. He knew that Lee was right. Phnom Bok, Phnom Bakheng and Phnom Krom were three sandstone temples that were dedicated to the Trimurti—the three primary forces of creation, destruction and preservation. They had been built in the reign of King Jasovarnam I around the year 910. Most tourists tended to ignore this triangular gem because it was located far from the usual circuit. Also, you had to climb 633 steps to reach the top of the 673-foot-high hill to get to Phnom Bok.

'Angkor is mostly about Vishnu,' said Lee. 'But the trilogy of temples is about all three forces—Brahma, Shiva and Vishnu. It is the only part of Angkor that is dedicated to all three!'

It would have been logical for the Pallava kings to maintain their stock of potion in distant Cambodia, given that they were related to the ruling family by blood. And if there were three urns containing Bamahao, Shipo and Pishinou, where else could they be except within the confines of a temple complex worshipping all three?

88

I stayed in Nalanda for two years, studying under Silabhadra. I then sought his permission to leave for an extended tour of the rest of Yindu. He graciously granted me permission but requested that I come back to Nalanda before returning to Cina. I promised him that I would. Never did I imagine that it would take four years and 3,000 miles of travel before I returned to Nalanda.

One of the attractions of this extended tour of the Yindu peninsula was that I could visit the birthplaces of Buddhist philosophers such as Nagarjuna, the sceptic; Dharmapala, the guru of my teacher Silabhadra; and Dignaga, the logician.

During my tour, I spent time in Irana,[111] to the east of Nalanda, as well as the region that faced the eastern seas. This area consisted of dense jungles and was home to elephants, black leopards, rhinoceroses and wolves. But it was also home to ten monasteries and over 4,000 monks.

I then visited the kingdom of Gaohati.[112] I was surprised to learn that it would take only two months to reach the border of Si Chuanlu in Cina from here, but the route was treacherous owing to poisonous vapours and demons. The people of Gaohati valued jackfruit and grew these in abundance. The king, Kumara, was a Brahmin but treated both Buddhist monks and Brahmins with reverence. The people told me that the Six Kingdoms[113] lay to the east of Gaohati.

---

111. Bangladesh and the modern-day state of West Bengal, India.
112. Modern-day Assam, India, with its capital at Guwahati.
113. Modern-day Myanmar, Thailand, Cambodia and Vietnam.

On my way south, I stopped at the port of Tamrallipti,[114] from where Faxian had embarked on the journey back to Cina. The people here informed me that there was an island at the southernmost tip of Yindu called Simhala.[115] It was the land where Mahendra, the son of Emperor Ashoka, had brought Buddhism. It was said to have a temple built over a tooth of the Buddha, and I was very keen to see it. It was possible to go to Simhala by sea from Tamrallipti, but terrible weather and strong sea currents made it a hazardous journey. Instead, I was advised to follow the land route to the southernmost part of Yindu and then cross the Rocky Strip,[116] which separated Simhala from Yindu.

I took this advice and travelled south to the kingdom of Udra.[117] At the Great Seaport,[118] I imagined I could see the twinkling lights of the temple at Simhala, but I was probably mistaken because it was thousands of miles away. In Udra I came across Pushpagiri,[119] a monastery that contained one of the oldest stupas built by Emperor Ashoka. I then trekked through South Kosala,[120] the home of Nagarjuna, the founder of the Madhyamika school, which espoused the philosophy of the 'middle path' between existence and non-existence. The king here was a Kshatriya by birth but Buddhist by faith. His official patronage was reflected in the hundred monasteries that dotted the kingdom and were home to 10,000 monks.

I now headed to Andhradesa,[121] which lay between the Two Mighties.[122] This was the home of Dignaga, the author of the

114. Tamaluk, forty-one miles southwest of Kolkata, India.
115. Modern-day Sri Lanka.
116. Palk Strait, between India and Sri Lanka.
117. Modern-day Odisha, India.
118. Modern-day Puri, Odisha, India.
119. Located in the Langudi Hills in Jajpur District of Odisha, India.
120. Parts of modern-day Chattisgarh and Odisha, India.
121. Modern-day state of Andhra Pradesh, India.
122. Krishna River and Godavari River.

'Treatise on Logic' that I had studied in Kasmira. I then went on to Dhanakataka,[123] *but the monasteries here were mostly deserted. Only around twenty were still in use, and I spent the better part of a rainy season with the monks who lived in these, 3,000 or so in number. I also took the time to visit the Great Stupa*[124] *nearby, which was known for its exquisite vihara carvings.*

I proceeded to Dravida,[125] *from where I made for Kanci,*[126] *the capital of the Pallavas and a strong hub of Buddhism. Kanci seemed to be at the very height of its glory. Hundreds of Mahayana viharas and over 10,000 monks thrived in addition to hundreds of Deva temples. Among the wonders of Kanci was a hundred-foot-high stupa built by Emperor Ashoka. The people of Kanci were courageous. They held dear the principles of honesty and truth. Most of them had a reverence for learning. The city was also home to many non-Buddhists, but Buddhism did not seem to have declined in any way.*

There was a specific reason behind my desire to visit Kanci. The treasure chest I had unearthed with the monks of Kiapishi had borne a sword that was engraved with the word 'Kang-zhi'. I had assumed that it referred to Gandhara, the fragrant land. It was Vajra who suggested that the hostage prince might have been referring to Kanci, which was known as a city of flowers and incense. Certainly, the similarity in sound was remarkable. I knew that many of the learnings of the monks at Shaolin came from the great practitioner Bodhidharma, who was said to have been a prince of Kanci. My instincts told me that my position of Di San Sou Chuan would be secured only through my actions at Kanci.

I reached Kanci and was soon granted an audience with the great Pallava emperor Narasimhavarman. The king occupied a grand palace, entirely made of wood and brick, unlike the Pallava

---

123. Modern-day Vijayawada in Andhra Pradesh, India.

124. Amaravati Stupa, close to Vijayawada, Andhra Pradesh, India.

125. Modern-day Tamil Nadu, India.

126. Modern-day Kanchipuram in Tamil Nadu, India.

temples, which were made of stone. I walked through a central corridor that was flanked by massive wooden pillars that had carved lions — the Pallava insignia — at their base.

Up ahead, the king sat on a low wooden throne, bedecked in exquisite jewellery. From his ears hung cylindrical kundalas and diagonally across his chest was a thick golden band encrusted with precious stones. On his head was a narrow crown that was embellished with jewels and fresh flowers. There were jewels all over his body too — on his necklace, armlets, wristlets and girdle. He wore a long silken sash wound around the waist with a semi-circular loop in front. He radiated positive energy and dynamism.

The king was gracious and treated me with respect, but his attention was focused on defeating his arch-enemy, the Chalukya king Pulakeshin. I wondered aloud whether I might help him in some way.

A devout Buddhist happened to be staying in Kanci at the time. Manavarma, the prince of Simhala, had been exiled from his kingdom. I had several meetings with him because I was interested in visiting his land to see the Temple of the Tooth. But this was seemingly impossible now, what with the bad weather, famine and civil war in Simhala.

Manavarma and I became dear friends, and I gently suggested that he assist King Narasimhavarman in his fight against Pulakeshin. In return, the king might help Manavarma regain his throne. The idea appealed to him, and he immediately set about getting reinforcements that were personally loyal to him and could bolster the armed forces of Narasimhavarman.

The king then called me for another meeting and asked for my advice on whether he should attack Pulakeshin. I replied, 'The philosopher Lao Tzu says that weapons are instruments of ill omen; they are not the instruments of the princely man, who uses them only when he must. Peace and tranquillity are what he *prizes.' Narasimhavarman took my advice and waited.*

Not long afterwards, Pulakeshin once again attempted to seize Kanci and a battle was fought between the Pallavas and the Chalukyas. This led to a long conflict between the two kingdoms. Narasimhavarman defeated Pulakeshin in several battles, including one that was fought just twenty miles east of Kanci. He followed up that victory with an attack on the Chalukya capital, Vatapi,[127] during which Pulakeshin was killed. Emerging victorious, he was bestowed the title of Vatapikondan, or 'the one who conquered Vatapi'.

89

In Phnom Penh, the capital city of Cambodia, a Chinese visitor with a straw hat perched on his head reached the gates of the American embassy in the Sangkat Wat Phnom area. He courteously asked for the counsellor for political affairs. He was careful to conceal most of his face with the hat and sunglasses. The security guard looked at the visitor suspiciously. Given the terror threats that American diplomatic establishments faced around the world, the guards had strict orders to not allow entry to visitors who did not have an appointment.

The embassy was a simple but fairly large white-stuccoed structure on four levels surrounded by well-manicured lawns. The visitor could see the structure through the steel gates where he stood.

'I'm sorry, sir,' said the guard. 'I cannot let you in without an embassy ID or an appointment pass.'

'I may be killed if you do not allow me to meet the counsellor for political affairs,' said the visitor nervously. 'I do not need to come inside. Could you call him outside

---

127. Modern-day Badami in Karnataka, India.

to meet me?'

The guard unbuckled the walkie-talkie on his belt and spoke into it. 'There's someone at the gate to see the counsellor for political affairs,' he said. 'He has no appointment pass. He claims that his life is in danger.'

The voice at the other end spoke and the guard listened. He put away his two-way radio and told the visitor, 'The gentleman you wish to see is out on a social engagement. However, the cultural attaché is stepping outside to meet you. Please wait for a moment.'

The visitor thanked the guard and stepped aside, to stand under a tree. He took out a handkerchief from his baggy cargo pants and mopped his face. He kept his hat and sunglasses on, though.

A few minutes later, a podgy red-faced American wearing a bush shirt that was a couple of sizes too small for him walked out. 'May I help you?' he asked. 'I'm the cultural attaché to the American embassy here.'

'Thank you for coming outside,' said the visitor. 'Unfortunately, what I have to say can only be shared with the counsellor for political affairs.'

'Why him in particular?' asked the attaché.

'Because he is the official representative of the CIA here in Phnom Penh.'

The attaché was quick to respond. 'Please come inside and sit in the lobby,' he said. 'In the meantime, I'll try to reach him on the phone.'

The visitor thanked the guard on his way in as the steel gate rolled aside. He was frisked at a booth just past the gate. Then, still accompanied by the cultural attaché, he entered the embassy through a colonnade of thick brown granite. To the left of the metal and glass doors was mounted a large seal of the United States on a granite fascia.

The attaché invited him to sit on a sofa in the visitors' area and signalled to the security guard, who walked over to keep watch on this strange man who refused to take off his sunglasses and hat even when he was inside the cool interiors of the embassy.

After about forty-five minutes, the counsellor for political affairs walked in. He took off his sunglasses as he headed towards the visitor and held out his hand. The visitor got up from his chair and shook hands. 'Come to my office and we can talk,' said the counsellor, leading the way.

Once they had sat down, the visitor was offered a bottle of chilled water, which he accepted gratefully. He took off his hat and sunglasses, then wiped his face clean.

The counsellor immediately recognised him. The photograph had reached him earlier.

There was a moment's silence, a hint of hesitation before the visitor pulled out his passport from the pocket of his bush shirt and placed it on the counsellor's desk. 'My name is Lee Zhou. I'm the leader of a special Chinese expedition to Angkor. I've been in touch with Mark Richards in Delhi through his antiquities dealer. Mr Richards must already have sent you my particulars. I would be grateful if America grants me asylum.'

90

Pam, Rao and Anu left the meeting feeling dejected. It had been unpleasant and pointless to argue with General Thakur. They walked over to Pam's car and got inside. Suddenly a fourth figure opened one of the rear doors and got inside with them. 'Drive towards Hauz Khas,' commanded VTK. 'I'll explain later.'

They drove silently and parked in a quiet spot by the old

tank. VTK turned towards Rao. 'How many people knew of the so-called Nessus effect? The fact that two ancient potions could produce toxicity and have it counteracted by a third?'

'It was known to me and now to Pam and Anu because of our recent discussions,' replied Rao. 'It was also known to Pam's father, Colonel Kishan Khurana.'

'Was it mentioned anywhere else? In the hearing of anyone else? Or in the briefest correspondence with anybody?' asked VTK.

'It was mentioned once within the document I gave to Pam,' replied Rao.

'The only other person who read that document was Jaya, the head of RAW's China and Southeast Asia desk,' said VTK. 'And yet the term was just used by General Thakur while we were having that heated discussion. How did he know of it unless Jaya told him? And why would Jaya tell him? Unless they are working together?'

Pam was hesitant to talk. She wondered whether she could trust VTK. After all, he had known about the GPS chip. But she decided to take the bull by the horns.

'Jaya is the one who sent me on a wild goose chase,' she said. 'She told me that the document was merely a translation of *Journey to the West*. As it now turns out, it had lots more to offer besides a few passages from the novel.'

Pam paused. She knew she had to get her fears out of the way. 'How did *you* know that there was a GPS chip in the Pallava coin I gave Dr Rao?' she asked flatly. 'I didn't tell anyone. I certainly don't recall mentioning it to you.'

VTK looked wary. He was unsure about how much he could say in front of Rao and Anu.

'These two people have spent their lives working for India and have been punished for it by traitors,' said Pam defiantly. 'I don't think they need to give us certificates of loyalty.'

VTK nodded. 'Whatever we discuss now stays right here. The implications of a leak are not to be contemplated.'

Taking a deep breath, he said to Pam, 'You *did* tell someone about that GPS chip. You told Mark Richards. It was Mark's team at CBTT that installed the chip for you.'

'And Mark told you?' asked Pam, feeling betrayed beyond measure.

She remembered her conversation with Thakur after he sent her the photograph of Mark meeting the proprietor of the antiquities shop in Janpath. *There is some suspicion that the Chinese-origin proprietor could have links to foreign intelligence agencies. I can't be certain that there is a problem regarding Mark but neither can I tell you that there isn't. Put some distance between yourselves and do not share any new information with him.* Was there anyone left whom she could trust?

'Yes,' replied VTK emphatically. 'Mark told me. Not only that, he gave me access to the live GPS location just like he gave it to you.'

VTK looked at Pam's crestfallen face, then added, 'That should come as no surprise, given that Mark works for Mossad. And Mossad works closely with both India and America.'

Secrets were spilling out now without filters. Pam could feel the ground slipping from under her feet. 'Mossad?' she asked.

'Indian and Israeli intelligence have been working together for years,' said VTK. 'Why do you think Mark was hired by CBTT's parent AXTech, a company headquartered in Tel Aviv? And why is CBTT a joint venture with the Indian government? It is a subtle transfer of high technology from Israel to India. Why did Mark's company try to hire Dr Rao in the past? For the very same reason. Even in the days when India and Israel did not have official ties, Mossad and RAW were working together. In fact, one of my earliest training stints was in Tel Aviv.'

'I thought that before Mark moved to the corporate world, he was with the US Marines and then the CIA,' said Pam weakly.

'He was. When he was with the CIA, he spent some time as a young operative in Thailand. Unfortunately, the Khmer Rouge, which had just been driven out of Cambodia, had established themselves in the jungles of Thailand. The Americans were publicly denouncing the Khmer Rouge but privately assisting them, albeit warily. Mark was involved in infiltrating the Thailand branch of the Khmer Rouge to keep the agency posted. When they found that Mark was an infiltrator, he was captured and tortured at one of their camps. It was a Mossad operative who pulled him out. Mark owes Mossad his life.'

Pam struggled to absorb all the information now swimming inside her head. She decided she would have to take her chances with VTK.

'Do you know that the names Jaya and Shengli mean the same thing—victory?' she asked.

VTK's expression was a sight to behold. Pam could not tell whether it was a reaction to this new information or whether it was self-loathing for not having made the connection himself.

'All this while, she's been right under my nose,' he said, his voice barely above a whisper. 'Why did I not see such a simple connection?'

'She was very clever,' said Pam. 'She asked me not to reveal the contents of Rao's document to anyone as she wanted to check that there were no hidden codes. Actually, all that she wanted was for the document to reach Chinese hands first and to ensure that no one else would contradict her explanation to me.' Pam paused in thought, then asked, 'Who is this Chinese-origin shopkeeper whom Mark met?'

'A smuggler. He usually smuggles antiquities but sometimes also smuggles people. His contacts in countries like Cambodia, Vietnam, Thailand and much of Asia are very strong. And because of his value to the agencies, no one ever bothers raiding his store to curb his smuggling. Mark engaged him because we needed to safely move three Chinese nationals.'

'Who?' asked Pam.

'I shouldn't be telling you any of this. But I guess today we'll have to break some rules so that we can actually sort out the mess we're in. The most recent person we needed smuggled out was Erkin Chong, the head of China's ADAM and EVE projects.'

'A defection?' asked Pam.

VTK nodded. 'Erkin is a Muslim Uighur from Xinjiang. The man is an absolute genius and, in spite of all the odds, won scholarships to finish a master's and then a doctoral programme at Stanford. He would have never gone back to China except for the leverage that the Buzhang had on him.'

'What leverage?' asked Pam.

'His mother was put into a re-education camp. Erkin is a key component in China's twin strategies of human engineering and artificial intelligence. When the CIA's network in China was destroyed by the Chinese MSS, Erkin was recruited through Mossad. Ironic that a Muslim's strings were being pulled by Jews!'

'Where is Erkin now?' asked Pam.

'He's just been smuggled out via South Korea to a Mossad–CIA safe house in London. He'll soon be transferred to the US.'

'And the other two?' asked Pam.

'We had to get Erkin's mother out of the re-education camp she was being held at. Without that assurance, he was unwilling to budge. We've succeeded in that endeavour too.

'The last is Lee Zhou, the Chinese head of the Angkor Wat exploration mission. We weren't sure what his team would discover. As it turned out, they found nothing. But we couldn't take a chance. Our soldiers were dying and we had to figure out a way to improve the odds. As we saw it, there were only three ways to do that. One, put a spoke in China's scientific research. Two, play spoilsport in Angkor. Three, find the potions in India and use them for Indian soldiers. We worked on all three possibilities.'

The pieces of the puzzle were coming together in Pam's mind. 'That day, when the shooting occurred, I was suspicious of Mark because the CBI team told me that the bullet trajectories indicated I was the intended target. I wondered whether Mark had supplied the shooter with the location of the eatery where we met.'

'That's nonsense,' said VTK. 'Thakur was operating his own informal intelligence network. He did not trust me or RAW to keep him fully informed. What was conveyed to you was CBI misinformation—at the behest of Thakur and through Kumar—to get you to mistrust Mark.'

VTK paused. 'The Leninist Liberation League were not going after you,' he said. 'In fact, the Chinese were hoping you would discover the urns. That's why they had you, Dr Rao and Anu under constant surveillance. The Buzhang wanted Mark—not you—eliminated because with him gone, China's secrets would be safer.'

Pam remained quiet as she digested that last bit of information.

'Do you know who ensured that you were assigned this case?' asked VTK.

'General Thakur was the one who called me into the COSC deliberations initially,' replied Pam.

'He was simply following instructions from the prime minister. Thakur was not keen on assigning the case to you. It was the PM, through me, who ensured that your name was put forward by the army chief at the COSC meeting.'

'But why would the PM need me?'

'Because you are Colonel Kishan Khurana's daughter. He knew that if there was anyone he could trust to draw out the Chinese sympathisers in India and yet bring Dr Rao around, it would be you.'

Rao smiled at Pam. 'The PM's hunch was right. I would never have shared information with anyone else. Your father is—was—like a brother to me. Had both of us been allowed to proceed as planned, the Indian Special Forces would have been the envy of the world. In fact, I even gave you the original location of the urns—my three monkeys called Bok, Bakheng and Krom. *Virile above and plus below, the three monkeys and the centre aglow.*'

'I was just too dense to see it,' said Pam. 'Even Jaya alluded to the possibility of deeper meanings in your text. Stupid of me to ignore her.'

'It was to prevent enemies from knowing the original location,' said Rao. 'I was following in the footsteps of Wu Cheng-en. By bringing the monkey character into *Journey to the West*, he too was alluding to the fact that Xuanzang had something that could give him monkey-like strength. Possibly that was the reason the book was written under a pseudonym. It was a way of keeping others, especially those perceived as enemies, from finding out more.'

'India does not need enemies from outside,' said Pam. 'There are enough within. Like Jaya.'

'And Thakur,' said VTK. 'Only someone with his seniority could have sabotaged Rao's programme. And he was intelligent enough to always keep an anti-China profile. Even now, he only wanted those urns so that he could eventually use them for the Chinese, not for our Indian soldiers.'

'But how do we save our soldiers from another attack if there is no potion?' asked Pam.

'No need for that,' replied VTK. 'Erik Chong's debriefing has begun in London. The Chinese only have two of the potions, not the third, so the EVE programme is going nowhere. The men who are consuming the existing mixture are dying from the Nessus effect that we just discussed. In any case, the Chinese are least interested in holding the barren territory they captured. They're treating India as a playground for testing their global capabilities.'

'They also have robots from the ADAM programme,' countered Pam.

'That programme is in a mess,' said VTK. 'Too many bugs. Selective misleading press leaks are declaring great success in the programme, but that's a move by the Buzhang to counter the Chinese president. The two men have serious ideological differences. That in itself is sufficient deterrence.'

91

When Pam visited Mark in the hospital, he had been shifted from the ICU to a private room. She crossed the corridor and met the CBTT personnel who had taken turns keeping vigil over him while he recuperated. She thanked them profusely and even hugged Mark's secretary, who was a little taken aback by her exuberance. Pam then opened the door and walked into Mark's room.

A nurse was checking the flow of Mark's IV line. Pam and he stared at each other in silence until the nurse finished her work and left the room.

As she stood there looking at him, she recalled the words of the great philosopher Khalil Gibran, that a river could only get over its fear by entering the ocean. The moment it entered the ocean, it would realise that the experience wasn't about merging *into* the ocean but *becoming* the ocean. Pam wondered if she was ready to be that river. After an extended silence, she spoke. 'Were you snitching on me?' she asked softly.

Mark nodded his head. 'Not to the Chinese, only to Mossad and VTK.'

'Why?'

'Ever since my terrible experience in Thailand, where I was tortured, then saved by Mossad, I've been leading many of Mossad's projects. Israel has strong military ties to China, but they feel emotionally connected to India because both are democracies that are fighting Islamic radicalism. One of my objectives has been to tip the Indo-China power balance in favour of India. I needed you to draw out Rao. In parallel, I needed to ensure that your discoveries would not reach the Chinese. I was unsuccessful because of Jaya, but ...'

'But?'

'The Chinese do not have Pishinou,' said Mark. 'Plus we've ensured that Erkin Chong and his mother are out of their clutches. We've also managed to pull out Lee Zhou, and he assures us that no potions were found in Angkor.'

'You destroyed my trust in you, Mark,' said Pam. She saw the sadness in his eyes. 'And how is it that you seem to know the latest happenings in the case?'

'I was also attempting to protect you, Pam. You're too proud to accept anyone's help. It was easier to protect you by stealth.'

'I don't want your favours!' she shot back. The only one who could affect her like this was Mark. 'Why do you think I owe *you* any gratitude?'

'You don't. VTK must have had his reasons for wanting me to look out for you. When you suddenly called me for assistance in your investigation, I took it upon myself to keep you under a protective umbrella. At times you felt you were being watched. You were. Not only by Thakur and Jaya's thugs, but also by my operatives.'

'How did that help?'

'Dev was killed by Jaya. The thugs who kidnapped Rao and Anu were Jaya's men. The thug who died in a truck explosion was killed by his own master, Jaya. But you're safe. That must count for something.'

Dev is dead? There was a part of her that felt responsible for his death.

Deep in thought, she got up to leave.

'I love you, Pam,' Mark said weakly as she walked to the door.

She paused. Every fibre of her being wanted to turn back and love him for the rest of her life.

'I love you too, Mark,' she said as she opened the door and walked out. 'It's just that I'm not sure I can trust you.'

92

'You have been a friend to me and to the Pallava kingdom,' said Narasimhavarman. 'Ask for whatever you want and it is yours.'

'I have only two requests, O king,' I said as I stood before him. 'One, your victory was made possible by the support of Manavarma. Please help him win back his kingdom.'

'It shall be done,' said Narasimhavarman. I was later to learn that he launched two attacks on Simhala; the second was successful in reinstating Manavarma as king.

'And what is your second request, O wise one?' asked the king.

'My emperor, Taizong, devotes his energies to repelling the attacks of barbarian Turks from the north, but we need your help.'

'How?'

'We have two elements of the elixir, Bamahao and Shipo, brought to us by Faxian and Bodhidharma. But the third, Pishinou, is missing,' I explained. 'If you would share an urn of the third element with me, it could help the emperor stabilise the kingdom.'

Narasimhavarman thought about it for a moment and then said, 'One day in the future, my descendants will look back and call me a fool for having done what I'm about to do. But the relationship between Narasimhavarman and Taizong should be one of cooperation and friendship, not enmity and mistrust. Both our empires are great in their own ways. You have earned the vessel, O monk. You shall have the potion in the spirit of friendship with the Pallavas. Make sure that it is used wisely.'

I thanked the king profusely. Now that I had the thing I had sought so long, I was free to finish the rest of my travels in Yindu with a light heart. From Kanci, I made my way north along Konkanapura[128] to a seaport called Kshaharatapuri[129] on the western coast of Yindu. From there, I toured the region known as Maharashtra.[130] I visited the glorious Buddha rock-cut temples of Vakataka[131] and then Moholo,[132] the home of the Sanskrit

---

128. India's western coastline.
129. Modern-day Mumbai in Maharashtra, India.
130. Modern-day Maharashtra, India.
131. Ajanta Caves in Aurangabad, Maharashtra, India.
132. Malwa region of Madhya Pradesh, India.

bard[133] who was renowned in India. Travelling northwest, I reached Bharukaccha[134] in the peninsula of Valabhi,[135] where the merchants traded gold, silver, copper, rare pearls, silks and carpets with the Land of the Western Women.[136] I then made my way back to Nalanda.

Silabhadra was delighted to see me. I spent the next two months studying with a monk who was considered an expert in grammar and logic. Afterwards, I studied under Jayasena, an eccentric who excelled at the esoteric meanings within Buddhist texts. Subsequently, I was offered a post of part-time lecturer and researcher at Nalanda, but I refused because I knew that getting back to Cina with the potion was a very high priority.

One night I had a terrible dream in which I saw Nalanda laid waste and fires roaring through the buildings. I awoke bathed in sweat. I began to wonder how I would get back to Cina with all the material that I had collected and, most importantly, the urn meant for Shaolin.

In the morning, I called upon my Jain soothsayer friend, Vajra. He told me not to worry. He would use his connections to get Emperor Harsha and King Kumara to help me. I did not know either monarch personally and had never even been introduced to them. I wondered how Vajra would manage this.

I was taken aback when, soon afterwards, King Kumara of Gaohati invited me to his kingdom. I had been to Gaohati before on my journey to South Yindu but had not met him during that trip. This was now an official invitation. Even though the king was of the old faith, he treated me with immense care and respect. I was made most comfortable in the capital city for over two months.

My visit was cut short by a message from Emperor Harsha. He had just returned from an extended campaign and had heard

---

133. Poet Kalidasa, who lived in Ujjain in the fourth or fifth century.
134. Modern-day Bharuch in Gujarat, India.
135. Modern-day Gujarat, India.
136. Hormuz Island, Iran.

that I was with the king of Gaohati. He ordered that I be sent to him immediately. King Kumara was a vassal of Harsha, so he organised an elaborate flotilla of boats and personally escorted me to Poloyaka, called Prayaga by its residents. Harsha was in the midst of the Kumbh Mela, a pilgrimage that drew people from far and near, to take a dip in the waters of Fu-shui.

The emperor met me at midnight, accompanied by hundreds of men holding flaming torches and several others who beat golden drums synchronised with the emperor's footsteps. He had invited thousands to a festival in which he gave away all his possessions with the exception of his war horses, elephants and military stores. The emperor walked over to me, bowed low before me, scattered flowers at my feet and recited several verses penned by him in my praise. Such was the affection and respect heaped by the monarch on me.

Some weeks later, Emperor Harsha and King Kumara organised a great debate, which was attended by the kings of eighteen vassal kingdoms, 3,000 Buddhist monks and 3,000 Yindu and Jain scholars and priests. Emperor Harsha provided a sumptuous banquet and gave costly gifts to each of the invitees. My friend Vajra was suitably rewarded for having brought me to the courts of the two monarchs.

Harsha performed a fine balancing act in matters of faith. He performed the rituals of sun worship every day and participated in daily prayers to Shipo while also supporting many Buddhist endeavours.

Harsha asked me many probing questions about Cina. I like to think I played an important role in ensuring sound diplomatic relations between him and Emperor Taizong.

93

It was six in the morning when they rang the doorbell. Thakur was still in his pyjamas. As soon as his orderly opened the door, a dozen commandos stormed into the house.

'What is the meaning of this?' he sputtered. Tea spilled from his cup and his cigarette fell into the puddle. His face had turned puce. Thakur was entirely unused to being at the receiving end of such action.

'You need to come with us, sir,' said the leader of the commandos.

'Upon whose instructions?' Thakur demanded to know.

The commander looked coolly at him. 'Upon the instructions of the prime minister. He wants to know why you've been screwing the nation besides screwing your old flame.'

'I'll have you shot for speaking to me like that,' said Thakur, but by now his arrogance was fast dissipating.

Thakur was allowed to change under the watchful eyes of the commander. He then got into the waiting car. He sat between two officers like a common criminal.

As the car shifted into gear, Thakur was transported back to 1962. The India-China war was playing out in the Karakoram mountains, some 14,000 feet above sea-level. The cause was the disputed region of Aksai Chin. India averred that it was part of Kashmir, but China claimed that it was part of Xinjiang. The trigger was the Dalai Lama's flight from Tibet to India, where Prime Minister Nehru granted him sanctuary.

War broke out. India was hopelessly unprepared. The war lasted only a month, but 1,383 Indian soldiers and 722 Chinese soldiers died. Thousands were wounded. As many as 3,900 Indian soldiers were captured and imprisoned by the Chinese. And what did it get India? Absolutely nothing. China took over Aksai Chin. Had it not been for the threat of American intervention, a ceasefire would have been impossible.

Thakur was a young soldier aged twenty-three when he was captured. He and many others were held at a POW camp near Chongye monastery in Tibet.

The Chinese officers used both threat and persuasion to break the loyalty of the Indian soldiers. Thakur was kept in solitary confinement in a small, cold cubbyhole of a room and made to listen to Radio Peking broadcasts to the exclusion of everything else. And his only reading material was Chinese communist literature. But there was food on time, even though it was always rice and radish. And he had to be thankful for the clothes on his back. Each day, his Chinese supervisors would explain to him why China's government and its policies were far better than those of India.

Gradually, his captors increased the number and kind of favours—a cigarette, hot water for a bath, a square of candy. But each of these little favours was accompanied by a two-hour interview in which he was asked to recap how badly prepared India had been for the war. Indian soldiers were wearing gym shoes at 15,000 feet. They had run out of artillery, ammunition, equipment and food. Prime Minister Nehru had refused to use the Indian Air Force without offering any explanation. Equations between senior commanders of the Indian armed forces had been poor, and this had led to petty politics when the focus should have been on winning the war. Nehru had repeatedly ignored warnings and remained in an echo chamber that had him persuaded that India and China were brothers, not foes.

Gradually, Thakur had begun to see things differently from the young and naïve soldier who had been sent to fight an unwinnable war. Each day, his captors would tell him about the glories of communist China and Mao. By the time he was released in 1963, Thakur sympathised with the Chinese cause. His views on the India–China relationship also underwent a change. He believed the

Indian government had mishandled the border issue with China and was convinced that the Chinese would never have fought a war with India if India had handled the situation better.

But the Chinese also taught Thakur something very important: to never reveal his true feelings to anyone. One of his mentors there often reminded him, 'The man who waxes on about loving his wife usually loves his mistress more, and the one who fights against homosexuality would never do so in front of his secret male lover.' Thakur would be of no value to them if his intentions were suspect. He would be their man in India in private but would have to take an anti-China stance in public. That was the only way he could assist the communist cause.

Thakur eventually made it safely back to Delhi. Not as a war hero, but as one among several brave soldiers who had done their best in spite of bungling by their political masters. He followed the advice of his Chinese masters to the letter, warning successive administrations about the Chinese threat, predicting the bonhomie between Pakistan and China and making public statements about the need for Indian preparedness.

His tongue spoke for India but his heart beat for China.

94

Jaya hummed as she took her morning walk in Lodhi Gardens. It was a ritual that never varied. If she was travelling, the location would change, but her morning routine would not. It was her hour of solitude before the hustle and bustle of the day commenced.

On most days she would walk alone. Familiar faces only nodded to her as they passed by, knowing full well that she preferred not to engage in conversation. Plus, there was a Doberman bitch on leash with her. The bitch, brought into heat with drugs, had proved useful in distracting the Rottweiler while eliminating Dev.

Her routine was fixed. Wake up at six in the morning and have a mug of tea. Do yoga for an hour before setting off for an hour's walk. Return home and spend the next two hours devouring newspapers from around the country while smoking her first few non-filter Camel cigarettes of the day. She remained fit owing to her routine, fit enough to drive a motorbike while casually tossing a grenade in the required direction.

Thirty minutes into her walk, she was intercepted by two burly plainclothes officers. 'You're required to come with us, ma'am,' one of them said. 'Please don't make a fuss; the area is swarming with our men.'

'Who are you?' she asked, but she already knew the answer.

They walked up to the ubiquitous red Maruti parked just outside the gates. She got inside willingly, a prayer on her lips, her hands clasping the locket around her neck. Anyone who knew her would have found her actions odd because Jaya was an avowed atheist. Her father had been passionately devoted to Ma Durga, but all that it had got him was an early death from cancer. The years she had spent in JNU had only reinforced Jaya's belief that God was merely an excuse for the lazy and a tool for the astute. Her years in intelligence had exposed her to the world's disgusting underbelly, which had been the final nail in the coffin of faith.

Seated in the stuffy car, Jaya's head spun with beautiful memories. She had been a student at JNU pursuing a master's degree at the School of Language, Literature and Culture Studies. By then Thakur had moved up the ranks in the defence establishment and was rapidly emerging as a prime candidate for army chief. He was invited to give a lecture at JNU about India's defence strategy. One of the young ladies seated in the first row had been the starry-eyed Jaya, who thought that idealism could win any battle.

By then, JNU was already known as a bastion of Marxists. Political life in the university was intense, and it was impossible to graduate without deep-seated beliefs in one kind of politics or another. Jaya was no exception. She had approached Thakur hesitantly after the lecture to get his autograph, which had led to an innocent cup of coffee at a nearby restaurant.

Thakur was already married but had found himself falling in love with a woman more than twenty years his junior. They began spending their evenings at the unused guest house of one of Thakur's friends, reading Mao, Lenin, Marx and Engels. The nights were just as memorable.

And then Thakur's wife had found out about their affair. She threatened to go public and thus destroy any career prospects he had within the government. Thakur had quietly informed his friends in Beijing. Miraculously, Thakur's wife was killed the next day in a road accident. Jaya attended the funeral, weeping and providing solace to Thakur. They were now a team that could not be prised apart; their relationship had been sealed with a blood sacrifice. They met regularly at Lal Kot to share information, away from prying eyes. Sometimes they made love in the car.

Jaya had been initiated by Thakur into the select group that would spend the next few decades passing on India's secrets to the Chinese. It was not only a profitable profession—risky, perhaps—but also promised the potential reward of India going the communist way. Jaya's needs were simple and financial incentive mattered little. It was idealism that had always been her guiding light. Meanwhile, Thakur had become senior enough within the defence establishment to create roadblocks for the Indian military whenever required.

Jaya muttered a prayer under her breath, her voice rising and falling, and she kissed the locket around her neck fervently, over and over again. Suddenly, she bit into the locket, a sealed glass ampoule between thin metal sheets. The ampoule released a concentrated solution of potassium cyanide into her mouth. By the time the officers managed to get her to a hospital, she was dead.

Long live the revolution.

95

The Buzhang slept late that morning. The official reception hosted by him in honour of the visiting army chief of Pakistan had run late. The Buzhang knew that Pakistan was unimportant in and by itself. It would only become important if it turned into an infection that would fester and eventually kill India.

He was unaware that in the wee hours of the morning, a secret meeting had taken place at Zhongnanhai. It included the president, the premier, as well as key members of the state council. An aide to the president had shared photographs of the special ward at the hospital in Dengfeng County, Henan. They were depressing pictures of rows of steel-framed beds containing frail old men wearing striped hospital gowns. They looked like they were waiting to die.

It had taken a very delicate operation to pierce the secret ward at the hospital and take photographs using a camera fitted into a doctor's pen. The Buzhang controlled the space zealously, and the doctor would have been killed if his activities had ever been discovered.

The aide played video footage from the research lab in Beijing. The oversized bolts at the research centre had done their job of recording and documenting activities.

The footage showed a robot abruptly stopping its routine and going crazy, as though it was having a tantrum. The men in the conference room watched as it slammed the wall with its fists and tried to kick open the electronic door.

'I asked him to stop the experiments,' said the president. 'I even asked him to shut down the re-education camps. But he doesn't listen. The results are here for everyone to see. We have over 2,000 young men who are on the verge of death owing to the ancient potions fed to them by the Buzhang's scientific team. We have millions of Muslims in camps and we're finding it impossible to explain to the rest of the world what can possibly justify detentions on such a large scale. Frankly, I'm tired of his ways.'

The president looked at the men seated at the table. They included three Buzhang loyalists, but no one spoke in his favour. Last night, each of them had been shown their own intelligence dossiers, three files that had been painstakingly researched and put together by the president's aides. The first had made millions on a construction project; the second was into hurting women during his frequent S&M sessions; and the third's carelessness had caused thousands of job losses owing to his misplaced loyalty to a Chinese billionaire. All three knew that the price of survival was throwing in their lot with the president, who had promised to overlook their mistakes. At their meeting with the president, each of them had had a version of Roosevelt's famous quip quoted to them: 'If you've got them by the balls, their hearts and minds will follow.'

The president sighed. 'The relationship between China and India has been a complicated one, no doubt. But we should not forget the amazing cross-pollination of ideas between the two regions from ancient times. Faxian, Bodhidharma and Xuanzang showed how much value we are capable of adding to each other. Had it not been for bungling by the British, who defined our mutual borders foolishly, many of the modern-day disputes could have been avoided. We are the two most populous regions in the world, and our countries constitute thirty-five per cent of the world's population. And yes, there will be disputes. But can't we find ways to forge ahead while working on our differences? And do we need superhuman men to do that? My mentor, Deng Xiaoping, would have wanted us to solve our problems sensibly.'

The Chinese premier, who was trusted by the older members of the Communist Party, spoke up. 'We are way ahead of India economically and militarily. We should stop thinking of them as competition. India's progress could be a way for us to further accelerate our own economic progress. Imagine what such a relationship could do. We need to stop thinking of Mao Zedong versus Deng Xiaoping. Instead, we need to focus on taking the best ideas from both and making them work.'

The president looked around the room. 'The Japanese talk of the three mystic monkeys who see no evil, hear no evil and speak no evil. The world has forgotten that the notion first came from our own Confucius, who spoke of four, not three, elements. The fourth was to do no evil. I believe that the time has come for us to live by that fourth element.'

'Shall we take a vote?' he asked, once he was convinced that everyone was on his side.

The men voted for the arrest and incarceration of the Buzhang as he slept.

96

I requested that I be permitted to return home, but Emperor Harsha kept finding excuses to hold me back. Eventually, the monarch relented and provided me with a military escort, horses and an elephant to carry back all the material that I had collected on my travels. He also provided me with 3,000 gold pieces and 10,000 silver pieces to defray the costs of my return journey. Besides all the other treasures, I had procured sugar candies for Emperor Taizong. I took the king's leave with a heavy heart, unaware that he would be dead just four years after my departure.

I had the option of returning by the sea route as was done by Faxian, but I was reluctant, given that I was carrying so many priceless treasures. My party made its way back to the northwest of Yindu through Jalandhara and Tachashilo, using the same route I had taken thirteen years ago. In Jalandhara I was joined by a hundred monks, who wanted the safety of a large travel group. As an added precaution, we would send an advance party to ensure that the route was clear of bandits.

Having travelled 900 miles from Poloyaka, my party got into boats to cross the river Yindu at Utokiahancha. The boats were piled high with scriptures, relics statues and gifts. Alas, there was a storm just as we reached the middle of the mile-wide river. One of the boats capsized and fifty manuscripts and sacks containing the seeds of many Indian plant species were lost. Luckily the bulk of my cargo, including the special urn acquired at Kanci, remained safe. The king of Kiapishi happened to be nearby, and when he learnt that I had been carrying seeds from Yindu, he explained that the river was known to become angry when anyone tried to transport seeds that were native to Yindu. I ended up staying in Kiapishi for two months while replacement manuscripts were sourced. I had a visitor while I was there, my old friend who had taken such good care of me, the king of Kasmira. There was a reason behind his visit. Like Harsha, he too wanted to establish diplomatic relations with the Tang empire.

Eventually, I crossed the Snowy Mountains through the Kavakhya Pass,[137] at a height of 13,000 feet. When we started

---

137. Khawak Pass, near the head of the Panjshir Valley through the Hindu Kush Range to northern Afghanistan.

out, one hundred porters, in addition to horses and asses, were put to work carrying my precious cargo. Sadly, the icy winds and slippery slopes terrified the porters, many of whom abandoned the journey and ran back. Soon, my caravan was left with just seven priests, twenty followers, one elephant, ten donkeys and four horses. We struggled through the frozen waste, snow fills and furious winds for several days before we could descend into Antolapo.[138] There were three small monasteries located there, and we stayed for a few days before proceeding to Huo, where Prince Tardu, whose marriage I had arranged, awaited me. He was extremely hospitable and arranged an escort for our party. Joining us were some merchants too.

The route that we now took to Cina was not the same as the one we had used thirteen years ago. Instead of the northern caravan road to Samokien, we followed the river Po-tsu to Kasha.[139] On the upper reaches of the river, we stopped at the kingdom of Potochangna[140] because the mountain roads were blocked with snow. We eventually made our way through the high-altitude roads until we reached the Great Dragon Lake,[141] with its fresh, dark-blue water. Giant ostriches inhabited the shores of this lake. But we were attacked by robbers on our way to Kasha, and my mighty elephant plunged into a river and drowned.

We finally reached Kasha, an oasis town that was very important on the Silk Road. I visited the bazaar and was delighted to see fine woollen carpets and woven garments. Kasha was a territory of the Tang empire and was ruled by a governor deputed from Cina. From Kasha my party proceeded to Yutian,[142] where I stayed at

---

138. Andarab, located in the southern part of Baghlan Province, Afghanistan.

139. Modern-day Kashgar, Xinjiang, China.

140. Historic region of Badakhshan comprising parts of what is now northeastern Afghanistan, eastern Tajikistan and Tashkurgan County, in China.

141. Lake Zorkul in the Pamir Mountains, which run along the border between Afghanistan and Tajikistan.

142. Modern-day Hotan, Xinjiang, China.

a Hinayana monastery for almost seven months. The people of Yutian loved singing and dancing. They were also experts in silk-weaving, an art that had been jealously guarded by Cina for many centuries, until a ruler of Yutian married a princess from Cina. There was a strong influence of Yindu in this region, with many of its residents claiming to have come from Tachashilo.

I found a merchant in Yutian who was on his way to Chang'an. Through him I sent a letter to Emperor Taizong, seeking his forgiveness. I told him I was returning as a loyal subject who had played a small role in spreading the glory of the Tang empire far and wide. I also slipped in the fact that I was carrying with me vast treasures and, most importantly, an urn meant for the Shaolin temple.

Seven months went by before I heard from the emperor. It was a very positive and encouraging reply. I breathed a sigh of relief. In his letter, he wrote that he was delighted to hear that I had made the arduous journey to distant lands and was returning with even greater wisdom and knowledge. He said that additional horses had been arranged for me and that the authorities at Yutian, Shazhou, Shanshan[143] and Chemo[144] had been instructed to help me reach Chang'an.

97

Two weeks later, a group of tourists visited the Chidambaram temple in Cuddalore district. Among them were Rao, Anu and Pam.

It had come as a revelation to Pam that her driver doubled as a tour guide at the temple when he wasn't ferrying customers in his car. He knew the layout of the temple like the back of his hand. He did not waste time on preliminaries

---

143. Kingdom located at the northeastern end of the Taklamakan Desert.

144. Cherchen, a river oasis town along the southeastern rim of the Taklamakan Desert in Xinjiang, China.

of the sort that he used with tourists. He did not point out the massive hall of 1,000 pillars, the huge reservoir or the golden roof made of 21,600 tiles. Nor did he waste time explaining the intricacies of the movements of Nataraja, the dancing Shiva.

Rao had been very clear. 'We need to see the block of stone that was sent by Suryavarman II, the king who built Angkor Wat, to the Chola king Kulottunga I, to be incorporated into the temple's structure.'

Ever since that fateful day when Rao and Anu had been abducted and Pam had reached the Sanjeeviraya Hanuman temple along with her driver in a bid to rescue them, a strange sort of acquaintanceship had developed between the driver and Rao. Pam found it strange, because she thought the driver was rather creepy.

'Here we are,' he said now, assuming his tour guide avatar. He read out the inscription for them in Tamil.

Rao translated, 'This stone, presented to our king by the king of Kamboja, was placed, as per the instructions of our king, in the front portion of the temple and subsequently fixed in the upper front row of the stone wall of the shrine.'

In Pam's hand was a handheld LiDAR scanner, but she was reluctant to use it in the presence of the driver. She despatched him to get a few bottles of mineral water.

As he left, Pam looked at the Suryavarman stone through the screen of the LiDAR device. Rao and Anu watched the process intently. And within minutes they saw it! There were three cavities deep within the stone. Snugly fitted into them were three urns.

'The real urns,' Rao said quietly. 'This block of stone was hollowed out from its original resting place between the three temples of Phnom Krom, Phnom Bakheng and Phnom Bok. It contains all three potions, including the

Vishnu potion. It's because this block of stone—the vault of Vishnu—had already been moved here that the Chinese team could not find the urns in Cambodia.'

'But why?' asked Pam. 'Why send them here?'

'Suryavarman reigned during troubled times,' explained Rao. 'Life was a series of military exercises, particularly the ones against Dai Viet—now Vietnam. By then, the kingdom was also paying a price for Suryavarman's building spree and his overinflated ego. Thousands of slaves had been used to build Angkor Wat, and the king was always under threat of assassination. Suryavarman understood that getting the potions out of Cambodia and back into India would be the wise course of action. Hence his gift of a block of stone to the Chola king.'

'It seems incredible,' murmured Pam.

'The Khmer kings owed their ascendancy to Dravida,' said Rao. 'These potions had helped kings such as Khambujaraja establish the kingdom of Khambujadesa. Bhima, the younger brother of Simha Vishnu, would never have succeeded in overpowering the many competing claims to the throne, in the latter part of the sixth century, without the help of these potions. A descendant of Bhima, Nandi Varman II—who was brought back to Kanchi to ascend the Pallava throne—also used the potions to vanquish his rivals. Preserving the potions was the single most important role of the Khmer and Pallava kings. '

Pam quickly shut off the LiDAR device. 'This is a Shiva temple,' she said to Rao. 'Ideally, shouldn't this temple have Brahma, Vishnu and Shiva because Hanuman's power is derived from all three? Yes, I did read the relevant portions of *Rasagovinda* like you told me to.'

'But it does,' said the driver, who had quietly returned with bottles of water. He handed Pam a bottle and continued, 'Within the inner courtyard is a shrine that contains the statues of both Brahma and Vishnu. In that sense, Chidambaram is one of the very few temples that worships the Hindu trinity of Brahma, Vishnu and Shiva.'

'Were you listening to us?' Pam asked suspiciously. Something was not right about the driver. *Why is he eavesdropping?*

Rao cleared his throat. 'I think there's something I need to tell you, Pam,' he said very softly. 'My apologies for not saying this earlier ...'

'What?' asked Pam, a little irritated by the interruption.

'The person who is your driver and now your tour guide ...' Rao began.

'Yes?' asked Pam impatiently.

'He's also your father.'

98

Pam was in shock. She did not know how to react. The man she had worshipped all her life was not dead after all. The surge of happiness at this knowledge was followed by a deep sense of anger. Why had he allowed Pam and her mother to believe that he was? And how had he been written off as dead when he wasn't? Why had he done it?

She looked at him carefully as he took off his Ray-Bans and cap. For the first time she took in the little details. Yes, he was wearing his usual khaki bush shirt and trousers, but they were neatly pressed, much like a military man would have them ironed. His thick salt-and-pepper beard and bushy moustache—even the small ponytail—were neatly trimmed. It was evident that the cap, sunglasses, bushy beard, moustache and ponytail had been carefully cultivated to conceal his face from prying eyes.

He smiled at her. And she looked back at him, hypnotised. She had his smile, his nose, his lips. The dimples on her cheeks were exactly the same as his. He had kept himself fit, but it was clear that he was in his mid-sixties, an age that would tie in with his recorded 'death' at the age of thirty-five.

And then Pam threw a tantrum of sorts. It was as though she had regressed to infancy and was obstinately demanding something that only her father would accede to.

'You destroyed our lives,' she wailed. 'Mom and I were devastated when we were told you had died. And all along, you were alive! Not once did you think about your wife and daughter or about the hell we went through.'

'I don't expect you to understand, Pam,' said Colonel Khurana, his eyes welling up. 'You're right to be angry. But the truth is that I had no way of saving your lives without disappearing.'

Pam was not interested in his answer. She stormed into the courtyard and leaned against one of the pillars, sobbing without control. He followed her.

'Why?' demanded Pam as he stood before her.

'Because I had discovered the monkey tribe,' said Khurana. 'And my dear friend Rao and I had succeeded in reformulating those Pallava potions. I had even deciphered the tribe's prayer.'

'How?' asked Pam.

'Listen carefully,' said Khurana as he recited the words he had sung to her when she was little.

Baa-maa-ko-ki-joo-ka-lo
Wee-noo-ko-ki-moo-pa-lo
See-waa-ko-ki-soo-pa-lo
Haa-noo-ko-ki-poo-da-jo

'Think of the beginning of each line in that song,' he said. '*Baa-maa* refers to Brahma; *wee-noo* refers to Vishnu;

see-waa is Shiva; and *haa-noo* is Hanuman. The prayer was simply stating the obvious—that Hanuman's qualities were derived from the trinity. It was the tribe's version of the Gayatri mantra, dedicated to Brahma, Vishnu, Shiva and Hanuman.'

'But that still doesn't explain why you had to disappear,' argued Pam.

'The problem was that Thakur, Jaya and the Chinese wanted the potions at any cost. I knew that it was just a matter of time before I would be abducted and possibly even tortured. The greater fear was that they would go after you and your mother and use you as leverage.'

'The danger to you was the same as the danger to Professor Rao, yet *he* didn't disappear.'

'You're right,' said Khurana. 'But Rao did not know the coordinates of the monkey tribe hamlet, nor did he have access to the apes and their herbs. All four elements—the urns, the texts, the apes and their herbs—were needed. The urns so that the original Pallava formula could be checked; the texts so that the potions could be reformulated; the apes so as to study the various effects of the herbs; the herbs so that the Pallava formula could be cross-verified with the original plants from Hanuman's time. Without any one of those four, it would have been impossible to revive the ancient technology on a large scale. The Pallava documents do not describe proportions, quantities or processes. I was the essential cog that could enlist the help of Ikoalikum.'

'And the bullet?' asked Pam. 'The funeral?'

'All fabricated. I was on that boat and a shot did ring out, but it was fired by one of my own colleagues, the ship's doctor. Not at me but in the air. I was quickly taken by him to his onboard clinic. When the ship docked, I was smuggled out in a crate. An autopsy report was filed, but that too was fictitious. The ship's doctor got someone at the

Armed Forces Medical Examiner's office to make the file disappear. To prevent any questions, a "cremation" was performed, of a sealed casket, in an electric crematorium. My personal belongings were handed over by the doctor to your mother. Other than that, every effort was made to make the Chinese and their lackeys believe that I had actually died.'

'I must say that the doctor was surprisingly helpful,' observed Pam.

'He too was a dear friend, like Rao. He was one of our poetry club members too. And he's presently the prime minister of India.'

It was several minutes before Pam regained her composure.

'The doctor opted for early retirement from the military after the incident,' explained Rao. 'He then entered politics and turned out to be surprisingly good at it. He had always been a good orator, and very well read. His passion for poetry allowed him to connect with people at an emotional level. Over the next three decades, he reached the highest office in the land.'

'But why didn't he do something about you and the programme if he knew all this?' asked Pam.

'I'd gone missing. Even the PM didn't know where I was. Rao had become a recluse and was unwilling to entertain the notion of restarting his programme. The PM also knew that there were Chinese moles in the system and he needed them flushed out. That's why—using VTK and Mark—he brought you in, a rookie whom he could trust. A rookie who could get me and Rao back into the system.'

'And none of you gave a damn about what happened to me or my mother all this time,' snapped Pam. Her heightened sense of abandonment was on full display.

'After my staged death, a trust was established to help you and your mother. The PM looked after it personally. Sure,

I was physically absent from your lives, but I was always there in my own way. I had my own moles in the defence establishment. When I was tipped off that you would be coming to Chennai, I became your driver so that I could protect you. I couldn't stop looking at you. It had been so long. And I could see so much of myself in you.'

Pam's tears were unstoppable. Khurana stepped forward hesitantly, unsure how she would react to his advance. But before he could take the final step, Pam hugged him and broke down, crying like a baby.

She would never let him disappear again. Ever.

99

Café Turtle, tucked away inside Khan Market, was relatively quiet at this time. Mark and Pam occupied one of the corner window tables. It had taken persistent follow-ups on Mark's part to get Pam to come. But the clincher had been Pam's father.

'When I was no longer in your lives, a foundation called the Vegavathy Trust stepped in to help you financially,' Khurana had said. 'Why do you think the trust chose to provide assistance specifically to you and your mother?'

'I was told that they help army widows,' said Pam.

'Only one family was ever helped,' said Khurana. 'And that was ours. It was set up by Rao, the PM and me to look after you and your mother. The name should have rung a bell for you. Vegavathy is the name of the river along which Rao's academy is located in Kanchi. Mark helped too.'

'I understand the trust being established for us,' said Pam. 'But what does that have to do with Mark?'

'After I disappeared and Rao went into hibernation, the trust was managed by the PM. He eventually assigned the responsibility to VTK and Mark. Mark has always been looking out for you. Not just by way of security cover.'

'You knew Mark?' asked Pam.

'During Mark's stint in Cambodia with the CIA, Rao and I had gone there on an exploratory trip. We were introduced to Mark by VTK. We soon discovered that the original urns had been moved out of Cambodia many hundreds of years earlier. After a great deal of research, we discovered that they were concealed in the Chidambaram temple, but Rao and I decided that the location should not be revealed to anyone, not even to Mark or the PM. That's why I became a tour guide: so that I could keep watch over it.'

Pam found herself looking at the man who had quietly been looking out for her. They sipped their café lattes in silence, looking through the windows at the avenue of trees across the road.

'Erkin met his mother yesterday,' said Mark suddenly. He located a photograph on his phone that showed mother and son hugging. It had been taken at an undisclosed location. He swiped forward to a video in which Erkin's mother was holding her son's hand and reciting a prayer.

Allahumma inni a'udhu bika min zawali ni'matika
wa tahawwuli 'afiyatika,
wa fuja'ati niqmatika,
wa jami'i sakhatika.

'O Allah, I seek refuge in You against the declining of Your favours, passing of safety, the suddenness of Your punishment and all that which displeases You.'

Pam smiled. 'What about Lee Zhou?' she asked.

'Gone to Israel. He's hoping that Mossad can help him get his family out of China.'

'What was your discussion with the Chinese proprietor at Janpath about? The photograph Thakur shared with me showed you shaking hands with him, and then in animated discussion.'

'My exact words as I recall were, "I've discussed the matter. And obviously we've agreed to the terms. The Buzhang will do everything to prevent these men from crossing over to our side. However, we have to ensure that it happens."'

'All right. What happens next?' asked Pam.

'There will be some strain in Indo-China relations. But I guess that political leadership on both sides will eventually need to understand that the two countries would benefit more from working together than at cross purposes.'

'And the Chinese information network and the programme?'

'Jaya is dead. Thakur is in custody. Through him, VTK is trying to figure out if there were other leaks. Your parents are happily reunited while Rao is back in business with your father. They had a meeting with the PM yesterday. The urns at Chidambaram are going to be extracted and the special forces programme restarted.'

'What about the tribe?'

'We do not need to disturb them except for a small window of observation. Isn't that the best thing we can do—leave them and their way of life alone?'

Pam nodded in agreement. 'I'll never forgive you for keeping secrets from me, though,' she said.

'Ever heard of Francis Bacon?' asked Mark.

'Who's he?'

'Was,' corrected Mark. 'He was an English statesman who served as attorney-general and lord chancellor of England. He once said something that applies to all of us intelligence types.'

'What?'

'"He that would keep a secret must keep it secret that he hath a secret to keep,"' said Mark cheekily. 'And talking of secrets ...'

'Yes?'

'The biggest secret is that I've decided to retire. I'll be fifty next year, and I feel like I've lived a lifetime.'

'What will you do?'

'Buy a little cottage in Goa. Eat again at that seafood joint, share Malana Cream joints with hippies, overdose on strawberry daiquiris and feni, make waffles with extra maple syrup ...'

'And?'

'Live the life of a beach bum. And marry you. That is, if you still want me.'

100

I was treated to a hero's welcome in Chang'an. Word of my miraculous journey to Yindu had spread and Chang'an filled up, its streets choked with curious visitors. A large group of monks had arrived to help carry all the things that I had brought with me. A parade had been organised. Our procession started from the Street of the Red Bird and ended at the Monastery of Great Happiness. Scholars, monks, officials and excited citizens lined the path that we traversed, sprinkled flowers and incense before us. Banners congratulating me on the expedition were held up along the route.

When I saw the number of monks who were required to carry all the materials, I too was amazed. I had brought back bone fragments of the Buddha and seven statues, some as high as seven feet and made of varied materials including sandalwood, gold and silver. Also in my procession were 657 palm-leaf manuscripts in various Yindu scripts. These were contained in 520 cases and included 224 Mahayana sutras, several Hinayana treatises, thirty-six works of logic and thirteen works of grammar.

The emperor was away on a military campaign in the northeast but wanted me to come to his second capital at Dongdu. He met me at the Palace of Phoenix in Dongdu and greeted me warmly. Memories of my meeting with him in the court of the Great Luminous Palace flooded my mind. I remembered kneeling before him in the qi-shou position and being commanded to rise and approach him. I remembered him whispering into my ears, 'The folly of Qin Shi Huang needs a solution.' Now, his eyes were wide open and I knew that he was waiting for an answer to the riddle. Through that riddle, he had unofficially sanctioned my journey to Yindu although he publicly forbade it.

I said to him, 'The folly of Qin Shi Huang lay in thinking that immortality could be the result of a tonic. Yes, Bamahao-Shipo-Pishinou can add years to one's physical life, but immortality of spirit is already present in all of us. We just can't see it.'

The emperor smiled. He was curious about my journey and wanted to know all about the countries I had visited. He was dumbfounded by the distances I had covered. I explained to him that his fame had spread far and wide and that my expedition was only made possible by that. He was mesmerised by my narrative of kingdoms, kings, climates, foods, traditions, people, cultures, history and religions. On several occasions, he was reminded by his councillor and brother-in-law that the army awaited, but he ignored them. He simply wanted to listen to the tale of my journey while sucking on sugar candies brought back from Yindu.

Suddenly he got up and walked outside, asking me to follow him. His advisers thought that the emperor was ready to survey the troops. But no, he wanted to travel to Mount Song. Hasty arrangements were made for him to travel to the Shaolin monastery located there. He asked me to accompany him in his imperial palanquin, a rare honour. 'I'm doing you no honour,' he declared. 'I wish to get a few hours without interruptions so that I may fully comprehend the extraordinary expedition you have undertaken.'

When we reached Shaolin, the monarch was greeted ceremoniously by the monks, who already knew who I was and why I was there. They immediately led us to the secret room behind the Shadow Cave of Bodhidharma. In front were three platforms that held two urns. A bunch of smoking incense sticks were placed in front of each. The first platform was labelled 'Bamahao'. It held the urn that Faxian had brought to Cina and that had been placed in the White Horse temple, only to be transferred many years later to Shaolin. The second platform was labelled 'Shipo' and held the urn that had been presented by Bodhidharma to the monks of Shaolin upon his admittance. The third platform had been labelled 'Pishinou' but was bare. With great care and ceremony, the monks of Shaolin placed the urn brought by me on this third platform and lit sticks of incense before it.

The emperor then turned towards me. I quickly knelt before him. The two seniormost monks of Shaolin stood to his right and left. The emperor said to me, 'You have done our people proud, like Faxian and Bodhidharma. You are now Di San Sou Chuan—the third vessel.'

Alphabetical List of Ancient Place Names With Modern Equivalents and Related Footnote Numbers

Adhisthana: Sri Nagara, modern-day Srinagar, Kashmir, India. 83

Akini: Yanqi, coinciding with modern-day Karasahr in Xinjiang, China. 33

Andhradesa: Modern-day state of Andhra Pradesh in India. 121

Antolapo: Andarab, located in the southern part of Baghlan Province, Afghanistan. 138

Anxi: Modern-day Guazhou in Gansu Province, China. 21

Ayute: Ayodhya, Uttar Pradesh, India. 97

Bharukaccha: Modern-day Bharuch in Gujarat, India. 134

Chandrabhagar: Chenab River, one of the major rivers of the Punjab, flowing in Pakistan and India. 84

Chang'an: Modern-day Xi'an in Shaanxi Province, China. 11

Che-shih: Modern-day Tashkent, Uzbekistan. 40

Chemo-Cherchen: Cherchen, a river oasis town along the southeastern rim of the Taklamakand desert in Xinjiang, China. 144

Chenliu: A town situated in Kaifeng County, Kaifeng, in Henan Province, China. 3

Chinabhukti: Modern-day Firozpur in Punjab, India. 86

Cina: China. 6

Congling: Pamir Mountains, located at the junction of the Himalayas with the Tian Shan, Karakoram, Kunlun, Hindu Kush, Suleman and Hindu Raj ranges. 35

Congling Pass: Bedal Pass between Kyrgyzstan and Xinjiang, China. 37

Daqin: Rome. 12

Daxia: Tokhara — parts of Afghanistan, Tajikistan and Uzbekistan. 107

Desert of Red Sands: Kyzylkum desert in modern-day Kazakhstan, Uzbekistan and Turkmenistan. 45

Dhanakataka: Modern-day Vijayawada in Andhra Pradesh, India. 123

Dongdu: Modern-day Luoyang in Henan Province, China. 1

Dravida: Modern-day Tamil Nadu, India. 125

Foho Navavihara: Velayat-e-Balkh in Afghanistan. 56

Fu-Shui: Ganga River, India. 55

Gandhara: Modern-day Peshawar Valley, Kabul Valley, Swat and Chitral. 43

Gaochang: Modern-day Karakhoja in Xinjiang, China. 29

Gaohati: Modern-day state of Assam in India with its capital at Guwahati. 112

Gashun Gobi Shamo: Gobi Desert in China and Mongolia. 26

Goguryeo: Korea. 106

Great Pure Lake: Modern-day Lake Issyk Kul in eastern Kyrgyzstan. 39

Great Seaport: Modern-day Puri in Odisha, India. 118

Great Stupa: Amaravati Stupa close to Vijayawada, Andhra Pradesh, India. 124

Hantenggeli Feng: Mount Khan Tengri, part of the Tian Shan Range. 38

Heavenly Mountains: Tian Shan Mountains in Xinjiang, China. 28

Hexi Zoulang: Hexi Corridor in the Gansu Province of China. 16

Huang He: Yellow River, the second longest river in China. 2

Huo: Modern-day Kunduz, Afghanistan. 49

Huoyanshan: Flaming Mountains, sandstone hills in the Tian Shan Mountains of Xinjiang, China. 30

Husekialo: Hushkara Monastery—the village still exists as Uskar on the banks of Behat River, two miles to the southeast of Baramula. 81

Irana: Region covered by Bangladesh and the modern-day state of West Bengal in India. 111

Iron Gate: Narrow pass between Samarkand and Balkh. 48

Isipatana: Sarnath Deer Park, Varanasi, Uttar Pradesh, India. 95

Jalandhara: Modern-day Jalandhar, Punjab, India. 54

Jiangling: Modern-day Jingzhou, Hubei, China. 5

Kanci: Modern-day Kanchipuram in Tamil Nadu, India. 126

Kanokushe: Kanyakubj, modern-day Kanauj in Uttar Pradesh, India. 92

Kantolo: Part of Gandhara, an ancient state in the northwest of the ancient Indian subcontinent, modern-day Afghanistan and Pakistan. 69

Kapilavastu: Modern Tilaurakot in the Lumbini zone of Nepal. 101

Kasha: Modern-day Kashgar, Xinjiang, China. 139

Kashi: Modern-day Varanasi, Uttar Pradesh, India. 102

Kasmira: Modern-day Kashmir, India. 53

Kavakhya Pass: Khawak Pass, near the head of the Panjshir Valley through the Hindu Kush Range to northern Afghanistan. 137

Kiaoshangmi: Kausambi, modern-day Manjhanpur, Uttar Pradesh, India. 99

Kiapishi: Ancient Kapisi, modern-day Bagram in Afghanistan. 60

Konkanapura: India's western coastline. 128

Kshaharatapuri: Modern-day Mumbai in Maharashtra, India. 129

Kubha River: Kabul River in Afghanistan. 64

Kuci: Also called Kucha (or Kushan), modern-day region of Aksu, Xinjiang, China. 34

Kulu-to: Kulant Peeth, or modern-day Kulu-Manali in Himachal Pradesh, India. 88

Kunlun Shan: Kunlun Mountains on the northern edge of the Tibetan Plateau. 36

Kusavati: Kushinagar, Uttar Pradesh, India. 96

Land of the Western Women: Hormuz Island, Iran. 136

Liangzhou: Modern-day Wuwei in Gansu Province, China. 20

Lumbinivana: Lumbini, Nepal. 93

Maharashtra: Corresponds to today's state of Maharashtra in India. 130

Menggu: Mongolia. 108

Menggu Land of Grasses: The grasslands of Mongolia. 17

Moholo: Malwa region of Madhya Pradesh, India. 132

Monastery of Hostages: Shotorak Monastery north of Kabul, Afghanistan. 62

Motulo: Modern-day Mathura in Uttar Pradesh, India. 91

Mount Song: Mountain in China's Henan Province. 8

Nakaloho: Nagarahara, modern-day Jalalabad in Afghanistan. 63

Niranjana River: Phalgu River in Bihar and Uttar Pradesh, India. 105

Pataliputra: Adjacent to modern-day Patna, Bihar, India. 104

Place of Shining Light: Modern-day Bamiyan, Afghanistan. 58

Po-tsu River: Amu Darya River (or Oxus River), which flows through Afghanistan, Tajikistan, Turkmenistan and Uzbekistan. 50

Polomenkuo: Land of the Brahmins, another term for India. 67

Poloyaka: Prayaga, modern-day Allahabad, Uttar Pradesh, India. 98

Potochangna: Historic region of Badakhshan comprising parts of what is now north-eastern Afghanistan, eastern Tajikistan, and Tashkurgan County in China. 140

Pu-ho: Modern-day Bukhara in Uzbekistan. 47

Pulushapulo: Modern Peshawar, derived from Sanskrit 'Purushapura' or 'City of Men' in Pakistan. 70

Pushpagiri: Located in the Langudi Hills in the Jajpur district of Odisha, India. 119

Qinghai Plateau: Tibetan Plateau. 18

Rajagaha: Rajgriha, modern-day Rajgir in Bihar, India. 110

Sakala: Modern-day Sialkot in Pakistan. 85

Samokien: Modern-day Samarkand in Uzbekistan. 46

Seat of Saints: Jaulian monastery in Haripur district of Khyber Pakhtunkhwa Province in Pakistan. 79

Shadow Cave: Near the village of Charar Bagh in Afghanistan. 68

Shangdang: Modern-day Changzhi city in southeast Shanxi Province, China. 4

Shanshan: Kingdom located at the north-eastern end of the Taklamakan desert. 143

Shazhou: Modern-day Dunhuang in Gansu Province, China. 24

She River: Syr Darya River, known by the Greeks as Jaxartes River, flowing through modern-day Uzbekistan and Kazakhstan. 44

Sichuan Lu: Modern-day Sichuan Province, China. 9

Sigh Koh: Shibar Pass connecting Parwan Province to Bamiyan Province. 59

Silver Mountains: Argu Tagh Range in Xinjiang, China. 32

Simhala: Modern-day Sri Lanka. 115

Snowy Mountains: Hindu Kush Mountains that stretch through Afghanistan to northern Pakistan and into Tajikistan and China. 57

South Kosala: Parts of modern-day Chhattisgarh and Odisha, India. 120

Spring of Wild Horses: Modern-day oasis of Nanhu in the Gobi Desert. 27

Sravasti: Modern-day town of Bhinga in the Shravasti district of Uttar Pradesh, India. 100

Suiye: Modern-day Tokmok in Kyrgyzstan. 41

Supofastu River: Subhavastu, modern-day Swat River. 73

Ta-mi: Modern Termez in Uzbekistan near the Hairatan border crossing of Afghanistan. 51

Ta'er: Ruins of Souyang city in modern-day Guazhou County. 22

Tachashilo: Takkasila, modern-day Taxila near Rawalpindi in Punjab Province, Pakistan. 75

Takelamagan Shamo: Taklamakan Desert in southwest Xinjiang, China. 19

Tamosufana: Tamasavana monastery near Jullunder. 87

Tamrallipti: Tamaluk, 41 miles southwest of Kolkata, India. 114

The Great Dragon Lake: Lake Zorkul in the Pamir Mountains, which run along the border between Afghanistan and Tajikistan. 141

The Rocky Strip: Palk Strait between India and Sri Lanka. 116

The Six Kingdoms: Modern-day Myanmar, Thailand, Cambodia and Vietnam. 113

The Two Mighties: Krishna River and Godavari River. 122

Thousand Buddha Caves: Modern-day Bezeklik caves in Xinjiang, China. 31

Tubo: Tibet. 109

Turfan: Modern-day Turpan in Xinjiang, China. 14

Udakakhanda: Modern Muzaffarabad in Pakistan Occupied Kashmir. 72

Udra: Modern-day Odisha, India. 117

Urubela: Bodh Gaya, Bihar, India. 94

Utokiahancha: Modern-day Hund, a small village in the Swabi district of the Khyber Pakhtunkhwa Province of Pakistan. 74

Vaisali: Tirhut division of Bihar, India. 103

Vakataka: Ajanta Caves in Aurangabad, Maharashtra, India. 131

Valabhi: Modern-day Gujarat in India. 135

Varahamula: Baramula town along Jhelum River, downstream from Srinagar, Kashmir, India. 82

Vatapi: Modern-day Badami in Karnataka, India. 127

Vipasa River: Beas River in Punjab, India. 89

Vitasta River: Jhelum River, which flows through northern India and eastern Pakistan. 80

Western Turkic Khaganate: Modern-day regions of Kazakhstan, Uzbekistan and parts of Kyrgyzstan, Tajikistan, Turkmenistan, China and Russia. 42

Xila: Greece. 61

Xiyu: The Western Regions, the lands beyond the Yumen Pass. 15

Yangcheng: Modern-day Dengfeng in Henan Province, China. 10

Yazhou: Asia. 13

Yenmouna River: Yamuna River in North India. 90

Yindu: India. 7

Yindu Pass: Khyber Pass in Pakistan. 71

Yindu River: Indus River, which runs through Ladakh, Gilgit-Baltistan, Kashmir and Pakistan. 65

Yizhou: Oasis of modern-day Hami in Xinjiang, China. 25

Yumen Guan: Yumen Pass or Jade Gate located west of Dunhuang, Gansu Province, China. 23

Yutian: Modern-day Hotan, Xinjiang, China. 142

References

I always aim to provide a comprehensive list of books, papers, journals, videos and websites that I have used while developing my narrative. Some of these sources may even express views that run contrary to the story. The idea of any book within the Bharat series is to provide a starting point for further exploration. I am hopeful that my readers will use this list of sources for further reading and discovery.

1. *Buddhist Centre—Hsuan Tsang,* https://thebuddhistcentre. com/system/files/groups/files/week_4_-_hsuan-tsang_ xuanzang.pdf.

2. *Buddhist Records of the Western World,* Samuel Beal https:// www.wisdomlib.org/south-asia/book/buddhist-records- of-the-western-world-xuanzang/d/doc220262.html.

3. *China Buddhist Encyclopedia—Xuanzang,* http://www. chinabuddhismencyclopedia.com/en/index.php/ Xuanzang.

4. *Da Mo Zu Shi—Master of Zen—Bodhidharma,* https://www. youtube.com/watch?v=GQiK8m_Z8fo.

5. *Empires of the Silk Road: A History of Central Eurasia from the Bronze Age to the Present,* Christopher I. Beckwith, Princeton University Press, 2011.

6. *Encyclopaedia of Ancient Indian Geography, Volume 1,* Subodh Kapoor, Genesis Publishing, 2002.

7. *Futuristic Sci-Fi Military Technologies That Already Exist,* Himanshu Sharma, https://listverse.com/2019/06/10/10- futuristic-sci-fi-military-technologies-that-already-exist/.

8. *Gayatri Mantras of the Several Gods* http://www.hindupedia. com/en/G%C4%81yatri_Mantras_of_Several_Gods.

9. *Great Tang Dynasty Record of the Western Regions,* Edited by Bianji, Translated by Li Rongxi, BDK America, 1996.

10. *Hanuman: Valour, Wisdom, Humility and Devotion*, APN Pankaj, Prabuddha Bharata Vol. 113 No. 10, 2008, https://advaitaashrama.org/pb/2008/102008.pdf.

11. *Incredibly Futuristic Weapons and Modern Fighting Vehicles*, Adrian Willings, https://www.pocket-lint.com/gadgets/news/142272-28-incredible-futuristic-weapons-showing-modern-military-might.

12. *India-China Doklam Standoff*, Gopal Sharma, Sumit Enterprises, 2018.

13. *Indian Herb 'Sanjeevani' (Selaginella bryopteris) Can Promote Growth and Protect Against Heat Shock and Apoptotic Activities of Ultra Violet and Oxidative Stress*, Nand K. Sah, Shyam Nandan P. Singh and others, Department of Biotechnology, Madhav Institute of Technology and Science, Gwalior, 2005, https://www.researchgate.net/publication/7580332_Indian_herb_'Sanjeevani'_Selaginella_bryopteris_can_promote_growth_and_protect_against_heat_shock_and_apoptotic_activities_of_ultra_violet_and_oxidative_stress.

14. *Influence of Caste System in Clothing—Medieval South India Before Sultanates*, Purushu Arie, 2018, https://purushu.com/2018/08/influence-of-caste-system-in-clothing-medieval-south-india-before-sultanates.html.

15. *Intervention in Sri Lanka: The IPKF Experience*, Gen. Harkirat Singh, Manohar Publishers, 2007.

16. *Isolated Tribes*, https://www.sciencemag.org/tags/isolated-tribes.

17. *Journey to the West*, Wu Cheng'en, Edited and translated by Anthony C. Yu, University of Chicago Press, 2012.

18. *Journey to the West: A Play*, Mary Zimmerman, Northwestern University Press, 2011.

19. *Kaoboys of R&AW: Down Memory Lane*, B. Raman, Lancer Publishers, 2009.

20. *Mahabalipuram: Costumes and Jewellery*, Gift Siromoney, Madras Christian College Magazine, Vol. 39, April 1970, https://www.cmi.ac.in/gift/Archeaology/arch_jewellery.htm.

21. *Maritime History of India*, Rear Admiral K. Sridharan, Publications Division of Ministry of Information and Broadcasting, 2017.

22. *Monkey: Folk Novel of China*, Wu Ch'engen, Translated by Arthur Waley, Evergreen Books by Grove Weidenfeld, 1994.

23. *Naga Story: First Armed Struggle in India*, H.C. Chandola, Promilla/Bibliophile South Asia, 2012.

24. *Ocean of Churn: How the Indian Ocean Shaped Human History*, Sanjeev Sanyal, Penguin Random House India, 2017.

25. *On Yuan Chwang's Travels in India 629-645 AD*, Thomas Watters, London Royal Asiatic Society, 1904.

26. *Pallavas Kingdom: Origin and Life under the Pallavas* http://www.historydiscussion.net/history-of-india/the-pallavas-kingdom-origin-and-life-under-the-pallavas/2535.

27. *Pallavas*, G. Jouveau-Dubreuil, Translated by S. Swaminadha Dikshitar, Asian Education Services, 1995.

28. *Prisoners of War*, Sam Cowan, https://www.recordnepal.com/wire/prisoners-war/.

29. *Real Tripitaka and Other Pieces*, The Arthur Waley Estate, Routledge, 2013.

30. *Sanjivani Quest: An Uttarakhand Village Hasn't Forgiven Hanuman for Defacing Their Holy Mountain*, Mrinal Pande, https://scroll.in/article/812802/the-sanjivani-quest-an-uttarakhand-village-hasnt-forgiven-hanuman-for-defacing-their-holy-mountain.

31. *Shadow Image in the Cave—Discourse on Icons*, Eugene Wang, https://www.academia.edu/5911631/The_Shadow_Image_in_the_Cave_Discourse_on_Icons.

32. *Shaolin Kung-fu's Indian Connection*, Aditi Shah, https://www.livehistoryindia.com/snapshort-histories/2019/02/20/shaolin-kung-fus-indian-connection.

33. *Silk Road During the Tang Dynasty*, http://factsanddetails.com/china/cat2/sub90/entry-5441.html#chapter-4.

34. *Silk Road Encyclopedia*, Jeong Su-Il, Seoul Selection, 2016.

35. *Silk Road Explorers*, http://factsanddetails.com/china/cat2/4 sub8/.

36. *Silk Road Journey with Xuanzang*, Sally Hovey Wriggins, Westview Press, 2004.

37. *Sino-Indian Relations: A Tale of Two Asian Giants—Historical Analysis of Discord and 1962 Border War, Cooperation, Competition, Conflict, 2017 Doklam Standoff, Unresolved Territorial Dispute*, Daniel Godkin, US Government, Kindle Edition, 2019.

38. *Special Features of the Popularization of Bodhidharma in Korea and Japan*, Beatrix Mecsi, Institute of East Asian Studies IV (XX) Elte University Budapest, 2016, https://www.researchgate.net/publication/297755673_Special_Features_of_the_Popularization_of_Bodhidharma.

39. *Story of Angkor*, Jame DiBiasio, Silkmorm Books, 2013.

40. *Story of the South Indian Prince Bodhidharma Who Founded Zen Buddhism and Shaolin Kung Fu*, https://m.dailyhunt.in/news/india/english/wittyfeed+india-epaper-witty/the+story+of+the+south+indian+prince+bodhidharma+who+founded+zen+buddhism+and+shaolin+kung+fu-newsid-65206509.

41. *Sunnah: The Book of Supplications*, https://sunnah.com/riyadussaliheen/17/14.

42. *Temples of The Pallavas in Kanchipuram District: A Historical Study*, V. Purushothaman, Department of History Pachaiyappa College Chennai, 2016, https://shodhganga.inflibnet.ac.in/handle/10603/180609.

43. *Thondaimandalam: Costumes and Jewellery*, G. Siromoney, 1973, https://www.cmi.ac.in/gift/Archeaology/arch_thondai. htm.

44. *Three Wise Monkeys: Mizaru, Kikazaru and Iwazaru*, Ivana Andonovska https://www.thevintagenews.com/2017/06/03/priorityrwmizaru-kikazaru-iwazaru-three-wise-monkeys/.

45. *Tracking Bodhidharma: A Journey to the Heart of Chinese Culture*, Andy Ferguson, Counterpoint, 2012.

46. *Transgenic Rhesus Monkeys Carrying the Human MCPH1 Gene Copies Show Human-like Neoteny of Brain Development*, Lei Shi, National Science Review, Vol. 6, Issue 3, May 2019, https://doi.org/10.1093/nsr/nwz043.

47. *Travel Records of Chinese Pilgrims Faxian, Xuanzang and Yijing—Sources for Cross Cultural Encounters Between Ancient China and Ancient India*, Tansen Sen, Education About Asia Vol. 11 No. 3, 2006, http://afe.easia.columbia.edu/special/travel_records.pdf.

48. *U.S. Ground Forces Robotics and Autonomous Systems (RAS) and Artificial Intelligence (AI): Considerations for Congress*, Feickert Andrew, Library of Congress, 2018, https://www.hsdl.org/?abstract&did=819279.

49. *Uyghurs: Strangers in Their Own Land*, Gardner Bovingdon, Columbia University Press, 2010.

50. *Where Hanuman Stands Alone*, http://aalayamkanden.blogspot.com/2012/02/where-hanuman-stands-alone.html.

51. *Xuanzang and Bodhidharma: Pilgrimage and Peace-building in Buddhist China and India*, Ian S. McIntosh, International Journal of Religious Tourism and Pilgrimage Vol. 4 Issue 6 Article 14, 2016, https://pdfs.semanticscholar.org/8d9e/a04aaa453b9c20b6cedd3c7387fbca5c2cf5.pdf.

52. *Xuanzang's Journey to India*, Chang Zheng, China Intercontinental Press, 2010.

53. *Xuanzang's Pilgrimage*, CCTV English, https://www.youtube.com/watch?v=AVEJzp4h_MY.

54. *Xuanzang's Record of the Western Regions*, Translated by Samuel Beal, https://depts.washington.edu/silkroad/texts/xuanzang.html.

55. *Zen Teaching of Bodhidharma*, Red Pine, North Point Press, 1987.